HAUNTING MR DARCY

A Spirited Courtship

KARALYNNE MACKRORY

Quills & Quartos
PUBLISHING

Edited by Christina Boyd and Ellen Pickels

Cover by Jack Lalaine, End2End Books

ISBN
978-1-951033-09-5 (ebook)
978-1-951033-10-1 (paperback)

A long time ago in a college far, far away my heart met its other half and has been beating fiercely ever since. I love you, Andy.

❧ I ❧

The deep, resounding *thwack* of the study door closing with exaggerated force caused Fitzwilliam Darcy to wince. In his agitation, he had swung it harder than necessary, and now the ache in his head intensified like an echo of pain inside his skull. With a restlessness that had built in him over the past few weeks, he impatiently pulled at his cravat, doing considerable damage to the fine silk before he twisted it into a ball, ready to lob it across the room.

"Aargh!" Darcy expelled as his muscles stretched and fulfilled their master's command, tossing the garment into the air. The light silk unravelled and spun slightly, twisting and turning like the mesmerising dance of a fire before floating harmlessly to the floor mere feet from him. Laughing humourlessly, Darcy sighed. "A fine metaphor, I should say."

He walked the short distance, picked up the garment again, and stood looking at it. He had returned from yet another insipid London ball, and like the others he had uncharacteristically attended in the recent weeks since his return from Hertfordshire, he had extended himself so far as to participate in the festivities: dancing, engaging partners in conversation—all of it. All of it in an attempt to purge a certain lady from his thoughts, a certain lady he had met a few weeks before with his friend Charles Bingley at Netherfield. Like the anguished and impassioned discard of his cravat, all his efforts to disengage her from his thoughts by thrusting himself into society came floating down, spinning to naught—spinning away all his energised activity to settle her right back into his thoughts and heart without any real change.

Darcy's hand holding the crumpled silk fell to his side as he walked to the sofa near the wall. His legs folded, his shoulders slumped, and his hands came to create a nest for his head. For a while, he sat there, holding the cravat to his face, and attempted to calm himself and halt his developing megrim. Miss Elizabeth Bennet had bewitched him, and even after escaping her charms by following Bingley to London after the Netherfield ball, he had yet to forget her. So very easily, he could recall the soft brilliance of her skin and the beautifully contrasting dark hue of her curls. It was an intriguing brown—so dark, it could almost be called black—yet when the sun lit it, there was clearly a warm, delicious coffee with slight hazelnut highlights that hid at her temples. Her hair, he imagined, was as soft as the silk in his hands.

Darcy lifted his head to look at the cravat again. Slowly, he brought the silk to his cheek, imagining he held her mass of hair to his face—inhaling her scent, a unique vanilla-lavender blend. Instead, the smell of lemons and sandalwood taunted his senses; his own cologne mocked him, a fair reminder he was yet again playing the part of the fool. With a frustrated groan, he pulled his hand away, shaking his head as he collapsed against the back of the sofa, and stared at the ceiling.

This is utterly ridiculous! Why can I not purge myself of this... this...obsession! Darcy groaned again, knowing with certainty it was more than an obsession but not quite prepared to admit it aloud. He still had faith that he was not in such danger as to make redemption impossible. He could liberate himself and forget Miss Elizabeth Bennet. He could and he would. And once he did, he would be better off for it. Again, he reminded himself that she only need serve as an example—a template. He could take her spellbinding traits and charms and simply find them in another, more suitable lady.

He forced his thoughts back to the ball from which he had recently returned. There were many handsome women there—all from the correct station in life—with connections and wealth to make a most proper Mrs Darcy.

Darcy thought back to his dance with Miss Dennis at the ball. She had intrigued him with her dark hair and light complexion. He allowed himself to admit that she almost resembled Elizabeth and that it was one of the reasons he had asked her to dance. His choice based on such a resemblance was purposeful, he told himself, because if he were to find Miss Bennet's replacement, he ought at least to be attracted to the lady.

They took their places in the set, and Darcy reminded himself of his purpose in attending that evening. Looking across at his partner, he attempted a congenial smile. She properly blushed and returned a slight smile of her own. She was pretty despite brown eyes that were not quite right, he told himself. He thought that perhaps dark chocolate brown eyes with little flecks of gold would suit her better. And if she could just have a slight dimple on her left cheek that appeared, teasingly, when she smiled, she could be called very handsome, indeed. Suddenly, Darcy had stiffened, his face falling into a stern frown. He realised once again that he was trying to make this lady into Elizabeth instead of finding a lady to replace her in his thoughts.

He saw that his sudden change of expression discomposed Miss Dennis for she quickly lowered her head, taking her gaze with her. The music started, and they began the simple movements of the dance. Darcy knew he ought to make amends for his boorish behaviour just then and searched his mind for something to say.

His lip twitched with humour as he said, "I believe we must have some conversation, Miss Dennis."

She smiled and assured him that whatever he wished to be said should be said. The pattern separated them for a moment, and when next he was upon her, he mentioned the elegance of the dance.

"Indeed, it is lovely, sir."

Darcy sighed and looked away as the gentlemen circled right. When next they met, that same wicked humour struck him again, and without fully realising it, he attempted to relive his dance with Miss Bennet at Netherfield and said, "It is *your* turn to say something now, Miss Dennis. *I* talked about the dance, and *you* ought to make some kind of remark on the size of the room or the number of couples."

His partner seemed startled, and instead of replying with a witty rejoinder as he had hoped, she fell silent and her face paled. Sighing once again, Darcy attempted an apology and explanation when next they faced each other, joining hands for the allemande.

"Forgive me, Miss Dennis, for my poor attempt at humour. I did not intend to give you discomfort."

He barely heard her reply, and he realised he hardly cared. Already he was feeling the familiar pull of his heart, the weight settling on his shoulders, and the ache developing in his head. Miss Dennis was lovely, surprisingly kind and seemingly possessed little of that vulture-like avarice often possessed by the ladies in London. Yet, despite all these things, he could not be satisfied. She could not replace Miss Elizabeth, of that he was certain. He was beginning to believe that nobody would, and that was a thought that terrified him, for Elizabeth was not a suitable option for a wife, and he was determined to find one.

The rest of the dance proceeded with an awkward silence that suited Darcy just fine. He was in no humour any more to give consequence to young ladies who could not fulfil his requirements. And this time he did not mean wealth, connections, and social status but rather wit, beauty, and joie de vivre.

Immediately upon presenting Miss Dennis to her relations, Darcy made for the cloakroom. He retrieved his belongings and, dismissing a call for his carriage, instead told the servant to have his groom send the carriage home. He would walk.

He pulled up the collar on his greatcoat when he saw a light snow had begun to fall. In the short distance from the London residence of Lord and Lady Hoemke, the host and hostess of the ball, to Darcy House, the light snow turned into a heavy coating on his shoulders. The walk became slick with a layer of ice, and Darcy occasionally slid briefly as his lengthy, frustrated stride propelled him home. Upon reaching Darcy House, he entered without a word to his surprised butler, whipped off his coat, hat, and gloves—tossing them aside to a small bench in the hallway—and headed to his study.

Darcy kicked off his shoes and lay back across the sofa, coming to rest with his arm hung across his eyes as he brought his thoughts back to the present. *At least, tonight I did not imagine Elizabeth!* A feeble laugh escaped as he recalled the ball he had attended not a fortnight earlier where he had a most frightening encounter. He had been walking around the outside of the room when he heard Elizabeth's same tinkling laughter. Quite under their own command, his legs propelled him towards the sound, only to find the owner of the laugh was not Elizabeth but a striking woman with golden hair and blue eyes. The only proper thing to do after such a direct encounter was to seek an introduction. A Miss Ellsworth was owner of that deceptive laugh. His dance with her had been remarkably enjoyable. She was skilled in the art, but he soon found that she laughed too much. Every word he spoke produced the sound that—his closer inspection made quite obvious—was a little higher pitched than Elizabeth's and far less endearing, he decided.

It was a pattern Darcy was beginning to recognise. He would seek out ladies possessing some aspect of the charms he favoured so well in Elizabeth, only to find that their differences, however slight, were enough to keep him from furthering the acquaintance with the lady. And here he was at the start of the new year, more than a month since he had last seen Elizabeth, and he was no closer to expunging her grasp upon his heart and mind than when he was in her presence.

A knock at his study door pulled Darcy from his discouraging thoughts, and he contemplated ignoring it when it opened without invitation, a peek under his arm revealing his cousin Colonel Fitzwilliam. Darcy groaned and quite rudely said, "Go away, Richard."

"Well now, Darcy! I say, is that any way to repay my generosity?"

Darcy pulled his arm from his eyes and pierced his cousin with his gaze. "And what form of benevolence, pray tell, do you delude yourself into believing you have bestowed upon me?"

"I have saved you from the wrath of my mother, of course," the colonel said pragmatically as he poured himself a glass of port. He raised the glass to his cousin in salute and then drank it down before filling it again. "May I pour you a glass?"

Darcy shook his head in exasperation and sat up. "Please, help yourself."

Colonel Fitzwilliam laughed and stated that, indeed, he would help himself.

"What is it that I have done to gain the ill favour of Lady Matlock that necessitated your intervention?" Darcy groaned as he began stripping off his formal waistcoat and silk stockings. He only stopped when he had made himself more comfortable in shirtsleeves and breeches.

"This is not the first ball hosted by a friend of hers that you have abruptly left without taking your leave." The colonel paused as he found a comfortable seat near the fire. "Your poor manners caused no small insult this time, and I, gallant as I am, made excuses for you. I mentioned you looked as if you were getting another of your megrims."

"As it is, I am," said Darcy. "Thank you. I found myself in need of fresh air and, in the end, decided my mood was best soothed by leaving. I did not realise I had created such a pattern of poor behaviour. I shall write Lady Matlock tomorrow and apologise."

The gentlemen were silent for a time, and Darcy again leaned back against the sofa to stare at the ceiling. His cousin eyed him as he savoured his drink. Darcy's behaviour of late had been troublesome in a number of ways. First, it was not in Darcy's nature to attend many events of the Upper Ten Thousand, especially balls. Since returning to London, his cousin had attended quite a few each week. Second, Darcy, if compelled to attend, did not, under any circumstance, dance. However, at each of the balls the colonel also had attended, he had marvelled that his usually taciturn cousin danced a few sets each time. It was beginning to draw attention from the *ton* too. Rumours were floating that Fitzwilliam Darcy of Pemberley was looking for a wife. And lastly, Darcy's manners were usually impeccable. Colonel Fitzwilliam scanned his cousin; his dress was usually impeccable too.

"I always imagined I would be married before you, but at the pace you are setting, it looks as if you may beat me to the altar in the end."

Though startled slightly, he merely spoke to the ceiling. "*That* looks ever more unlikely."

"So it is true. You are looking for a wife?" Colonel Fitzwilliam could not hide the surprise in his voice. He had simply intended to rile his cousin. He had not anticipated that his teasing would ring true.

Darcy's bored tone was incongruent with his words. "I am looking for a wife." He then added under his breath, "A suitable one."

The colonel sat up and leaned towards his cousin. "Fiend seize it! You are either a trifle disguised tonight or you are in love!"

His cousin's words shocked Darcy, and he, too, sat up immediately to deny it, only realising too late that his reaction confirmed it all the more. The two men stared at each other in a battle of wills that eventually ended only when the colonel began to laugh.

"And by that comment, I assume the lady in question is not suitable."

Darcy glared at his cousin, angrier with himself for being so careless with his words.

"At least tell me she is a gentlewoman."

"I have no wish to speak of this. Kindly finish my port and see yourself home."

The colonel's amiable expression suddenly turned serious. "Is she a gentlewoman?"

"What kind of cad do you take me for? Of course she is. Now pray, leave me be."

Darcy's irritation increased as his cousin relaxed and settled himself deeper into the chair he occupied. He loved his cousin and was grateful to have his wise perspective when it came to their shared guardianship of his sister, Georgiana. Usually, Colonel Fitzwilliam's jovial temperament struck just the right balance to his own generally sombre mien so as to create a mutually endeared friendship that went beyond the familial. But at times like tonight, in the mood he was in, his cousin severely grated on him. He wished tonight only to be left alone.

The colonel, sensing he had pushed his cousin far enough for the evening, conceded gracefully with a promise to return to the subject at hand. "I would very much like to hear about this 'unsuitable' lady. It is a remarkable thing in and of itself that you have fallen for anyone, and I should like to hear what strategy this lady employed to capture your heart."

Darcy's silence was not unexpected.

"And I am particularly intrigued by your notion that she is unsuitable—if, as you say, she is a gentlewoman. You are a gentleman; so far as I see, you are equals."

"Good night, Richard."

Colonel Fitzwilliam laughed as he stood to replace his glass at the sideboard. "Good evening, Darcy. Sleep well." Upon reaching the door, he turned and paused, looking at his cousin carefully. A touch of concern marked his brow.

Darcy lifted his head to return his cousin's gaze. Their silent communication was brief, and it almost made Darcy change his mind about confiding in Fitzwilliam about Elizabeth—almost. He could see his cousin's concern, yet for now, Darcy could not contemplate the pain of that conversation.

Colonel Fitzwilliam nodded his head in farewell but then remembered something and checked his watch. "You did leave quite early tonight. It is not even midnight. But since I am leaving, I shall say 'Happy New Year' to you now and wish you a good year. Do not forget to make a New Year's wish!" He laughed and returned Darcy's silent wave before sliding through the darkened doorway. Darcy's dilemma was quickly replaced in his mind by the image of a beautiful Miss Andrews still at the ball. If he hurried, he could make his own New Year's wish come true and secure a dance.

For quite some time, Darcy looked at the door through which his cousin had exited. He heard the entry clock strike the quarter hour. His cousin's words had an unexpected effect on Darcy. *If I had a wish for this new year, I would wish for an end to my search.* Then foolishly he added, *and to see Elizabeth one last time.*

He stood and walked to the sideboard to pour himself a drink. He hoped it would help ease the pain that still made a home for Elizabeth in his heart and mind. After finishing his refreshment, he returned to the sofa and lay down. He heard the clock strike midnight, and his thoughts as he drifted to sleep were of her.

❧ 2 ❧

Elizabeth Bennet's laughter died away when her line of sight drifted from her dance partner to her sister Jane, dancing down the set from her. Jane had a pinch about her eyes that imparted her true feelings behind a serene countenance, and had Elizabeth not been such an intimate of her sister, she might not have noticed. Suddenly, a surge of protective emotion rose in her breast, and anger simmered at the way things had turned out for Jane.

Ever since the Bingleys and Mr Darcy left for London, her sister had been exposed to the derision of the world for disappointed hopes and suffered misery of the acutest kind. Her former suitor, Mr Bingley, was blamed for his caprice and instability. Elizabeth was certain that Mr Bingley loved her sister and just as certain that his friend and sisters had everything to do with their separation.

She did not miss the irony that they were even then attending a Meryton assembly—the New Year's Eve assembly—a twin to the one several months earlier at which Jane had met Mr Bingley for the first time. The noticeable difference at this assembly was the absence of single gentlemen in possession of large fortunes and in want of wives —certainly not with all those elements combined. Elizabeth looked at her partner, the charming Mr Wickham, and confirmed that, although there were many good single gentlemen, they certainly did not possess large fortunes, and those in want of wives were among those without fortunes.

Even if such a man were to come into the neighbourhood, Elizabeth was certain it would not matter much to Jane, for she was, though heartbroken, still as much in love with Mr Bingley as ever.

When the dance came to an end, Mr Wickham escorted Elizabeth to Jane; her dance partner had left to retrieve refreshments. After accepting Mr Wickham's offer to retrieve a glass of refreshment for her as well, Elizabeth turned to her beloved sister.

"You are not well, Jane." Concern poured from her as she took in the hollow look in Jane's eyes while reaching for her hand.

Jane turned her hand up to hold her sister's and tried to swallow the sudden emotion surging in her breast. "I am having a difficult time with my memories; that is all, Lizzy. I shall be fine soon, I assure you."

"Oh, Jane." Elizabeth squeezed her sister's hand and, seeing that her gesture added to the emotion Jane was experiencing, eased the pressure. "Shall we not go home now? I am a bit fatigued, and I am sure there is time enough to return and send the carriage back for our sisters."

Jane turned to her sister and smiled thankfully. "You do not have to cut your evening short, Lizzy. I know you enjoy the dancing. At the last assembly, gentlemen were scarce, and to my certain knowledge, more than one lady was sitting down in want of a partner."

Jane's attempt at levity was valiant, and Lizzy laughed for her benefit. "Indeed, I recall the evening quite well. With the addition of the militia, the misfortune of a scarcity of eligible gentlemen is resolved."

"Much has changed in such a short time, has it not?"

The quaver in Jane's voice proved she was adequate for neither the conversation nor the lively atmosphere. Elizabeth decided then that she would accompany her sister home despite her sister's protestations. She could see the evening had been a difficult one for Jane, and it need not continue in that manner. When Mr Wickham and Jane's previous dance partner returned with glasses of punch, Elizabeth asked Mr Wickham to call for her family's carriage.

"But you are not leaving, Miss Elizabeth. The night is still young, and the clock has not yet struck twelve."

"Lizzy..." Jane started.

"Mr Wickham," Elizabeth responded while kindly silencing Jane with a smile, "indeed we are. I fear I am not feeling well, and Jane has agreed to accompany me home."

She watched and was surprised by the look of frustration that flashed in the gentleman's eyes before his usual charm re-established itself.

"Can you ladies not wait at least until midnight that we might have the honour of wishing you a Happy New Year?" Mr Wickham implored prettily.

Elizabeth was momentarily struck by Mr Wickham's insistence. She had overheard many officers mention that they were hoping to steal a kiss from a lady when the clock chimed twelve. Mr Wickham had been in the group of gentlemen, and although he had not said it himself, he had laughed. She had dismissed it as a brazen notion of young, overeager officers. She wondered briefly whether Mr Wickham's lapse in manners was due to his desire to steal a kiss at the New Year. She shook her head, dispelling the thought. *Mr Wickham is much too gentlemanly to condone such youthful indiscretions.*

"You are too kind, Mr Wickham. Indeed, though, I do not feel well enough to stay any longer. If you would please call for our carriage, I would be much obliged."

Mr Wickham pursed his lips and bowed in resignation but not before Elizabeth perceived again the irritation that seemed to flicker on his countenance. She looked at Jane and noticed that her sister was gently biting her bottom lip as was her habit when she was in the throes of emotion. She needed escape from the evening, and Elizabeth immediately forgot the strange behaviour in her officer friend in deference to her worry for Jane. After securing their cloaks, Elizabeth left Jane briefly to inform their mother of their departure. Mrs Bennet was not best pleased with the arrangements and demanded Jane stay and dance with another or two of the officers.

"For surely it would do her good to have them show her a bit of preference."

Elizabeth had anticipated such a protest and settled her features into a concerned mien.

"Mama, I fear the evening is fatiguing to my sister, and her beauty is diminished by her weariness. I am taking her home so that it does not become generally believed that she has lost her bloom."

Elizabeth rolled her eyes at the ease with which this fallacy escaped her tongue and its immediate success with her mother. Almost as soon as the words left her mouth, Mrs Bennet was insisting that Elizabeth waste no further time and take Jane home to rest.

"Take care that she has Hill make her one of her tea blends to place on her eyes when you get home, and Lizzy, see also that she has a glass of wine before bed. It will help her rest well, and then perhaps she will feel refreshed for any officers that may come and call upon the morrow. Of course, had Mr Bingley not left..."

Elizabeth turned and left before she heard the rest, all the while shaking her head at the absurdity of it all. Her mention of Mr Bingley's absence, however, did bring back to Elizabeth's mind the frustration she had towards that gentleman's party. It was with these energised thoughts that Elizabeth reached Jane's side again just as Mr Wickham arrived to announce their carriage was ready.

"I SHALL MOURN THE LOSS OF YOUR PRESENCE FOR THE REST OF the assembly, Miss Elizabeth, but I see you are determined. I shall not say another word but, instead, bid you a good night." Mr Wickham made an elegant bow over her hand and kissed her glove.

Elizabeth was pleased and flattered by his words. She laughed merrily, instantly convincing herself that she had misread his earlier countenance, never believing that his dramatic prose or his charming words were anything but harmless flirting.

"Thank you, sir. I pray your evening is not spoilt."

Mr Wickham then stepped forward, reached for her cloak's hood, and placed it on her head. "It is a cold night, Miss Elizabeth, and the snow is already quite heavy. Do take care, or you will catch your death. Good night."

Elizabeth blushed but managed a tolerable reply. Eager to get Jane home and out of society, Elizabeth indicated her readiness to go.

With that, Mr Wickham handed Jane and Elizabeth up into their carriage and signalled the groom to drive on. The horses' hooves slid momentarily on loose snow and ice but then caught hold, lurching them forward into the dark night.

Elizabeth turned to her sister and secured her hand. "We are alone now, Jane; you need not hide your feelings."

That was all it took to unlatch the gate of Jane's emotions. Elizabeth could hear her sister's sudden sobs, and with a familiarity known to sisters, pulled her into an easy embrace while she cried. Jane's pained heart was especially difficult for Elizabeth as she knew there was nothing she could do to ease her heartache. She was suddenly pleased that her sister would travel to London in the coming week to visit with Aunt and Uncle Gardiner for a time. It was hoped that Jane might see something of Bingley there, and then all would be made well. Until then, Elizabeth knew that what Jane needed most was the love of her favourite sister.

"Do you think it would help to speak of it, Jane?"

Her sister's muffled reply was almost lost in the sound of the cold wind rustling against the carriage. "I was just thinking of the last assembly."

"It was a mistake to come tonight, I fear."

"No, no, it was not—if only to teach me what a fortunate memory I now have of that night in September. Mr Bingley shall ever more be held in my mind as one of the most amiable and handsome gentlemen of my acquaintance."

"You are too good. But if it pains you, we do not have to speak of that night."

"It does not pain me. I am afraid I let my memories overwhelm me, 'tis all."

Elizabeth, unable to bear her sister's haunted expression, attempted a bit of humour. "I believe Sir William enjoyed the festivities this evening more than last time. His dancing became a trifle unbalanced after his fourth glass of punch."

Her observation lightened Jane's countenance, and the sisters even managed to laugh together for a few moments. "His exclamations of 'Capital!' could be heard across the room by the time we left."

They chuckled together again and spent a few minutes in light conversation discussing the hilarities of their neighbours, both aware that under the surface more sombre feelings still lapped at Jane's heart.

"And I do believe this assembly found me with an improvement in my beauty, for I heard not one gentleman declare me only tolerable or not handsome enough to tempt him."

"He was very bad to have said that." Jane laughed at the imperious tone taken on by her sister's last words.

"It was very bad of him, to be sure." Elizabeth giggled with a nudge to her sister. "Perhaps as my revenge, I shall declare that man's misfortune—and my New Year's wish—is for Mr Darcy to want something he cannot have!"

"Lizzy!" Jane, now feeling her good spirits returned by the liveliness of her sister, pretended to rebuke Elizabeth. "You ought to be careful what you say on the eve of a new year. All wishes are granted on the New Year to those whom Fate deems deserving."

The sisters fell into laughter at the oft-spoken superstition their Aunt Philips most diligently expressed each year before the assembly, plaguing her nieces to make wishes for finding a husband.

"Ah, but you forget. Fate cannot grant the wish unless the person making that wish is destined to fall in love in the coming year. And since you are quite twice as handsome as me, it is likely I shall never find myself in love unless it is with *your* ten children."

"Lizzy!" Again, her sister exclaimed her name among a fit of laughter. "Ten children! Pray, find me a husband first!"

Together the sisters erupted in mirth. Just then, the carriage jolted to the side abruptly, and they felt it slide briefly on the ice. It was only a second before they felt the wheels recover again and straighten, but the momentary fright sobered them completely.

"It is such a cold night," Elizabeth whispered. "I think we ought to tell John to return for our mother and sisters immediately for the weather is getting much worse. Soon, I fear the roads will be impassable."

Jane remained silent, and after a minute, Elizabeth turned to look at her. It was too dark to see her face, but a feeling of foreboding slipped around Elizabeth's heart. She reached a gentle hand up to her sister's face and frowned when her suspicions were confirmed as her hand encountered tears.

"Jane..."

"Lizzy..."

They both spoke at once, and without humour, they laughed at their combined entreaties.

Jane began again when it was clear Elizabeth was waiting. "I made a wish last New Year's that I might meet someone this year, and it came true. I fell in love with Mr Bingley."

"Oh, Jane." Elizabeth embraced her sister again, tears stinging her own eyes.

"I think Fate granted my wish, though I daresay I am not certain in the manner I had hoped." Jane sighed with longing, and Elizabeth clenched her eyes to keep them from watering further. Her sister's pain was her own, and she very much wished she could offer relief.

"You shall see him when you go to London. He returns your love; I am certain of it."

They remained silent for a spell, listening to the laboured breaths of the horses, the howl of the wind, and the discordance of their personal thoughts. *If given the chance, I shall right this wrong*, Elizabeth vowed. The carriage lurched again, and the sisters held tighter in an attempt to steady themselves. This time, the carriage continued to slide, and fear burst into the hearts of both as they felt a sudden jolt. They heard the snap of a carriage wheel as it crashed into the trees on the side of the road. A fearful squeak escaped Elizabeth as the carriage tipped abruptly to one side. In the way of horrifying moments, she felt as if time had slowed and every detail of the accident was being captured in her memory with vivid acuity. The blanket floated up around her in the air, and she turned to see light from the carriage lamps now pour through the window where the drapes also seemed to swim into the frosty night air. Jane had her eyes squeezed shut and her arms extended towards Elizabeth. Elizabeth, too, saw her own arms—empty of Jane—extended, as they were thrust apart by the jolting of the carriage. And then the crawl of time sped suddenly to a fearful pace as Elizabeth felt her shoulder hit the side of the carriage. Then her head knocked painfully against the ground as the glass of the window shattered beneath her.

The lamp light through the carriage window above her seemed strange. It did not seem natural that she should be looking up to see the window. She tried to move, but her arms felt so heavy, and the weight on her chest was oppressive. She struggled to keep her eyes open, for she suddenly was feeling quite sleepy. When the light from the lamp outside the window flickered and then sputtered out, she found she welcomed the dark, for her head was beginning to pound mercilessly.

The weight on her chest moved, and she realised it was Jane. *Jane!* Her mind cried but she could not get her mouth to say the word.

"Lizzy..." Jane's groggy voice sounded miles away. "Lizzy, are you all right?"

Elizabeth struggled to find her voice. It seemed her mind was too tired to speak and the connection to her mouth no longer there. *I must speak.* She could hear her sister's pleas, and now distant voices were coming from outside. Elizabeth mustered the last of her energy and resisted the sleepiness enough to manage a quiet whisper.

"I am cold. It is so very cold."

"Lizzy! Stay with me; you are going to be well. Help is here, and we are rescued. Lizzy, stay with me!"

To Elizabeth it seemed as if Jane was moving away from her. *Do not leave me, Jane.* Her thoughts were becoming sluggish now, and she could not find her voice. The lethargy began to drown her again. It engulfed her like a thick, dark blanket, and she welcomed the night that consumed her. The pain was now fading, and sleep beckoned. Somewhere the distant, hollow sound of the church bell echoed midnight.

❧ 3 ❧

Raising her small hands to her face, Elizabeth rubbed her eyes to see whether she could clear the scene before her. Eyes focused again, she allowed her unbelieving gaze to wash over her surroundings. It was as before, only with every passing minute, she became more aware of the unfeasibility of it all. Yet there were emotions stirring—feelings engulfing her. She was simply in the most amazing, most beautiful place she could ever imagine. Never in her life had she experienced such a sense of belonging and warm contentment as she then felt. The entire space had a pull on her as if her very soul was saying this place was just as it ought to be—just as its creator intended. Drawing in deeply, Elizabeth held her breath and closed her eyes once again to savour every detail.

It often happens that, when one is deprived of one of their senses, the others immediately come to the fore. Such was the case with Elizabeth as she stood, arms relaxed at her side, slightly extended with palms facing up as if expecting some sort of heavenly endowment to gently settle on her shoulders. She expelled her breath and became aware of the warm leather scent that danced around her, swirling with the traces of wood smoke. Turning her head to the side, she thought she might have even detected a hint of lemon in the air. A wide, genuine smile spread across her features as she opened her eyes again.

It was quite possibly the most beautiful view upon which she had ever rested her eyes. The place had the ability to feel open, imposing, and cavernous yet also warm and welcoming. The colours were muted yet rich and inviting. *Surely, this is heaven.* Laughing quietly— for any louder sound did not seem reverent enough for such a place— Elizabeth spun with childlike innocence, her delight captured easily in her eyes and upon her countenance. She was having the most delightfully bizarre and astounding dream.

"Dream of dreams," she whispered.

No other explanation could account for finding herself in a place she had never before seen. Nodding her head, Elizabeth confirmed in her mind, that yes, indeed she must be dreaming. *Yet, I cannot fathom that my imagination could create such a place.* Allowing her eyes to drift to the vision before her, she acknowledged to herself with a cheerful smile marked with humour that *her* heaven would most certainly be this place: a place filled to the brim with knowledge, adventures, and excitement—a place she should like to spend a great deal of time. In her dream of dreams, Elizabeth found herself standing in the centre of a luxurious and expansive library.

The room was darkened except for the lively glow cast by the fire in the hearth, its warmth reaching almost to her as she stood in the centre of the room.

Bookshelves surrounded her from floor to ceiling, and their thick leather bindings reflected back at her like a tapestry of browns and reds. The lush carpet beneath her muffled any noise her movements might have made, and the furnishings of the room were matched perfectly to the soul of the room.

She lowered her eyes to her gown and delighted in the soft brilliance of it. It almost seemed to glow, yet she thought she had never seen it before. She was once again astonished with the depths of her imagination. Her dreams were rarely this vivid, yet what else could it be? Even now, she was detecting elements that were impossible except in the make-believe world of dreams.

As evidence, when her slim fingers reached to touch the glowing fabric of her gown, her hand slid, sunk, and eased through the cloth as if it were but a fabrication of her mind. The glowing ivory of her gown rippled and flowed unlike any other gown she had worn. Yet, if she stepped to the side, as she did just then, it moved and lapped around her legs just as it ought.

Elizabeth smiled in dreamlike wonder, for dreaming she must surely be since, in the realities of wakefulness, such impossibilities and striking inconsistencies did not exist. For several minutes, she explored this newfound wonder, gliding her hands in and out of the side of her gown as if merely swimming her hand through still waters.

"Beautiful wonder of wonders..." she murmured as she explored the phenomenon further, her face alight with fascination. "Never have I dreamed such a dream. It is beyond belief."

Pausing, Elizabeth was struck with the intense desire to explore this dream further and discover any other wonders it might garner. She ventured immediately towards an inviting armchair coupled with its twin near the fire. But almost as soon as she commenced her walk across the room, she had to stop—for *walking* she was not. She seemed to float, gliding without resistance across the space. Yet again, another inconsistency. She moved her limbs as if walking, and the motion propelled her as it should; nevertheless, she could tell that she was moving with a grace unknown to her wakeful self. She marvelled anew at the strange sensation as she tried her paces across the rug and back—all the while, smiling to herself at this wonderful dream she was having.

Somewhere she heard a clock strike the hour, and judging from the darkness pouring in from the windows and the sound of the clock chimes, it was two in the morning. She shook her head slowly at the details of this dream. She felt none of the listlessness of other reveries.

With renewed desire to explore her dream world before she woke and it was lost to her, Elizabeth resumed her journey to the armchair. Upon reaching her destination, she extended her hand to the side of the chair, and just as she expected, her hand slipped right through. Laughing, she realised that she did not know what to expect, yet she did at the same time. It was the most bizarre experience of her life. She turned her back to the chair and held her breath as she lowered herself, hoping that, since it was *her* dream after all, she might be able to will herself to sit on the object. With a *humph*, she landed on her backside on the floor, her head just tall enough to protrude most shockingly through the cushion of the chair as if on display in a horridly grotesque way.

Her face contorted in frustration as she sat inelegantly on the floor. Her arms crossed petulantly until she realised it was only embarrassment she felt at her clumsiness. The absurdity of it all made her brows relax, and she began to laugh quietly at herself. For a second before rising, she imagined what a sight she might make: a disembodied head resting on the cushion. The thought caused further hilarity and suspended her attempts to stand. She noted that, though she could not sit in the chair, she still could almost experience its softness, comfort, and luxurious construction.

The duality of her experiences in this dream was most delightful. She could wear the dress yet not really touch it. She could walk but moved as if gliding rather. She could not recline in the chair; however, she knew with surety of its comfort. Strange and stranger still.

Realising this meant that she might be able to move through *anything*, she took a most unceremonious turn about the room, crossing through divans, side tables, and ottomans. Each time she felt the basic qualities of the object without really being able to *feel* it. *It is almost as if I am a ghost!* Elizabeth laughed to herself at the notion before the thought halted her. She froze quite awkwardly in the middle of the chaise longue.

"I could not have died," whispered Elizabeth. "For, surely, I would remember such an event." She racked her brain for any such happening and found her memory devoid of any trauma.

Elizabeth relaxed, her shoulders slumping. Her last memory was that of retiring to her room for a brief respite before the New Year's Eve assembly. So dreaming she must be. She certainly did not remember anything else. The idea triggered something in her mind though, a tickle of something that she grasped at, yet it floated away as many thoughts tend to do during dreams. It did make her look down at herself for some reason. Again contemplating her gown, she noticed for the first time the unique pucker of the sleeves and the stitching around her neckline. It was definitely a dress she had never known before. The thought was like a butterfly flying about in that haphazard manner they do, never quite in one place long enough for her to capture what she was missing before it floated off again.

Unable to probe further, she decided to continue her exploration. "A dream such as this must not be wasted."

Until this time, she had remained mostly on the thick rug that encompassed much of the centre of the rectangular room. On one of the two longer walls was the large, inviting fireplace, its mantel coming to just above her head. The opposite side consisted entirely of bookshelves, interrupted only by a dark cherry-wood door. She briefly wondered whether there was more beyond this library for her to explore but set that thought aside for the moment. The furniture clustered around the rug and beyond the room expanded further to the short walls on both ends. One side housed additional built-in shelves—heavily laden with their leather-bound treasures—and another door. Elizabeth imagined the large set of windows opposite this wall brought in a fair amount of light for reading. She could easily picture herself on a warm day sitting in the sunlight with a book in her hand, and the image made the room all the more heavenly to her.

Noises from outside the window drew her attention. Until that moment, she had made all the sounds in the dream and been utterly alone. Curiosity and wonder caused her to wish to look out beyond the windows, but as she walked in that direction, she reached the last sofa and could go no further. It was as if there was a glass wall or some overpowering force keeping her from venturing beyond that point. She attempted multiple times without success and wondered whether the laws of the dream meant she could not go beyond the rug. This idea settled a disappointment on her of no small magnitude as that meant she could not reach any of those books along the outsides of the room.

Elizabeth turned around, walked to the opposite edge of the rug, and paused. She now had her back to the windows and faced the small wall of books with one door. Taking a deep breath, she readied herself to try to leave the rug on that side, fully expecting that she would be prohibited as she was before. To her astonishment and delight, no such hindrance held her, and she was able to walk all the way to the bookshelf. *Stranger still!* she thought as she glanced back over her shoulders towards the wall with windows and the faint sounds of carriages, horses, and even the occasional voice in the night.

Returning her gaze to the books before her, Elizabeth began to read the titles on the shelves, her previous frustration and confusion over her prohibition from the far side of the room completely forgotten when compared to such delights! The shelves possessed a varied collection of poetry, seemingly arranged only by genre. Walking slowly, she found she moved from poetry to history. The history section did not give way until she reached the fireplace. The tastes of the owner, she assumed, tended towards that subject, for the collection before her was expansive and all-inclusive. This gave her pause, for presumably *she* was the owner of the library as it was *her* dream. Surely, she should be allowed to choose the content housed within.

Her hands were clasped behind her as she bent and read the gold-embossed titles—some from various historic wars, others detailing the lives of the English monarchs, and still others being histories of numerous foreign countries. Pleased and intrigued, Elizabeth reached for a book, a history of Italy.

Her fingers nearly touched the book when she paused, disappointment flooding through her as she remembered she could not lift the book from the shelf. To be in a library full of books and not read one sent emotions flooding into her like nothing she had before experienced. Elizabeth further noticed that, in her dream world, her emotions were intense and seemingly enhanced beyond her norm.

She considered the book for a moment, and then her brow rose, and she whispered to herself as she stood, hand extended towards the book, "I wonder..."

She allowed her fingers to skim *through* the book's spine, and suddenly she was filled with the words of the book. It was as if they were poured out of a bucket over her as her thoughts filled with vistas described in vivid detail of Venetian waterways, conquests of land, and artists of such wonder that she trembled with pleasure in all its splendour. She pulled her hand back, and it was if she had experienced the whole book without turning so much as one page.

"Marvellous!" Elizabeth spoke with excitement, the volume of her voice for the first time reaching a conversational level.

Immediately she walked a pace and reached towards a book that lay on a small table. It was a chronicle of Wellesley's actions on the continent. She placed her small hand atop it, allowing her fingers to sink into the leather. Just as before, Elizabeth was washed with his account of the Battle of Vimeiro, described in graphic detail as she experienced the British defeat of the French. She pulled her hand away, delighted. Although histories, particularly war histories, were not of interest to her, she found experiencing this amazing impossibility exhilarating and the topic rendered exciting for her.

Her laughter rang out into the silence of the room and echoed off the walls. No longer able to contain herself with any form of decorum, Elizabeth rushed from book to book—touching each briefly as she experienced wave upon wave of their secrets. Of all the enchantments this dream afforded, this was beyond them all, and her happiness was immeasurable.

Tears streamed down her cheeks as her emotions overwhelmed her. The feelings were both spectacular and indescribable. Such an otherworldly marvel suited her exactly in disposition and talents.

Her liveliness and satisfaction expressed themselves most becomingly upon her face as she explored the library, briefly touching volume after volume, hardly giving herself enough time to relish the blanket of words from one before moving on to the next. It was a beautiful impracticality and one she wanted to experience as much as possible before she awoke.

DARCY'S EYES OPENED IN AN INSTANT. DISORIENTED, HE WAS motionless as he stared into the blackness above him. Slowly his surroundings settled on him again, and he remembered the ball, the visit from his cousin, and the headache that he now happily realised was gone. He was in his study and had obviously fallen asleep on the sofa against the wall. A sound woke him, and although he now knew where he was and how he had arrived there, he still felt disoriented for the sound he had heard was as impossible as it was beautiful.

There it is again! Darcy's head jerked to the side. It seemed to come from the other side of the wall. That wall divided his study from the library, and the sound, although muted, had definitely seemed to come from the library! He slowly pulled his large hands up to his temples and rubbed them; headache or no, he was imagining things now. The night was full upon him, and he could have slept only a few hours. The house was deathly silent except for the few times he had heard the sound. Beyond his belief, he knew it to be the enchanting gaiety of Miss Elizabeth Bennet's laughter.

His body tense, Darcy strained to listen to the darkness around him. For a while, there were no more sounds, and he began to relax back into the cushions of the sofa. Its shorter length was not comfortable for his tall frame, but nevertheless his fatigue gave way. Darcy rubbed his face and expelled a heavy breath through his fingers. He was obviously weary and needed more sleep. Having come home from the ball frustrated, still beholden to his memory and infatuation with Miss Bennet, it was no wonder he had fallen asleep thinking of her and no strange thing still that he would imagine her laughter like the remnants of a dream drifting away as he woke.

Darcy turned on his side, trying to make better purchase of the small space. He considered that he ought to go to his chambers, but he was too drowsy to make the effort. His muscles were just beginning to melt against the comfort of the sofa when he heard the sound again, louder this time and distinctly realistic. His eyes snapped open, and he sat up immediately. The disconcerted gentleman rubbed his hands through his hair and then against his ears as if to dislodge the frantic feelings coursing through him. Darcy stood then and walked directly to the door leading to the library.

He knew it was foolish, ridiculous, and insane, but he also *knew* he had heard the sound that time. He looked down at his naked feet and detected no other light coming through the gap beneath the door. The library would be empty, the hot coals of the fire likely on their last hour of warmth. There was no way Miss Elizabeth Bennet could be on the other side. Yet idiotically he yearned. He leaned his forehead against the door and breathed deeply. He needed to govern himself and his silly obsession. His overtired state, too, was surely to blame, yet he could not help feeling a profound disappointment in himself as he found his hand reaching for the doorknob anyway.

And then it happened; the sound—the most bewitching, delicious voice he knew—wafted through the door once again to reach his ears as he sighed in contentment. Insane or not, it was a tone distinctly created to pull at his heart, addle his mind, and in the immediate case, propel him through the door.

His eyes were drawn immediately to the glow before him. His Elizabeth, swathed in ethereal glory, stood facing him. His eyes devoured her beauty, breathing in her delicate features and settling it all with contentment inside him. She looked as she ever did except for the radiance of her person. Her hair was pulled up in a magnificent pile of curls straining for escape, and its brilliance against her alabaster skin made his breath catch. She stood next to a bookshelf, her hand extended towards it. It was not until his eyes drifted up to behold her fine eyes—eyes as familiar as the heart beating in his chest —that he allowed himself to contemplate the truth of the matter before him. He was imagining her in perfect detail, and his infatuation with her had surely reached proportions beyond sanity.

He watched as she immediately lowered her eyes, breaking their gaze, and with confusion written all over her face, dipped into a perfect curtsey. He smiled at it all. His muddled state did not forgo the details, it would seem. Belatedly, he performed his own bow when he saw that she seemed to expect it. He almost laughed aloud at the absurdity.

His heart beat faster, and although a fear was beginning to assert itself in his mind that he was headed to Bedlam, he could not but be pleased with his source of insanity. He laughed aloud, causing Elizabeth to startle from her frozen state and speak. *I am surely attics to let! For her voice sounds just as I remembered!*

"Mr Darcy!" Elizabeth exclaimed; equal parts of confusion, chagrin, and disappointment battled for precedence within her breast.

This is my dream, for heaven's sake, and who is to show up and ruin it—one Fitzwilliam Darcy of Pemberley! It was just too much. Like everything else in her dream so far, it was a mixture of the impossible and astounding. Out of habit, she had curtseyed, and after he finished what seemed to be an exaggerated and prolonged perusal of her person—*Odious man!*—he returned a bow. Now she had spoken, and he seemed rooted in place, hand on the doorknob, and in complete dishabille.

Elizabeth was angry that his state of dress—or rather *undress*—caused her cheeks to heat, more angry still that she was dreaming of him in such a state, and still more that his handsome features were distracting her from her anger. It made no sense, and she threw up her hands in exasperation.

This seemed to awaken her unwanted guest who blinked a few times and said, "I cannot believe it. I should fear for my state of mind, yet I find myself quite charmed."

Elizabeth, surprised, raised a brow and looked upon him with the same degree of astonishment. "It is I who should fear for my sanity, sir. For I was having the most marvellous dream, and then somehow I have stumbled upon a means of stealing its allure."

He seemed to delight in hearing her speak but paid no attention to her words. Instead, he walked directly to her, much too close for propriety, his stare boring into her. She took an automatic step backwards but to no avail. He would come closer. She watched his eyes roam over her face and settle on her lips, and once again, she experienced the exasperating flush in her cheeks. *Can I not have some control over this dream? Am I to be humiliated in my own wonderland?* She could stand it no more and turned her head away. Her eyes went wide when she heard his next words.

"You are every whit as beautiful as I remembered," he whispered, much to her further astonishment, causing her to gasp at his declaration.

"Sir! I..." *What is happening? Mr Darcy complimenting me and, not only that, in a most discomposing manner.* As if she needed further proof that she was dreaming.

She sidestepped around him and walked several paces away. When she turned, she noted that he had followed her movement, still with a look of amazement as if *she* were being imagined by *him*.

For several uncomfortable minutes, they looked upon each other. Elizabeth struggled to explain not only his presence in her mind but also that she was not as unhappy as she ought to be. She conceded he was a handsome man, and although relief flowed through her that at least her mind had not conjured up the toady Mr Collins, she still could not be happy at his presence.

The deep timbre of his voice broke into her cascading thoughts. "I am usually a temperate man, Miss Bennet, but perhaps this evening I have imbibed more than my wont."

He looked at her, and though he seemed not to need a response, she felt compelled to say something to such an altogether baffling statement. "I fear I do not take your meaning, sir."

He smiled, and adding to the strangeness of this dream, Elizabeth found it caused her to breathe unsteadily and instinctively smile back. Her dream was still her own, for though she wished her mind had not brought him about, at least it had changed his character to possess a bit more charm.

He casually walked towards the armchair she had previously "occupied" and sat down with an ease that spoke of familiarity. One leg came to cross the other at his exposed ankle, and his hands drew together to rub his chin. He still had not responded to her, and there was something about his eyes that suggested he was savouring the moment. His actions furthered her confusion, and she looked at him with a sudden impatience.

This, too, like everything thus far, seemed to amuse him, his eyes lighting with fascination. Finally, he opened his mouth and spoke. "Pray tell, Miss Bennet, how is it that you have found yourself to be in my library?"

Elizabeth gasped and looked around her. Her head jerked back to Darcy, and she exclaimed, "*Your* library, sir? That cannot be, for *I* imagined this place."

Darcy's brow lowered a fraction at her speech but quickly resumed its sardonic air as he continued, "*My* library, madam."

Elizabeth contemplated his question as she frantically looked around. Surely, this could not be *his* library, for she was the one dreaming and... Ease flowed through her; of course, all manner of strange things had occurred thus far, and she took comfort in this as just another element of it. *Though perhaps nightmare is more accurate*, Elizabeth thought with a touch of humour.

She answered him honestly. "I know not, sir. But in such cases, it matters not how one arrives, I believe."

"In such cases? It is now *I* who cannot take *your* meaning."

"In the case of dreams. I am dreaming."

To her surprise, this made him laugh. She watched amazed as he leaned forward and covered his face as his laughter came up deep from within him and washed over *her* like a warm embrace. She knew not why, but the sound was as intoxicating as it was new. She could not recall a time when he had laughed in her presence in Hertfordshire.

"Indeed, it seems I must have partaken too much. For although I do not feel the least bit bosky, I must be in my cups. Miss Elizabeth Bennet is dreaming of *me!*" He erupted in laughter again.

"I fail to see the humour, sir."

Mr Darcy lifted his head and, dark eyes bright with humour, stared at her. "You say you are dreaming, madam, but surely that cannot be for it is *you* who haunt *my* dreams."

DARCY WATCHED AS ELIZABETH BLUSHED DELICIOUSLY AND turned away from him. He was losing his wits, but he would worry about that later. For weeks, he had struggled to forget her. Somehow, his struggle had manifested itself in such mental anguish as to produce hallucinations of her, and wonderfully good ones they were. He marvelled at the accuracy of his memory. Her manner was just as bewitching as it was in Hertfordshire, and she was even as impertinent as he remembered.

Upon closer inspection, he did notice a few changes. The dress, although most handsome on her, was not one he had seen her wear before. Of *that,* he was certain, for he recalled every occasion they were in company together, and she had never worn such an angelic dress. Surely, he would have made a point to remember it if she had. There were a number of other small nuances too. She seemed almost to glow in the darkened room, fuelling his conviction that she was a product of his imagination.

Not wishing to think at all upon the consequences of such a notion as his being bound for Bedlam, Darcy focused his mind on enjoying the illusion while it lasted. She was probably a product of too many glasses of wine at the ball and a lack of rest. Darcy frowned;

he only recalled having one glass of wine with the supper meal. There was the small glass of port he had earlier after Colonel Fitzwilliam left him, but such would not constitute dipping rather deeply.

"Will you not have a seat, Miss Bennet?" Darcy said as he reclined further into his seat. If she had been real, he would have remained standing until she was seated as any gentleman would, but she was not real, and he would enjoy her company whilst seated.

He watched her look towards the chair he offered near the dying embers of the fire. "I cannot, sir."

"Cannot?" With a brow raised in challenge, Darcy enjoyed seeing how this provoked her eyes to flash with something like the intensity they did when he would spar with her at Netherfield. *Oh, how I love to provoke you, Elizabeth!*

He watched as she gazed steadily back at him, increasing his heart rate and making his lips twitch. She seemed to come to a decision in her mind, and then she lifted her chin and, with a mischievous smile, walked towards the chair. He leaned back and put his arms behind his head, enjoying the graceful way his mind was conjuring her movements.

Then he watched, frozen in place, as she walked into the chair and stood in the midst of it, her legs disappearing within it. Darcy bolted upright and jumped behind his chair in fright. His wide, shocked eyes quickly met her satisfied ones, and he croaked, "How...? What...?"

His eyes darted from Elizabeth's to the spot where her body disappeared into the cushion and back up to her face. She did not seem to be at all surprised by the feat, yet his mind was racing at the utterly impossible scene he was witnessing.

Elizabeth sighed, walked again out of the chair, and then turned to him. "As I said, sir, I cannot." She seemed to be growing in frustration, yet he could not understand it. It was he who had reason to be upset; she was not real, yet he could see her, talk to her. Fatigue taking over his momentary fright, Darcy slid inelegantly into the chair again, this time dropping his head into his hands.

"Why is this happening to me?" he groaned.

He was a good man, an honourable man. He was a responsible

agent of his estate and brother to his sister. He had not gone to Hertfordshire to become beguiled by a country miss, nor did he see why he could not forget her. Darcy laughed without humour. Looking up through the slits of his fingers at Elizabeth's form still visible to him, he thought, *Forget her! Ha! It is my mind now alongside my heart that might be in some danger.*

His phantom spoke then and, he imagined, with a hint of compassion in her voice. "Sir, I can see my presence distresses you, and I assure you that, if it were in my power to remove myself from you, I would."

Darcy lifted his head and looked at her. He could not fault himself for creating such a beautiful escape from reality. If he were to lose his mind, it would be a comfort to know it was in pursuit of Miss Elizabeth. He sighed and stood, closing the space between them in a few strides. He noticed she held her breath at his advance, and a part of him wished that this reaction was not an invention of his deteriorating mind.

"Come, Miss Bennet. I fear it is late, and the morning will come soon enough. If it is, as you say, that you are dreaming, then you will soon wake. And as for me, sleep will cure my half of this strange sojourn."

Elizabeth shrugged her lovely shoulders and nodded her head. "What shall we do to pass the time then, sir?"

Looking down onto her comely face, Darcy realised his New Year's wish had come true. He was getting to see Elizabeth once again. A smile tugged at his lips, and he resolved to enjoy the last of the evening. With luck, he would fall back asleep and wake rested enough to have his sanity restored. Then, he determined, he would endeavour to extinguish this fascination with Miss Elizabeth Bennet before he truly did lose his mind.

Darcy smiled and gestured around him. "What think you of books?"

To his delight, she laughed. "Oh no, I am sure we never read the same or not with the same feelings."

Darcy settled himself back into his chair and again waved his hand towards the long rows of shelving. "I am sorry you think so, but if that is the case, there can at least be no want of subject." He paused, taking in the brilliance in her eyes. "We may compare our different opinions."

"Very well, sir. What is your opinion of this book here?" He watched her walk towards the small table where he had left the book he was currently working through about Wellesley's battles. His eyebrow rose as he turned to her.

"You have read the account? I am quite astonished."

Her smile was mischievous, yet she answered smoothly, "I briefly felt my way through it."

Darcy appreciated the way her lip twitched when she spoke, almost as if hiding a secret. Still he tried to remind himself that, as she was a part of his own imagination, she would have no secrets and he should not be surprised to have her choose a book he was reading. Sadly, it was only more proof that this was all just a break from reality for him.

Still he wished to savour this time with her and so sat back and began a discussion. He was surprised to note that, although he was imagining her presence before him, his mind did not conjure her to agree with him on all accounts. Her opinions were sound, and though they did not always agree, he found the conversation stimulating. She was certainly a remarkable lady, hallucination or not.

ELIZABETH WAS ASTONISHED THAT THE DARCY IN HER DREAMS was less patronising than she expected. He seemed to find her opinions and viewpoints interesting and even enjoyed being challenged.

It was well after the clock struck four that their discussions began to wane. Elizabeth could see that this warmer, more charming Darcy was losing his battle with sleep. The fact that she remained without fatigue made her smile. For all his reasons she was in his library, she was not the one fading. As they spoke, there were times that he leaned his head back against the cushions of the chair and listened to her. He would still respond, eyes closed, and Elizabeth found that she was surprisingly glad for this, as it became harder not to focus her eyes on his features the longer she remained in his company. She remembered Jane's asking her whether she thought he was handsome after having danced with him at Netherfield, and she had responded,

'He handsome? I should as soon call Mr Collins a wit!' But now that she observed him in the soft glow of the fire, she was becoming much too aware of the falsity of her statement.

"Come, Mr Darcy. I fear it is time for you to retire." Her suggestion had double motives, for she wagered that, if he were to retire, she could once again be alone to enjoy her dream in solitude.

"Mmm..." was all the response she was to expect.

Elizabeth smiled at him. It was easy to be charmed by this Darcy —for he was half-asleep! "Sir, I am sure you are not comfortable where you are."

"'Tis a shame that I shall not see you again tomorrow, Lissa-bethh." His words slurred.

Elizabeth gasped, and her hand rose to her heart. She ought to rebuke him for using her Christian name. But then she remembered it was a dream, and he was clearly not himself in his exhaustion. Laughing, Elizabeth shook her head. The bizarre nature of the dream was softening her towards the man she swore to hate for all eternity!

"Perhaps if you were at least to change seats, sir. You will not find rest in that chair." Why am I concerned for his comfort? He is not even real! Elizabeth determined to care no more, but then Darcy rose unsteadily to his feet and nodded at her.

To her growing alarm, he walked towards her. Unaccountably her heart began to beat faster, and she clutched at her neck, feeling her blush spread again across her cheeks.

"Beautiful...Elizabeth," he breathed near her ear, only just not touching her. "I bid you...a good night."

And with that startling adieu, she watched him step aside and slide easily into the chaise longue beside her. His steady breathing told her he had already fallen asleep. Only then did she release the breath she had been holding.

"ELIZABETH, DEAR SISTER, PLEASE WAKE UP," JANE PLEADED near the bed in which Elizabeth was lying. She looked up with wet eyes at her father and Mr Jones standing near the bed. "Why has she not wakened, Mr Jones?"

The older man, who had tended the Bennet family ailments for all her life, looked kindly and compassionately back at the eldest daughter.

"Miss Bennet, she has suffered a terrible blow to her head, and I fear it will be some time before she wakes. It has only been a few hours since you both were brought home. She must rest, and furthermore, I must prescribe the same for you. You have your own injuries to attend. Come, the morning is approaching, and there is naught that we can do tonight."

Mr Bennet stirred from his frozen state. His night had been thrown into a whirl of alarm and activity as he was pulled from his sanctuary to the sounds of his groom calling for aid, his carriage having overturned just outside the gates. Mrs Hill, the housekeeper, had come swiftly with his greatcoat, and he was quick to don it along with his gloves and hat. With fear possessing his heart and propelling him with the speed of a much younger man, he reached the outside of his estate gates to find his carriage on its side and hear his eldest plead for Elizabeth to stay with her.

The resulting fervour of activity produced first Jane from the carriage with minimal injuries; then, much to his horror, he saw his second daughter lifted out with great care. Her body was limp, and she was insensible.

The hours that followed were a blur of activity as men righted his carriage and sent messengers to Meryton to notify Mrs Bennet and call for the doctor. Elizabeth was placed in her room; a maid changed her from the sage gown she wore into a nightgown and draped blankets atop her that had been warmed by the fire. His wife and other daughters would stay with Mrs Philips in Meryton until the weather improved.

His ears now registered that Jane was speaking with Mr Jones. Mr Bennet tried to focus on what the doctor was saying, but his eyes kept looking at his Lizzy.

"Come, Jane, you must heed the doctor and get some rest. There is nothing we can do tonight."

Mr Bennet watched as Jane nodded tearfully. She gathered the shawl from about her shoulders and walked past him to her room, her arm tenderly held against her as she protected her only injury, a sprained wrist. He turned to Mr Jones once they were in private.

"Sir, speak plainly with me, I beg. Will my Lizzy be well?" His voice faltered at the end.

The doctor placed a hand on Mr Bennet's shoulder and turned his head to look at Elizabeth. "Only time will tell, sir. Let us hope for the best and let her rest for the night. We will know more in the morning."

Mr Bennet nodded numbly, and the doctor left him. He dismissed Hill to get some sleep and insisted that he would act as nurse that night, determining not to leave his daughter's side.

❧ 4 ❧

For some time, Elizabeth remained silently watching Darcy sleep. It was perplexing to her that the content of this most marvellous and troubling dream would feature him so prominently. Her puzzled thoughts struggled to understand it. She did not even like the man. His treatment of his late father's favourite, George Wickham, was uppermost in her mind. She also had her suspicions about the manner in which the whole party at Netherfield left so precipitously when Mr Bingley's plan, as she understood it, was to return shortly from his business in London. *I must be knocked senseless to be dreaming of Mr Darcy! Ha!* A tickle of something floated through her mind but was gone before she could hold onto it, effectively removing any bemusement she felt.

Once again, her thoughts propelled her eyes to look upon his form, lying in repose on the chaise longue. The disapproval she held of his manners and character wavered slightly, like the flutter of leaves in the breeze, when her gaze travelled to his face. Grimacing, Elizabeth admitted to herself that she had always found him hand-some, and that fact had made his arrogance, conceit, and disdain for the feelings of others all the more tragic and frustrating to her. He was a man to whom, presumably, the world had given everything, yet he was still such as he was. He was a man who was used to having those around him orchestrated to his liking, who looked down upon those lesser than he was with disapproval, and who—*sigh!*—was charmingly boyish and handsome while asleep.

Elizabeth huffed and turned her back to him with a stomp of her slipper. She shook her head and rubbed her face as her heart filled with disappointment and dismay at the level of power he seemed to have garnered over her in this fantastical world in which she dwelled. *Why do I dream of Mr Darcy? What does this mean?* She turned her head to peek at him again over her shoulder. Stubble darkened and roughened his straight jaw, and his nearly black curls were variously flattened against his head or standing on end. She felt her frown soften and the crease between her brows disappear.

If she listened carefully, she could hear a quiet snore, and this, more than anything, amused her greatly, his words while she stayed at Netherfield coming comically to her mind: *"I have faults enough, but they are not, I hope, of understanding."*

"Indeed, Mr Darcy," Elizabeth whispered, not wishing to wake him. "You snore!"

Elizabeth laughed at her own humour though it did not last long. She was beginning to notice the room was lightening with the coming dawn. The light coming through the far windows brought with it a growing unease deep in her heart, for the dream was not concluding, and that worried her greatly.

Wishing with a sudden desire to rid herself of this bizarre experience even if it meant losing her many amazing new accomplishments —the book experience still her favourite—Elizabeth began pacing the rug in contemplation. She pinched herself quite determinedly to attempt to wake herself, but still she remained frustratingly fixed in the dream. Furthering the disquiet of her mind, she did not feel the pain of her pinches. In addition, she had remained awake all night in this dream and was not fatigued. Her mind spoke hesitantly of the idea that she might not actually be dreaming but stuck somehow, unbelievably and irrevocably, in Mr Darcy's library.

That idea created such a panic in her breast that she immediately and resolutely forced her thoughts away from that avenue. It could not be, and so it was not.

In her distracted state, she had not noticed that her pacing had brought her further into the room than she had previously been able to venture. When she realised that she was so near to the windows as to be able to discern the street below, her movements stilled immediately. Her new location prompted her to dispel momentarily the gloom building in her mind as she had new spaces to explore.

To her astonishment, no imaginary force held her back from reaching the far portions of the room, and she looked on distractedly out the window as she contemplated this new variance. *Perhaps this fresh-found freedom means I am near waking.* Smiling at the idea, Elizabeth watched the early morning hours bring forth servants and merchants delivering produce in the predawn discharge of their duties. As she strained to look down the length of the street before her, she began to recognise the area as Mayfair. The disquiet she felt earlier returned, evidence building for Mr Darcy's case that she was in his London library. *But surely, if I had created this library and him inside it...* Her thoughts drifted as she rationalised that she could still be dreaming and thus conjuring this little portion as well in order to explain the former.

Turning from the window and from the debate within her head, Elizabeth allowed herself the distraction of reading the titles of the books on that side of the room. Her new occupation was sufficient to keep her fears at bay, and she once again lost herself in the pleasure of her fantastical way of experiencing the volumes.

While encountering anew in a most delightful manner the plays of Shakespeare through the touch of her fingertips, a door along the long wall opened, and a maid entered, startling her. She was labouring under the weight of a tin of coal and making her way to the hearth. Elizabeth stood frozen where she was—unable to determine whether she should make her presence known. The idiotic dilemma brought a smile to Elizabeth's face as she considered the juxtaposition in which she found herself. If she were to make herself known to the maid, it would only place her presence alone with the single gentleman, sleeping not far from her, under public scrutiny; yet, if she were dreaming, that would not matter. However, the choice was taken from her as she watched the maid finish her duties and turn right to her.

Elizabeth knew that it was the role of the servants to act as if they were invisible. Albeit, it became clear to her that this maid behaved as if *Elizabeth* were the invisible one. She was about to say something when the maid spoke.

"'E's sleepin' down 'ere again," she whispered as she shook her head.

Elizabeth answered, "Yes, I believe he had a late evening."

The maid tut-tutted disapprovingly and reached for a small blanket strewn across the back of the chaise longue and spread it carefully over Mr Darcy's shoulders. A cool sensation settled over Elizabeth as she realised that the maid had yet to acknowledge her. The cold dread building in Elizabeth's chest propelled her forward until she was standing directly in the maid's path. The maid picked up her tin of coal to leave and paused only briefly to look back at her master, shaking her head again. Then, to Elizabeth's utter astonishment and absolute panic, the woman walked right through her!

With a swirl of her skirts, Elizabeth spun around to see the maid shiver slightly and continue to exit the room.

"Oh no, no, no!" Elizabeth took a few steps towards the maid and then turned back to glance at Mr Darcy. A profound dread settled into the very fabric of her being, keeping her rooted once again in the centre of the rug as she began to contemplate the implications of what she had just experienced. She had not felt a thing when the maid had passed through her. Nevertheless, even that small acknowledgement meant little when she realised that the dream she believed she was having was quite possibly, and most distressingly, not a dream at all!

Her hands rose to her face as her head began to throb. *It cannot be. It is impossible.* For all the strange and implausible things Elizabeth had experienced that evening, this was the one possibility she could not accept or allow herself to believe was happening. She knew deep down, with a conviction she could not explain, that she had not died and become an apparition in Mr Darcy's library. She had no memory of dying, and thus it could not be so! A part of her wanted to continue to believe that this was the most elaborate, most distressing dream she had ever experienced.

A strong desire to leave that place took over Elizabeth then, and she quickly made for the same threshold the maid had passed through. She was nearly there when, once again, she was knocked backwards by an invisible barrier.

"But I could reach this end of the room before," she squeaked.

This alarming discovery caused Elizabeth to pace the room, finding now, much to her astonishment, that she was limited from much of the room on the *other* side! The confusing perimeter had changed since the beginning of the dream. Contemplating what might have changed, she realised that the only difference was Darcy's entrance into the room.

"Oh goodness, no!" Elizabeth exclaimed, her anxiety turning into anger as she theorised that she might be tethered in some indiscernible way to Mr Darcy! She quickly checked this new hypothesis and realised that it, indeed, appeared to be the case. To her utter shock and absolute fury, she was prevented from venturing further than ten paces from him. *That odious, loathsome man! Who only looks upon me to find a blemish!* Here Elizabeth resolutely disregarded the memory called forth to her mind of his proclaiming her beauty only that morning.

The tumult of her mind was now painfully great. She knew not how to support herself, and from actual weakness, she sat down and cried for half an hour. Her astonishment, as she reflected on what had passed, was increased by every review of it. That she should be tied to Mr Darcy! That this experience might in actuality, and quite frighteningly, not be a dream at all. It was not until she had recovered somewhat from her distressing recollections that she realised she was sitting, or hovering rather in a seated position above the chair into which she had collapsed. She stood then and considered the chair— the same one she had drifted through not hours before. The discordance of results from then to now only added to her list of confusions. Determining then to have one thing in which she had control, she discovered through several attempts that she could sit rather than drift through the chair if she avoided acknowledging the portion of her mind that *experienced* the chair—its softness and construction.

In childlike triumph, Elizabeth shouted an exuberant, "Aha!"

Her small victory was quickly washed away as her previous, distressful preoccupations resumed.

Her cry aloud caused Mr Darcy to stir, and as she continued in very agitating reflections thereafter, the sound of him waking further caused Elizabeth to realise how unequal she was to encounter his observation. Indeed, not wishing to see him at all, Elizabeth hurried her way around the back of the chair to stand among the drapes, making sure she noted their texture so that she could easily slip through them and disappear from view.

A CALMING LETHARGY WAS SETTLING NICELY IN HIS ARMS AND legs. It had been many weeks since he had slept so soundly, yet he could tell that he had slept only a few hours. With eyes still closed, Darcy stretched and savoured the remnants of languor lingering in his muscles. Slowly, he opened his eyes and, upon realising his location, suddenly became wide-awake. Events of the previous evening flooded his consciousness.

He sat up and, pulling his legs out in front of him, leaned his elbows against his legs. The entire evening was excruciatingly wonderful. He knew he ought to worry for his state of mind, and indeed, he would later, but for now, in the quiet moments of first recollection, he wanted only to savour the evening's pleasures. He had to give his mind and memory credit, for although on the verge of obvious collapse, they had created her distinctly as beguiling as he knew she was in the flesh.

He smiled at the memory; his mind had not altered her one wit to be more agreeable and compliant like the other ladies of the *ton*. It was a confirmation to him that this characteristic was most important to him. He wanted a wife, not a mirror. *In fact,* he thought with some humour, *I should have made her a tad more agreeable.* But soon, the roguish smile Darcy wore softened as his face reflected the memory he had of her initial reaction to him. His mind had taken no pains to make it seem as if she expected him or perhaps took pleasure in his appearance. If he had a say in this denigration into lunacy, he would have conjured her up to welcome him. Shaking his head, he smiled sardonically at himself. Here he was recalling, with pleasure instead of concern, the obvious evidence of his madness—and even taking pains to make it more to his liking!

For the first time, Darcy looked up to scrutinise the room. He knew he had heretofore avoided such because half of him hoped and half of him agonized that he might see her. Indeed, upon seeing he was entirely alone, he could not shake the sense of loss he then felt. Rubbing in the proximity of his chest, Darcy studiously denied the absurd feelings and instead forced himself to imagine that he felt relieved to see he was alone. It meant that he was obviously faring better mentally.

He stood then, straightening his wrinkled clothing as well as he could and finding in that real disgust. He was usually much more careful with his appearance and could only think this obsession that was causing such havoc in his life—*and mind*—had caused him to forget himself. He had seemingly cared little for his appearance for quite some time—indeed, since he had left Hertfordshire. *It is a good thing last night's illusion was not really Elizabeth.* He shuddered to think of her seeing him in such a state. It would have been the height of humiliation for him. He decided then that the first part of his journey back to full reason was to see to his appearance now and in the future. He would forget Elizabeth!

With renewed determination, Darcy stood and walked resolutely through the library door. With a silent gasp, Elizabeth dug her heels in the carpet but to no avail, for she found herself being pulled along behind him. Knowing she was unable to get away, she angrily crossed her arms and scowled at his retreating figure as she trailed unwillingly behind him. She clenched her teeth to see that, despite her disinclination to follow, she moved gracefully behind him in a stance of silent disobedience—for all the good it did.

She had half a mind to call attention to herself, to halt his retreat. Contrarily, she was too irate to address him, however much she relished the idea of startling him. So instead, she maintained her posture and allowed his exit. Her perturbation was momentarily dispelled when she, too, exited the library only to gaze upon one of the most beautiful homes on which she had ever set her eyes. The dark cherry-wood panelling contrasted serenely with the marble flooring, and the furnishings were both subdued and expensive. Elizabeth noted with grim reluctance that the home seemed to suit its master well. She smiled to herself then and thought, with a fair bit of humour, *Of all this, I am to be spectre!*

MR BENNET ACKNOWLEDGED THE TIMID KNOCK ON THE DOOR and watched as his eldest daughter's slim shoulders and silken blonde head peeked into the room.

"May I come in, Papa?"

"Of course, child. I should like some company." His tired eyes returned to their vigil over Elizabeth's sleeping form. He looked at her hair swept around her on the pillow, creating a blanket of dark curls.

Jane walked quietly into the room and took up the seat on the other side of Elizabeth. She reached for her sister's hand and squeezed. With tears in her eyes, she looked upon her dearest sister. Her guilt weighed heavily on her mind as she took in the dark bruising along the side of Elizabeth's head. Jane's eyes then travelled to the binding around her sister's arm, preventing it from moving from her side. She winced at seeing this injury, knowing she caused it when she fell on her sister during the accident.

Tenderly, Jane smoothed a curl from her sister's forehead. She spoke so quietly that Mr Bennet almost missed it. "If not for me, our Lizzy would not be like this."

Mr Bennet's furrowed brow added to his questioning tone. "What is this? What nonsense you speak."

Jane lifted her red-rimmed eyes to her father as the tears once again began to flow. His compassionate countenance was too much to bear, and she confessed. "I was not well. I was unhappy at the assembly...missing a certain gentleman. Elizabeth offered to come home with me so that I might not have to endure more."

Mr Bennet, although weary from his long night near Elizabeth's sickbed, stood and walked resolutely around to meet Jane. He pulled her shaking shoulders up to stand and engulfed her in a father's embrace. Her sobs grew more distinct, and he pressed his lips in a stern line to keep from exposing his own overwhelming emotions. As soon he was a master under good regulation, he spoke tenderly to her.

"My dearest Jane, do not trouble yourself over this. Let your heart be light, for you are not to blame for this. Lizzy should not like to hear you say so."

He held Jane back to look into her face. She did not meet his eyes, but he indicated towards the bed. "I know she is in there. She may not be alert, and she may not be healed enough to wake, but she is not lost to us."

"The carriage"—Jane hiccupped—"When it fell...I landed on Lizzy."

Mr Bennet helped his daughter to sit again and stood this time behind her, his hands on her shoulders as they watched Elizabeth's sleeping form. "I cannot say how, Janey, but I feel it, indeed I know it: she will be well."

Jane, leaning against the strength of her father both physically and in spirit and faith, nodded numbly. She reached her hand up to cover his on her shoulder and clasped it. She smiled weakly at the childhood endearment he used with her just then. Together, they offered silent prayers for Elizabeth's recovery.

5

Unwittingly, Darcy took Elizabeth on an abbreviated tour of the house as he made his way. Upon exiting the library, he entered into a wide passage that led to what seemed to be the front entry. If she had wished to make herself known to him, she was unable, for at that moment she was struck quite mute at the beautiful paintings that lined the vestibule and corridors through which he travelled. She nearly called out to him to stop as she wished to gaze a little longer at many of the paintings, but the gentleman seemed quite determined to reach his destination and at the earliest instance.

Her unguided tour concluded when he came to the end of a passageway, entered through a doorway, and closed it behind him, leaving her on the other side. Until that time, Elizabeth had been absolutely fixated on the rich colours and muted elegance of the residence through which she glided. Not once, she noted, did Darcy look back at her, and though she half expected it at any point along the route, she found she was glad for it. She was certain she would not wish for him to see the awe that was surely on her face as she admired his home.

The invisible pull that compelled her forward momentum halted just as she reached the closed door. Grateful for the momentary break to feel as if she were once again mistress of her own destiny,

Elizabeth took the time to prepare herself for what she was certain would be a bizarre and troubling encounter. However, much to her annoyance, before she would declare herself quite ready, the tug of her person once again propelled her through the solid door.

She entered just in time to witness the gentleman—to her horror, embarrassment and shock—pull his shirt over his head and stride into another room, exposing her eyes to the breadth and strength of his back. It was then that Elizabeth realised, in the most alarming manner, that she stood in what appeared to be his bedchamber. Panic seized her as she turned and struggled against the boundary line. Her thoughts were a jumble of dread and maidenly shame. Elizabeth's fists pounded on the unseen wall as her eyes squeezed shut and a blush scorched her face. *Pray, God, have mercy on me! Let me but disappear!*

Her pleas had at least the benefit of easing her panic as, without hope, her shoulders slumped, and she realised she was already invisible except to the one person for whom she wished to be. Her cheeks still blooming with the deepest of blushes, Elizabeth travelled the boundary line in a mortified state for soon she recognised the sounds of water splashing in a tub from the other side of the door. Never in her life had she felt so exposed and uncomfortable.

Wake up, wake up, wake up! she bleakly cried to herself. Her hands ran through her hair, dislodging its careful coiffeur. The feel of her hair tumbling to her shoulders ceased her anxious movements. She quickly re-pinned her hair, feeling absurdly calmed by the mindless process. She could not add to the impropriety of being in the gentleman's chamber by having her hair unbound. Laughing without humour, Elizabeth settled into hopeless pacing across the rug, constantly testing the invisible border and praying it would move.

DARCY FELT NEW RESOLVE SETTLE UPON HIM AS HE FINISHED his bath and allowed his valet, Rogers, to begin his shave. Leaning back to allow the man access, Darcy closed his eyes and contemplated a list of rules he must follow if he were to successfully extinguish his admiration of the most unsuitable Miss Elizabeth Bennet. *First, I must not think of her.* The early morning hours of lunacy, although quite possibly the most candid experience of his life, were indeed facilitated by his constant mental fixation on her. Darcy vowed then to think of her no more. He would not think of her soft curls, her dark eyes, or most especially how the firelight danced in them. He would not think of the charming way she tilted her head to the side when she contemplated something or the intriguing habit she had of troubling one of the sweet curls near her ear.

"Blast!" Darcy swore as he realised he had already slipped into breaking his first rule.

"Pardon, sir, are you hurt? I do not think I cut you," responded his valet.

Darcy cleared his throat and closed his eyes again. "You will excuse me, Rogers. I was not speaking to you. Carry on."

Rule Number Two: no more tender feelings for her. And Rule Number Three: no more undignified behaviour. In the past few weeks, as Colonel Fitzwilliam had severely pointed out to him, he had displayed a total want of propriety so frequently, so almost uniformly, as to offend his nearest relations. It would not do.

Rogers made quick work of his toilette, and as soon as it was time to dress, Darcy took pains to choose clothing that would accentuate his fine, tall person, handsome features, and noble mien. No more would he disregard his duty to his appearance. His rules determined and firmly in the forefront of his mind, Darcy dismissed his valet and walked with quick strides into his bedchamber. Whereupon, seeing the image before him, he promptly forgot both his determination and his rules.

Elizabeth spun around at the sound of the door opening. Her countenance warmed again at seeing him impeccably dressed and staring dumbfounded at her. She turned her back to him, embarrassment and mortification swelling in her breast again at the unseemly situation in which she found herself.

"This is quite enough! I demand that you rid yourself of my presence immediately, madam!"

Elizabeth gasped in shock at his arrogant speech. Her hands clenched into fists at her side, and she half turned to address him. Her mouth went slack as she witnessed him quickly pull the dressing room door shut behind them. His intent, she presumed, was to keep his valet from witnessing their confrontation. It did not soften her fury at the man. Her embarrassment, however, was still fresh, and she resolutely, and with renewed blushes, turned her back to him again.

"I would most gladly, sir, if you would but allow me!"

"Indeed! I find that most astonishing; that you would think it is I —" Darcy's speech stopped mid-sentence as he realised it was indeed he that kept her there. *Whatever happened to The Rules, man?* His agitation then presented itself most acutely in the manner in which he began to pace the room. "I have resolved not to think of you. Therefore, you cannot be here."

"Ha! If only it were that simple. Pray tell, sir, what means of trickery have you employed to keep me here? Is it your intent that I should be compromised?" Elizabeth warmed to her argument. Her accusations came more from the unthinkable situation than from real belief.

Darcy's head snapped up most succinctly at that, and his stare pierced her. His voice was grave, low, and steady. "Those accusations are beneath you, Miss Bennet. And besides, I have already stated that your presence here is not my wish."

Darcy sighed, dropped his head, and ran his fingers through his wet hair. His voice was different, defeated as he spoke next. "Pray, Miss Bennet, forgive my unpardonable rudeness."

He then huffed. *Why do I care whether I am gentlemanly or offend my own hallucination? 'Tis utter madness!* The jostling of his emotions and thoughts had begun to cause his head to ache. Suddenly, he stopped, slid into a chair, and looked at her sadly. "Why can I not forget you?"

Elizabeth drew in a shaky breath, and with her exhale went all her fiery hostility. She was hopelessly lost in a world of impossibilities and tethered to the last man in the world she could ever be prevailed upon to accompany with the least degree of pleasure. It seemed neither of them wished for this enforced incarceration. Her emotions raw from the turmoil of the long evening and the bleakness of the situation before her, Elizabeth succumbed gracelessly into a nearby chair and cried.

Her tears drew the gentleman's attention, and his features softened further. "What foolishness have I stumbled upon that I can draw tears from you in my delusions?"

Before Elizabeth could answer, the door from the dressing room opened and his valet stepped out. "Sir? I heard you speaking. Did you have further need of me?"

Darcy dismissed the man with a wave of his hand, eyes never leaving Elizabeth. "Perhaps, just a glass of water for—" Darcy stopped himself before idiotically requesting a drink for the imaginary lady in his bedchambers. "Ah, a glass of water please," he croaked, thankful for the distraction of his valet. His cheeks reddened as their location occurred to him for the first time. Rogers seemed to hesitate as he looked about the bedchamber and then again at his master. Darcy turned to the man with a raised brow.

His face gave nothing away at that moment, and Rogers nodded, bowed, and left, promising a speedy return with the refreshment.

With his man gone, Darcy was once again aware of the intimacy of their location. He could not look at her for the feelings coursing through him. He wished he could say they were all virtuous, but he was more the fool if he thought that having the beautiful, bewitching, and beguiling Miss Elizabeth Bennet in his bedchamber would not affect him. *I am a bloody buffoon!*

"This will not do, Miss Bennet. You are not real, and the sooner I can convince myself of that fact, the sooner I shall be free of this lunacy."

Elizabeth shook her head, her tears forgotten in renewed exasperation at the gentleman. She ventured to look at him then. He sat with an air of feigned calm, one hand cupping his jaw, his fingers covering his mouth as he spoke. It was all quite distracting.

"Sir, I assure you. I am as real as you are." Her brows lowered as she considered her strange new abilities. "At least, I think I am," she whispered to herself.

"Aha! I heard that." Darcy sat forward, leaning towards her, his words slow and deliberate as if he were saying them to convince himself rather than her. "See, Miss Elizabeth, you are nothing but a lovely apparition, a product of my imagination. And I assure you that I am most determined to see myself to reason."

"If I am only part of your delusion, sir, then answer me this: How is it that I can think and act upon my own free will?"

Darcy frowned, stood, and began pacing in meditation. Coming to a conclusion, he thus answered her, his hands moving about as he spoke through his reasoning. "Disguise of every sort is abhorrent to me, Miss Bennet. Therefore, my mind would not create the object of my admiration to be other than that which she is. Thus, your impertinence is to know no bounds and obviously my insanity likewise." Darcy was only half satisfied with that answer as it gave further proof to the disintegration of his faculties.

Elizabeth's heart began to beat unsteadily at hearing him call her the object of his admiration. Much to her dismay, the idea settled most stubbornly in the proximity of that traitorously beating organ. Still, she wished to dismiss and hide the effect of his words and so answered him laughingly, sarcasm giving tone to her words and helping to dispel the flushed feelings his words had induced.

"My beauty you had early withstood, and as for my manners—my behaviour to you was at least always bordering on the uncivil, and I never spoke to you without rather wishing to give you pain than not. Now be sincere; do you admire me for my impertinence?"

The sides of his lips twitched slightly in a smile. His eyes danced with humour and captured her in that stern gaze he had always bestowed upon her in the past. There, in the most improper and intimate setting in which she found herself with the gentleman, Elizabeth began to see his stare in a new light. It was both alarming and invigorating.

"For the liveliness of your mind, I do."

Rogers at that moment chose to return and, after giving Mr Darcy a glass of water, quickly retreated again. The pause in conversation required for such a disturbance, brought both parties quickly back to the grim matter at hand.

"Mr Darcy, I feel we must be serious, for a solution must be found. I cannot live under such restrictions, and it is highly improper besides. If it is as you say that you—or rather your mind—are in control of this quandary, then I demand that you release me."

"Would that I could, madam, believe me. What are these restrictions you speak of?"

Elizabeth rolled her eyes in a very unladylike manner. "Obviously, I refer to the limits of how far I may venture from you."

"Do you mean to tell me that you cannot leave my side?"

"I would not be in your bedchamber otherwise, sir!" Elizabeth's cheeks heated once again, and she turned her head sharply away.

Darcy was silent for a moment as he contemplated her words. He purposely walked the distance to the far side of his chambers, his eyes going wide when he saw Elizabeth being towed along behind him.

"Fascinating. It would seem my journey to Bedlam knows no limits." And with that, he walked the other direction, once again pulling her along after a certain distance. He then laughed in an agitated manner.

Elizabeth crossed her arms when his strides began to again traverse the room. "Are you quite finished, sir?"

Darcy stopped and sighed. "I fear this is just another bit of proof that you have been manufactured by me; your very existence requires me."

Elizabeth wanted to argue with him. She wanted to restate how real she knew she was. Yet she could not explain why she was there any better than he could. Her only argument lay in knowing her own thoughts, and at that moment, her thoughts were turning towards home. *I just want to go home. Oh, how I miss my family.* Elizabeth sighed sadly and looked upon her unwanted anchor. She knew she should be sensible to the great compliment such a man's admiration meant, but at this time, she could not. He was still arrogant and presumptuous, all the while declaring his responsibility for their situation and disregarding her protests. It was simply too much. There was some reason their lives were intertwined in this way. And just like that, the butterfly of a thought fluttered in her mind again, but it was gone just as quickly.

Resigned, Elizabeth spoke. "What is it you presume to do?"

Darcy walked towards her then, and she felt his closeness in a not unpleasant way. She swallowed the sensation and lifted her chin to him, hiding her beating heart with a disguised façade.

His eyes washed across her face as he readied himself for what he knew he must do. He must endeavour to keep Rule Number One and not think of her. If he could ignore her presence, then she would go away.

"Most assuredly, I must not think of you any more. It is this fixation I have developed that has brought you about, and so I shall not acknowledge your presence. From now on, you are not here, Miss Bennet. I cannot see you or hear you."

Elizabeth tried not to laugh, but she could not help it then. Her hilarity increased when she saw his countenance turn to a scowl as his stride took him to this bedchamber door.

"That is your plan, sir? Forgive me if I do not have faith in its success."

She barely held her laughter at bay when she saw that he was determined to ignore her comments, yet she saw his shoulders straighten with that same resolve.

"Well, by all means, carry on, sir." She giggled at her own wit as she said, "Pray, do not *mind* me."

Elizabeth then sat back, amused at his dogged willpower while he propelled her through the house once more at a purposeful pace.

MRS HILL KNOCKED ON THE BEDCHAMBER DOOR AND OPENED IT to find Jane and Mr Bennet together with Elizabeth. Smiling tentatively, she spoke gently. "Mr Jones is here to evaluate Miss Lizzy again, sir."

Mr Bennet woke from his troubled thoughts and turned to his housekeeper. "Very good, you may see him up, Hill."

A few minutes later, the doctor entered the bedchamber and greeted the occupants. "How did she fair the night, sir?"

"She did not wake if that is what you ask. At one point I worried she might have developed a fever as her cheeks became flushed." Out of the corner of his eye, he could see Jane gasp as she heard this report, for he had not wanted to add to her worry. He quickly went on. "However, when I felt her head, she was not feverish at all."

"Well, I should say that is good news. It means our patient is healing."

Everyone looked at Elizabeth then, only to see she was scarlet once again.

Jane rushed to Elizabeth's side and felt her head, "Oh, look she is flushed again. Mr Jones, do you think she could be getting feverish this time? Just look at her, Papa, she is quite red!"

The doctor quickly went to examine Elizabeth but, upon feeling no sign of undue heat, declared she seemed in no danger. "Though it puzzles me why she would have these moments of redness infuse her cheeks."

"It is almost as if she is blushing," Mr Bennet observed.

"Indeed, I think you describe it accurately, sir," Mr Jones affirmed.

Mr Bennet watched as the glow on her cheeks intensified, giving her face a vivacity that had heretofore been missing. It strengthened his hope that she was not lost to them. Intrigued still, he thought, *Of what are you dreaming, my Lizzy, to make you blush so?*

6

With an amused smile dancing about the edges of her mouth, Elizabeth glided comfortably behind Darcy as he again made his way through the house. Although she could see he was determined to ignore her existence, a fact that diverted her greatly, she could also tell that, indeed, he was having quite a difficult time of it. She detected the slight constriction in the muscles of his neck and shoulders when, along the route, her laughter rang out to him.

"Do slow down, sir," Elizabeth said with mischief. "I see no cause for such haste. There are several of these paintings I should like to look upon."

She knew he would not acknowledge her words, yet she was further pleased to note that his pace did slow slightly. Indeed, however much her statement had been made in jest, Elizabeth found that she was in actuality wishing for some kind of object to fix her attention on for any length of time. Being swept along this way made it altogether too easy to fix her attention upon the man himself and his broad, strong shoulders. As she did so, she also observed that his denial was fragile at best.

This unexpected admiration of his fine figure caused her no small discomposure. She did not want to acknowledge any attraction for the gentleman, for that proved too close to approval. She tried instead to focus all her attention on provoking him by any means. Doing so seemed to serve two purposes in her mind: it would get him past this stubborn refutation of their situation so they could discover how to break the bond that had forged between them; and second, it helped to divert her mind from those dangerous feelings. The latter seemed more pressing to Elizabeth the longer she was fixed to his presence.

How aggravating it seemed that she should be stuck with such a man. His behaviour had always been most irregular. From the beginning, he was arrogant and aloof. When next in his presence, he had begun to scrutinise her in a most disturbing manner—she presumed always looking to find fault. And as their acquaintance lengthened, he convinced her of his disagreeable nature to such an extent that it was not a month after they met, she decided he was the last man in the world she could ever be prevailed upon to marry. *Marry? I...absurd!* Elizabeth shuddered and shook her head to dispel the shocking thought. It was proof that her continued captivity with him was addling her wits. *Perhaps we are both run mad!*

More shocking still, Elizabeth mused, as he continued to lead her along the galleries of his home, he seemed to have developed a preference for her. It was an inclination and admiration that both flattered and stunned her. It was also a change in him that Elizabeth did not wish to dwell on, for she could not be ignorant of the compliment of having garnered the affections of such a man. And she was certain that his good opinion had not been in existence in Hertfordshire. Indeed, he was most disagreeable to her there. He argued and debated with her almost constantly, eavesdropped on her conversations with others, and pierced her with his dark eyes nearly every time they were in company together. *For heaven's sake! He argued with me during our dance at the Netherfield ball!* Yet she could not deny the things he had said to her here. Since she could not yet acquit her mind of the notion that this was not the most agonizing and enchanting dream she had ever experienced, the only plausible explanation was that the recesses of her mind were responsible for coming up with this fantastical scenario. That alone caused Elizabeth to shudder with acute discomfort. For why her mind would wish to dwell so severely on such a man was not a question to which she cared to know the answer at present.

At length, Elizabeth discerned that the pull upon her had slowed considerably and she was coming to a stop. Thankful for the new distraction from her thoughts, she allowed her eyes to take in her location. She was in a large foyer with warm, rich wood mouldings and cream-colored silk wall dressings. The shimmering light from the candles of the wall sconces against the early morning light flickered their glow around the quiet, elegant space. Elizabeth could now detect the delicious aromas of breads, eggs, and other breakfast sundries nearby.

Darcy stood with his back to her before a set of double doors. His stance was eerily fixed as if he was waiting for something to happen. Elizabeth looked about her and did not see any servants to open the door. That was her first presumption to explain his pause before entering the room before him. It occurred to her then, as a smile crept about her features, that he was much too still for any ordinary setting. Indeed, she saw that the hands at his side were engaged in a feverish rubbing of the fingers. With growing amusement, Elizabeth realised that she had been silent during her earlier ruminations and now, as she looked upon Mr Darcy, she saw that his head was tilted to the side slightly as if he was listening for some sound—for her. She crossed her arms in front of her and waited. She knew it would only be a matter of time before the gentleman gave in to the temptation to see whether she had disappeared and thus contented herself with a smug look of satisfaction.

Indeed, much to her delight, Mr Darcy's will gave over only a moment later. She watched incredulously as he stilled further, slowly looking over his shoulder. His stormy look met her raised brow and amused shake of her head. She could see in his eyes a most odd combination of frustration and annoyance; a flicker of what might be construed as relief passed as well. His glance over his shoulder lasted mere seconds before he turned once again, determining, she presumed, to continue his denunciation of her presence.

Laughing merrily, Elizabeth was not surprised to see him clench his hands into fists before soundly pushing the door open. Elizabeth's laughter faded away as she entered what looked to be an elegant breakfast room. The aromas she detected earlier now overwhelmed her senses as she looked around her at the sumptuous spread displayed for Mr Darcy's pleasure on the sideboard along the wall. True to his quest, Darcy went forward and, pretending she was not about, procured himself only a cup of steaming coffee before settling himself in the tall-backed chair at the end of the table. A newspaper had been placed there already.

"I daresay such a feast would have the potential to make me quite round should I have the good fortune to experience it daily," Elizabeth mused, not surprised that he made no reply.

She walked closer to the dishes, and although she realised she felt no actual hunger pains, she did almost feel a thirst and desire for the food before her.

Darcy diligently ignored her comments, but he found, much to his frustration, that he had been watching her for at least a full minute as she leaned over to examine the different foods before realising he was doing so. With a jerk of his head, he looked away and then picked up his paper. Unfolding it with unnecessary energy, he bent his head to frame the paper around him. This efficacious barrier allowed him to keep his eyes away from the tantalizing vision of the curve of her neck extending over the sideboard, her closed eyes, and the altogether sensuous look about her delicate face as she inhaled the aromas of the breakfast table. Stifling a groan, he forced his mind to focus on the paper before him and attempted to engross himself in its written word. His hands tightened around the edges of the paper in a death grip since his ears could not ignore the sounds coming from near the sideboard.

"Mmmm!" Elizabeth breathed in the warm scones as she walked along towards the other pastries.

Surprisingly, her actions and audible enjoyment of the aromas before her were not part of her purposeful game to distract and annoy Mr Darcy. She was simply in raptures over the display of delicacies before her. Yet her innocent actions were most successful in disturbing the gentleman.

"This seems most inconvenient," Elizabeth mused pensively as she thought for the first time what a disagreeable situation she was experiencing being in a room full of delicious fare and unable to partake of any.

Straightening, Elizabeth turned for the first time back to her companion. She smiled as she saw nothing but his white knuckles straining against the delicate paper. A wicked idea came to Elizabeth. Slowly, she walked closer to him and bending at the side of Mr Darcy, allowed her head to pass through the paper to his side of it.

"Anything of interest?" she quipped as he sprang back in surprise.

"Aargh!" Darcy jolted upright and dropped his paper. Elizabeth's head coming through the centre of his paper had given him a most alarming shock and tipped the scales of his tenuous composure.

For the first time since leaving his chambers, he allowed himself to look into her eyes. A fleeting thought for the enchantment that danced in them was arduously shut out as Darcy steeled himself once again to her, all the while his heart pounding from her unearthly jest. Her face was close to his, which did nothing to calm the beating in his chest. To his relief, her enjoyment soon quieted as she, too, realised their proximity. Darcy's lip twitched as her cheeks coloured with warmth, and she stood abruptly, walking with feigned composure towards a nearby window. This power gratified him in small measure before his face grew stern and he willed himself again to adhere to his rules. *I simply must ignore her until my mind grows tired of this lunacy*—delightful lunacy, though it was.

Elizabeth remained at the window for some time while her own emotions settled. Never had her face been so close to his, and the trifling distance did his looks no disservice. When she had realised as much, her heart galloped, and her mouth felt dry. His dark eyes fixed on hers furthered her disquiet as she realised, with no small amount of amazement, that she had almost missed his gaze since they had left his chambers—and it had not even been that long ago! She fingered the embroidered neckline of her dress as she thought through the puzzling mixture of emotions she was experiencing. In an attempt to settle herself in more familiar territory, she tried to recall his past offenses, finding the task arduous and ineffectual. She had simply meant to disturb and bother Mr Darcy with her little joke with the newspaper. With renewed amusement, Elizabeth presumed that her attempt had been most successful. She recalled the way he shot upright and dropped the paper as if it burned him. He still would not learn, it seemed, that his plan to ignore her was not going to work.

Elizabeth smiled as she turned to look upon Mr Darcy, who was again attempting nonchalance as he reached for the silver tray of cream and sugar in front of him. She could prove to him that she was real and that his avoidance of her was useless, but she needed to do so without allowing him to rob her of her senses in the process. *This is Mr Darcy, for heaven's sake! Not the charming Mr Wickham or the amiable Mr Bingley.* He was detestable, presumptuous, and obnoxious. What did it matter that such a man was also devilishly handsome?

"It matters not!" Elizabeth said aloud. Her companion did not react but instead, she saw, scooped a heavy spoon of sugar into his coffee. It was the second of such scoops she had seen him stir into his cup.

"I never care for coffee myself," Elizabeth said by way of conversation, not in the least bothered by his continued disregard.

"I prefer my tea black—no sugar or cream." Deciding a continuous monologue might do as well, Elizabeth walked towards the gentleman. "I cannot abide sugary, hot drinks."

Darcy chastised himself for almost responding then that he well knew her preferences as he had noted them as early as her stay at Netherfield. Keeping his face blank, Darcy merely stirred a third scoop of sugar.

"My goodness, sir! With so much sugar, it will resemble syrup more than coffee." Her face contorted in a grimace of distaste.

Elizabeth reached to place a hand upon the table then, her fingers accidentally brushing the discarded newspaper. The sensation she felt was a flood of political news and a myriad of tedious social gossip. The blandness of the newsprint was absorbed as she remembered her new glorious accomplishment. The reminder gave her pause to consider whether she might try something new.

Reaching her hand towards Mr Darcy's cup of coffee, Elizabeth murmured, "I wonder..."

Casually, the gentleman moved his cup to his lips, as if only to partake of the drink, rather than keep it from her, though she knew the latter to be the case. Her entertainment at this subterfuge displaced her disappointment at not being able to see whether she could *experience* the beverage as she had so many other objects.

Before she could think to try again though, the door opened quietly, and she watched with rapt attention as a graceful, striking creature entered. Her gold tresses glowed in the morning light streaming through the windows, and though her head was bowed, Elizabeth could see immediately that she was exquisite. Slowly her gaze left the newcomer to settle on Mr Darcy. Elizabeth was stunned to acknowledge an almost immediate feeling of profound displeasure steal around her breast, constricting her breathing and causing her jaw to clench shut when she saw that the entrance of this beautiful lady into the dining room caused the most uninhibited look of pure joy to envelop the gentleman's countenance—a look, her heart whispered, not unlike the one he gave her when she first encountered him in the library the night before. Still, Elizabeth could not explain nor understand why seeing him look so happy in this lady's presence disturbed her. She was not a cruel person, and although she did not like Mr Darcy, she did not wish him unhappy; yet this unknown lady made him happy, and Elizabeth did not like it one bit.

Unconsciously, Elizabeth crossed her arms about her and fixed her features to conceal the surging tempest inside her.

To her right, Mr Darcy stood immediately and quickly closed the distance to the intruder. Elizabeth's mouth gaped as she saw him engulf the lady in a warm embrace and bend to kiss her cheek. The torment this scene caused inside Elizabeth was too overwhelming to account, yet she could not take her eyes off the tender scene.

"Georgiana, my dear. Good morning," Mr Darcy said sweetly as he released her.

"Good morning, Brother. I...I did not think to see you so early this morning. It was my understanding that you were out last evening."

Elizabeth drifted in a dazed state to sit in a corner chair during this exchange. *His sister!*

Darcy turned with Georgiana and elegantly guided her to a chair next to his own. "You have not been misinformed, dear. I was out quite late. May I prepare you a plate, Georgie?"

"Are you quite sure I am not disturbing you?" Georgiana looked at his crumpled newspaper and half-empty cup of coffee.

"No, I should like to have your company. 'Tis disagreeable to dine alone." Darcy spoke with a calmness that seemed unnatural to his sister. It puzzled her since she knew that he frequently preferred to breakfast alone lately. In truth, Georgiana did not know that her entrance into the room was the first time he had not been achingly aware of another presence in the room. Georgiana would prove to be a much-needed distraction.

"As it is, I have a meeting with my solicitor soon, and so it is I who will not disturb your meal for long," Darcy said with a smile to his sister. "I have not yet broken my fast in any case."

"Very well, then. I am always glad for your company." Georgiana beamed at him.

The tumult of emotions disturbed Elizabeth greatly. That she should at first feel jealousy—for that is what she knew she had experienced upon Georgiana's entrance—was distressing enough, yet the liberating feeling of relief that coursed through her when she realised that this beautiful woman was only his sister—*his sister!*—was even more unsettling. Why should she care that Mr Darcy displayed such tender emotions for someone else? It took her several minutes of quiet reflection to calm herself and resolutely dispel the unfamiliar feelings. During her quiet contemplation, Darcy and his sister enjoyed morning pleasantries with each other.

As Elizabeth slowly came to the present, she sat back with a new purpose to observe the siblings. Her mistaken assumption about Miss Darcy was easy to explain, for the young girl was as fair in her colouring as her brother was dark. Where his hair was curly, hers held only a gentle wave. When Elizabeth looked closer still, it was clear to her immediately that this could be no other than a relation of Mr Darcy's for the girl shared his discerning eyes. Darcy then said something to his sister that Elizabeth did not catch, but it made the girl giggle. Her smile, too, resembled her brother's, though Elizabeth thought it was perhaps less engaging. Although it enhanced her beauty, her features did not light up as Mr Darcy's did on the rare occasions Elizabeth remembered having seen him smile. Examining her further, Elizabeth could see Miss Darcy took pleasure in her interaction with her brother, that they were close, and that the girl held him in fond affection. She found herself smiling at the two of them and being captivated by this charming side of Mr Darcy.

She also noted with some confusion that this Miss Darcy was not the girl she expected if she were to believe Mr Wickham's description. Though she did have an upright, proud air about her, Elizabeth detected that it was more an element of schooled discipline and that she seemed unsure of herself rather than arrogant like her brother. Added to this was the clear regard the siblings had for each other, further evidence that Miss Darcy was not at all what Elizabeth had been led to believe.

Mr Darcy, she noted was different too. Gone was the proud visage to which she was so accustomed. He was most solicitous of Miss Darcy as he asked her preferences and served her selections. When he placed the heaping plate before Miss Darcy, her eyes bulged at the portions.

"Good heavens. I shall be sick if I eat all of this."

Darcy's responding smile seemed slightly off to Elizabeth, causing her to observe him closer. He laughed with only the slightest edge to the sound and assured her she need not eat it all. When he turned to get his own plate, Elizabeth saw Miss Darcy look over her plate and then send a puzzled look towards her brother. *Interesting*, thought Elizabeth. It seemed to her that perhaps Miss Darcy thought that her brother's behaviour was atypical as well.

Elizabeth smiled as she speculated that Darcy was happily using his sister as a distraction. Her suspicion was confirmed when she caught his fleeting glance as he returned to his seat. His face fell from its pleased look; he closed his eyes and breathed deeply, his back to his sister. Elizabeth realised the disappointment she saw then on his face was for still seeing *her*, and she experienced a twinge of pain that he should take such displeasure in her company, the glaring difference between his feelings towards his sister spurring her resentment further. Though if she could have known his thoughts, she would realise that it was not displeasure that he felt in her company but rather the opposite—to an extent with which he was not comfortable.

She watched when he opened his eyes again. He purposely avoided her direction and feigned a look of contentment as he turned to face his sister once again. Elizabeth was not a person given to petty behaviour, but she uncharacteristically decided then, in her wounded pride, not to leave the gentleman alone during his breakfast with Georgiana.

Elizabeth stood and walked towards the table. She was satisfied to note the stiffening of Mr Darcy's shoulders. The siblings were discussing the previous night's festivities, and Darcy was recounting the society he had met at the ball. Elizabeth listened as the girl asked about a cousin, a colonel in the army. Contenting herself to observe, Elizabeth circled the table waiting for an opportune moment.

"And did you make a New Year's Eve wish, Brother? Do you think Fate will target you this year?"

Elizabeth was amused at the innocent tease. With practice and a little confidence, the girl might be absolutely charming. Elizabeth, curious about her brother's response, looked at him. She frowned, mirroring the expression she found on his face. It seemed he was displeased with Miss Darcy's attempt. Noting Georgiana's bowed head, Elizabeth could see that the young girl also took notice of his reaction. Darcy was simply remembering that he had indeed made a New Year's wish and, with a glance at the apparition across from him, noted Fate was definitely targeting him.

"You will make the poor girl cry with such a sour face. She was only teasing you. Have a heart, sir," Elizabeth chastised.

She knew he heard her because of the slight wince of his face and the immediate redirection of his eyes from his plate to his sister. The softening of his features then made Elizabeth wonder whether some thought other than the tease had caused his earlier grimace.

"Forgive me, Georgie."

"No, it was I...I should never have behaved so imprudently just now." Georgiana trembled.

Darcy, awash with shame for his behaviour, was quick to reassure her. "Oh, my dear, think nothing of it. I was not offended in the least at your tease." He offered her a generous smile to prove it. "I was momentarily distracted, is all. I am sorry, but I believe I am not good company this morning."

Miss Darcy ventured further, taking heart in his renewed approbation. "I have been worried of late. You do not seem yourself."

Darcy blew out a long breath. "You are correct. I have not been, but I assure you, I am working most heartily to change that."

Elizabeth was touched by his sincere demonstration and so was his sister. Her resolution to annoy him temporarily set aside, she decided instead to allow Darcy a moment's peace. For the next quarter hour, Elizabeth merely observed the siblings again. She noted that the longer she stayed out of sight, for she placed herself behind Mr Darcy, the less his shoulders were fixed with tension. She also noticed the cadence of his voice took on a more melodic rhythm as he settled into comfortable conversation again. Much to her astonishment—alas, adding to the many things that astonished her since awaking in this bizarre state—she found she was envious that she had never met this relaxed, conversant Darcy. He had always had a tension in his voice when conversing with her. Elizabeth mused on this change for some time while she watched him with Georgiana. It called to mind something she had heard before about the gentleman: *"He can be a conversable companion if he thinks it worth his while."* Mr Wickham had said that, and Elizabeth could see the truth before her.

In her distraction, Elizabeth found herself veering once again to the sideboard, the luscious aromas still wafting towards her in enticing waves. Setting aside the puzzling character of Mr Darcy, a character she was still having a difficult time trying to illustrate, Elizabeth looked at the variety of foods before her. In an attempt at discretion, Elizabeth placed her back to the other occupants of the room. She decided once again to see whether she might *experience* the food as she had wished before Miss Darcy had interrupted with her entrance. She reached tentatively towards a lemon pastry on the platter closest to her. To her delight, she could taste the buttery goodness of the pastry, and although lemon had always been her favourite, she could not think of a time when tasting it seemed such a delicious and enchanting experience. The crème was rich, smooth and had a lightness that she wished she could actually have in her mouth. *Marvellous!*

Experiencing these pastries was different from *reading* the books in the library, for she could touch them again and experience more of the book, or rather, different parts would stand out each time. With the food, she could taste the lusciousness of it, but it did not satiate her. It was a strange sensation to feel hungry, or more, to know you were hungry but not really to feel the pangs of hunger. It was as if her mind was disengaged from her body; she knew she wished for food and drink but could not feel her body's recognition of it.

Not wishing to give any more attention to her disquiet in this regard, Elizabeth quickly touched another item. The fascination of tasting different foods effectively kept her from wallowing in her growing doubts and fears.

Her attention was called back to the others in the room when she heard the scrape of Darcy's chair as he stood. Turning around, Elizabeth knew she looked like a guilty child, but luckily for her, the gentleman was still avoiding her.

"Thank you for the lovely repast, Georgie."

Miss Darcy blushed at the praise. And Elizabeth blushed at the tender kiss she saw him place on his sister's head. She quickly turned around, hoping to distract her wayward thoughts with additional treats. There was a delicious-looking plum cake at the far end of the table. Elizabeth went immediately for it only to find the boundary line pulling her away. She turned in protest towards Darcy who was exiting the room.

"But I wanted to taste the plum cake!"

With a pout, Elizabeth once again crossed her arms about her and glared at the back of Mr Darcy who, although she was sure he heard her plea, was most ungentlemanly ignoring it.

AGAINST HIS WILL, AGAINST HIS REASON, AND EVEN AGAINST HIS character, Darcy found himself smiling at her petulant tone as he strode from the breakfast room without so much as a pause. Her beguiling presence was truly haunting him. He knew he had done a poor job ignoring her that morning. Her defiant remarks about his intentions to do so only made him more determined. To block out the musical sound of her laughter when they left his chambers, he had forced himself to recite the kings of England in chronological order. After a while, it seemed to work, for he could no longer hear her. He had almost believed he had accomplished his goal when he had reached the breakfast room.

But of course, it could not have been that easy. He had, indeed, felt disappointment when he turned and found her so impertinently standing behind him. Yet, in the morning glow of the candles that had been lit to chase the night away but not yet extinguished, she had looked every bit as bewitching as before and indisputably still there.

Biting his lip and suppressing a smile, Darcy recalled her little prank with the newspaper too. If he were not attics to let, he would laugh at her wily trick. Again, he had to give himself credit for making her such a lively minx. Oh, how he had wished at that moment for her to be the real Elizabeth! He most certainly would have taught her a lesson in decorum—a not very decorous lesson either.

The idea of her being real was what brought Darcy back to reality. Their situation—the whole, sordid mess—was proof enough that there was a definite illusory sensation to whatever was happening. Neither of them acted entirely with propriety with regard to the other. She spoke more impertinently; he was unguarded. What if his little make-believe lady was real? Darcy shuddered at the thought. Certainly, there had been moments that he would have gone to great effort to behave differently. He coloured at the forward remarks he had made so far with this Elizabeth. *Am I to act in accordance with the dictates of society with my manifestation of Elizabeth?* He had to smile, for part of him found their lack of restrictions exhilarating.

Darcy stopped abruptly on the journey to his study and spun to look at Elizabeth. He almost smiled when he saw her, for he knew somehow that she would still be there. It was not as if he had done a thorough job keeping Rule Number One. For a moment, the two just gazed at each other. Darcy's perusal of her was intense and studied. He was not sure what he was looking for, but nonetheless, his eyes took in every detail.

He watched with detached amusement as her eyes drew his attention to a cocked right brow. When their eyes met, she performed a perfect curtsey—perfect in its mockery.

"Mr Darcy, sir." Her lilting voice reached his ears.

Darcy returned her salute with a bow of his own. "Miss Bennet."

Their eyes once again locked until Darcy could hold back no longer. With a toss of his arms in the air, he once again spun in place and laughed manically as he continued on his way.

"This is certainly madness!" he spoke aloud. *What did I think—I could stare her out of existence? A fine job of that I did in Hert-fordshire.*

Mr Bennet was just emerging from his rooms when he heard the rumble of voices chorusing up the stairs, heralding the return of his wife and other daughters. After a long night with Elizabeth, with but a short reprieve from her bedside to quickly bathe and see to his appearance, the last thing he needed was the drama of the rest of his family.

He could hear his wife calling frantically for Hill, addressing the footman for another task, and calling for another to fetch her husband. Mr Bennet had half a mind to turn on the spot and hide in his chambers. But he could not, and he certainly did not wish to have her go to Elizabeth's bedside in such a state. With a sigh, he descended the stairs to greet his wife.

When he arrived, he could see Jane had not yet come down and was grateful for that mercy as he was sure Mrs Bennet's agitations would only be heightened with the sight of her eldest daughter's bruises and injured arm.

"Oh, my dear Mr Bennet," she said as she saw him enter the room. "We have had a most delightful evening, a most excellent ball. I wish you had been there. Jane was so admired, though she did leave early; everybody said how well she looked, and Elizabeth danced with Mr Wickham though it was my Lydia who really caught his eye. Mr Wickham thought her quite beautiful and danced with her twice. Only think of that, my dear: he actually danced with her twice, and she was the only creature in the room that he asked a second time."

"Enough madam! Did you not receive my missive last evening?" Mr Bennet was exasperated with her talk of partners and dances when his Lizzy lay upstairs, lost in a world beyond.

"Of course I did. And as you see, here I am. I did not venture into the storm and stayed at my sister Philips's house."

Mr Bennet looked at his wife with utter shock at the callous way of her speech. He looked towards his other daughters only to find them caught up in their own ruminations of the assembly. His feelings got the better of him then, and he spoke with more force than he had intended. "Mrs Bennet, be so good as to share with me exactly what message you received." When she went to speak, he added, "Word for word, ma'am."

Mrs Bennet detected the angry tone in her husband's voice and, although she did not see why he ought to be upset, answered him with more forbearance than she felt he deserved. "Mrs Philips's maid passed along the message she received from our groom that we were to stay in Meryton, the roads being dangerous and likely to overturn the carriage." With a lift of her chin, she ended with, "As you see, sir. We have done just that."

Mr Bennet sank heavily into a nearby chair. "The roads were indeed dangerous last night, madam. And the carriage being overturned, I fear, not likely but definitely."

The room went uncharacteristically silent. Mrs Bennet's voice was barely a whisper as she spoke haltingly. "Where is my Jane? I have not seen her yet. And Lizzy, why have they not greeted us?"

Jane came into the room then, her arm held closely and tears in her eyes. "I am here, Mama."

Mrs Bennet stayed fixed where she was, her normally fickle heart beginning to beat a steady rhythm. She spoke to her husband while looking at her daughter. "Mr Bennet, what has happened to my Jane?" The low tone of her voice was the only indication that she was affected by the sight of her bruised and injured daughter.

"I am well, Mama," Jane intervened, ready to assure her mother.

"Mr Bennet, why are you so silent?" And then remembering his earlier words, she said with heavy emotion, "What did you say about the carriage?"

The two locked eyes, and Mrs Bennet's began to swim when she looked into the fatigued, heavy eyes of her husband. "Sir, I will kindly ask you again: Where is Lizzy?"

Mr Bennet stood then and came to his wife. With a sadness in his eyes, he looked at her puzzled and worried face, and taking her hand said, "Come, dear, I will show you to her."

7

The glass was warm, the liquid a shimmering amber. As Darcy swirled it, he watched the candlelight dance and flicker through it. It was the most fascinating glass of brandy he had ever had and mostly because he was determined to make it so. Watching it meant he was not watching anything or *anyone* else. The sounds of the men around him nibbled at his ears although not sufficient enough to distract his thoughts entirely but enough to keep him properly adhering to Rule Number Three: avoid undignified behaviour. That was the whole purpose in coming to his club in the first place. He had spent the day in various pursuits, and nothing had kept his eyes from drifting to her ever-present form. Smiling at his cleverness, he again lifted the glass to his lips to take a sip. Throughout his day, he had found that if he were surrounded by people, or at least in company with another person, he could effectively numb his mind to her allurement and almost close his ears to the melody of her voice—which was what he was attempting now.

He recalled with a grimace meeting with his solicitor earlier in the day. It was not long after he had left the breakfast room that his butler, Mr Carroll, had announced Mr Maddings's arrival. The portly gentleman's entrance was never so generously received nor so welcome a sight to his client's eyes. Darcy usually took satisfaction in working through his books and managing his estates. It was an honour to continue the legacy that his father had left him—but never so much as now when doing his duty also allowed him to accomplish his goal.

Early in the new year, he had always had a standing meeting with his solicitor to review his accounts and plan for the coming year's expenses, investments, and legal needs. It gave Darcy an opportunity to have the man update his essential documents and work the year's income into the brackets. The meetings were uneventful and strictly business. The men had never discussed personal details not directly necessary for the solicitor's legal drafting.

Darcy raised his hand and, with a flick of a finger, summoned the club's footman for another drink. He dared not lift his head for he knew what he would see—or rather *whom*. His thoughts returned to the meeting with his solicitor and, with its recall, the memory of her presence. Whether he was ignoring the fact or relishing it was hard to say. He was a weak man when it came to Elizabeth, and although he was engulfing himself in the society at White's for the sole purpose of blocking her out, he could not entirely forget—and so he purposely remembered.

"Mr Darcy, sir. Good morrow and a happy New Year," Mr Maddings had said as he wobbled across the study rug, a heavy satchel in one hand and the other extended to him.

"Thank you, Mr Maddings, and a good day to you too."

Darcy stood and enthusiastically gave his solicitor a shake of the hand then motioned for him to take a seat across the desk from him. Out of the corner of his eye, he could see Elizabeth—who had been browsing the selections of books he kept in his personal study— straighten and turn to observe the newcomer. She had until then been driving him to utter distraction with her lilting laugh over one book or a witty comment about another. It was all he could do not to respond, let alone allow himself to restfully gaze upon her lively countenance, showing much mischief and joy as she walked about the room. Most difficult of all was to keep from questioning her about her method of reading the books. It appeared to him that she never picked up any book but merely glided her fingers through them. *Lucky books.*

The other gentleman cleared his throat, startling Darcy. He had lost himself in studying her again. Her eyes were filled with humour when he found that she had caught him too. Realising that it must look as if he were staring at his bookshelves for no reason, he turned resolutely back to Mr Maddings and tried to stifle the grimace he felt for behaving so. *Drat. Rule Number Three.*

"Pardon me, I..." Darcy coughed inelegantly into his fisted hand and with a determined air continued. "Shall we begin?"

Darcy resumed his seat as the other man stood and handed him a stack of papers across the desk. Mr Maddings then came around to stand at Darcy's left as he began their interview. His unimpassioned tone gave Darcy hope that he, perhaps, had not behaved too strangely.

"Very good, sir, you will see in this draft that I have first tallied the investments and monies you possess with the profits from last year. In this column here..."

Darcy wanted to, nay, *needed* to pay closer attention to his solicitor, but his words began to drift into the background as Darcy became aware of Elizabeth's coming up beside him on the right. Suddenly, he felt trapped between the two. He could say nothing to her without confusing the gentleman and making a fool of himself. Besides, was he not trying to ignore her so that she would vanish? Instead, he positioned himself in such a way as to rudely block her view with his shoulders. It was not as if he cared whether his ghostly Elizabeth knew his income. Rather, it was an attempt to block *her* from *his* view.

He felt himself stiffen when he heard her whisper from behind his shoulder and near his ears.

"My, my—you are a very rich man."

Every nerve in his body became alert to her nearness. He remained as still as possible and squeezed his eyes shut. When he opened them, it was with a renewed focus on his solicitor.

"Despite the heavy rains this year, your harvest was good, and I see no reason why you cannot increase your holdings here as you wish..."

Mr Maddings droned on, pointing to another column or occasionally lifting the paperwork to find a different document.

"It is good that the neighbourhood in general was so deceived, sir, as to your true worth. Even my mother might have endured your conceit had she learned it."

He detected the teasing tone of her voice and knew that her imprudent speech was another attempt to unsettle him. She was taking every opportunity to force him to acknowledge her, but he was stronger than she was. He was positive this was the only way to resolve his bout with insanity, and so, though his lips twitched with amusement, he made no response. He did note with relief that her voice showed she had moved further away though—*thank God!*—still out of his sight.

Darcy applied himself then with renewed vigour, catching the last of his solicitor's words.

"...should you be wishing to increase Miss Darcy's dowry."

"No, no. Although we had discussed it, I am certain it is sufficient."

"Very well, sir." Maddings continued as he made a note in his book, "And I presume you may wish to take a wife at some point."

"Oh yes, Mr Maddings, for it is a truth universally acknowledged that a single man, in possession of a good fortune, must be in want of a wife," Elizabeth said with evident humour as she walked around and made direct eye contact with Mr Darcy, her eyes positively glowing with mirth.

"You presume too much," Darcy said with more force than he intended as he tore his eyes from Elizabeth's and looked at his solicitor. Immediately upon seeing the man's reddened cheeks, Darcy was repentant. The man was simply ensuring Darcy was secure in whatever life events he might have. He could not be knowledgeable of Darcy's recent struggles against his infatuation with Elizabeth nor her clear unsuitability. The man did not even know that Elizabeth had spoken to him, for only Darcy could see or hear her!

"Mr Maddings, I must ask that you excuse my unpardonable rudeness just now. I simply have had a fair bit in...on my mind of late." *More like a fair lady.* "And I took it out on you most ungraciously."

The man paused only briefly before replying in haste. "Think nothing of it, sir."

They then resumed their business with more attention on Darcy's side. Before he had realised it, an hour had passed in review and strategy for investments and the corrections and additions to the drafts Mr Maddings had brought with him.

It was clear to Darcy that his earlier show of temper had sufficiently convinced the lady to end her charades, for though she lingered—obviously—nearby, she took mercy on him and did not again attempt to provoke him.

When the footman delivered his new drink, Darcy took it immediately and brought it to his lips to hide a smirk lingering as the memory faded but not without bringing to mind the look of her undisguised surprise, and perhaps begrudging admiration, when Mr Maddings reviewed his charitable obligations and the organisations to which he was the benefactor. The smile fell as Darcy realised that any approbation he garnered from this fictitious Elizabeth was neither useful nor meaningful as soon he would be rid of her. Besides, he did not need even the real Elizabeth Bennet's good opinion. It mattered not what she thought of him, for she was simply not suitable. And he needed to accept that.

"Quite the dour face you show there, Cousin."

Darcy startled at the thump on his back from Colonel Fitzwilliam.

"Mind if I join you this evening? I went by Darcy House and was informed by our sweet Georgiana that you were dining out."

"You are, of course, welcome. It is your club as much as it is mine."

"I see that you have already dined," he waved towards the cold, half-eaten plate in front of Darcy. "But you will not mind if I do?"

"You may do as you please. You always do," Darcy said with good humour. Without realising it, he had allowed himself to look over at Elizabeth for the first time since coming to his club.

Upon arrival, she had voiced numerous fascinations and observations about his club. Her witty remarks were as humourous as they were distracting; twice he had found himself almost responding to her observations but had caught himself in time. It would not do to have people see him talking to himself. He could just see the bets that would be placed in the book. *How many days until Fitzwilliam*

Darcy is admitted to Bedlam?" Instead, he had garnered an empty table in the corner, ordered a meal and a brandy, and then scolded himself into studiously not allowing a single look at her. Now he could see that her interest in her surroundings had not waned. Only Darcy could see that she was also now curious about the newcomer to the table.

Just then, she winked at him and curtseyed for Colonel Fitzwilliam, waiting cheekily for an introduction that obviously would not come. *Bothersome minx*, Darcy thought even as he smiled into his glass and turned again to his cousin. Richard was just finishing his order to a footman.

"I did not know you had plans to call on us, or I would have taken pains to remain at home."

Colonel Fitzwilliam laughed jovially, pulling a genuine smile from Darcy. His amiable nature almost always brought out either the best or the worst of him, and tonight he was determined it would be the best.

"Would you now? Forgive me if I find that humourous. Surely, you do not think me stupid?"

"I beg your pardon?"

"Other than our little 'chat' last evening in your study, you have most earnestly been avoiding me since you returned from Hert-fordshire."

Darcy frowned, and while he was aware that Elizabeth had moved closer at the mention of her home county, he was more concerned that his cousin would not provide the lift to his moods that he wished for after such a long, exhausting day of mental tug of war with his grip on reality. The day weighed on Darcy: from the surprise encounter in his chambers after his bath to the entire episode in the breakfast room and the visit with his solicitor. It was, indeed, a battle of wills that he was beginning to fear he was losing. Nothing he did seemed to diminish her allure in the least. He had even thought at one moment in the afternoon that physical exercise might help tire his mind of its playacting with his senses. He had gone, determined and hopeful, to the Fencing Academy on Bond Street, but he only lasted there a few minutes—especially when he saw the wide eyes and pink cheeks Elizabeth displayed as she looked at all the men in shirtsleeves practicing their swordplay. No, it was only gentlemanly of him to keep her exposure to *that* at a minimum. At least that is what he told himself. He did not even consider Gentlemen Jackson's next door for he knew the men there wore even less. Instead of finding the physical release he wished for to help temper this fight, he found himself ridiculously jealous of the look on Elizabeth's face when she caught sight of the fencers. *Idiocy! I am possessive of even my own hallucinations!* Becoming aware that his mental ruminations had been noticed by Colonel Fitzwilliam, Darcy endeavoured to be more attentive.

Searching his memory for his cousin's last words about trying to avoid him, Darcy thus replied with feigned nonchalance, "I am sorry you think so. It was not my purposeful intention to—"

"Oh, give over!" Colonel Fitzwilliam said with another laugh. "It certainly was, and I now know why. Do you not remember your little revelation last evening?"

Darcy could feel his cheeks colour slightly, and he shifted in his seat uncomfortably. "I do, and if you will humour me with another topic, I would be most pleased to remain in company with you this evening."

Darcy watched his cousin's brows rise while considering the challenge. His food arrived, and true to its power over his cousin, the meal won over Colonel Fitzwilliam to Darcy's side, for he then said, "Very well, for the time being, Darcy, but only because this smells divine and I do not wish to spoil my appetite in verbal wrestling with you over your lady love."

"*Ooh, how intriguing. A lady love—do tell!*" Elizabeth's laughter caused Darcy to wince, and although he detected an edge to it, he paid it no more attention.

Elizabeth took up a chair at the table and observed the two cousins curiously. She liked this cousin of Darcy's at once, for he had a lively, cheerful manner, convincing her immediately that this was a man whose company she would enjoy. Darcy seemingly ignored her except for the slight tightness about his eyes when she laughed with his cousin. She dearly wished she could make the acquaintance of that gentleman in truth, for he was a man prone to good humour, and she dearly loved to laugh.

It was not until much later in the evening, after many hours of intelligent conversation—conversation that astonished Elizabeth with yet another unexpected and begrudgingly admirable aspect of Darcy's character—that Elizabeth even learned the name of Darcy's cousin. It had happened when, surprisingly enough, an acquaintance of *hers* came up to the two gentlemen.

"Mr Bingley! Hello, my good man. Please join us," Colonel Fitzwilliam said loudly when he saw the man enter the room.

Elizabeth watched with a tinge of regret for Jane as a jovial Mr Bingley strode towards their table.

"Colonel Fitzwilliam, a pleasure, sir!"

Darcy also greeted his good friend warmly. When Bingley joined their table, he again smiled at everyone though Darcy could see it did not reach his eyes—and had not since leaving Netherfield. A guilty thread wrapped around his conscience, and a nagging doubt picked at Darcy as it had, on occasion, for weeks. Furthermore, Darcy sincerely hoped—though it made no sense as she was only a creation of his own mind—that Elizabeth did not notice the pinch to Bingley's features. Darcy did not want to examine why he should worry about her when she was not really the sister of Miss Bennet, not in the flesh. His actions to separate the two were done with the best of intentions and probably were also for the best.

Darcy did not stay long after Bingley's arrival though the company of two such amiable men *was* adequate distraction despite the musical laughter and impertinent interjections Elizabeth made occasionally. The growing discomfort he was feeling with regards to Bingley made him leave—that and the sheer exhaustion from the day's efforts at forging his way back to sanity. He dared not stay in company longer; more than once he had caught himself smiling towards the empty chair to his left when Elizabeth commented. He was certain at least his cousin had noticed. No, Darcy just wanted to claim his bed and sink into sleep's oblivion.

"Gentlemen," Darcy said standing. "I believe I shall leave you now."

"Good evening, Darcy," Bingley replied with sincerity, making Darcy wince slightly.

"A pleasure as always, Cousin. It will not be a long farewell for either of us, for I shall see you both tomorrow at my mother's ball. You still plan to attend?"

Though wishing he could evade the obligation under his new circumstances, Darcy knew it could not be avoided. "Of course. I shall see you both tomorrow. Adieu."

The ride home was uncomfortable at best. Such sweet torture only added to Darcy's growing impatience for sleep. He had no choice except to either close his eyes or look at Elizabeth seated directly across from him. And when she spoke, her voice drifted in the small space, wrapping him like a warm blanket.

"I must say that I am having a most fascinating and educational experience. I never should have believed I would see the inside of the hallowed gentlemen's clubs and academies."

Though Darcy kept his eyes firmly shut, he could almost picture the blush spread across her cheeks as she spoke of the Fencing Academy; the slight tremor in her voice gave her away aptly. He schooled his features to show no emotion though, despite his fatigue, he was experiencing many.

Their carriage pulled up to his house then, and with his escape in close proximity, Darcy hastened up the stairs to the open door and his waiting butler. With barely a greeting, he tossed his greatcoat, hat, and gloves to the servants and took the stairs two at a time to his chambers.

Elizabeth, now accustomed to the invisible thread between them, kept up her dialogue. *"You will have to pardon your master, Mr Carroll. He seems to be quite put out this evening."*

Elizabeth startled and then laughed when it looked almost as if the butler had heard her as his bow to acknowledge Mr Darcy was perfectly timed in response to her words. Though she, too, knew herself to be tired, despite the intriguing aspect of not feeling like she was, Elizabeth had decided that, until Darcy acknowledged her, she would endeavour to pay no heed to the growing discomfort and mounting evidence that she was perhaps trapped in something other than a dream.

When they arrived in his chambers this time, Elizabeth was better prepared to enter though perhaps not immune. The moment she crossed the threshold, her cheeks heated, and her heart raced.

Thankful in that moment for his studied avoidance, Elizabeth was glad to see that he had immediately gone into his dressing room with a resounding slam of the door. Therefore, although she was in the man's bedchamber, she was at least alone for a time.

When he returned, she was altogether too mortified to say anything for he was once again in his breeches and loose shirtsleeves. She was aware that he was quite similarly affected by her presence, for he, too, blushed even though he made no attempt to look at her. Quite suddenly, he stopped. She saw him clench his eyes tightly shut. He was in the act of climbing into his bed when, suddenly, his eyes opened, full of fire though not necessarily anger.

He then proclaimed loud enough to startle her, "ENOUGH! THIS WILL NOT DO!"

Stunned momentarily by this outburst, Elizabeth quickly smiled incredulously and shook her head with growing humour. She watched him manoeuvre behind the posts of the bed and, with a few physical grunts and groans, managed to edge the bed from the wall.

"What are you doing, sir?"

"A man has the right to sleep undisturbed in his own chambers!" he replied with agitated strain.

Elizabeth began to laugh then as she watched Darcy, after much effort, manage to push his bed into the centre of the room. His sheer physical strength was not lost on her, but she found her laughter a good disguise for the warmth spreading across her face. His valet must have heard the commotion for he entered the room only to see Darcy's redecorating.

"Sir? Can I help you?" The incredulous tone of the valet had Elizabeth clutching her sides with renewed mirth as tears began to swim in her eyes.

"Rogers! Yes, come here man and help me move this blasted bed. It is damned heavy."

The valet came to his aid immediately, and together they made greater progress.

"Forgive me if I speak out of place, sir, but may I ask why you are wishing to move your bed?" Rogers huffed through his exertion.

"A man deserves to sleep alone if he wishes. It is just plainly as simple as that," Darcy replied between shoves.

Elizabeth chuckled again at the confused look of his valet who must have been well trained, for despite not understanding Darcy in the least, he said no more. For Elizabeth's part, she found that, the further the men moved the bed to the other side of the room, the closer she was able to venture to that side as well. Soon they were finished and with a wipe across his forehead, Darcy thanked and dismissed his valet.

Turning then to Elizabeth, he locked eyes with her. His heavy breathing and dark eyes caused her own breathing to hitch and the laughter to die in her throat. He walked towards her then with purposeful strides, his eyes focused in a heated exchange with hers. As he neared, her heart beat faster and faster, her hand coming up to her neck to hide the pulse. He said nothing as he came right up to her. He stopped, and she watched his eyes roam hungrily over her face. He leaned in slightly and Elizabeth found her breath quite taken away under his paralysing gaze. After only a moment, he turned and walked around her.

She spun around to see him open the door behind her and, with a wave of his hand in a gentlemanly gesture and a partial bow, indicated she should pass through the doorway.

All curiosity, Elizabeth walked through the open door and found, presumably, the mistress's bedchamber. She turned around just in time to see him bow once again and say, "Your rooms, madam."

Jane entered Elizabeth's bedchamber and found her mother near her sister's side. In a turn of events that surprised everyone, Mrs Bennet had sombrely stayed with Elizabeth nearly the entire day. Jane pulled her shawl closer about her shoulders as she crept further into the room. The night's darkness was defeated only by the glow of the candles beside the bed.

"Hello, Mama," Jane said as she took the seat near her mother.

"She has taken a bit of broth, which is a good sign Mr Jones said. We are to help her swallow some as often as we can."

Jane nodded. She recognised her mother's need to report—to feel some control over the situation. "I heard him speaking to Papa. 'Tis a good thing. He said that she would not be so pink nor have grumbling in her belly if her body did not wish to heal."

"Yes, I suppose you are right, child."

"Do you not see?" Jane urged her mother who still looked as if to despair over Elizabeth's state of being. "She would not be hungry if she was not going to come back to us."

Mrs Bennet smiled wanly at her eldest daughter and patted her cheek. She understood Jane's good nature would believe any hopeful news from the doctor. She had her own doubts, and they were riddled with a private pain.

"You should rest, Jane. You will need your sleep to heal as well." Mrs Bennet turned towards her second daughter's resting body. "I shall stay with Elizabeth until Hill returns with more water for the basin."

Jane nodded but, before standing, turned to her sister and, holding her warm, still hand, said, "Lizzy, dear. We need you to come back to us. Take the time you need to rest, to heal"—her voice hitched with emotion then—"but do come back to me...to us...soon."

Mrs Bennet waited until the door closed behind Jane before she turned her eyes back to Elizabeth. Mr Jones had said that it could not hurt, and perhaps may indeed help, to talk to Elizabeth—to remind her and encourage her to wake. Mrs Bennet hoped he was right.

Tentatively, Mrs Bennet leaned over to rest on the bed near her daughter and, with a shaky voice, said, "Lizzy...I..." She swallowed and sitting up again lifted her jaw. "You are a very headstrong, foolish girl who does not know your own interest. But I shall make you know it."

Mrs Bennet's bravado was considerably reduced in its force by the tremor in her tone and the tears pooling in her eyes. She clasped her daughter's hand in hers and bringing it to her cheek, placed her other hand on Elizabeth's cheek.

"You will come back to us, my Lizzy." With a sniff, she added, "Or you will not hear the end of it from me, child!"

8

Standing near the window in Darcy's study, Elizabeth watched the fevered activity on the street below as she contemplated her troubling reality. She had now spent two days in this dreamlike world and still had no way of knowing how she got there, how she was to leave, or most distressing of all, why she was tethered to the man studiously ignoring her at the desk behind her. With a private smile, Elizabeth remembered his acknowledgement last evening when he moved the bed and ushered her into her own chambers. It was thoughtful, though at the time she found his actions amusing—mostly because she knew that his wish for peace from her was what provoked his redecorating. With the light of dawn came a renewed determination, it seemed, on the gentleman's part to continue this charade of ignoring her as his plan to facilitate her disappearance. Elizabeth rolled her eyes and even emitted a small laugh at the ridiculousness and stubborn impracticality of the idea.

She had to acknowledge her disappointment that he had reverted to avoiding her. The longer she was captured in this state, the more certain she felt that the only way she—nay, they!—could solve this riddle was to work together. That he was again pretending she did not exist and doing it better than he was yesterday was only frustrating her further. She wished she knew his thoughts so that she could provoke him with better success. That morning when she had managed to successfully brush her fingers through his sickeningly sweet coffee, he had not even blinked an eye. Her comment on his preference for so much sugar caused not so much as a twitch of his lip. All she received for her efforts today was a shiver of disgust at the taste of the coffee that engulfed her— and without any other foods around at the time to wash away its lingering essence.

Now much of the day had passed, and Mr Darcy had spent it all as if she were nothing more than a spectre, not a lady of his acquaintance. Elizabeth frowned as she turned around to look at the gentleman. She was no longer sure she was not a spirit, and that thought frightened her greatly. Her frown remained while her eyes took in Mr Darcy's composed, elegant person. His blue superfine coat fit his shoulders superbly. The folds of his cravat were impeccable and up to par with the height of fashion. He was a man who certainly looked the part of a gentleman.

She walked closer to him and took up the seat across from his desk. His head was bent in serious study of the papers before him. Occasionally, his hand scratched his face or pushed back a lock of hair. Mesmerised, she could not look away when he fought that errant lock of dark hair, exposing a faint scar near his hairline that she had not noticed before. It had the same aged look of some childhood scars. A wave of tenderness surprised and assailed her senses then as she contemplated what this man might have been like as a little boy. She could almost see his knee breeches covered in dirt and a makeshift fishing rod in his hand, the same unruly curls framing his boyish face.

Embarrassed at her unexpected thoughts for Mr Darcy, Elizabeth tried to brush them off with a bit of humour as she always did when she was uncomfortable.

"I could grant you the loan of one of my hairpins, Mr Darcy. Or I am certain Miss Darcy would have an extra. I find they are extraordinarily useful at keeping hair out of the face."

She was not surprised when he did not react, though that did not keep her from feeling some disappointment. Without artifice, Elizabeth leaned closer as she studied his face. From this vantage point, she took notice of the caramel flecks in his eyes despite the dark lashes attempting to hide them as he read the papers.

A knock at the door startled Elizabeth, and she jumped upright, a bloom coming to her cheeks. *It is I whose wits are addled!* Grateful for the distraction and eager for some diversion to steer her thoughts to more reasonable avenues, Elizabeth looked towards the door with some anticipation. She closed her eyes only briefly when she heard Darcy's resonant voice herald the visitor to enter. It was a voice to which she had become attuned, and she had not heard it all day except for the rare occasions he needed to speak to a member of his staff. Adding to her muddled thoughts, she found she missed it.

"Mr Darcy, sir. I apologise for the disturbance."

Darcy stood then to stretch his shoulders and responded with warm familiarity. "Not at all, Mr Carroll. I should have taken a break some time ago. What is it?"

Elizabeth admitted that, the longer she saw Darcy interact with his staff, the more she had to admire his calm, gracious way of managing his estate. He was kind to his servants, and they obviously respected him in return. The familiarity she saw between him and his butler only added to the evidence that Mr Darcy was a careful, considerate master. This was as surprising to learn as it was pleasing.

Good humour was reflected in the hazel eyes of the middle-aged gentleman before her. The grey hair at his temples added to his dignified appearance, and the smile lines around his eyes defied it.

"I came to inform you that Miss Bingley is here, calling on Miss Darcy, sir."

Elizabeth looked at Darcy for his response and smiled when she saw his face fall and his eyes roll unexpectedly in a rather juvenile manner. He sighed before asking, "And might I hope to hear that her brother is in attendance as well?"

The wishful tone of his voice made Elizabeth laugh, for she had never considered that he might not experience pleasure at the acquaintance.

Mr Carroll's mouth twitched in a half smile, and he responded good-naturedly. "You may hope all you wish, sir. I fear that it will do little good. She and Mrs Hurst arrived five minutes ago—quite alone."

Darcy groaned and, nodding to his butler, said, "Very well.

Notify my sister that I shall attend her shortly. And thank you for informing me."

"It was your wish that I do so, as I recall, sir." The two exchanged amused smiles and Mr Carroll went on: "Would you...be wanting some prior fortification, sir?"

Darcy's brow rose in amusement. "Fortification, Mr Carroll?"

The butler smiled, giving way to his good humour. "To my certain knowledge, you possess a very fine wine cellar, sir, and at the very least a bottle or two of French—"

Darcy's loud guffaw interrupted the man then, and Elizabeth watched, in heightened amusement herself, as the butler smiled—obviously expecting Darcy's reaction to his jest.

"A tempting idea, my good man—indeed, very tempting." Darcy sighed dramatically. "But alas, I am not so fearful of the consequences of one afternoon tea with the lady. And besides, I promised Georgiana that I should not leave her alone when Miss Bingley calls."

Mr Carroll bowed in acknowledgement and began to back out of the room.

"To the front, then Mr Carroll. Lead your troops to battle."

Elizabeth laughed openly at Mr Darcy's nonsense. She was beginning to find that he improved upon further acquaintance. If this display of comedy was an aspect of his character, it was a welcome discovery to her.

"*Onward soldiers, indeed. The foe is as fierce as she is foolhardy.*" Elizabeth chuckled; her smile remaining when she saw that, for the first time that morning, Mr Darcy's smile stayed, almost certainly in response to her words.

DARCY PAUSED OUTSIDE THE DOOR TO THE MORNING ROOM where his sister and her guests were visiting. It was not a visit he anticipated with much pleasure. Miss Bingley's ingratiating behaviour to both Darcys had always been endured with patience rather than pleasure for the sake of his good friend for Mr Bingley did not deserve to have Darcy cut his sister.

"Oh, come now, Mr Darcy, why the delay? Surely you exaggerate the gravity of the situation."

Darcy smiled in spite of himself when he heard her words from behind him. He had done well enough today at telling himself she was not real. It helped to disabuse him of the need to look upon her ivory skin or react to her impertinent speeches. He waited longer at the door without entering to see whether he might provoke her into talking again. He knew she could not resist teasing him, and it was always with a mixture of anticipated excitement and vexation that he received it. Sadly for him, the vexation was not due to displeasure at being teased but at the realisation that he rather delighted in it. *Foolish man that I am.* His lips pressed together to keep his smile from becoming more pronounced when she spoke again just as he had predicted.

"They are in fact very fine ladies, not deficient in good humour when they are pleased, nor in the power of being agreeable where they choose, but proud and conceited, I grant you."

Darcy was at first taken aback by this view of his friend's sisters, for although he had never enjoyed their company, he had always considered them to be well-educated, proper ladies. He found this sketch of them at once profoundly accurate and, to his further displeasure, only highlighted to himself the deficiencies in his previous approbation of the ladies. Their incivility towards Elizabeth in the past had always been due to his admitted admiration of her, he thought, but upon hearing Elizabeth's opinion of Miss Bingley and Mrs Hurst, he recalled their general behaviour towards society in Hertfordshire with new eyes.

Not wishing to dwell too much on this new discovery at the moment, not entirely because it brought with it recollections of his own poor behaviour amongst Elizabeth's neighbours, Darcy squared his shoulders and—without acknowledging that he had heard, been distracted by, and was provoked by Elizabeth's speech—ventured into the room. Obviously, the lady followed.

"Miss Bingley, Mrs Hurst. May I bid you ladies a good morning?" Darcy said while performing a perfect bow.

Miss Bingley stood upon his entrance and, abruptly leaving her conversation with the lady she had come to call upon, drew herself next to him. After curtseying with the refinement of any student educated at one of the first private seminaries in London, her cloying smile was aimed at him.

"Indeed, Mr Darcy, we are having a wonderful tea with your dear sister." She smiled over her shoulder at his sister; the look now struck Darcy with its insincerity.

How had I not noticed before?

Thwarting her attempts to loop her hand through his arm, he held his hands behind his back and smiled tightly at her. Noting the pale complexion of his sister, Darcy walked casually into the room.

"Georgiana, dear," he said as he bent to place a kiss on her cheek. Upon straightening, he took up a place behind her seat and rested a comforting hand on her shoulder.

"Miss Bingley and Mrs Hurst were just discussing tonight's engagement."

"Ah yes—Lord and Lady Matlock's winter ball." Darcy was gladdened to hear his sister's voice held little distress. Georgiana had confessed some months ago that the Bingley sisters made her uncomfortable with their constant compliments and praise. He had suggested that it was merely their natural admiration of her, and naturally, they should praise her many accomplishments. Nevertheless, he had agreed to accompany Georgiana whenever the Bingley sisters visited. Now he wondered whether their flattery was another attempt to ingratiate themselves with him.

"Indeed, we were just saying that it is such a shame that Miss Darcy is not out and will not be in attendance this evening. I am certain she would catch the eye of every gentleman if she were." Mrs Hurst spoke with an ennui that betrayed her true sentiments.

"The way they fawn over your sister, sir, is frankly disgusting. Even I can see that she does not wish for such compliments," Elizabeth said with such sympathy that Darcy almost turned to look upon her; indeed, the temptation was so strong that his grip on the chair in front of him tightened in the struggle.

The warmth in her voice, the perception she showed for Georgiana's true feelings, and the genuine scorn she attributed to the Bingley sisters only heightened his regard for her. A fissure of calm wove around his heart, melting his efforts to evict her from that portion she owned. Still, he schooled himself to give away none of this new turmoil in his breast. *It cannot be.* He sighed to himself and squeezed his sister's shoulder gently, glad she had one true champion in Elizabeth, his mental creation of her being as considerate as he would have expected of the real Elizabeth.

"I thank you, Mrs Hurst. Georgiana is, indeed, a striking young lady—though, you must admit, perhaps a bit young for society. Of that, I am grateful," he said looking down at her upturned face. "I should not like to have her leave me so soon."

Miss Bingley, tired of a conversation in which she had no share or in which she did not stand in prominence rather, stood abruptly and, with exaggerated regret, said, "Sir, forgive me for neglecting your tea. Allow me now to pour."

Darcy's jaw tightened at Miss Bingley's assumption and transgression of his sister's role of hostess and mistress of his home and, instead, inclined his head at the lady. He must have betrayed his anger, for he felt Georgiana place her hand on his tense one upon her shoulder. Immediately, he relaxed and loosed his hold. Now it was sister giving comfort to brother.

"I say, she goes a bit far, do you not think, sir?"

"Indeed," he responded to both Miss Bingley and Elizabeth.

Miss Bingley, gratified by his response was quick to pour the tea and procure him a plate of pastries from the table. He thanked her in stilted tones when she handed the refreshments to him. Taking the opportunity to seat himself, he took up the companion chair to his sister's when Miss Bingley returned with superior satisfaction to her own seat near her sister.

Darcy brought his cup to his mouth and, tasting the tea, held back a grimace.

"Not enough sugar for you, Brother," Georgiana teased.

"Not enough sugar for you, Mr Darcy," Elizabeth teased. The two ladies having spoken at once caused Darcy to almost spew the drink down his cravat and waistcoat.

"I begin to like your sister, sir," Elizabeth said with a laugh.

"Oh I am sorry, William," Georgiana said with a slight chuckle when she saw him cough. "Here—let me make amends."

Darcy watched as his sister discreetly switched plates with him and crossed to the refreshment table. He watched her return the lemon pastry Miss Bingley had procured for him and replace it with one of the raspberry tarts he preferred. She knew that he did not like the lemon. When she returned, she easily switched plates again before the Bingleys could take note.

"Then again, I may have to question her judgment, Mr Darcy. She took away that lovely lemon pastry. And it looked so delicious. Such a shame."

Darcy smiled at this, knowing Elizabeth's preferences had always included lemon-flavoured delicacies; he found himself absurdly wishing for that abandoned pastry despite his sister's considerate actions.

He winked at his sister and, wishing to move the visit along to its inevitable and long-anticipated conclusion, turned towards his guests. "I believe you were speaking of the ball this evening. You ladies, I am sure, have many preparations to make. It was kind of you to take the time away from your afternoon of pampering to pay us a visit."

Miss Bingley either did not take the subtle hint or purposely ignored it. "You paint the picture that we ladies spend all day in preparation. 'Tis not kind, sir," she said coquettishly.

Her little flirt was purposely ignored as Darcy stood then to place his full cup of tea on the table. He should not have brought up the topic of the ball again for he was sure she hoped for an invitation to dance, and at the moment, he was not in any mood to request it.

To his surprise, Miss Bingley followed him to the table under the guise of disposing of her own dish. He looked back at his sister and saw that she was in quiet conversation with Mrs Hurst, so he could not return without looking quite rude to Miss Bingley. He was tempted to do so anyway, especially when she came closer than propriety allowed and whispered conspiratorially to him.

"I must speak to you on a matter of delicacy, Mr Darcy. And as our sisters are engaged, I hope you do not mind that I do so now."

Darcy refrained from the cutting remark he wished to give and instead nodded his assent. The quicker she finished, the sooner she would leave. Out of the corner of his eye, he could not help noticing that Elizabeth had drawn closer.

"My thanks, sir. I shall be quick for we have little time." She stepped yet nearer to him, causing his shoulders to tense at the proximity. "About a fortnight ago, I received a letter from a certain acquaintance we both share in Hertfordshire."

Her significant pause here caused the tension to spread to his neck because he was conscious of whom they were speaking and also because *his* Elizabeth was listening. Even mentally claiming Elizabeth's imagined spirit as his own could not calm the disquiet spreading in his mind. He could not explain it, but even though it should not matter that his Elizabeth hear Miss Bingley—being a fabrication of his own creation, her very being was entirely from the recesses of his own mind—he still did not relish the idea of her hearing any of this conversation. A foreboding unequal to any he had ever felt began to weigh heavily on his heart.

Miss Bingley continued despite his lack of response. "Miss Bennet has written me, sir, and the subject of her correspondence is most troubling to our *cause*. I would wish to hear your opinion on the matter. She informs me that she is due to arrive in London soon for a short duration's visit with her aunt and uncle in Cheapside!" She said the last with such derision that Darcy winced at her rudeness.

"Of what 'cause' does she speak, sir?" Elizabeth interjected with some heat.

He could not help himself then; he looked upon her. Her cheeks were gloriously pink, her eyes were alight with an angry fire that only added to their brilliance, and her beauty positively hit him with a force he could not deny even in her growing fury. For a moment, he just looked upon her. She raised her brow at his lack of answer, and he watched her cross her arms as she waited.

"Sir, what should I do? I have not replied for I wished your counsel. Do you think it wise that Charles risk seeing her at this early stage? I fear all our attempts at separating and protecting him from her will be for naught if he sees Miss Bennet in London."

"I should have known; indeed, I think I may have." Elizabeth's quiet tone only underscored her growing rage, and Darcy could not help but fear the consequences of this revelation.

He knew she had understood the matter correctly. He, with the help of Miss Bingley, had separated her sister Miss Jane Bennet from his friend. His intentions had been compassionate on the part of Bingley, but he could see that none of that mattered to her. Already, she was refusing to look at him any more. He watched her pace back and forth across the floor before him, her delicate hands pulling through her hair. He had spent the last few days wishing for his sanity, and now that it looked as if his own actions might cause her to leave him, he feared the pain of it happening.

"Sir? Did you not hear me?" Miss Bingley's attempt at returning his attention to her reminded Darcy of his strange appearance when staring at nothing across the room.

Though he did not wish it, the words began tumbling from his mouth without regard. It was almost as if his mind, wishing for so long to be rid of Elizabeth, had come to a decision and said the very things he knew might make her image leave him.

"Do not write back. If she comes, you must act surprised at her appearance as if you did not receive the letter. Do all you can to make it clear that you wish to cut the acquaintance." He still looked at Elizabeth, seeing her outrage and angry tears. With shame, he pulled his eyes away.

"No, no, no!" she cried.

He closed his eyes briefly to gain control and, upon opening his eyes, allowed himself to see her once more—to take in her beauty, brilliance, and look of betrayal before adding the final nail to the coffin of this insanity. "And say nothing of this to Bingley. He must not know she is in town."

"Papa, Papa! Come quickly, it is Lizzy! I fear something is wrong with her!" Kitty exclaimed in such animated tones that her alarm quickly reached the ears of the entire household.

With everyone converging on her at once, she lowered her head in embarrassment. She never liked when the attention was solely on her, and that was why she usually enjoyed spending her time in Lydia's shadow.

"Well, what is it, child?" Mrs Bennet exclaimed, even as all her sisters, her father and even Mrs Hill began rushing towards her, their bodies propelling her along with them towards the stairs.

"I...I was just reading to Lizzy, when..." Kitty stammered in embarrassment. Her rarely displayed affection for her sister made it difficult to admit to having spent time with Lizzy. Indeed, her cheeks flushed with the acknowledgement of her tender emotions.

The group continued their hurried ascent up the stairs towards Elizabeth's bedchamber. When the door flew open, the household poured in. Silence fell upon them all.

Jane, reaching for Elizabeth's hand, looked back at her father. "Her heart is racing, Papa."

Concern and worry engulfed everyone as Mr Bennet knelt at the bedside to place his hand at Elizabeth's cheek. Her face was flushed, and he felt that indeed, her pulse was fast and profound. Turning towards Kitty, he said, "Kitty, child, what is it that happened?"

Kitty looked at her sister's still form and bit her lip. She walked carefully to her father's side as if in a daze as she remembered the startling moment just minutes before. "I was reading to her, sir." Swallowing emotion, she continued with difficulty and said, "And she became restless. She was tossing back and forth—oh, it was so frightening! I tried to calm her, to talk to her as Mr Jones said, but she would not respond to me. And then she stilled and spoke quite forcefully. She yelled, 'No, No! No!' I was scared, and then I called for you." Kitty dissolved into tears, fearful that her attempts to help Lizzy had made her worse. Everyone then returned their eyes to the injured sister who was no longer moving or speaking but deathly still and fearfully quiet.

With prayers and exclamations ranging through relief, excitement, and dread, the group together looked upon the startling change in the patient with mixed emotions. Jane was confident it meant that Lizzy was healing. Mr and Mrs Bennet were worried for the thrashing and exclamation, but they felt relief that there had been some response. Mrs Hill was fearful that the strain would further complicate her favourite miss's recovery. Only Lydia, silent and grave, saw the tear that emerged and fell from the side of Elizabeth's closed eye, glide ominously down her cheek, and disappear unseen into the pillow.

❧ 9 ❧

Miss Bingley and Mrs Hurst left soon after the former's confidential interview with Mr Darcy though the gentleman could scarcely be relied upon to remember the particulars. The chaos marking his emotions was so extreme that it was some time after their departure that he had even become aware of their absence. He remembered only her. Her face, pinched in pain, turned from him finally, shoulders arching in anguished sobs. It was almost enough for him to wish her anger to return. Darcy steeled himself to it though; it was what was necessary, he told himself, to end this tragic play—to force his mind to give up Elizabeth. He purposefully had caused this anguish, hoping self-preservation might win and eradicate the spectral Elizabeth.

For Elizabeth's part, her heart had been so pressured and bruised that she could not vouch for her own wellbeing. She felt faint, extremely tired, and lost in a way she had not since arriving in this most dreaded dream-state. She felt a pain in her head and a duller throbbing in her shoulder that made no sense to her as she had no recollection of injuring herself there. Still those ailments were but fractions of the great pain lancing through the confines of her heart. *Hateful man!* To hear that he had been the means of ruining, perhaps forever, the happiness of her most beloved sister. It was just too much to bear. Her heart longed for her sister acutely, causing an ache most profound. This longing only added yet another emotion—a distress at her inability to eliminate her irrevocable connection to that hateful, arrogant, and awful man. Worse still was the fact that she knew she had begun to admire him. It was perhaps the reason for the majority of her sorrow. Disappointment in him reigned supreme, and the man she had begun to think he was could not be, not in the face of such proof—not in the face of such hurtful words.

He had orchestrated Mr Bingley's separation from Jane, and when given the chance—the opportunity to correct the wrong—he had perpetuated it. She could not help but feel that it was a purposeful act to push her away, to seal his terrible plan. Anger flared in her breast again, for not once had he asked her opinion. Not once had he deigned to ask *her* what could be done or how *she* felt about their unwanted bond. He claimed to admire her, yet he would not ask her thoughts on the matter. Not even his reasoning that she was a figment of his imagination could acquit him now from her censure, for she did exist. She was not his—in heart or mind. She existed, if only by proof of the anger and pain she was now experiencing.

She could hear his sister asking him whether he was well. Elizabeth cared not for his answer and closed her mind to his response. She felt momentarily for the girl, Miss Darcy, for she could not know what kind of man her brother was. His sister's admiration for him was untainted by any knowledge of his audacity.

His response was short, and soon Elizabeth felt the tug of bondage to the man pulling her out of the room. She would not look at him, and so she turned her head to the side. Her eyes filled with tears, and once again, she had cause to hate the dark sorcery that held them together, this time with a passion she had never before felt.

For the rest of the afternoon until it was time to change for the ball, Darcy remained in his study. Although he tried not to look at her, hoping to facilitate the eradication for which he wished, he could not help but see the distance she kept from him. It was not so much a physical distance—as that was a determined amount—as an emotional distance. Gone were the shocking statements, provoking smiles, and humourous attempts to draw his attention. After a while, he could take it no more, and he moved towards the sofa near the wall in his study. There he knew she would take immediate refuge in his library on the other side of the wall. She had kept to the furthest perimeters since his discussion with Miss Bingley. As he expected, she disappeared through the wall into the library. He could not expect this olive branch on his part would be noticed by her. Still, despite his avowed wish, it rankled that she disappeared so quickly.

Sinking heavily into the sofa, Darcy's head fell into his hands. Slowly, a suspicion that had been taking root in his mind—though one he had avoided acknowledging—came at once to his thoughts. This situation had more to it than merely a phantasmal creation of his deteriorating mind. For some reason, unbeknownst to either of them, they were destined to be together, at least for a time. Most distressing of all, perhaps this Elizabeth, *his* Elizabeth, was not really his in nature but her own—the real Elizabeth Bennet of Hertfordshire. This avenue of thought only increased Darcy's distress, for it meant that she had indeed felt the hurt of his actions, but worse still it meant that her presence there might indicate that something terrible had happened to her—that she perhaps may be gone from this world except to have her spirit haunt him.

Suddenly racked with a pain more profound than any other emotion he now juggled, Darcy's eyes welled with tears at the thought of his Elizabeth passing on, the brilliance and life swept from her eyes. It was not a thought he could well stomach, and forcing it from his mind, he collapsed against the sofa and, covering his face with his arm, attempted to slow his laboured breathing and still his aching heart.

They were ironically back to where they had started: he on one side of the wall and she on the other. The only difference was that each was aware of the other in the acutest way.

THE RIDE TO LADY MATLOCK'S HOUSE WAS THICK WITH tension. In a turn of fate that seemed designed by the devil himself, Darcy was unable to send his regrets, perhaps claiming some illness. Colonel Fitzwilliam, seemingly possessed of supernatural precognition and suspecting decampment on the part of his cousin, came to Darcy House with the express purpose of riding with him to the ball.

Darcy, wishing less to face his cousin's inquisition than to attend a *ton* event, readied himself with little care and climbed into the equipage. Elizabeth still kept her distance and never so much as looked in his direction. Colonel Fitzwilliam's own serious mien proved to Darcy his poor mood was not hidden sufficiently.

Though he would act as if the intrusion on his personal affairs bothered him, in truth Darcy was grateful for the close friendship he had with Richard. His judgment and good humour were often welcome and had helped him to come to the right decision about serious matters in the past. The overwhelming chaos that had enveloped his life since waking early New Year's Day was the most profound life event Darcy had experienced to date and also the only thing he had ever ventured to keep from his cousin.

The weight of it stood before them like a wall of secrets that Darcy could not like but also could not help. It would not do to have his cousin and best friend know of his lunacy, if indeed it were such. If it were the other, more distressing idea—*that I am being haunted by the woman I... No, I cannot say it*. It could not be true, either the sentiment or the reason for her presence.

None of the passengers, either physical or spiritual, said anything along the way to the ball. And upon reaching their destination, Darcy immediately exited the carriage and escaped into the throng and revelry. His purpose soon found—a glass of his uncle's scotch—he took up a position along the back wall of the ballroom.

He could not see Elizabeth as she purposefully took advantage of the pillar against which he leaned, continuing in absentia from his other senses. He heard no laughter, no witty remarks about the guests, or any inane comments about the number of couples or size of the room. It was a silence that echoed loudly in his ears. He lifted the drink to his lips again as his stormy eyes took in the festivities before him.

Elizabeth focused all her energies into feeling and experiencing the cool texture of the marble pillar. Sinking into it, she was grateful for the obstruction it provided. She could not see him and, unless he spoke, could almost believe herself rid of the horrible man.

For some time, the pain in her breast was cooled by the lack of sight. It was as if she could breathe again after the disappointment she had earlier experienced at his hands, a disappointment more profound than if she had been indifferent to him. But soon her peaceful recollections were disturbed by the sound of Mr Bingley greeting his friend.

Curiosity drove her forward, and she emerged enough from the pillar to take in his appearance. She did not imagine that he looked less lively and acted less cheerful. She felt she was not biased in this, and though she would not deign to say as much to her unwanted companion, she hoped he would notice.

"These balls begin to hold little enjoyment for me these days, Darcy." Bingley paused to sip his own drink. Laughing without real feeling, he continued. "Perhaps I grow too much like you, my friend. After so many of these town events, there is not much of interest any more to capture my attention."

Elizabeth had the satisfaction of seeing Darcy wince at the feigned laugh that followed Bingley's words. "I sincerely doubt that you have any need to fear becoming like me, Bingley, for your amiable nature will always render events such as these easy while I shall always feel ill at ease amongst so many people."

Bingley shrugged but added, "Still, I perhaps now see the virtue in standing about the perimeter of the room as you do. It is damned uncomfortable—a crush like this." His tone registered frustration.

The men remained silent for a moment. Darcy was acutely aware of the change in sentiments from his friend, who once said he would not be so fastidious for a kingdom when it came to crowded ballrooms or their inhabitants.

Bingley turned to his friend and with sincere remorse said, "Forgive me for my intemperance just now. I must be in a foul mood. Perhaps I ought not to be in company. I have grown tired of London. 'Tis suffocating really. I have been thinking of going to Scarborough to visit my relations for a time."

Darcy gave his friend a pat on the shoulder. He was a good man. Even though he had barely raised his voice, he still felt the need to apologise. Darcy thought of Miss Bennet's impending trip to London and seized the opportunity to protect his friend's still-tender heart.

"Yes, perhaps it may be a wise choice. I had thought of retreating to Pemberley myself," Darcy said by way of agreement, though now the idea had merit.

Bingley nodded his head, firming his resolution, it seemed. "I think I shall go up north to my relations. Caroline can remain in town with the Hursts. You are a good friend, you know. I can always rely on your judgment."

Darcy smiled tightly in response and emptied his glass. The nagging guilt and doubt he had once acknowledged only yesterday at his club was now more profound than ever. A part of him wanted to stop his friend, call him back when he departed. But what good it would do, Darcy did not know, for it did not change the fact that Miss Jane Bennet did not love his friend. He was still quite certain of that. Her easy, contented behaviour while in Bingley's presence portrayed only amiability not love in his opinion. They both would be destined, it seemed, to be addled by a lady in the Bennet household. As soon as Bingley left, Darcy noticed Elizabeth once again sink back into the pillar. Equal parts relief and disappointment warred for precedence in his heart at her desertion.

After some time, Darcy decided to walk the perimeter of the room. His movement was calculated to force Elizabeth from hiding. It was cruel of him, or perhaps more accurately, it was selfish of him. He felt trapped upon a difficult precipice. On one side, he wished to see her, and on the other, he knew his earlier actions had been designed to rid himself of her. His circuit was without design except to avoid places where she might hide from his vision. He stopped occasionally to speak to an acquaintance as he made his way in an attempt to act naturally.

However, Elizabeth was not without her own form of revenge either, he noted. On one occasion when he had stopped to speak with Mr Kingsley, a friend from his university days, she ventured so much as to speak, though he could not like what she said.

"He is a handsome man, is he not?" Elizabeth said as she lifted onto the tips of her toes to lean closer to the gentleman's face. Darcy watched her overt admiration as she commented on Mr Kinglsey's fashionable attire, becoming smile, and pleasing manners.

Darcy discerned her intent to make him jealous, and despite that, he feared it was working, for as quickly as he could without being deemed uncivil, he removed himself from his friend's company and resumed his walk, pulling her decidedly away from the handsome and pleasing Mr Kingsley.

He returned to the pillar, whereby her departure into it was welcome to both parties. He decided to remain there for the rest of the evening.

"A rousing success, would you not agree, sir?"

Darcy almost groaned when he felt Miss Bingley's arm snake through his and her voice disturb his ears. He noticed that Elizabeth did not venture out with the appearance of this acquaintance. He did not blame her; at the moment, he wished he, too, could hide in the pillar. The thought of doing so brought humour to his mind for the first time in hours as he pictured what *she* would do if he could invade her hiding spot.

"Miss Bingley."

"Come, Darcy, I must have you dance. I hate to see you standing about by yourself in this stupid manner. You had much better dance!" she said playfully with a swat of her fan to his shoulder.

If she thought her humourous prodding was going to get her an invitation to dance, she was mistaken. "I am sorry to disappoint you, Miss Bingley, but I have decided not to dance this evening."

The lady laughed uncomfortably as her motive had been all too apparent. After it seemed that he would not further the conversation unassisted, she decided to introduce a topic she knew would interest him. "It just so happens, that suits me perfectly, Mr Darcy. I do not wish to dance at the moment either. I have some news, though, that might ease that scowl upon your face."

Darcy's frown deepened, but he looked down at her anyway. Satisfied with his attention, Miss Bingley continued with gleeful tones. "We are saved! For I have had another letter from Miss Bennet just this very day. It arrived, amusingly, while I was at tea at your house." She then laughed at her own drollness, grating upon her companions' nerves—both the seen and unseen.

Darcy was suddenly intent on what she might have to say. He was not worried that Elizabeth's ire might be further stoked, for he was certain he could not add any more to her ill opinion, but something Miss Bingley had said struck him. She had said they were saved, which only could mean they would not have to worry about Miss Bennet's arrival in London. His earlier ruminations about Elizabeth's possibly coming to some disastrous end now caused his heart to beat wildly. He must know she was well.

"And...Miss Bingley, what is it that Miss Bennet writes?"

Miss Bingley considered what to tell. She had not thought to share any of the letter's contents with Mr Darcy as she was certain that his own infatuation with Eliza Bennet had not fully come to heel. It would not do to have him know of her unfortunate accident. He might do something rash like run off to Hertfordshire!

"Oh, merely to say she cannot come to London after all," Miss Bingley evaded easily. "You see all our worry was for naught." Her laughter was hollow.

"Was there anything else?" Darcy urged, noting that Elizabeth had come out of the pillar again with a strange look on her face, confusion in her eyes. He noted in the edge of his vision that she rubbed along the side of her head as if it pained her—as she had when they had argued earlier.

"Why is Jane not coming?"

"Does Miss Bennet give a reason for her change in plans?"

"Nothing of interest, I assure you."

Recklessly, Darcy pressed further. "And her family, they are in good health?"

"Oh perfectly, I am sure." Miss Bingley, though comfortable with disguise of any sort, had a difficult time meeting his eyes after this last prevarication. She wished she had not brought up the topic after all. With relief, she noted that she was spared from further inquiry by the approach of Darcy's cousin. She surmised that Colonel Fitzwilliam did not like her, yet she could never fault him for his manners.

"Miss Bingley, Darcy. I hate to interrupt your tête-à-tête but I came to give Miss Bingley a message from my mother."

The lady perked up at the news, ever eager to ingratiate herself with members of the *ton*. She curtsied to the gentlemen and, releasing Darcy's arm, said, "What does her ladyship need, Colonel?"

Colonel Fitzwilliam smiled benignly at her and replied, "She merely wished to speak to you. You will find her near the refreshments."

Miss Bingley flushed with pleasure and quickly made her escape in the direction of the refreshment room. Darcy looked upon his cousin with a sceptical brow.

Laughing, Colonel Fitzwilliam replied to the unspoken statement. "You will owe me now, Darcy, for dispatching the gel, but I am afraid I have done an injustice to my mother just now."

"And how is that?" Darcy could not help himself, and his mouth perked up into a smile.

"She absolutely did *not* ask for Miss Bingley and will, no doubt, *not* thank me for sending the lady."

Darcy laughed and, feeling his mood lift ever so slightly, said, "I thank you for your sacrifice on my part, and if I can repay you in any way, perhaps with a place in my home when she disowns you—"

"Indeed, well I have just the thing." The colonel was quick to interject in a way that made Darcy nervous. Upon seeing his cousin's frown return, Colonel Fitzwilliam added, "I think you take my meaning. For now I will not pressure you, but tomorrow I will seek you out, and you *will* speak to me."

Darcy opened his mouth to respond, but his cousin cut him off.

"Not tonight. Go home now. You are in no mood for company, and I shall once again make your excuses should my mother notice your absence." Laughing suddenly, he said, "But with Miss Bingley in her attendance, she may be unable to notice."

Darcy did not laugh nor did he argue. He quickly made his escape and requested his carriage as he retrieved his belongings. Soon he was on his way in yet another tension-filled carriage ride. Darcy knew himself to be a fool, for although it had been his plan all along to try to rid himself of her by any means available to him, after only a few short hours of her avoidance of him, he found he could take no more. The tables had turned with her avoiding him, and he did not like it one bit. His resolve to ignore her presence had begun to dissolve long before the revelation of his part in Bingley's removal from Hertfordshire. His counsel to Miss Bingley, which he was beginning to severely regret, was one last desperate attempt at a dying plan. Now that he could see his plan had not worked, he realised with a jolt that he was no longer interested in her leaving him. Remembering a phrase he had once heard, "Once you lose your sanity, you do not miss it," Darcy decided he was happier with Elizabeth near him and speaking to him than he was having her so distant and in opposition to him, or worse, gone altogether.

Upon entering his home, Darcy made straight for his library. He would go where they had last had such happy moments together, hoping the atmosphere would help serve his purpose and allow him to repair the mess he had made for himself.

He took up the seat near the fire that he had occupied two nights before and looked upon her stubborn stance. She had her back to him, and although he wished he could see her face, he was perfectly content to wait until she could not take it any more and faced him. After nearly a half hour of this, Darcy, with a smile, began his own form of provocation.

"I had always thought your hair was beautiful, but tonight, in the light of the fire, it strikes me as particularly so."

He had the pleasure then of seeing her stiffen at his words. It was not perhaps the reaction for which he hoped but was glad nonetheless for any effect.

"Though it is the illuminating tone of your fair skin, as smooth as silk, that I find most handsome this evening. Well, of course that and your fine eyes." Darcy warmed to his topic though not without consequence: he was finding himself increasingly beguiled by the woman the more he gave voice to the thoughts in his head.

To his disappointment, he saw her walk through the sofa—startling him as it always did when he saw it—and sit on the other side. He presumed she sat upon the floor to hide herself from his view.

"Come now, Miss Bennet. I cannot have you sitting on the floor. You had much better seat yourself in the comfort of a chair."

He sighed when again she made no response to his words. Though disliking the thought of angering her further, he knew that the only thing that could resolve this discord between them was to address the subject head on. "I have angered you. Do you not wish to address me?"

The lady huffed loudly from behind the sofa, making his lips sneak up into a smile. With a foolish courage, Darcy pushed yet further. "And this is all the reply which I am to have the honour of expecting! I might, perhaps, wish to be informed why, with so little endeavour at civility, I am thus ignored. But it is of small importance."

Darcy secretly was satisfied that this speech finally gave way to a reaction from Elizabeth, but his satisfaction quickly was squelched upon seeing the stormy look upon her features as she stood and spun around to address him.

"I might as well enquire," replied she, "Why, with so evident a design of offending and insulting me, you chose to tell me that you liked my hair, my skin, and even my *fine* eyes? Was not this some excuse for incivility if I was uncivil? You tease and mock me, sir!"

Darcy's brow rose in surprise. "Indeed not, madam. I spoke those things in earnest."

Elizabeth coloured, but having the coals of her temper stoked by the idea of confronting Darcy, she spat, "But I have other provocations; you know I have. Do you think that any consideration would tempt me to speak to the man who has been the means of ruining, perhaps forever, the happiness of a most beloved sister?"

Darcy coloured briefly, but the emotion was short for she continued on, walking towards him until she was almost upon him. He had to tilt his head up to look at her face. "I have every reason in the world never to speak to you. No motive can excuse the unjust and ungenerous part you acted *there*. You dare not, you cannot deny that you have been the principal if not the only means of dividing them from each other, of exposing one to the censure of the world for caprice and instability, the other to its derision for disappointed hopes, and involving them both in misery of the acutest kind. I have heard it from your own lips and those of Miss Bingley this very day!"

She paused and saw, with no slight indignation, that he was listening with an air that proved him wholly unmoved by any feeling of remorse. He even looked at her with a smile of affected incredulity. Slowly he rose to stand before her. She took a hasty step back as his standing brought him quite nearer to her than was comfortable.

"Will you deny that you have done it?" she repeated.

Darcy took in the luminosity of her complexion as she fumed about his actions with regards to his friend. Never had she looked so beautiful. With assumed tranquillity, he then replied, "I have no wish of denying that I did everything in my power to separate my friend from your sister or that I rejoice in my success."

Elizabeth, incensed at his ready answer, insufficient as it seemed to her, decided at once to share with him the extent of her dislike for him, readily ignoring the warnings of her heart.

"But it is not merely this affair," she continued, "on which my dislike is founded."

"Dislike?" Shocked, Darcy stepped closer to her; they were now nearly chest-to-chest.

"Indeed, dislike! Long before it had taken place, my opinion of you was decided. Your character was unfolded in the recital I received many months ago from Mr Wickham. On this subject, what can you have to say? In what imaginary act of friendship can you here defend yourself? Or under what misrepresentation can you here impose upon others?"

Darcy stood silently looking at her, his expression that of a tempest. Under this heated battle of wills, she detected that his eyes held a touch of pain and sadness. Her ire quickly cooled like coals tossed in the snow. It had sputtered with indignation, and now faced with his inscrutable expression and sorrowful eyes, she wavered. After a long while, but not before Elizabeth could discern she somehow felt disloyal to Darcy, he spoke.

His voice was void of emotion, somehow making his words more penetrable. "You take an eager interest in that gentleman's concerns."

Although wavering still, she foolishly pressed on. "Who that knows what his misfortunes have been can help feeling an interest in him?"

Darcy left her standing there and walked to the fireplace. Placing his arm across the mantel, he stared into the flames. "His misfortunes!" repeated Darcy contemptuously. "Yes, his misfortunes have been great indeed."

He did not wish to discuss Wickham, and having Elizabeth bring it up made Darcy question whether his assumptions about the reasons for and manner of her presence were wrong. For he knew that, given the opportunity, his mind shied away from anything to do with that man; it was just too painful a subject to think upon. No, he could not have created Elizabeth to introduce such a subject if she were under the direction of his mind.

"I will not speak of this now, Elizabeth. Do me the favour of allowing me the chance to defend myself on that charge at another date. For now, I fear I am not up to the pain of it."

"But of Jane and Mr Bingley?" Elizabeth whispered, having lost all momentum under the softness of his reply.

Darcy sighed and indicated they should sit. The disturbing calmness in his voice and the civil way in which he suggested it, caused Elizabeth to capitulate. She sat slowly, unsure how to describe the immense feelings pushing at her ribs. He began to describe to her the reasoning behind his interference in that quarter. He had observed Miss Bennet, objectively he thought, and had found that, although she seemed to receive his friend's attentions with pleasure, it was not with any particular degree of regard. She protested then, pronouncing that her sister was shy and not the type to display her feelings candidly. He recognised her superior knowledge with a nod. Though it pained him to wound her, he detailed his other reasons for disparaging the match, stating specifically the impropriety shown by many members of her family.

To say that Elizabeth was disheartened was generous; she was devastated by his account. His view of the two parties was biased, presumptuous, and unfortunately correct. She could not fault him there any more, and it grieved her—oh, how it grieved her!—to know that Jane's disappointment had, in fact, been nearly as much the work of her nearest relations and reflected how materially the credit of both must be hurt by such impropriety of conduct. She felt depressed beyond anything she had ever known.

That is not to say that Elizabeth did not fault him for his mistaken logic and presumptuous actions, but she could not further hold him accountable given the other weightier evidences.

After all that could be expressed, explained, and mourned over was, the two sat in silent contemplation—the disquiet of their minds not nearly the same, however, for reasons only they knew and could understand.

Darcy was left after this recital with such an assortment of emotions that he scarcely could decide upon which to focus. At length, he wondered on what phantasmal force could have brought them together.

"Why are you here, Miss Bennet?"

Elizabeth was grateful for the time being to have him return to addressing her so formally. He had called her by her Christian name once during their earlier argument, and it had not gone unnoticed. Because it also elicited strange feelings inside her, she found herself happy to have him return to formality.

"I do not know, sir. I thought at first this was a dream—a strange, impossible dream."

"And now?"

Elizabeth reflected on it, still undecided about what held her there. "I do not know, sir. At times I am certain it is a dream, for there are things I can do that could not be possible but for that explanation. However, at other times..."

"At other times...?" he prompted.

Sighing, her brow troubled, she replied, "At other times, I feel as if I am merely disconnected from life."

"Disconnected? I fear I do not take your meaning?" Her words sent a chill through him.

Elizabeth shrugged and rubbed her head where the pain came and went. "That is the best I can describe it, sir. I simply cannot put words to it. Disconnected. Lost. It is the same."

Darcy sat forward then, another question prompted by her actions. "You rub your head, Miss Bennet, as if you have injured yourself. Are you hurt?"

Elizabeth dropped her hand to her lap, suddenly self-conscious. But she would answer him honestly. "'Tis one of those 'other times' I fear. At times—mostly when I am experiencing heightened emotions—it seems my head hurts and occasionally also my shoulder."

She felt his eyes upon her and, keeping hers lowered to her lap, decided to ask her own question now that they had learned to be civil. "And you, sir, why do you believe I am here?"

Darcy blew out a long breath, stood to pour himself a glass of brandy, and resumed his seat with a casual grace and attitude she had yet to see in him. His easiness relaxed her.

"I am yet uncertain too. I believed there was a chance that I was losing my mind; indeed, a part of me still believes it may be the case."

"How would that explain my presence, sir?"

Darcy looked at her then, his eyes penetrating and focused as they often had been in Hertfordshire. His eyes shifted away when he began speaking. "I am not a man given to recklessness, Miss Bennet. I do not jump heedlessly into any situation. However, despite myself, I have found that I...I am in the possession of a...a rather strong attachment to you. Indeed, I am bewitched."

Elizabeth blushed and stammered idiotically. "But you cannot think...?"

Darcy shrugged helplessly. "I have tried to forget you—tried to replace you in my thoughts and heart. It cannot be done, I fear. I am beginning to think I do not want it to be done. But I have obligations to my family, to my status..." He looked away in shame for his words. Having given voice to them, he realised he felt they held little strength any more. It was as Colonel Fitzwilliam had said New Year's Eve: she was a gentlewoman, he a gentleman. They were equals. Yet, he still had some reservations.

In an attempt to hide the emotions his words had elicited in her, she summarised with good humour. "So I am either dreaming rather fantastically, or you have gone quite mad. I am afraid that neither seems adequate nor favourable."

Laughing hopelessly, he replied, "Indeed, my dear, indeed."

LYDIA LOOKED AROUND THE DARKENED HALLWAY AND, SENSING that all were quiet in their slumber, tiptoed to her sister's room. Silently she slipped into the small chamber, feeling her way to the bedside with the limited light from a single candle near the slumbering form of the housekeeper, who had taken to sleeping in Elizabeth's room in case anything was needed.

Being careful not to wake Mrs Hill, Lydia sat herself on the bed next to her sister. She felt foolish coming at night like this, and indeed, it was the first time since her sister's accident that she had come. Her earlier witness of Elizabeth's tear tugged uncharacteristically at her heartstrings. Looking at Lizzy now made Lydia uncomfortable, and she did not wish to contemplate any feelings of that sort. She was given to frivolities and silliness because she was allowed to, and though she often received censure from the sister before her, it was always done without disdain.

Not knowing what to tell her sister but wishing she could do something to help in any way she could, Lydia had contemplated what she might tell Elizabeth before she snuck into the room.

"I bet you are terribly bored, Lizzy. Lah! I should think I would be if I could not get out of bed." Lydia cleared her throat quietly. She paused suddenly, feeling quite foolish for whispering to her sister's almost lifeless body.

"I saw Mr Wickham today in Meryton. He asked about you. But I would not triumph yet, Lizzy. He was speaking with Miss King, that freckled little thing." Lydia scrunched up her nose in disgust. "And that only a few days after he paid such attention to me at the assembly. And you as well, I suppose," she added awkwardly.

The reminder of that evening and the accident that precipitated from it effectively stole any further words Lydia might have said. Feeling ill at ease again, she only ventured a quick, "Get better, Lizzy." Lydia was at such an age where friendships and acquaintances were always increasing, and though she cared for her sister, she had not yet learned to be unselfish in her desires. "If only so that we might have the officers for dinner. You would not wish us all bored, would you?"

❧ 10 ❧

"'Tis a strange state of affairs we face, is it not, Miss Bennet?" Darcy asked as he leaned forward and rested his arms on his legs.

Elizabeth sighed and reached unconsciously to a curl near her ear as she answered. "Indeed, most strange, especially considering neither of us seems to have an adequate explanation for it or any reason to wish for the other's company."

Darcy looked towards the dying embers in the fire before them. He stood and knelt before the fire, his back to her. "All true for the first but perhaps less so with the second."

"I might remind you, sir, that you believe my existence to be a hallucination of yours, a drift from reality—one that you have studiously tried to rectify for a few days now."

"Your memory is most astute," Darcy replied, using the occupation of building up the fire as an excuse to be turned from her.

"I am not accustomed to speaking to one's backside." Elizabeth laughed quietly when she saw that her words caused him to stiffen and even become unbalanced as he crouched near the fire.

When he steadied himself, he turned to look at her over his shoulder, a smile at his lips. "You will have to pardon my rudeness then.

While you seem to be unaffected by the growing chill in the air, I, however, am not."

Elizabeth smiled, but she was not fooled by his explanation. "You will, of course, excuse my ignorance of such things, for gently bred ladies do not tend to the fires...though I have seen a fire built before but *never* with such meticulousness. You take your work most seriously, I see. You will soon be driving winter itself away with all the coal you are placing so carefully, sir."

The gentleman merely chuckled, his shaking shoulders distracting Elizabeth.

"No, I must say I believe you are avoiding an explanation of your words. You in truth do *not* wish for my company or else you would not have fought so valiantly for its removal."

Darcy stood then, still smiling as he wiped his hands on his handkerchief. Turning towards Elizabeth once again, he said, "Perhaps I did not wish to give voice to sentiments that have proven in the past to be unwelcome." Their tones were light and teasing, and although his words were truthful, they were not said with any kind of malice.

"And I have given you reason to believe your sentiments were unwelcome."

Sitting down then, Darcy met her eyes. "Unwelcome, insincere, and disrespectful, I believe."

"I said no such thing!"

"No, you are correct. Your words were that I teased and mocked you with my compliments. Why then should I not be fearful to give voice to any admiration or desire for your company with such a repayment expected?"

Elizabeth coloured, remembering her earlier words spoken in a heated temper, and since their conversation was now polite and friendly, she felt remorse for the way she had addressed him.

"Well then I beg your pardon, sir, if you felt I had not given your feelings their due credit. At the time, I knew only that your words were spoken in an attempt to provoke me into speaking to you."

"Well, I shall not say that you were mistaken entirely. My words were meant to provoke, but they were no less true. I do think you are a handsome woman."

Darcy smiled when she flushed, but he was taken aback by the sudden question in her eyes and her response. "Why is that?"

She had spoken in an off-handed manner as if she were thinking to herself. With raised brows, Darcy said, "I have never been asked to explain my preferences on this subject before, but I shall attempt to if you truly wish it."

Elizabeth was quick to stop him with an uneasy laugh and another blush. "I beg your pardon, sir. I spoke rather to myself there. I was not asking...indeed, it is not necessary that you..." Elizabeth swallowed deeply and stomped her foot in a manner that the gentleman found endearing. "That is to say, I was wondering to myself, actually, why it is that you speak so candidly about your...inclination towards me. When last we were in company in Hertfordshire, your decided *dislike* was most apparent."

Darcy sat upright, caught by her candour. "Dislike? I assure you I have felt many things with regards to you, but 'dislike' was never among the lot."

She tried to ignore his words—and the flip she felt in her stomach upon hearing them—as she was now determined to have this puzzle in her mind solved. "But certainly you must admit you are much less reserved now than you were then, sir."

Darcy smiled, clasping his hands near his jaw. "Is the reason not obvious?" His smile grew more pronounced as he continued. "Despite your assurances to the contrary, from the beginning of this little predicament in which we find ourselves, I have always thought you were only a figment of my imagination. I am not accustomed to guarding my opinions from myself."

"But I assure you, I am very real."

Darcy shrugged. "So you say. However, since neither of our theories can be proved or disproved satisfactorily, I see no reason to act with the propriety normally expected of me while in the presence of a lady." He punctuated his words by casually kicking off his boots. Smirking at her, he reclined back into the chair then crossed his feet in front of him on the footstool.

Surprising even herself, Elizabeth laughed openly at him. She had to admit he had a point. Why should either of them expect even the most normal behaviour of the other when their situation was anything but?

"I think on this point we may have to agree to disagree, Elizabeth. May I call you 'Elizabeth'? I must admit I have long since dispensed with formal addresses when my thoughts tended in your direction. Now with the oddity of our arrangement, I find the formality silly in the extreme." He ended his provocative speech by crossing his arms casually behind his head.

Elizabeth knew not what to say; she had always thought the only man to whom she would grant that liberty would be her husband. She searched her heart and mind and was surprised to find she felt no aversion to it. Still, she hesitated. *Did such things count in dreams?*

Darcy laughed at her indecision, throwing his hands up in the air before furthering his argument. "For heaven's sake, madam, you have not been able to move further than a few yards from me for two days and, until a solution can be found, will remain thus tethered for the foreseeable future."

Elizabeth smiled and shook her head in exasperation at him, and though she was resolved to allow him this liberty, before she could indicate so, he spoke again.

He leaned towards her, his voice lowered, as he said in mock seriousness, "And you *have* been in my chambers."

"Ah, speak no more, sir!" Elizabeth coloured and laughed, covering her ears with her hands. Somehow, she knew he had not made the point to cause her to be uneasy but only to tease her, yet her embarrassment was extreme. She liked this friendly, even teasing, Darcy much more than she ought. "Very well, sir, you may."

Darcy again relaxed into the cushions of his seat, a self-satisfied smile on his lips and a heated contentment about his eyes. "Thank you, Elizabeth."

She coloured again at his purposeful use of her name. Her eyes could not meet his though, and she felt her heart's unsteady tempo. She smoothed the invisible wrinkles from her gown and fumbled to regain control.

Darcy sensed her discomfort, and although he relished her brightened cheeks and marvelled at the satisfaction he felt using her name —almost as if it were the most precious of gifts—he wished to put her at ease again. This was the most pleasure he had garnered since awakening New Year's Day to discover in his library the beautiful, laughing sprite before him. He had started out denying her presence as he had tried to deny his feelings for her. He had acted the fool with Miss Bingley earlier in a misguided attempt to rid himself of her image. His actions, though stupid and mistaken, had led to a glorious argument with Elizabeth—one that rendered him stunned with her increased beauty and stung by her accusations, especially regarding Wickham—yet now they were amiable, civil even and, if not entirely comfortable, at least friendly. He would not wish to change that. For the first time, he was determined to allow himself to enjoy this little insanity for as long as it lasted.

While searching for something to say, he noticed her fingers fidgeting with her dress. He watched as they floated in and out of the garment and his curiosity came to the fore, giving him a means for conversation as well. "How do you do that?" he said, gesturing towards her hands and smiling when they ended their play.

Elizabeth folded her hands more properly across her lap and answered with a shrug, hoping to come across as casual. "It is rather like magic, I guess. One of the first things I discovered upon entering this dream state."

Darcy, truly interested now, said earnestly, "Tell me how you came to be here, as you see it."

"I actually do not remember arriving in your library, if that is what you mean." Elizabeth unconsciously rubbed at her forehead as she spoke. "In fact, I remember only that I laid down to rest before the New Year's Eve assembly, and next I knew, I was here, in the dark of your library."

"So you believe you are even now dreaming of me...err...of all of this"—he lifted his hands in a sweeping motion—"while you rest before the dance?"

Elizabeth's face flashed with a moment of confusion before she answered. "It is the best I can do to explain."

"How do you explain the passage of time then? New Year's Eve was two days ago." He spoke softly, the weight of their conversation falling upon him. He waited while she thought about her answer and noted again that she rubbed the side of her head.

Eventually she sighed and, with sadness in her eyes, said honestly, "I cannot explain it, sir, except to say that anything is possible in a dream. Dreams often distort or stretch time. It may be that I am still dreaming; only in reality, Father Time has been less generous with what time has been spent. Perhaps I shall awaken and find it is time to ready myself for the ball."

Darcy was about to protest, based upon his own real experience of the last few days, knowing he was very much awake, but she forestalled him.

"I know this explanation is not satisfactory to you, given your interpretation of our shared experiences, but we have, on this point, agreed to disagree." She flashed him a censuring smile that he found absolutely charming. He nodded as in acquiescence.

A most wicked and tempting plan then entered his mind, and he settled his features into a severe frown in preparation of its execution.

"I believe I owe you an apology. I have not been fair to you."

His abrupt change in topic confounded her momentarily. Her serious tone matched his as her forehead wrinkled in concern. "I should like to think that I would always welcome any apologies you might wish to give me, but in this case I feel you must explain yourself, sir."

Darcy shook his head, his brow lowered in a grave manner. "There you go again. Elizabeth, please accept my most sincere apology."

This time his companion detected the humour lurking in the depths of his eyes and, with a secret smile of her own, decided to play along with him. She responded with the same sombre tones. "I think I understand your concern now, sir. And I agree. This travesty cannot go on."

She watched his eyes flash with triumph and barely kept from laughing.

"I am glad to hear it. Considering your earlier concession, it was the height of rudeness for me not to respond with equal generosity." Darcy sighed dramatically and his companion, unable to hold back any longer, laughed briefly before biting her lip in an attempt to pull her face into a more serious mien.

Though she did not know his purpose, she nodded her head and looked sternly at him. "True, any less would not be gentlemanly of you."

"Then it is settled. You will call me by my given name. I will not force you to refer to me so formally any more. It was rude of me not to offer it before."

Elizabeth gasped, surprised by the reason for his ruse and realising how neatly his charade had trapped her.

"Mr Darcy!" Elizabeth laughed, fighting a blush that tried to creep up her neck. It was one thing for him to argue his right to call her by her Christian name; by his own account, he was half mad anyway. One should not provoke the truly mentally unstable. But it was certainly quite another thing for her to refer to him so intimately, for she was not addled in the least—or at least she hoped she was not. She was beginning to question it given the feelings she was presently experiencing, feelings she had no notion before a few days ago of ever feeling towards this gentleman.

"Uh-uh," he said with a shake of his finger. "Not 'Mr Darcy' any more, Elizabeth."

"What if I said that I do not know your given name?" she responded, trying to buy herself some time to sort through her thoughts for a defence. Besides being humoured by his clever trick, she was still caught off guard.

"I would say that you are a storyteller."

Elizabeth laughed then, letting go of all her reservations. The abruptness of his response and confidence in his tone told her she had not fooled him for a moment. It was the challenge in his eyes, however, that made her lift her chin and finally say, "As you wish, sir."

"Sir?"

"Would you have me begin now?"

"Carpe diem, and all that, my dear," he said with a casual flick of his hand and a roguish smile.

Elizabeth sent him a half-hearted scowl at his endearment before deciding to give him a bit of his own merriment back. "Very well. 'Fitzwilliam' it is. A fine name if I am allowed to say. It puts me in mind of your charming cousin, Colonel Fitzwilliam."

Darcy growled. "I think I would prefer you to call me 'William.'"

"Are you sure? 'Fitzwilliam,' like your cousin who also bears that name, has a certain appeal."

Darcy marvelled at their witty repartee as she turned the tables on him. Though only half concerned that she was really charmed by his cousin, he still could not like the idea she might think of Richard when she spoke *his* name.

"Elizabeth," he warned, "you are *my* fantasy, not his."

Elizabeth merely shook her head at his words. They would never come to an agreement on who was right, but neither would they compromise on their own interpretations. His fit of jealousy was oddly comforting to her though, and so she gave in with a warmth settling in her cheeks.

"That I am, William; that I am."

Their conversation thus advanced into a comfort often found only amongst old friends. They did not always agree, and there were still barriers between them, particularly with Elizabeth giving her trust entirely to Mr Darcy, but the tension that had marked the last two days slowly dissipated into the darkness surrounding them as they sat by the glow of the fire.

She did not ask again about Wickham although she burned with curiosity and a need to understand how he might defend himself in that regard. Sensing that their tenuous and newly won truce was likely unable to withstand such a dialogue kept her from approaching the topic. Besides, the gentleman before her she was beginning to know was in contrast a very different sort than the one Wickham had described.

They also did not venture again into the reasons for their imposed connection. Neither, it seemed, was comfortable with the explanations of the other nor the implications of what it meant if their viewpoints were not correct. Though their thoughts returned often to the mystery at hand, they did not share them.

Darcy, in particular, was disturbed by something Elizabeth had said earlier in her explanation of her averred dream state. She said she remembered nothing beyond preparing for the New Year's Eve assembly. Though he did not want to think too heavily on it, it did add proof to her theory as she had memories beyond their association in Hertfordshire—memories beyond his leaving the county and thus ending their shared memories, memories she could not have if she were entirely a product of his cupid-bit imagination.

But the thoughts Darcy most diligently tried to avoid were his feelings towards Elizabeth. He could not admit more than an ardent admiration; he could not say it was love. By sheer determination, he avoided consigning the turbulent emotions roiling in his breast as that definitive name. To do so would seal his fate, and although he knew he loved being with her, loved speaking with her, and loved looking at her, admitting he loved *her* would allow him only one choice in the matter: marriage. Stubbornly, he wished to hold on to his choices, despite how foregone the conclusion appeared.

Instead, he distracted himself with asking her questions. He questioned her further regarding her strange abilities. The ability to read books by merely touching them amazed and intrigued him. Long into the night, he marvelled as she demonstrated time and again by reaching for a series of books. The delight and faraway look that stole through her bright eyes when she felt the book took his breath away. It was many books before he realised that he asked her to try her abilities simply to see that look come across her features as she *experienced* the book.

She asked him about his estate, how he came to be master and of the deaths of his parents. He was not offended by her intrusion into such personal matters. She asked with such a sweetness of temper and concern evident in her features that he found himself telling her things that he had never admitted to another soul: his pain at the death of his mother and then compounded at the loss of his father. He spoke of the weight that pulled at him when he contemplated his responsibility towards his sister, his wish to be a good brother to her even while he struggled with his role as father figure too. They talked about his close friendship with his cousin, and he admitted how he often felt envious of Colonel Fitzwilliam's easy nature.

"It is the same with Mr Bingley. I am not easy in company. I guess you would say that I should practise, but I have always been reserved, and no amount of practice will change that."

"They are both of very different natures to you; I would not dare presume to counsel you to be like them. Their characters complement yours. I am certain there are aspects of your personality that they envy," she said kindly.

"Would you tell me about your sister, Elizabeth? Was Miss Bennet really affected by my friend?"

Elizabeth was silent for too long, making him fear he had broached a topic that was too volatile in nature and would break their newfound camaraderie. But she eventually did speak, and though he strained to hear her whisper, he heard it nonetheless.

"She loved him very much and was heartbroken when he did not return to Hertfordshire."

"Then I have done my friend and your sister a great injustice."

Together they sat in silence, surrounded not only by the dark night but also by the darkness of their thoughts. Elizabeth was pained with a longing for her home and family so severe that she was rendered mute, and Darcy was contemplating the grave error he had made many weeks before in separating two people who loved each other.

"Come, Elizabeth, it has grown late. And although you have explained earlier that you do not sleep in your dream, in my world, I do," Darcy said, breaking the silence.

He stood then and offered his hand to assist her to her feet. She smiled, saying, "I thank you, but you will not be able to aid me."

"So you say, but have you ever tried? You mentioned earlier that you are able to sit if you do not think about *experiencing* the chair."

Elizabeth wondered whether his argument had merit though she had her doubts considering the way the maid had walked through her on her first day in the house. Still a part of her longed for some human touch, and so she put forth her hand.

Darcy held her gaze as he slowly extended his hand further to capture hers. When his fingers enclosed on themselves, grasping nothing but air, both felt a disappointment. The sadness in Elizabeth's eyes was hidden as well as the mirrored sentiment in his.

She laughed uneasily. "One day, William, you will have to admit when I am right."

Darcy smiled at her use of his name. Though she had blushingly used it a couple of times during their conversations earlier, never had it rolled off her tongue so naturally. It delighted him like nothing else. "Right. And beautiful."

LONGBOURN HAD LONG SINCE EMBRACED ITS INHABITANTS IN the warmth of sleep when one such resident, who for a number of days had slumbered in a restless though unconscious state, drew a deep, cleansing breath in the silent night air of her room before relaxing into a deep, *healing* slumber. It was the first such rest for the hapless, lost soul since her body had been battered, bruised, and tossed like a ship during a storm—the first since her carriage tumbled and finally settled on the icy shoreline of the road.

❧ II ❧

Elizabeth spent the rest of the long night-time hours admiring the chamber next to Mr Darcy's. She knew it to be the mistress's chambers and that one day it would house his wife. The very idea was both disconcerting and stirring to her. It was only a small improvement to be able to escape into this room when her companion retired for the night, and certainly she was glad not to have the mortification of residing in his private chambers as she had done before he rearranged the furniture. This room came with its own set of difficult emotions. At its best, it was a place she could feel she was alone for the first time since finding herself in Mr Darcy's library. But even that solitude was uneasy for Elizabeth, for she could not deny a certain pull of a different sort developing towards the gentleman on the other side of the wall, one that made the tether between them feel more of a comfort than a punishment.

She still felt a certain embarrassment being in this room, for it was an extension of that man, and she could neither understand nor necessarily welcome the blossoming approbation she was developing for him. His more candid admiration of her was as new as it was unexpected, given her impressions of their time together in Hertfordshire. Knowledge of *his* admiration was softening her heart, yet she felt as if she still ought to guard it from him. Something kept her from wishing to concede any feelings for him. Her long-standing opinion of him still pulled at her conscience. She was an intruder, unaccustomed to knowing the intricacies of a gentleman's life outside the tea parlour or dance floor. So strange were the emotions creating the mosaic in her heart that anything she could do to distract herself from evaluating them was welcome.

Thus, she turned her attention once again to the room she occupied. It was richly furnished with soft sea-greens and greys, a combination that she found soothing in its effect. When he had first moved his bed and opened this room up to her, all the furniture was draped with sheets, protected from dust. *No Mrs Darcy anticipated in the near future.* The thought brought a smile to Elizabeth's lips as she thought how Miss Bingley's grasping efforts were making little progress if the state of the room was any indication of her success.

Somehow, during the course of the day though, he must have ordered it cleaned and aired although Elizabeth did not recall his speaking to the housekeeper about it. Now the bedchamber she had all to herself for the night was removed of its sheets and dust. The air was permeated with the smells of furniture oil freshly applied, and there was even a bouquet of flowers in a vase at a small writing table near the fireplace.

Elizabeth moved towards the flowers and inhaled their sweet scent. Looking down at the delicate table before her, she could almost picture herself sitting there and writing to Jane about all she had experienced as if she were merely on holiday. That had Elizabeth laughing with sardonic humour. *A holiday tethered to Mr Darcy, indeed.* The turn of her musings soon gave way to more sombre feelings as she thought about what she could tell Jane or, more alarming, whether she would ever be able to see Jane again—or any of her dear family for that matter.

Turning from the table, Elizabeth looked about her as if suddenly panicked at the idea. Yet the longer she stayed in this dream state, the more difficult it was for her to organise her desires towards any one resolution. She felt as if she were on a small vessel driven by the winds of a storm. One moment she would wish for land, and the next, she felt at home where she was.

Towards the man himself—the object of this unreal probation

from reality—she had still more conflicted feelings. Her dislike of him was like a pair of well-loved walking boots: comfortable, predictable, and sturdy. It was easy to find fault with his arrogance and haughty behaviour. That was an easier sentiment to have as it kept her from examining her uncomfortable new feelings when he looked deeply into her eyes, spoke in that way towards her, or called her name. *Mercy!*—when he spoke her name, she could almost forget what he did to Wickham or his behaviour in her own village!

Remembering Wickham was like everything else, a difficult juxtaposition of conflicting thoughts. She could see that Wickham's description of Georgiana was faulty, and though he had said brother and sister were much alike, she could only agree that they were both diffident. And when she had confronted Darcy about Wickham earlier in the evening, he had not denied her accusations but simply begged her to postpone that conversation for another time. His words had slightly tempered her ire for he had avoided the topic, not because he was embarrassed by the dishonourable actions, but *"For now, I fear I am not up to the pain of it."* Why he should feel pain gave Elizabeth pause to doubt her complete trust in Wickham's report. Such doubts were causing the soles of those comfortable walking boots to separate and drop out and, indeed, making her feelings for Darcy that much more complex.

If there was one constant in this dream, it was that she felt everything acutely and simultaneously. She yearned for home and felt at home at the same time. Mr Darcy—William, as he had insisted— made her feel exasperated in both good and bad ways. She longed to be alone yet did not enjoy the separation from him. *It is enough to drive a person mad!*

Elizabeth's hand flew to her mouth as she burst into laughter at the thought. *Perhaps destiny would have us both attics to let.* Her laughter, though quiet, was all-consuming, and she collapsed into the chair at the desk, holding her sides as her eyes watered. The release of tension she felt from this was cathartic, and it rejuvenated her spirits. When her laughter subsided, she sought a means to bring it back and keep her dark thoughts and disorienting feelings at bay longer.

Her eyes drifted to the writing supplies beside her. She chortled at the thought of actually writing to Jane. She could just see the horror on her sister's face when presented with the unbelievable story of being tied to Mr Darcy and even having to follow him unwittingly into his private chambers. Surely, Jane would die of mortification, yet knowing her sister, she would also have something to say in concern for the gentleman's poor predicament. Elizabeth could only imagine Jane's sweet nature acknowledging William's difficult position.

Elizabeth considered that William was not the type of man to wish for anyone's pity and chuckled at the irony that he should receive it from someone he had regarded as having little feeling.

The knock that echoed through the room then effectively curbed Elizabeth's mirth, and she stood nervously, smoothing her gown and checking her hair in the mirror over the mantel before calling, "Enter." She rolled her eyes at the silly actions, the sudden strumming of her heartbeat, and the excitement she saw in her reflection in the mirror. She realised with some surprise that she was looking forward to seeing him again.

When he opened the door to the chambers, her thoughts were wiped clean at the sight of him in his outerwear. He was dressed for the cold outside, complete with his gloves and hat in hand. She looked at him in question.

"Mr Darcy, sir. You are dressed for departure. Pray, where are we to go at this hour?"

Darcy bowed and, with a small shake of his head, looked at her as he replied, "Are we once again back to 'Mr Darcy,' Elizabeth?" He was satisfied to see her colour, her eyes falling to her hands in front of her. "But I have not answered your question; let me do so now. We *are* going out this morning... Ah, I see that you do not believe me, but indeed, despite the hour, it is truly morning."

Elizabeth looked towards the heavy drapes at the window and noticed for the first time the grey light escaping around their edges.

"I stand corrected though it looks to be quite early. Where may I ask are we to venture at this unlikely hour? I cannot believe it is customary to arise this early in London."

Darcy had an air of excitement about him, and it was undeniable to his companion though she detected an underlying nervousness.

She stepped towards him then, and her senses detected the aromas of coffee and rolls from his room. Now she was truly diverted, taking several steps until she could peek into his chambers to confirm he had a tray of food at a table. "And have you already breakfasted, sir?"

She looked up at him and, realising she was near enough to have to tilt her head to see him, suddenly lost her breath, forgetting even her curiosity.

The gentleman stood there looking down at her with such warmth and happiness that, if her breath had not already escaped her, it would have been quite taken away. His tone was softer, calmer than the boyish excitement he used earlier in speaking with her. "I have. You are welcome to anything you like." He raised his arm then, indicating the tray, but his eyes remained fixed upon her, paralysing her. "Though I should tell you that we must hurry, for our appointment this morning is of utmost importance."

Elizabeth smiled, blushing, as she stepped around him into the room, not unconscious of the ease with which she entered the room that previously caused her such embarrassment. Though not completely comfortable, she noticed she felt perhaps less shy.

She ventured towards the table and the delightful aromas there, feigning calm after standing in such close proximity to Mr Darcy. Her companion followed and offered her a seat before taking up one of his own, a smile about his lips and a secret in his eyes. He watched her reach for a roll, its buttery warmth immediately flooding her senses.

"Your cook is a very good one," she stated as her fingers sunk next into a lemon pastry.

Darcy leaned back in his chair, crossing a leg on his knee at the ankle. Watching her, he said, "Is it like the books? This food—you can taste it?"

Elizabeth shrugged and unconsciously wiped her still clean hands on a napkin before her. He smiled at her practiced actions, despite the absence of any perceived crumbs on her hands.

"It is perhaps one of my favourite things, next to the books," she replied with childish glee, unaware that Darcy picked up the roll she touched and took a bite of it himself. "I hardly think that food in real life tastes as good as it does when experienced this way. It is almost as if I can pull apart all the elements of the morsel and appreciate them individually yet together."

Darcy nodded, not quite understanding but enjoying the light that the topic lent to her eyes.

"For instance, I can appreciate the flaky goodness of the crust, the tart of the lemon, and the sweetness of the crème, each presenting their unique contributions to the whole."

Elizabeth suddenly went silent, feeling modest at the excitement and enthusiasm she just expressed towards a sweet.

"Fascinating," Darcy said simply, not knowing himself whether he referred to Elizabeth or the pastry.

"The downside, I suppose, is that, no matter how many I taste, I cannot be full."

Elizabeth watched Darcy's brows lower in concern before he leaned forward and spoke earnestly. "Are you hungry, Elizabeth?"

It was an aspect of this ridiculous experience that he had not anticipated, and frankly, he did not like the idea of it. It left him feeling helpless—an emotion he had always hated. He felt it when his parents died, when Georgiana was deceived by Wickham, and at times during this entrapment with Elizabeth. Yet the very idea that she might be suffering at all was almost more provoking of that loathed emotion than any of those other instances had ever been.

Elizabeth could not like the storm that clouded Darcy's eyes and was quick to reassure him. "That is another aspect that is hard to describe, sir. I am not hungry although I know that I desire the fare."

Lost in his own thoughts, he did not respond. She leaned towards him, and dipping her head to bring his gaze to her eyes, she said, "William."

Darcy snapped to attention then, and despite his concerns, a slight smile tugged at his lips, her use of his name again doing wonders at restoring his previous good mood.

"Truly, I assure you. I feel no discomfort. I am not hungered in the least." She spoke slowly, making sure he registered each word. It warmed her heart that it seemed her words cleared the concern on his face. That he should worry so much for her stirred the embers of that warmth still further.

"I am glad to hear it. I do not relish the idea—indeed not."

Elizabeth nodded and looked at the food before declaring a revelation. "I have been tethered to you for a few days now, and I have never seen you eat the lemon tarts. Do not tell me that you have developed a taste for them now?"

Darcy laughed and shook his head. "I have not."

Raising her brow, Elizabeth queried, "Yet you have several here on your platter. I cannot believe that your efficient staff would know so little of your preferences."

"They were for you, Elizabeth."

"Oh!" Elizabeth coloured at what should have been obvious to her, yet she was charmed by his admission. "But will they not think it strange that their master, who does not like lemon tarts, has requested them for his breakfast tray?"

Darcy seemed unconcerned and simply said, "I am the master of this house, and strange or not, if I wish to have lemon tarts with every meal, I may certainly do so."

Elizabeth blushed with the idea that there might be even the hint of a secret meaning to his words. Abstractedly, she reached towards the mug before her and tasted the sharp bitterness of coffee. Immediately her face crunched up, and she withdrew her hand in disgust.

To her surprise, this action, too, caused the gentleman to laugh. "I suppose it is an acquired taste, though I think you may like it better with sugar. Or as it were, a lot of sugar, as is my preference."

Elizabeth smiled and shook her head at him. "I hardly think I need fear developing a taste for coffee when tea is available, sugar or no."

Darcy looked around the table with chagrin. "Forgive me. What a poor host I am. I did not even think to order tea. I hardly have it outside of morning rooms and parlours."

Now it was the lady's turn to laugh softly. "It is of no concern really. You need not order everything I like when I cannot partake of it in truth."

"Thank you for your graciousness. Still I take pleasure in making you happy, even if by means of a simple cup of tea."

His words settled a weighty awkwardness upon the two that Elizabeth could not like. She smiled kindly at him, attempting to make her reaction to his words seem as natural as they were said. She recalled with much curiosity their engagement and asked, "You said we were in something of a hurry, did you not?"

Darcy flinched and bolted from his seat. "Indeed we are! You have effectively distracted me as you often do—delightful distraction though you are."

"And you, sir, take great pleasure in discomposing me." She stood, colour infusing her cheeks.

"Ah, a tempting distraction again should I follow that avenue of discussion, but I am determined now upon my previous course. We do indeed need to make haste." Darcy smiled. "I will say this: I speak only the truth, these words you find 'discomposing.'"

"Though perhaps they are words you ought not to say to me at all, William. I never guessed you to be a shameless flirt."

The broad smile that then spread across his features, unearthing hidden dimples, stunned Elizabeth with his handsome transformation. "I am no flirt; *that* honour is my cousin's. And proper or not, I told you last evening that you cannot expect me to adhere to propriety with spectres of my own creation."

When Elizabeth began to protest as Darcy expected she would, he silenced her with a finger to her lips. Though neither could feel the touch, it was quite as effective as if they could. Elizabeth was rendered mute by the sheer intimacy of the action, and Darcy was spellbound by the thought of actually touching her lips. He leaned into her then and bending down to her eye level, whispered, "Allow me the pleasure, Elizabeth, of claiming you as my own for this moment. The fear of that time when you vanish as quickly as you came haunts me even now. Then I will be left only with the memories of these moments of candour. I *will* speak my heart and mind while I can. For later, I will experience true madness, I fear."

As if in a daze, Elizabeth spoke through the dryness in her throat. "Why did you not seek me out in Hertfordshire when we were both..."

Darcy was silent. Desolation and pain fluttered through his eyes as an intangible weight rested on his shoulders. She wondered at the transformation of this man before her from the ardent suitor of ghosts to the drowning man before her. She watched him fight an internal battle and then reach a conclusion. She waited for his reply, but none came.

Darcy straightened, shook his head slightly, and forced himself to smile. He spoke with feigned lightness as he baffled her with his change of topic. "You have done it again, Elizabeth. You have distracted me! But I am doubly determined this time, and you shall not prevail again. Come, dear girl, we are off on a mission."

Though disappointed and bothered by his evasiveness, Elizabeth laughed at his dramatic phrasing. "Will you not tell me what mission we so valiantly venture forth to fulfil?"

Darcy shook off the rest of his unease and laughed lightly as he turned towards the door, shaking his head as he went. "Not just yet, but I will say that it is of the utmost importance. We have not a moment to lose!"

He knew his plan would make her happy. He hoped he could be successful, but he also feared that the result of his actions may cost him a dear friend in the process.

Elizabeth chuckled to herself, effectively shaking off her malaise. "Indeed, it must be for us to leave the house at this ungodly hour."

Darcy's laugh reverberated towards her, echoing down the hall as they travelled through the house. They paused only briefly at the vestibule for Darcy to don his hat and gloves and then give a quick goodbye to the night footman, who was standing remarkably alert for being in the last hour of his stewardship.

The crisp air was refreshing, and Elizabeth noted by the light of the day that it was not as early as she had presumed, for the streets and houses around her only held the last vestiges of night. Indeed, sunrise was imminent, but it was still quite early by London standards.

"You know, it is partially your fault that we are off so early this morning."

"Is that so? I hardly can think how that could be." Elizabeth smiled indulgently at him. She found herself weakening under his charm.

"I might have wished to sleep in this morning after our late night discussions, but how was I to sleep with a witch in the next room, casting her spell on me with her laughter all night long."

Elizabeth bit her lip, unwittingly enchanting him further. "You must pardon me for keeping you awake then. I shall temper my laughter next time."

Darcy shook his head, protesting. "No, I hardly think that is possible nor is it desired on my part. I do not believe there will ever be a day that I will not enjoy that sound."

Elizabeth rolled her eyes inelegantly at the gentleman as she looked purposefully out the window, effectively helping her to calm her beating heart. For days now, she had endured like comments, yet each affected her quite as forcefully as the first.

After this, Darcy largely ignored any of Elizabeth's questions about their destination for the duration of the short carriage ride around the square to the next street over. The neighbourhood was just as fashionable as his was though perhaps the homes were slightly smaller in scale. Elizabeth's eyes were glued to the sights through the window, pointing out this or that to a silent, though smiling, Darcy. She wondered at his mood and their destination. This was almost a new side of him, and she found it added to the manifold qualities she admired. He was almost playful; yet, despite his humourous words of a 'mission,' their task was one that he took seriously and perhaps even caused him unease.

This last suspicion was confirmed as they pulled up to an elegant townhouse. She looked to Darcy again for an explanation, and she was met with an unguarded look of anxiety mixed with determination. It vanished almost as soon as she turned her gaze upon him, and it was replaced by the same tight smile he wore earlier in his chambers when she had asked him why he had not sought her favour in Hertfordshire.

"I do endeavour always to do right, Elizabeth. On occasion I find that I have erred, and it is then my duty to make the correction, even if at a great sacrifice."

"I do not take your meaning..." But her words died as she watched him exit and turn to hold the carriage door for her to descend also. She noticed the twitch of his hand as he almost lifted it to assist her. When she raised her head after exiting the carriage, she saw that a footman belonging to the residence was standing by, slightly confused at the way Darcy paused outside his carriage. If she had not felt the weight of his words, she might have teased Darcy.

They were presented at the door, and Darcy's card was accepted by a surprised doorman. The man nodded and, taking the tray with Darcy's card on it, walked away into the depths of the house. Despite the early hour, Darcy and Elizabeth noted a bustle of activity. Luggage and trunks were gathered at the base of the stairs, and servants were rushing about.

"It looks as if I have come just in time," Darcy said, noting the evidence that preparations were being made for a departure from London—and of some duration by the look of it.

The doorman returned and indicated that Darcy should follow him to the study down the hall. Although not quite as large as Darcy's, the room was elegant and masculine. She was intrigued yet further as she took a turn about the room and continued to wonder at their purpose there. She had ceased questioning Darcy for she noted an uneasiness about him that grew the longer they waited in the room. He sat in one of the chairs and restlessly tapped his knee with a quick tattoo of his fingers, occasionally running his hand across his face or his fingers through the curls at his neck.

They both turned towards the door when it opened, Darcy rising quickly to his feet.

"Darcy! Welcome, my friend. You are early for a visit, but what good fortune it is for me. You find me preparing to take my leave of London. I am glad to get to pay my farewell in person instead of a note as I had intended, given the hour." Charles Bingley smiled and jubilantly reached to shake his friend's hand, his words spilling forth in a reckless manner due to his excitement.

Elizabeth smiled at his easy nature and laughed at the enthusiasm he showed in such contrast to his downcast behaviour both at Darcy's club and at the ball last evening.

"Bingley," Darcy said as he shook hands with the gentleman. "I have come to speak to you about a matter of some importance."

Bingley immediately, though not quite effectively, tried to temper his exuberance as he nodded his head and indicated they should sit. Elizabeth watched this in curious wonder at their purpose there. She was not long in the dark about the matter of importance, however.

"Of course, Darcy. I always have time for you. I am glad that I was here for your visit then. Come, would you like a glass of port or something?"

Darcy shook his head, "Tempting despite the early hour, but I shall decline, thank you."

"Oh right, right. Coffee, then?" Bingley laughed, his expression returning to show his good mood. "What is it you needed to speak with me about?"

Clearing his throat, Darcy began with some hesitancy. "You are leaving this morning?"

"Indeed, it is as I mentioned to you last evening. I am bored with London." Here a slight pinch about Bingley's eyes appeared, masked only slightly by his broad smile. "I decided my plan last evening had merit, and I am off to Scarborough for a spell to visit relatives."

"I thought you always disliked visiting your relations there."

Bingley shifted in his seat, his mood losing a bit of its amiability. "In the past, perhaps I would have said that was true. But the idea now has such appeal that you can see I am quite excited about it." He smiled again though it did not reach his eyes.

Darcy breathed deeply before plunging forth on a course that he feared might make this the last visit he ever had with his friend. "Bingley, I want to ask you about Hertfordshire."

Bingley's smile stayed fixed upon his strained features. He looked down at his trousers and smoothed a crease there. "Ask away, my friend."

"Some months ago, I told you some things about a certain lady who resides in that county."

"I remember, I assure you." Bingley's tension was now so poorly hidden that Elizabeth's brow lowered as she looked upon the pair helplessly.

Bingley stood then and, walking to the sideboard, poured himself a glass of port despite the hour. "I assure you that I do not need reminding of my folly in that quarter if that is your purpose now."

"Indeed, it is not. Forgive me if I presume too much upon our friendship, but I wanted to ask whether you... Do you still care for the lady?"

Elizabeth and Darcy waited seemingly for minutes as Bingley

kept his back to them and made no reply for some time. Elizabeth worried for her sister, tears gathering at her eyes. She wanted him to answer, yet she feared what he might say. For Darcy's part, he was conscious of the pain he was causing his friend and the further pain he would soon inflict.

Bingley's answer reached them though he kept his back to his friend and the unseen guest. "I do," he sighed. "She may live in my memory as the most amiable lady of my acquaintance, but that is all. I have nothing to either hope or fear and nothing to reproach you with for your aid in helping me to see the way it was. A little time therefore... I shall certainly try to get the better."

At this, Bingley turned around, toasted his friend with a false smile, and downed his drink.

Darcy stood then and, with a fleeting look towards Elizabeth, took a few steps towards his friend. "I fear you *will* have cause to reproach me soon. I have something of a confession."

Bingley eyed his friend with an anxious solemnity as he nodded and returned to his seat. Darcy remained standing and paced a bit before continuing. "At the time of our departure from Hertfordshire, I was under the impression that Miss Bennet's feelings for you did not match your own. I had personal reasons to disparage the match, and although they were mean and petty to an extent, they were also founded on a deep concern for your wellbeing. I did not believe she cared for you as I wasted no time in telling you a month ago. I did have concerns for you with regards to her family and situation."

Darcy winced when he heard Elizabeth draw breath, but he was determined to continue. "I have since had many causes to reflect upon our acquaintances from that part of the kingdom, and I begin to have my doubts as to the assertions I gave you before."

Bingley spoke softly, but his voice was firm. "What is it you are saying? Out with it, man. Be clear."

"What I am saying is that I no longer am certain the lady did not care for you. I had my doubts then, but my belief in her indifference, I am certain now, was exaggerated by other factors that I am ashamed to say only suited my own purposes."

"What are these other factors of which you speak?"

Darcy's eyes turned automatically towards Elizabeth. For a

minute, he did not answer. Their gazes locked, but to his relief he only saw sorrow and none of the anger he expected. It gave him courage to continue.

"I found that I had developed..."

Bingley looked at his friend with a raised brow, his impatience evident.

Darcy sighed. "I found myself in possession of an admiration myself for a Bennet daughter."

"What!" Bingley jumped to his feet and immediately was before his friend. "Do you mean to tell me that you persuaded me against returning to Miss Bennet because you admired her too?" When his friend looked confused, Bingley spat, "I never suspected it of you, and I now am heartily disgusted at your deception."

Darcy looked at his friend and with alarm responded, "My admiration was not for Miss Bennet, as admirable as she is. I believe my words were that I had an admiration for a Bennet *daughter*. I admired her sister Elizabeth." His eyes returned to the lady spectre.

Bingley was silent for a minute before he began laughing sardonically, startling the other occupants of the room from their locked gazes.

"Do you mean to tell me that all of it—all of the disadvantages of the match with regards to Jane, her family, and situation—applied equally to you and that is why you endeavoured to dissuade me from returning to Netherfield?"

"They were factors but only so much as I believe they kept me from acknowledging my doubts. My main purpose was to protect you if Miss Bennet was indifferent. They—"

"No, I believe it is my turn to speak. Please feel free, however, to correct me if I have not understood you correctly. You believed Jane to be indifferent to me though you were not certain. But you fancied her sister, I suspect unwillingly, and so you tried to convince me to stay in London, effectively ignoring your doubts and favouring your wish for your own release."

"You have the right of it, Bingley," Darcy said with some embarrassment.

"You are a pompous ass," Bingley replied with a chuckle.

Darcy bowed in acknowledgement. "There is more, however, and it speaks even more to that assumption."

"Oh?"

"It requires a few more confessions on my part. In the weeks since leaving Hertfordshire, I have been unable to forget the sister. My admiration for her was—is—steady and perhaps maddening in its hold on me." Darcy looked at Elizabeth and, being unable to decipher her thoughts from her expression, continued. "In a hasty and fevered attempt to eradicate my feelings and thoughts of Miss Elizabeth, I did you a disservice yet again. Yesterday afternoon, your sisters took tea with mine. Miss Bingley told me that she received a letter from your Miss Bennet, indicating her intentions to come to London to visit her relations in Cheapside."

"Jane? Miss Bennet is for London?" Bingley sprang from his seat, his previous anger at his friend dissipated with the news.

"No, she is not. Your sister told me later last evening that she received another letter from Miss Bennet with a change of plans."

"You are making my head spin. First, Jane is coming, and then she is not?"

"I do not know why Miss Bennet changed her plans—only that she did. The disservice I rendered you was that I had told your sister to say nothing to you of Miss Bennet's intention to come to London."

Darcy braced for his friend's ire, but Bingley's spirits, buoyed with the idea of Miss Bennet coming to London, produced only a laugh. "But before she could, Miss Bennet changed her plans. What is the problem then? I fear I do not understand. It is a moot point now, and given your other enlightenments, I do not see any further harm done. In fact, you have done me a service just now."

Darcy sat tiredly and looked at his friend. "What do you mean?"

Bingley patted his friend on the shoulder. "You are slow today, Darcy. You have said that Miss Bennet may care for me. And you have told me her location. The way I see it, I am now in possession of two very important pieces of information."

Darcy breathed deeply and looked at his friend, relief easily read upon his face. "Then you are not angry with me for my interference?"

Bingley smiled ruefully. "Tell me this: Does your admiration of Miss Elizabeth make you crazy for want of seeing her?"

Darcy laughed humourlessly. "More than you know."

Elizabeth laughed then too.

"Then as far as I can see, your punishment is quite appropriate, and justice is served. Now, I am sorry to end this little interview, but as you see, I am in the middle of taking my leave of the city."

"*He is still leaving?*" Elizabeth said, concern in her voice.

Darcy looked at her, knowing her worries. "You still intend to go to Scarborough then? You do not intend to pursue Miss Bennet?"

Bingley laughed again, walking towards his study door. "Actually, I find myself with a sudden need to see my estate in Hertfordshire again. I am sure I have a letter from the steward somewhere that will justify it if it comes to that." He smiled broadly at his friend. "And besides, you know how I hate visiting my relations up north."

Darcy laughed then, the tension leaving his shoulders completely as he walked towards his friend. He reached out his hand to shake Bingley's outstretched one and said, "I think you are making a good choice. Go to her, woo her, and see if you cannot make her love you."

"Oh, I absolutely intend to do just that."

"*You will not have a hard task ahead of you, Mr Bingley; she is half in love with you already. And may I be the first to say you are welcome back to Hertfordshire!*"

Bingley stopped as he was walking Darcy to the door. "Why do you not come with me—do your own wooing?"

"I cannot, unfortunately. But I wish you the best in your efforts."

"Are you sure?" Bingley said with some concern.

Darcy looked behind him towards where Elizabeth was, distracted in her own thoughts. "I am," he replied gloomily. "But you will keep me posted on any developments?"

"I most certainly will, and you know you are welcome anytime should you change your mind."

"Thank you, Bingley."

With that, Darcy exited the house and climbed slowly into his carriage. His companion was quiet for a minute before she spoke. "You did a good thing there, William."

"I am sorry for giving you pain."

Elizabeth smiled kindly at him. "I shall not pretend to say that I was unaffected. I shall also not deny that knowing you have concerns about my family, ones that kept you from approving of Bingley's pursuit for Jane, is upsetting."

Darcy nodded.

"Why did you not wish to go to Hertfordshire with Bingley? Is it still because of my family?"

Darcy was quiet for a while as he thought about how to answer her. He realised his reservations regarding her family had ceased to hold any power with him, his strengthening regard for her effectively taking the power from those arguments. However, he still had concerns.

Darcy attempted to make light of the sobering situation. "And would you have me return, only to have the real you and the imaginary you both drive me mad? Elizabeth, I assure you, I am bewitched enough with one of you; I need not have two Elizabeths."

Elizabeth laughed at his answer. She could not convince him that she was the real Elizabeth nor was she sure she wanted to at that juncture. Her feelings for him were difficult to define. No—she agreed that their unique situation spoke to the wisdom of his words.

"SIMMONS! NOTIFY MY SISTER'S MAID THAT I WISH TO SEE Caroline in my study in one half hour, not a minute later. I do not care whether she has to be awakened; I will speak to her," Bingley addressed his butler after seeing his friend away.

"Yes, sir." Simmons turned to fulfil the orders, but he was forestalled when Mr Bingley spoke again.

"And please have someone from the stables readied to deliver an express to Hertfordshire. I must notify my housekeeper to open the house."

"Will you still be departing today for Scarborough, sir?"

Bingley laughed jovially. "Indeed not—I am to Netherfield, but I believe Caroline will soon find herself desiring to see our relations up north. In fact, Simmons, notify her maid to pack to that end. I feel certain that my sister will soon be wishing herself far from here."

Simmons held the smile he felt in check and simply replied, "Very good, sir," before leaving to carry out the orders.

"JANE! JANE! OH WHERE IS THAT GIRL?" MRS BENNET CALLED excitedly about the house.

Jane was sitting and reading to Elizabeth when her mother returned from a midmorning shopping trip to Meryton. She set aside her book and looked at her sister with a smile.

"What do you think this is, Lizzy? Mother sounds quite excited."

She reached to squeeze her sister's hand and laughed quietly as she thought of what Lizzy would have said had she been conscious. Finally, the vocal exertions of Mrs Bennet neared the door, and soon their mother entered the room.

"Jane!" Mrs Bennet flung herself into the chair beside her favourite daughter, waving a handkerchief about her face. "You will not believe the news I have to share with you!"

Jane smiled sweetly at her mother, waiting for her to continue. Mrs Bennet rarely required a response to continue.

"I was in town when an express rider came through Meryton, quite as if the very devil was chasing him!" Her heavy breaths caused her to pause then.

"Is that all? I thought at least the pigs had got out."

Mrs Bennet scowled at her daughter, wondering briefly that Jane sounded more like Lizzy just then. The thought of Lizzy distracted Mrs Bennet despite the seriousness of her message.

"How is Lizzy this morning, Jane? Any improvement in her?"

Jane smiled at Mrs Bennet, gladdened by her mother's improved sentiments towards her second daughter since the accident. "She is well, I believe. Still no change, but you can see as much yourself."

"Well, Jane, even Lizzy cannot stay long this way when she hears the rest of my news." Mrs Bennet warmed again to the intelligence she had lately learned in Meryton. "Indeed, pay attention, Lizzy, for you will be glad to hear this too, though not as much as Jane, I suspect."

Jane's brows creased when her mother winked at her in that way.

But she could not ponder its meaning any longer for her mother's words rendered her mute and frozen.

"The express rider came back through town on his return from his destination. And where do you think he went, Jane? He went to Netherfield! He is sent to tell the housekeeper that his master is returning—and very soon!"

Jane's heart beat wildly at the thought of Mr Bingley returning to Netherfield. It was an impossibility that she could not have guessed. Jane wondered whether Miss Bingley had shared her last letter with him, detailing the accident. Her hopes soared at the thought that he might return as a result. Of course, her modesty kept her from holding too much hope in his motives, but she could not deny that his return brought with it a warmth that had long since been missing.

"*Jane!* Did you not hear me? I heard it from the rider himself on his return for I saw him stop to water his horse in the fountain and manoeuvred myself close enough to hear him speak to Mr Roberts who was also watering his horse. That man is always trying to know everyone else's business, and you know I cannot approve of such ways, but I heard Mr Roberts ask the young man what his destination had been, and the lad replied it had been Netherfield. And then do you know, that nosey Mr Roberts straight away asked whether Mr Bingley was returning to Hertfordshire, and the young man confirmed that he was!"

Mrs Bennet, excited again by her discovery and certain that she was the first to have found out amongst her friends, left with haste to share the news with Mr Bennet and then off again to crow to her neighbours of her good fortune.

Jane slowly became aware that she was squeezing her sister's hand and looked down upon Lizzy's sleeping face. The bruising had faded substantially, and she looked almost perfectly healthy, if only sleeping. "So he is to come back, Lizzy."

Jane's eyes then fell to their hands as she thought she felt a slight squeeze from her sister in return.

❧ 12 ❧

"S traighten your shoulder, like so. That's it; now keep your arm level and attack."

Laughter bubbled out of Elizabeth at Darcy's focused look; nonetheless, she attempted to correct her posture. "I must say, this is much more difficult than it looks." Elizabeth flashed merry eyes at her instructor and continued. "Perhaps if I had more examples with which to compare myself, I might acquit myself better."

Darcy was neither fooled nor provoked by her words as she had intended, knowing she hoped that he might be disturbed. Nevertheless, he replied, "I assure you *that* is not necessary. I am more than capable of teaching you to fence as you have requested without subjecting you to further glimpses inside the Fencing Academy."

"'Tis a pity to be sure. There were so many *very* agreeable gentlemen."

Darcy stepped towards her until he was nearly upon her. His voice was low and menacing. "Is that so?"

His sudden proximity caused her arm to drop to her side and her breaths to come in quick succession. She stilled and slowly lifted her face to meet his. His dark brown eyes bore an intensity that thrilled her and liberated her senses. Although she had truly been interested only in the specifics of the sport at first, she had to admit her ques-

137

tions had led to a most delightful turn of events there in the ballroom in which she found herself being tutored by the gentleman standing closely to her.

She allowed herself to hold his gaze even as she twisted her brow up and sweetly tilted her head. "Oh, perhaps you are right. I might have been far too distracted at the academy to truly understand the sport."

"Right—and handsome," Darcy retorted, a smile pulling at the edges of his mouth.

"I beg your pardon?"

Darcy carelessly shrugged as he took a step backwards and away. Circling her, he casually swung his rapier as he spoke. "When one is entitled to hearing that they are indeed correct, I think it only fair that they ought also to have that something extra—that little something more."

"You think I ought to admit you are right *and* tell you that you are handsome?" Elizabeth said with a disbelieving laugh. "Such vanity!"

"It is only fair. I paid you such courtesy not two days ago when we left the library. I admitted you were right and beautiful. Or do you not recall?"

Elizabeth shook her head in bemusement. "You are worse than I had thought before. Very well then, Mr Darcy, you are right *and* handsome. Now, may we continue with my lesson?"

"With relish!" Darcy said, his eyes lighting with a satisfied spark and his lips turning up into a beguiling smile. He then stepped behind her and, lifting his hand, indicated she should again raise her arm. The intimacy of their pose—her back to his chest, his arm extended with hers—was heady, yet neither touched. "*En garde, prêt, allez.* Advance, good. Shoulders up, Elizabeth. You must keep your back straight!"

Elizabeth lunged forward, shuffling her feet back again and flicking her arm in the same downward motion he had shown her earlier. It was an exhilarating sport, and not just because she was learning firsthand from Darcy. Though she held no actual sword, her movements were full of grace and power.

A moment later, after another couple of manoeuvres, Darcy and

Elizabeth separated, hearts beating rapidly and breathing heavily, their exertions not entirely responsible for either.

"You are a quick pupil," Darcy said with evident appreciation in his voice.

"Thank you. I have a good tutor."

The two fell silent for a moment. The lady took the chance then to study her companion as she attempted to smooth her gown. She had enjoyed her lesson and marvelled at the playful side of Darcy that allowed it to happen. They had simply been speaking of the sport, and she had asked several questions. Then she thought she might tease him by asking him to teach her, assuming the proper Mr Darcy would not consider teaching a lady this most gentlemanly of sports. She had been wrong, for he had immediately accepted the challenge, and she could do nothing but feign a calm she did not feel.

Darcy had taken his jacket off earlier when they had begun the lesson, and the movement of his arms beneath the bright white linen of his shirt was distracting. She smiled though because, in the days since they had left Bingley to his precipitous trip to Hertfordshire, their time together had grown quite comfortable, not unlike his current attire. She found his manner easy though not entirely without formality.

They conversed most of the days away, their topics varied. They had many discourses on books, not always agreeing on the merits of a particular one, and they spoke often of themselves, securing further the ties of their bond.

She saw also that he was a diligent master to his work despite her presence, never neglecting business matters. He was also a thoughtful brother, seeking out Georgiana several times to include her in a walk or for tea. Elizabeth was often only a shadow about the room during these discussions, her respect and admiration for him growing as she watched him care for his young sister.

Elizabeth hid her smile, tucking her head to the side as she walked towards a mirror in the room. While she checked her appearance and secured a few loose tendrils, she recalled tea with Georgiana the day before.

Darcy had procured himself a plate, including the pastries they both knew she favoured. Despite the strange looks from his sister, he amicably discussed a book with Georgiana. It was one of Shakespeare's sonnets, and Elizabeth recalled now that one particular verse had quite affected her. At the time, she could not decide what had drawn her to the verse. It was as if the words had stirred some recognition of sorts.

Elizabeth's gaze met Darcy's in the mirror. He watched her silently, a serene smile upon his lips. She returned his smile, pink colouring her cheeks as she turned away. He had said nothing more about his feelings for her during their time together, and both parties avoided discussing their situation. Elizabeth was beginning to be of the same opinion as Darcy: she did not relish that moment when their mystic tether was cut.

Darcy's thoughts were also taking a serious turn though caused by a topic different in nature. As he watched Elizabeth fix the captivating ringlets that had fallen out of place atop her head, he struggled to think of any means to further delay speaking with her about a topic he found most distasteful and actually quite painful. Previous to their flirtatious fencing lesson, they had been talking amiably in his library. He had wanted to tell her about Wickham, but not knowing to what degree her heart might be drawn to that despicable man, he repeatedly delayed taking up the matter. He eagerly engaged in any other subjects she chose, even agreeing to teach her to fence as a means of postponement. The fencing lesson had turned into one of the most pleasingly torturous moments of his life. His feelings for Elizabeth had woven themselves so deeply around his heart that he would grant any wish of hers, even those clearly meant only to challenge or tease him.

It was this special regard for her that had him straightening his shoulders in preparation for speaking to her about Wickham. Darcy knew she cared for him, but to what degree, he knew not. And despite his lingering belief that she was but a product of his addled mind, he took pleasure in seeing the transformation of those feelings. Darcy worried that, after he revealed the true nature of her favourite —for that Wickham must be for her to so vehemently defend him in their argument during the ball—she might lose any kind regard she had for him in her disappointment over another. Worse still, he was concerned that Elizabeth, real or not, might not change her opinion of

Wickham despite his revelation, and thinking she favoured Wickham was agonizing to him.

Drawing in a deep breath, Darcy squared himself to his purpose. "Elizabeth, if you are quite satisfied with today's lesson, may I ask you to accompany me to my study? I would speak to you."

Elizabeth turned to look at him, noting his formal manner of speaking, and her eyes narrowed. Not liking the tension filling the air between them, she replied lightly, "I do not believe you have any need to ask my permission. You have always chosen where you wish to go, and I have had no choice but to follow."

Though her words were meant in a teasing manner, she noted his face grew firm and his eyes cooled. "Indeed, you have not. I wonder, if not for the—" He stopped there, watching her brow rise in question. He did not wish to know whether she would follow him of her own accord.

"Perhaps, Elizabeth, for the moment you might indulge me and choose to accompany me."

"As you wish, sir," Elizabeth said warily. Concern for his strained voice pushed into her thoughts. The transition from their easy light-hearted banter during the fencing instructions was disconcerting.

When they exited the ballroom in the direction of the study, they did not notice the small figure standing in the orchestra balcony above them. Georgiana Darcy, having heard her brother's voice as she passed the door to the balcony just a few moments before, entered the small alcove. What she saw concerned her greatly, for below her on the high gloss of the dance floor was her brother, seemingly giving himself a lesson in fencing. His movements were awkward and his words without context. He spoke as if to himself, for she saw no other, yet he said a name. *Elizabeth.* This latest piece of strange behaviour from him brought a blur to the young girl's eyes as she silently worried for her brother. Determining she could no longer stand idly by as William grew more ill, she quietly slipped out of the room and walked straight to her own chambers to write to the only other person she could trust with such a sensitive concern. She wrote to her cousin, the colonel, requesting his immediate presence.

"I WOULD HAVE YOU KNOW ABOUT WICKHAM," HE BEGAN without ceremony upon entering his study.

Elizabeth was startled by his abrupt introduction to the topic that, in all their history, had been one that was obviously distasteful to him. "You need not disclose anything to me," Elizabeth said compassionately. She could see the very real turmoil in his eyes and the tension in his jaw. After her enforced attachment to Darcy in this dream, she realised she no longer cared what he might have to say about Wickham. She knew he was a better man than Mr Wickham had portrayed, and although she could not discount the truth that seemed present in that fellow's features when describing his misfortunes at Darcy's hand, she could no longer find it within herself to disapprove of William.

"You are too kind, but we both know, despite the ease of the past few days, that this is a topic above all others that must be discussed."

Elizabeth acknowledged this with a heavy sigh and nodded her head. Not knowing beforehand what he might reveal, she could not have anticipated the extent of his full disclosure. The account of Wickham's connection with the Pemberley family was exactly what he had related himself; the kindness of the late Mr Darcy, though she had not before known its extent, agreed equally well with his own words. So far, each recital confirmed the other, but when Darcy came to the will, the difference was great. To think that Mr Wickham had purposely deceived her and garnered her sympathy under false pretences enraged her and produced profound disgust. However, the pressure on her chest that was growing ever more suffocating was produced by the guilt she felt in believing such a man over another. She had been pleased by the preference of one and offended by the neglect of the other.

Every word spoken proved more clearly that the affair, which she had believed impossible that any contrivance could so represent as to render Mr Darcy's conduct less than infamous, was capable of a turn that must make him entirely blameless throughout the whole. Of Wickham's former life, nothing had been known in Hertfordshire but what he declared himself. As to his real character, had information been in her power, she had never wished to enquire. His countenance, voice, and manner had established him at once in the possession of every virtue. She tried to recollect some instance of goodness, some distinguished trait of integrity or benevolence, but no such recollection befriended her. She could see him instantly before her in every charm of air and address, but she could remember no more substantial good than the general approbation of the neighbourhood and the regard his social powers had gained him in the officers' mess.

Wretchedly, Elizabeth looked up at Mr Darcy and halted his speech with the raise of her small hand. "You need not say more, sir. How despicably have I acted!" she cried. "I, who have prided myself on my discernment! I, who have valued myself on my abilities—who had often disdained the generous candour of my sister and gratified my vanity in useless or blameable distrust. How humiliating is this discovery!"

Darcy went immediately to her side, declaring his protest. "No, Elizabeth. I know not in what manner, under what form of falsehood, he has imposed on you, but his success is not, perhaps, to be wondered at. Ignorant as you previously were of everything concerning him, detection could not be in your power and suspicion certainly not in your inclination."

Though he did not wish to know how Wickham had imposed upon her heart, he did hope she would not take such blame upon herself.

"You are too kind, sir, but I have courted prepossession and ignorance and driven reason away where either of you were concerned. I deserve none of your consideration."

"Elizabeth." Darcy, seeing her head bent and her shoulders drooping, kneeled before her and, speaking again in calming tones, said, "Elizabeth, will you not look at me?"

When she raised her eyes to his, they were glossy with unshed tears that pulled at his heart and filled him with the desire to pull her into his embrace and comfort her. The imagined spectre, dream, or whatever game Fate had thrust upon the two of them had, until then, not caused him such anguish as it did now when he could not connect with her in any corporeal way. "Elizabeth, my dearest Elizabeth, please do not suppose you are to blame. He is a master of deceit, and you are a pure, kind-hearted soul whose natural empathy has done you a disservice in this instance."

After another quiet minute, Elizabeth spoke. "How heartily sorry I am for all the wasted time I spent in disapproval of you. Had I known, had I only known..."

Darcy's breath drew sharply. It pierced him to think how things might have been different had they both acted in some other way in Hertfordshire. Would he be so crazed with love for her had he not fought his inclination in the first place? And what of Elizabeth? Could he even have resisted her had she behaved with any real interest in him instead of her studied indifference that he vainly interpreted as attraction? He had thought he was raising her hopes in Hertfordshire; it was one of the reasons he left. They had both been foolish and blind with regards to the other.

"I hope I have not caused you too much pain. I know not to what extent he has injured you."

Elizabeth, wishing to clear herself in his mind in regards to what he must be thinking, spoke fervently. "Wickham has not injured me, leastways in the manner you think."

Darcy smiled though still plagued by the part of his history with Wickham that remained unspoken. She watched with growing concern as he stood and resumed pacing again. "There is more, is there not?"

Darcy halted suddenly and turned his head towards her. "It matters not. I do not wish to distress you further."

"I would like to know it regardless."

Darcy struggled with indecision as he looked into her eyes. It was the pureness in them that caused him to waver. He wished not to pervert her view of the world by disclosing further the degenerate character of his former childhood friend. Yet her face earnestly pleaded with him to continue. It occurred to him then that her wish to know was as much for herself as it was to ease him of the burden he felt.

With sudden clarity, he recalled the passage from the poem he read to Georgiana earlier—the one that had Elizabeth reaching suddenly for the book with a startled look. *"Showing life's triumph in the map of death. And death's dim look in life's mortality."* A chill spiralled up his spine as he once again considered what force brought Elizabeth to his side. Was it his own imagination as he thought or was it something more sinister? The horror of that thought caused him to close his eyes tightly, his heart clenching painfully. He feared the answer. A moment later, a peace stole about him, and Darcy, unsure of what force had calmed him, opened his eyes to see Elizabeth's small figure close to his, her arms wrapped around his waist, her cheek pressed against his chest. The sweet torture this discovery caused within his heart was severe. *If I could but feel her!* Slowly, Darcy reached his arms around her, wanting—aching—to feel her like nothing he had known before. Her goodness calmed him even as he pushed aside that ache, pretending instead that he did feel her warmth beside him.

Neither spoke for several minutes. He marvelled at her desire to comfort him. She marvelled at the way her regard for him had transformed over the time she had been tethered to him. He, too, realised that his feelings for her had undergone a transformation. No longer did he consider only his own situation but hers as well. She had removed his pride and taught him what it meant to please a woman worthy of being pleased. The next words of the poem then came forcefully to his mind: *"Each in her sleep themselves so beautify. As if between them twain there were no strife."*

Whether *she* was dreaming or *he* had gone mad, Darcy decided then that he could have no secrets from her. He revealed to her his anguished history with Wickham wherein it pertained to his young sister. With difficulty, he outlined Wickham's attempted seduction of her at Ramsgate and his strategic plan to revenge himself upon Darcy through the tender heart of Georgiana. Wickham's mercenary motives aside, his embittered hatred for Darcy was the real motivator. Her only sounds were soft sobs and gasps as he recounted the anger and pain of discovery, the guilt and helplessness of the moments after, and his heartache for his responsibility in it all.

Colonel Fitzwilliam entered his cousin's house with his brows knit in concern. Georgiana's summons was disquieting. She requested he come quickly and that he not tell Darcy of his visit. He was to meet her in her music room alone, which added to the strange nature of the entreaty. Her words were filled with the evidence of her unsettled state, and he wondered what she wished to discuss with him. It was obviously of great importance, yet she did not want her own brother to know. He feared she had more to disclose with regards to that blackguard Wickham! The very thought caused Colonel Fitzwilliam's hands to squeeze angrily about his riding crop, the wood beginning to splinter before he relaxed his hold.

It was not long into his interview with Georgiana that he, too, was filled with concern. Though grateful the topic had nothing to do with Ramsgate, Colonel Fitzwilliam could not be insensible to the implications of his discoveries from his young cousin with regards to Darcy's most recent behaviour. Before confronting Darcy, he sent for his cousin's valet and housekeeper. Gads, he hoped they were all wrong.

JANE ENTERED HER SISTER'S CHAMBER, HER HEART SO FULL THAT at first she knew not what to say. Exhausted from holding herself in check over the last half hour, she collapsed against the bed, her arms about the middle of her sister. She longed for nothing more than the calming and healing embrace of Elizabeth as she sorted the emotions she was experiencing.

When she was able to gather her composure, she poured forth the contents of her heart to her ever-quiet, ever-listening sister.

"He has come, Lizzy. I know not what to think other than that he has come. Mr Bingley called today, not a half hour ago. Oh, Lizzy, I need you. I *need* you. You must advise me as to how I shall act and what I shall say."

Seeing no response, Jane once again laid her head against her sister's chest, listening for the comforting sound of her beating heart. Tears swam in her eyes and finally spilled over onto the soft linen of Elizabeth's nightgown. While she listened to the steady beat, she whispered again. "I love him still, Lizzy. As God as my witness, I love him still. And I do not know how I am to keep my heart this time."

❧ 13 ❧

It had been several silent minutes since Darcy had finished his narrative about Wickham's despicable plot against Georgiana, and still Elizabeth had not spoken. They remained in a sort of embrace, each attempting to comfort the other through the harrowing account, each wishing desperately to actually feel the comfort of that embrace.

For Elizabeth, her mind was aching in acute confusion as she considered how completely her misguided loyalties had been placed. Although it had been many days since she had felt so severely against Darcy or favourably towards Wickham, the days had not the power to lessen her anguish regarding how wrongly she judged either gentleman, knowing that she had allowed herself to be so absolutely fooled. Her heart felt painfully tight and spoke to her of the regard she had developed for Darcy. He was, and had always been it would seem, a good sort of man, and she had previously not allowed herself to see it. The discovery of her misguided judgments caused Elizabeth to feel as if she were pulled in two different directions. Indeed, she was beginning to feel stretched thin, unable to discern one emotion before the next took hold, overwhelming her anew.

Her heart yielded to Darcy's power, yet mortification at her wrong-headed thoughts about him made her wish fervently that she might disappear from his view—indeed, that she might somehow leave this horrible, awful, wonderful dream.

The gentleman was no less affected by their discourse. He took no pleasure in recounting his history with Wickham, nor did he relish seeing Elizabeth so distressed. Yet her reaction was balm to his open wounds, soothing his pain over the ordeal, for he could see that her gentle way empathised with him and also with his dear sister. Her tenderness warmed his heart. And though he could not know her own pain at the knowledge of Wickham's deception, that unpredictable organ in his chest felt stronger for having shared his pain with her. Witnessing her kind compassion was as if the pieces of his heart were now melding together as one. His many regrets from the past dissolved only to become more powerful sentiments, his admiration and regard for Elizabeth and his convictions regarding her growing in strength as he stood there within the protection of her arms.

Whatever Elizabeth was, whether spectre or hallucination, he was haunted by her now more than ever, for her otherworldly power had reached into his proud heart and secured it for herself.

A commotion without brought both Darcy and Elizabeth from their private thoughts and alerted them to footsteps approaching the study door. Before either could gain better mastery of themselves, the door opened abruptly. Darcy and Elizabeth each immediately and embarrassedly took hasty steps back from each other, conscious of their compromising position.

"Darcy, my boy! A glass of your port, if you will!" Colonel Fitzwilliam declared unceremoniously as he entered the room, preceding a flustered Mr Carroll.

Darcy's gaze flickered anxiously from his cousin to Elizabeth twice, his cheeks matching her heightened colour before realising how utterly ridiculous his worries were. Ignoring his cousin, he locked eyes with Elizabeth, seeing the humour, telling him that she, too, felt the relief and realised the absurdity of their embarrassment. True, his posture might have appeared odd; however, no harm could be caused by it.

Elizabeth bit her lip, attempting to check her laughter. She had been mortified to be found in Darcy's arms. Such a breach of propriety was certainly not a laughing matter, yet when reality settled once again on her addled senses, she could not help but find herself quite amused that she had altogether forgotten her invisible state. Caught up in the moment, the instant had felt all too real for both of them. Now looking at Darcy, Elizabeth noticed the heat from his cheeks recede only to seep into his eyes. She was stunned, paralysed by the way his dark eyes pierced her then. Although a warmth of her own was spreading from her heart throughout her form from the strength of his gaze, she felt frozen in place.

"Are you well?" Darcy asked Elizabeth, remembering her distressed state prior to Colonel Fitzwilliam's entrance into the room.

Elizabeth smiled softly at him, her eyes bright with happy contentment. *"I am quite well, William."*

"Not all bad considering the devil of a day I have had, thank you for asking," the colonel answered before raising the glass he had just poured to his lips and emptying it.

Darcy frowned at hearing his cousin's voice, forgetting momentarily that Richard was there and had answered him as well. Darcy remained fixed in place, still regaining his composure and bearings with the sudden addition to their company. For the first time, he noticed his cousin was a little worse for wear, standing just to the side of Elizabeth. His butler was still in the open door.

Upon making eye contact with his master, Mr Carroll said, "Colonel Fitzwilliam to see you, sir." Although his statement was needless, his tone indicated disapproval of the colonel's unceremonious entrance as well as his taking liberty with Darcy's stock of spirits.

Darcy chuckled, surprised at the level of frivolity he suddenly felt towards the whole, ridiculous situation. "Indeed, Mr Carroll."

Colonel Fitzwilliam raised his refilled glass again as if in toast. "I do not think we shall have further need of you, Carroll."

The family retainer simply raised his brow and turned a proud chin towards his master, awaiting orders from that quarter before taking his leave. Darcy smiled understandingly at his butler; he was pleased also to see Elizabeth's amusement. "Thank you, Mr. Carroll. You will have to excuse my cousin. He seems to have lost his mind along with his manners."

Colonel Fitzwilliam sputtered, choking on his drink. Darcy turned then to him and, with a laugh and a pat on his back, teased his cousin. "What is the problem, Richard—cannot hold your liquor any more? If so, your officers will likely drum you out of the army."

The smile on Darcy's lips faded when his eyes met his cousin's serious and pained expression. His face was awash with concern, and Darcy's own countenance suddenly sobered. "Good God! What is the matter?"

The colonel shook his head and silently took up the seat near the fire, conveying the decanter of port with him. Darcy again importuned him to speak.

Richard, feeling tired and wary of the interview he was to have with his cousin, sighed and said, "Hold a minute, Cousin."

Darcy looked mildly surprised; never knowing his cousin to delay anything and sensing the seriousness plaguing his cousin, he was amazed to see him so reserved. Even in the most difficult times, Darcy had always known his cousin to keep his mettle about him and be a man of action.

"*He almost looks as if...*" thought Darcy.

"*He is overwhelmed,*" Elizabeth observed.

Nodding absently to her, he smiled slightly at the way their thoughts matched. "Overwhelmed" was an apt description and one he had never before used in regards to Richard. Even during the debacle at Ramsgate, his cousin had held a command over the situation that Darcy could not. Though he had been troubled as well, Darcy had admired his cousin's fortitude under the stress. He had not risen to the rank of colonel in His Majesty's Army without mastering hard circumstances with ease. This knowledge led Darcy to ask again the question he had previously meant for another.

"Are you well, Richard?"

His cousin waved away the question, lifting the decanter to refill his glass again. "If not *well*, I shall at least be *well foxed* when I have finished this."

Darcy frowned, walking towards the companion chair to the one Richard occupied. He was about to speak when his attention was caught as Elizabeth motioned for him to come towards her. Immediately, he turned and walked to her side, following as she led him to the window. With their backs to the room, the two gazed out the window at the twilight. Darcy looked down at Elizabeth in question.

Although unnecessary, Elizabeth still whispered in response to his unspoken entreaty. *"I believe, sir, that whatever is burdening your cousin can have nothing to do with me, and I was going to suggest that you take up the seat there."* She paused and motioned behind them to the sofa along the wall. *"That way I might leave you to your business with your cousin in privacy and slip into the library."*

"I do not think that is necessary."

"Oh I assure you, Darce—it is, indeed, entirely necessary." The colonel responded by raising the decanter up to actually kiss the glass.

Darcy half turned to his cousin, his concern growing yet manifesting itself as irritation. "By all means, drink until you have not a wit about you."

To his further irritation, Darcy heard his cousin laugh. He detected an edge to the sound that drew his brows together once again.

"At least in that, we shall be equals," the colonel said before laughing sardonically again.

Darcy breathed deeply, his jaw clenching. He turned silently towards Elizabeth and said, "I would have you stay."

He ignored the flippant reply his cousin made regarding his plan to go nowhere anytime soon and instead looked deeply into Elizabeth's eyes. He did not care for the idea of spending any time away from her, never knowing when the minute would come that would be his last. Whatever was troubling his cousin could not be worth being away from her. He waited until she came to a decision and nodded.

"If it is your wish, I shall stay." She smiled gently at him and turned so that she again faced the window, allowing him this degree of privacy with his cousin.

Darcy admired her a moment longer, taking in the beautiful curve of her neck, the soft brilliance of her hair in the light from the lamps and the smoothness of her skin. Sighing, he turned towards his cousin. As much as he wished he could spend the evening thus occupied, whatever was causing his cousin to be in such a state needed to be addressed.

Walking to Richard, Darcy took the decanter from his hands and, ignoring a protest, poured himself a glass before returning it to the table next to his cousin. He took up the seat from which he could observe both the countenance of Richard and the form of Elizabeth, standing near the window beyond him.

Darcy eyed his cousin over the rim of his glass as he took a moderate sip. The burn of the liquid down his throat focused him on the task before him. To his surprise, Darcy felt beyond his depths. Usually, it was Richard prodding him to talk and not the other way around. He thought of how to begin, and his lips twitched when he decided to use his cousin's own tactics.

While Darcy thought of flippant and ridiculous notions to provoke his cousin's ire in the manner used most effectively against himself in the past, his cousin was formulating his own troubled plan of action for pressing Darcy to acknowledge he was ill. His sister and staff all confirmed strange behaviour, and their collective voices amounted to one thing: his cousin Mr Fitzwilliam Darcy of Pemberley had lost his mind. The very thought blanketed Richard again in a cloud of fear and worry. He brought the drink to his lips again for a long gulp. A direct attack had never been the colonel's approach of choice before, but such would be his course tonight; he had not the fortitude to manoeuvre Darcy to reveal his secrets in his usual manner, nor would he have the clarity of mind if he waited much longer.

Richard began. "You have developed a taste for lemon tarts."

Darcy sat back, a little surprised at the obscure statement. "I... Yes... They have a certain appeal to me now."

Darcy kept his face unreadable, but his eyes flicked towards the window at the figure behind his cousin. Elizabeth turned and smiled cheekily.

Richard made no delay in issuing forth his next statement. "Yet you still do not consume them."

"What is this nonsense? Are you spying on my eating habits?"

"You did not answer my question," he responded, unmoved by Darcy's offended tone.

"I do not believe you asked a question," Darcy shot back.

Fatigue settled again upon Richard, and his patience snapped.

"Damn it, Darcy, I believe you take my meaning. You want an inquisition?—then you shall have one. Why do you request a food with your every meal or repast that you have heretofore detested yet never eat it?"

Darcy laughed uneasily, pretending to find his cousin ridiculous. "What does it signify? Are you my nanny now? Making sure that I eat all my peas," Darcy scoffed. "When you retire from the army, you ought to look into becoming a governess."

Richard huffed, moving to his next point. "What about your bed?"

Darcy shifted in his seat, becoming more uncomfortable but nevertheless maintaining his air of amusement. "My bed?"

Rolling his eyes heavenward, Richard spat out a word not often said outside of the gaming rooms at gentlemen's clubs. Darcy startled, years of ingrained decorum causing him to be conscious once again of Elizabeth's being within earshot of language no lady should hear.

"Watch your language!" he admonished immediately then regretted just as quickly. Darcy had never before cared about his cousin's cant and occasionally utilised a few choice words himself when flustered—but never in the presence of a lady.

He watched his cousin's brows shoot up in amazement. Richard looked about him at the empty room and returned his sardonic eyes to his cousin. "Seriously?"

Richard was beginning to feel the effects of several glasses of strong port and, thus freed from his usual self-control, purposefully offered up another round of expletives that would make sailors blush with the express purpose of provoking his cousin. So far that evening, Richard had not seen any unusual behaviour with the exception of his cousin's being posed rather oddly when he first entered the room. *If he is indeed addled*, Richard thought, *provoking him might force Darcy to see it himself.*

"That is quite enough!" Darcy growled loudly. He threw a pardoning glance at Elizabeth and was slightly mollified to see that she was covering her mouth with her hand, only suppressing a laugh rather than looking scandalised.

Sighing and falling back into his chair, Darcy rubbed his temples. "What is it you want?" he said tiredly.

His cousin's hard tone did not change as he replied, "Your bed, sir?"

"What about it?"

"Enough with the games. Why did you move your bed?"

"From nanny to decorator, Richard?" Darcy tried to jest, but upon seeing the stern face of his cousin, sobered and relented. "I assume you refer to the fact that I have repositioned my bed."

"Why?"

"I do not see why I need to give a reason. May I ask to what these questions tend?"

"Merely to the illustration of your character. I am trying to make it out."

Darcy once again looked beyond his cousin to Elizabeth, seeing that she, too, remembered a time they had engaged in similar conversation. Returning his attention to his cousin, Darcy said earnestly, "I do not see why you should have to illustrate my character. I should think you would already know it."

"Ah, but I do not get on at all. I hear such different accounts of you as puzzle me exceedingly."

"Is that so?"

Richard, drowsy from the large quantity of alcohol, lost a bit of the steel in his voice. "Just tell me why you felt the need to rearrange your room."

"I will need to speak with my valet, it seems. A man's privacy holds no value these days. It is too bad really; he was a good valet—a dream with a cravat," Darcy said flippantly. "I shall miss him. In fact, it would seem I have spies among many of my staff. But to answer your question, I found my sleep was disturbed when the bed was on the other side of the room."

Darcy saw his cousin was not satisfied and thus added evasively. "I have a better view of the windows now, and—" Darcy stopped abruptly when his cousin snorted in disbelief. "Blast it all. I do not have to explain myself to you in the least. I am master of this house, and if I wish to move my bed, I may certainly do so. Hell, I may even have every article of furniture redone in the hideous tones Miss Bingley always wears!"

This statement caused his cousin to break into laughter, easing the tension in the room considerably. Slowly Darcy joined him, especially when he heard the delightful, bewitching sound of laughter coming from the vicinity of the window.

However, Elizabeth was slightly worried on Darcy's account for this line of questioning, knowing that her presence was the cause of his strange behaviours, even drawing the attention of his staff. Though Darcy had easily explained away everything presented to him thus far, she feared it would get worse.

After another minute, Richard sighed and, in a calmer tone than he had used all evening, said earnestly, "Darcy, your staff is concerned. Georgiana is concerned. And I am concerned. You have been heard speaking to yourself—laughing even—and do not proceed to defend that point. I know you are not a man normally prone to laughter. And you have ordered foods you do not like—and still do not eat—to be present at all meals."

Darcy began to speak, but he was stopped when his cousin continued. "And you have asked that the mistress's chambers be cleaned and aired. In fact, I believe Mrs Carroll said you instructed her to make them 'ready for use.' Explain yourself now, sir."

Darcy remained silent. All that his cousin had said was true; yet what could he tell him? That he had gone mad—mad enough to see the lady of his dreams in his everyday reality? He looked at Elizabeth and drank in the calming effect of her beauty. Her eyes were lit with a kindness that settled into the tightness in his chest and relaxed him.

"I did not think I would ever need to defend my behaviour in the privacy of my own home." Darcy forestalled his cousin's attempt to interrupt. "No, I will thank you to remember that now it is my turn."

Darcy stood then and, taking the poker out of its holder, stirred the hot coals of the fire while he considered his cousin. He could tell that Richard was indeed quite worried, and if he could assure him that he had not gone mad, then he would do so, but *that* was simply not in his power. He turned his head to look at his cousin and, seeing that resolve in his eyes, decided perhaps to confess it all.

"A lady is at the heart of the matter—as I believe is the case for most men who find themselves acting strangely and without reason," Darcy said simply. Darcy lifted his head towards Elizabeth, and they shared a quiet smile. Her bemused expression was endearing, and despite this interrogation, Darcy could not find it in himself to wish his sanity to return. Darcy did not know what she was feeling, and although he had told her before that he admired her, he had never quite said the word "love." It was the final surrender to his addled state. Now, as he looked upon her angelic face, he could not help but wish to declare it. Knowing that his cousin still waited for more, he said, "A fact that you will no doubt find quite humorous. But before you begin mercilessly to tease me, allow me to explain from the beginning."

Elizabeth listened spellbound as Darcy described his first impressions of her. She learned that his comments at the assembly sprouted from a previous ill humour and not from any judgment on his part. He described the need for her that grew the more he saw or heard her, that he learned to favour her song to any other, and that the sound of her laughter left him spellbound. Her heart beat faster as he continued his discourse, enumerating all of her accomplishments, strengths, and allurements that he found tempting. The longer she listened, however, the more a strange occurrence began to pull at her awareness. She became conscious of a dull pain on the side of her head. His words were stirring, however, and she endeavoured to ignore the ache and listen.

"Is this the 'unsuitable' lady you proceeded to tell me you had feelings for on New Year's Eve?"

Darcy looked at Elizabeth when he spoke, his voice echoing sadness for having to hurt her with his confirmation. "She is indeed."

"You know I would like to argue with you over that point, but this is not the time. Obviously, we have more distressing points to discuss. Pray continue."

Darcy resumed his narrative, picking up with his need for escape from his growing feelings for Elizabeth. His account of his return to London and subsequent disquiet in general moved Elizabeth to tears. She sympathised, having lost long ago any offense at his actions, for she knew that his struggles had been great, and she had come to understand his reasons, knowing his concerns regarding her family to be justified if still a little heartrending. Oddly, the longer he spoke and the more detailed he became as he shared the contents of his heart, the more pronounced the throbbing in her head grew. She sat on the windowsill, her hand reaching to rub the spot as she focused more of her strength on Darcy and his words.

"I could not get her out of my head." Darcy stood and took a few steps towards Elizabeth, noticing she appeared slightly troubled. He had seen her on occasion rub the side of her head, and it had always nagged at him—the reason for it unknown to either.

The colonel fell backwards against his seat, brought the glass to his mouth, and emptied it in one gulp. Sighing loudly, he brought his cousin's attention back to him. "I cannot tell you what relief you have brought me with this news."

Darcy looked confused and turned his head to the side trying to understand his cousin's words.

"I came here today because I had been told that you may be ill."

"Ill? In what manner?" Darcy asked consciously.

"Ill as in headed-to-Bedlam ill. Good heavens, how glad I am to hear that you have only lost your wits over a lady." Colonel Fitzwilliam began to laugh wildly.

Darcy shifted his feet uncomfortably and looked at Elizabeth. She smiled in bemusement, knowing that insane is exactly what Darcy thought he had become. "I believe you have had too much to drink, Cousin."

This only made Richard laugh harder. "Indeed, I believe you may be right."

Darcy shook his head and continued to close the distance to Elizabeth. His eyes did not leave her even when his cousin spoke again.

"Is this Miss Bennet, about whom you have told me so much, perhaps named Elizabeth?"

Darcy nodded, his eyes softening as he looked at her. "Elizabeth."

Richard relaxed completely. It was the same name Georgiana had said she heard Darcy say while practicing his fencing earlier in the day. She had been concerned that he had been talking to himself but now Richard believed that what she saw was a man fighting his demons and struggling with an admiration he did not want, using physical exertion as a distraction.

"Well you are not the first man nor shall you be the last, I dare say," Richard began. Now relieved of concern for his cousin's state of mind, he resolved to sort out Darcy's state of heart as well.

"I believe it is time, my dear cousin, to let go of your reservations. You do not need money, and any concerns you have regarding her connections cannot be a problem when you have my mother."

Darcy turned from Elizabeth then and questioned his cousin, unsure of what Lady Matlock had to do with any of it. "What do you mean?"

"All these society events that she insists you attend have been her attempts at matchmaking."

"Surely, you jest!"

"I do not. You must have known this." Richard attempted to sit up but could not coordinate his limbs for the task.

"I assure you, I have not."

Richard shrugged. "Well, they have. I wager she would like to see both of us in the parson's mousetrap before long." He turned in his seat so that he could see behind him to where Darcy was standing a few feet from the window. "She just wants to see you happy. If this Miss Bennet lacks connections, by virtue of marriage to you, she will have connections to my mother, whom nobody of the *ton* dares refute." Richard tried to punctuate his words by snapping his fingers but the disobedient appendages had grown thick.

"I appreciate your assurances, but let me assure *you* that I do not need them." Darcy turned again to look at Elizabeth. "I care not what society thinks any more; indeed, I was a fool to let it lead me astray for so long."

Darcy slowly took a step closer to Elizabeth. His eyes roaming her features and resting finally on her eyes. "I am utterly and irrevocably lost to her already. The disapproval of society cannot change that nor would I wish it to."

Darcy could not help declaring himself further, sealing his fate with his words. "You must allow me to tell you how ardently I admire and love you."

Elizabeth felt the impact of his words like a song to her soul, awakening her like nothing she had ever felt before. Her head began to swim though, and her eyes began playing tricks on her.

"*William, I lo—*"

"A pretty speech, Darcy, and while I am sure I love you too..." Richard cut in, snorting drunkenly.

Darcy turned irritated eyes at his cousin for interrupting Elizabeth. Suddenly, fearing his cousin would again worry for his state of mind, Darcy quickly said, "I meant to say that you must allow me to tell you how ardently I admire and love *her*."

While Darcy was occupied misguiding his cousin again, Elizabeth felt a whooshing sound fill her ears and her head began to throb mercilessly. Her hands flew out beside her instinctively to steady herself as she felt the room begin to spin. Flashes of memories began to strike across her mind, forcefully jarring her consciousness from the present circumstances. She collapsed against the side of the windowsill, her head in her hands as she realised what was happening. The memories that now flooded her awareness were new to her yet familiar. It was like remembering a dream she had lost.

"*It was so very cold! I remember the cold most clearly now. The ground was hard and the frost seeped deeply into me, infecting my very bones.*" Elizabeth began numbly to describe the images coming swiftly to her mind again, even as her hands chaffed her arms as if to warm them.

Darcy's attention was whipped around immediately to focus on Elizabeth. Her words caused his heart to freeze uncomfortably in his chest. "Elizabeth! What are you saying?"

"*We left the New Year's Eve ball early; the room was so very full, and Jane was not feeling well.*"

"Uh...Darcy, are you well, man?" Richard, suddenly concerned by the fierceness of his cousin's face as well as the fact that he was talking to the window, stood unsteadily.

"*The carriage was going to come back for them.*" Elizabeth looked up with startled and fearful eyes. "*The snow started to fall just as we began for home.*"

"Darcy...?"

"Will you be quiet, Richard! For God's sake, allow her to speak!"

Richard fell silent, sobered slightly by his cousin's bizarre behaviour. Darcy turned abruptly back to the window and spoke fervently, panic lacing his voice. "Elizabeth, tell me what happened."

The lady felt as if she were in a fog, witnessing the terrible accident from afar but remembering and feeling the pain and terror of it as it happened. With glossy eyes, she looked up at Darcy, her mouth uttering the words that her mind could not hold back. "*The roads were icy and we slid a few times. I remember the screech of the wheels and the panicked noise of the horses. Everything went so quickly after that. Everything was tossed about and then fell still. I hit the ground here.*" She touched again the throbbing at the side of her head. "*And it was so very cold and dark too. I remember only the darkness after that.*"

Darcy fell to his knees, his worst fears taking hold of his heart and stealing his strength. "Oh God, not Elizabeth, not her." The pain in his chest pressing against him in a manner that left him breathless. *Elizabeth! Not her!*

"What is going on here, Darcy?" Richard was now at his side and, though foxed, still able to discern the gravity of the situation.

Elizabeth was silent for a while, considering Darcy's words and her own returned memory. She was agonized by an option she had not considered. All this time she had thought that she was merely dreaming, but dreaming had never explained everything. Certainly, it did not explain the parts of the dream where Darcy's own explanations held merit. A cold ribbon of dark, black fear wrapped itself around her heart as she considered the possibility that she might be an *actual* ghost—not an imaginary spectre to Darcy, not dreaming, but dead to both their worlds.

"*It cannot be. I am certain it cannot be,*" she stuttered numbly. Disbelief abounded in her thoughts, and she searched her new memories for anything that might assure her that she could not be dead. As she considered the grave thought, her conviction grew. Though she could not explain why she was with Darcy in spirit form without being deceased, somehow she felt all too alive to be dead. "*William, it cannot be! I am sure of it somehow.*"

Darcy lifted his eyes to her, and she saw they were rimmed in red, his features pale. "How can you be certain?"

Elizabeth shook her head stiffly. "*I do not know, but somehow I know that I am not dead.*"

"Bingley!" Darcy shot up from the floor, and headed towards his desk. "He might have written. I have not looked at my correspondence yet today."

"Bingley? Darcy, you are ssshpeaking nonsense. I demand you...

oomph." Richard rubbed his shoulder as he tried to right himself after stumbling into a bookcase. "Perhaps I am a trifle in my cupsssh."

The other occupants of the room ignored the inebriated colonel and rushed towards the desk. Darcy shuffled his hands through the stacks of papers on his desk, destroying their careful order. Papers slid across the polished surface and fell to the floor, floating like feathers to rest about their feet. Elizabeth, too, glided her hands through the papers, looking to feel any letters that were from Bingley. Images of estate matters detailed in letters from his stewards floated through her awareness but nothing from Bingley.

Desperately, they quit their search when nothing came up and looked at each other, each leaning against the desk between them. The thread of hope they had felt pulled taut enough to snap at any moment. A knock at the door startled everyone, the colonel included, who by this time had felt his head grow heavy and had chosen to lie down on the sofa.

Darcy rushed to the door and opened it to find a troubled Mr Carroll. He held in his hands a silver salver with a letter on it. "This has just arrived, sir, by way of express from Hertfordshire."

Seizing it immediately, Darcy looked frantically at Elizabeth. "It is from Bingley," he said when he saw his friend's familiar scrawl.

They both looked towards Richard who was struggling to sit up. Elizabeth turned again to Darcy with pleading eyes and said, "*Can we not go someplace more private?*"

Agreeing, Darcy turned towards his butler and dismissed him, relieved to note that, when he told Elizabeth the letter was from Bingley, it could have easily looked as if he were speaking to his cousin who thankfully was the same direction behind her on the sofa.

Darcy nodded and, looking beyond her to his cousin, said, "I am for bed, Richard."

Richard fell back gratefully against the cushions, already half insensible again. "I say, good idea. We will ssshpeak of this...in the morn..." He ended with an inelegant snore to the empty room, Elizabeth and Darcy not having waited for the end of his speech to escape up the stairs.

Upon reaching his chambers, Darcy threw open the door and

dismissed his valet who had entered when he heard Darcy come in. As soon as they were alone, Darcy broke the seal of the letter.

"Wait!" Elizabeth uttered, halting Darcy's attempts to unfold the letter. When he met her eyes, she whispered, "I do not know what that letter will say. It may tell us what we fear most right now, and there is something I must tell you."

The urgency of the matter faded away, and they were left with this feeling of being the only two in the world. Darcy allowed the hand holding the letter to fall to his side as his other came up to stroke across the space where Elizabeth's cheek would be if he could feel it.

"Would that I could touch you!" he said with such anguish that Elizabeth closed her eyes in agreement, a single tear escaping and rolling down her cheek.

"William, no matter what that letter says, I would have you know that...that I love you."

MR BINGLEY PACED THE LENGTH OF HIS LIBRARY AT Netherfield, his features awash with worry and his amber hair disordered by the many times he pulled his fingers through it. He agonized for Darcy and worried for his friend's reaction when he read the letter he had sent express post.

Sitting abruptly in the nearest chair, Bingley allowed his head to fall into his hands. He knew what it was to long for, desire, and love a lady he could not have. He knew what it was to anguish over her. He had only recently regained some hope for his own future with Miss Bennett. And now he was the one to break the news to his best friend —news that revealed, quite possibly, that Darcy might never see Elizabeth again in this life. Bingley had learned when he called upon Longbourn of the unfortunate accident that had left Miss Elizabeth unconscious for almost a se'nnight. Though her family were optimistic, he had questioned his housekeeper and learned the general belief in the neighbourhood was that it was just a matter of time.

❧ 14 ❧

"Dearest, loveliest Elizabeth," Darcy breathed, amazed at what he had just heard her say. His eyes roamed her features again to look for confirmation there of the declaration. It felt as if he were dreaming to hear such words.

"When?" he asked in a state of happy incredulousness.

Blushing, she said, "I cannot fix on the hour, or the spot, or the look, or the words, which laid the foundation, though not too long ago. I was in the middle before I knew that I had begun."

"Can it be true?" Darcy brushed the back of his hand down her cheek, trying to imagine the softness he could not feel but knew existed.

"It is true, whatever that letter says."

Both looked down at the letter in his hands, fearful once again of its power over their futures. Darcy slowly lifted it again and, with a silent agreement from Elizabeth, opened it.

After watching Darcy read for many minutes, and seeing his brows pulled together in what looked to Elizabeth to be confusion, she spoke. "What has Mr Bingley to say?"

Darcy shook his head in a jerking motion, frustration affecting his voice as he groaned. "Never in my life have I wished more that Bingley would learn to write properly. He leaves out half his words and blots the rest! And now when I must know what he writes, I cannot make out anything."

The strain of the moment caused Elizabeth to laugh eerily as she reached a hand out for the letter. "Allow me if you please."

As Elizabeth touched the edge of the parchment, thus releasing its contents to her awareness, the essential communication of the letter also became clear to Darcy. Both stilled as the intelligence dawned on them and flooded their thoughts. Meeting each other's eyes, they held perfectly still for some time in contemplation of the letter.

"You really are Elizabeth—"

"I am not dead—"

Speaking at once together, they both looked at the news of Elizabeth's accident in different manners. Darcy was relieved to know that his Elizabeth, though lying insensible in a coma, had not died in a carriage accident. Still his concern was great to learn of her accident and injury. If strictly examined, he would have to say relief was most prominent, considering how he had agonized that she had died when first hearing her memories.

However calmed he was by *that* news, he could not be insensible to the undeniable proof that this visage, this wonderment before him that he had thought was only a figment of his imagination was in truth Miss Elizabeth Bennet, the lady to whom he had lost his heart and mind. Until even then, despite her returned memory in the study, he had held some belief of there being another explanation that allowed her not to be the real Elizabeth, thus making it permissible for him to justify any manner of impropriety in his actions. The implications of her actual presence with him over the past few days hit Darcy with a force strong enough to make him look about the room for a place to sit.

His thoughts raced through recent events: the words he had said, the indelicate conversations spoken, and the behaviours shown. The impropriety of it all wrapped Darcy in a gulf of mortification. Though he could not regret the emotions or words he had expressed to Elizabeth, knowing that she was not simply a product of his imagination made those declarations unseemly under this new insight. His eyes grew wide as he contemplated that even now he occupied his bedchambers with the real Elizabeth Bennet. Groaning, Darcy covered his face. *Why am I forever making a fool of myself around this woman?*

Elizabeth was too elated with the intelligence the letter offered her to pay any heed to the alarm spreading across Darcy's features. For her part, she was thrilled to know that everything she had felt had been real. She was correct in her convictions that she had not died and instead was only unconscious. Troubling as that fact was, she was utterly delighted with the knowledge that there was still hope for her—hope for them.

"William! Is this not wonderful news? I am alive, and Fate has somehow brought my spirit here while my body heals."

Darcy did not react at first, his feelings too close to the surface to speak. Her use of his Christian name now filled him with guilt, knowing that, if he had just listened to her when she told him she was real, he might not feel this burden of knowing he had acted with such indecorum. It also confirmed she had not yet realised the implication of their situation. At least in that he could be grateful because he thought, once she considered their time together over the past couple of days—*gah, the fencing!*—she would scorn his ungentlemanlike behaviour. Remembering his roguish words and looks caused Darcy to groan again as he fell back in the chair and stared at the ceiling.

Elizabeth paced the room with jubilant energy. Unlike Darcy, her thoughts were on the future, rushing to make a plan for getting her spirit back to Hertfordshire where she was sure she could somehow reunite with her body. She did not know the method, but she was certain that together they could discover how it was to be done.

"Of course, we must somehow get you close enough to where my body is for me to..." Her jumbled words faded away as another thought took its place. "That will be tricky, especially if they have me in my chambers." She laughed with glee as the hope and excitement of resolving their current state of being surged through her. "I wonder if we might slip away at some point, perhaps when you take tea with the family..."

Darcy slowly became aware of Elizabeth's mumbling. He sat, watching the fire in her eyes light up her face, adding radiance to the rest of her smile. It caused him to yearn for her in a way that made his self-castigation begin anew.

"Miss Bennet." Elizabeth stopped and turned her bright eyes towards him, a bemused expression on her face for his formal address. The whole of her beauty caused him to swallow loudly. Suddenly, the knowledge of her being the actual Miss Elizabeth Bennet in the flesh—well not exactly, but metaphorically—seemed to catch Darcy's tongue. He was amazed and startled to find his previous ease in speaking with her had left him. A touch of reserve consumed him as it had in Hertfordshire, and the words he had intended to speak were gone.

"Yes, William?" Elizabeth prompted.

Darcy cleared his throat, stood, and straightened his waistcoat. Suddenly, he was wishing for his tailcoat as his state of dress struck him as highly improper. "I think I ought to retire for the evening. May I show you to your room?"

"Oh, of course. If we are to make an early start, you must rest," she said compliantly, turning towards her chamber door but spinning once again to face him as another thought crossed her mind. "You called me 'Miss Bennet'?"

Darcy halted only when he reached the door separating the two chambers. He closed his eyes, his hand resting on the doorknob, and drew in a deep breath before answering. "Indeed, madam. With our most recent discovery, I thought it only proper."

Elizabeth, much to Darcy's concern, did not move through the threshold to her own chambers. Instead, she crossed her arms about her body and frowned at him, holding her ground.

"You thought it proper, did you?" She huffed, trying not to feel offended or hurt by his formality in address.

She had grown accustomed to informality and could not like the reversal. Her hope for their future tilted slightly with the evil idea that now weaved into her thoughts like a disease. Now that he knew she was the real Elizabeth, he might not care for her in the same manner or to the same degree as before. Perhaps his previous reservations would hold sway again with him. His immediate actions now sickened her with the dread of that possibility.

"Eliz... Miss Bennet. It has been a trying day for both of us, and I fear that the knowledge of my actions towards you this week has... well, I am ashamed to think of them."

"I see," Elizabeth spat. Anger was easier to hold on to, helping her to keep her troubled feelings at bay.

Darcy could see that he had offended her and, though he did not wish to anger her, could think of no other way to explain his feelings.

Elizabeth now could not hide the hurt she felt and quickly walked towards the door he held for her. Her voice remained steady, for which she was grateful, as she said, "Then I suppose it is fortunate that tomorrow you shall be rid of me directly we reach Hertfordshire."

Darcy startled at her words, confused by the vehemence with which she delivered them and troubled at the idea that he might *"be rid of"* her. His heart softened, and before he could check himself, he spoke mellifluously to her retreating back.

"It is not my wish to be rid of you."

Elizabeth paused, her back to him. Swallowing the emotion she felt choking her and blinking at the tears she felt burning her eyes, she whispered, "Then why do you speak as if you do, Mr Darcy?"

Darcy was physically affected by *her* return to formally addressing him. He stood straighter, his head jutting back and his eyes blinking. It made him realise how much he disliked the sound of his name—his formal name—coming from her lips, especially after knowing the sweet pleasure it was to have her call him "William." Dislike it as much as he did, that did not change that it was correct. He would just have to accept that. At least her back remained to him, making it easier for him to find the words.

"It is difficult, Miss Elizabeth, for me to assimilate the knowledge of your actual presence here with the memory of my actions towards you this week. Had I behaved in a more gentlemanlike manner..." He allowed his voice to fade, hoping she understood now how heartily he wished he had acted with more decorum.

Elizabeth turned slowly towards him, her eyes stormy. "Do you regret spending this time together?"

"Not in the least, only the manner in which I acted towards you. I acted in ways, said things..."

Elizabeth steeled herself, unconsciously wrapping her arms

around herself as a protection, before speaking. "You are too generous to trifle with me. If your feelings are no longer what they were earlier this evening, tell me so at once. My affections and wishes are unchanged, but one word from you will silence me on this subject forever."

Darcy's eyes bulged with the realisation of what she was saying and feeling. Stepping closer to her, he immediately uttered, "I still love you if that is what you are asking. That has not changed."

"Then why are you so altered?"

Darcy sighed. "Miss Elizabeth, I had thought that you were part of my imagination. I did not withhold words I ought to have when there was no understanding between us. I have spoken of your beauty, of your charm, in an unguarded and improper manner. You are as yet standing in my bedchamber while I am not formally attired. All of these things are not proper, and it is my duty as a gentleman to do you the honour of behaving better than I have—than this."

Elizabeth now understood his distress, though not agreeing entirely with his stubborn resolve to change that behaviour. They had decided that theirs was a unique circumstance and thus required a unique distinction of what was considered proper. She was irritated with him and thus allowed him to see it as she stepped closer to him, following him again when he automatically stepped backwards to maintain a proper distance.

"You listen here, *Mr Darcy*, I do not see the past few days as you do. *Had* you behaved in a more gentlemanlike manner, *I* may not have seen the gentleman you are and might not have come to love you."

The force of her words melted some of Darcy's reserve, warming his heart again the way it had the first time he had heard her share her feelings for him. Still, the discovery of her true being was fresh in his mind and his indelicate behaviours ripe in his memory. It was a strange juxtaposition because it was his love and respect for her that caused him to wish to honour her by behaving more the gentleman now that he discerned she was real.

Elizabeth felt relief as she witnessed Darcy's face soften before her. He looked at her now in the way to which she had grown accustomed over the past few days. She watched as he lifted his hands to run them through his hair, drawing her eyes to the shape of his strong arms and shoulders. How she longed to care for this man in a way she was incapable of now.

"Miss Bennet." He shrugged at her raised brow upon hearing his continued use of her formal name. "Let me be clear. I have cherished every moment of these days with you, and other than being rather embarrassed to have been so candid with you at times—a man must have some pride—I am pleased to have had you here."

"I assure you that I understand your reasoning for acting so stupidly just now—"

"Stupidly?"

"Yes, sir. Stupidly. We have declared ourselves in front of your relations and been found in a compromising position, sir! Are we not beyond certain rules of propriety?"

Darcy smirked at her words. "You know as well as I do, Miss Bennet, that Colonel Fitzwilliam could neither see nor hear you."

Elizabeth returned his smirk. "Nevertheless, you seem to feel the need to act in a manner more suited to society's demands of a gentleman towards a lady, despite the fact that society cannot, at present, see me either. I, however, being the only one who can witness your impropriety, do not protest it. Thus, sir, pray tell me you are not acting stupidly."

Darcy chuckled softly, more in love with her wit and humour than ever before. He bowed to show his acquiescence. "You are, as ever, right, madam."

Elizabeth turned to walk towards her room, and shaking her hand, pointed a finger at him over her shoulder. "Nay, sir. Right *and* beautiful."

"Indeed, very much so."

Darcy smiled broadly, pleased to see that, despite the past few days, he still had the ability to make her blush, and he was surprised to find that he also had the desire.

"Get some rest, Mr Darcy." Elizabeth said his name cheekily. "We are for Hertfordshire in the morning."

Darcy watched as she slipped through the threshold. He stepped forward and closed the door, lifting a hand to rest upon its surface. He turned around and leaned against the door, surveying his room, his eyes resting on the new location of his bed. He knew that it was proper and only right that he should adjust his behaviour towards her now that they both knew the true state of their situation; however, he could not ignore her words. *As a gentleman,* he reasoned, *I need to respect the lady's wishes.*

Darcy grinned at the thought. Elizabeth certainly did not wish for him to act so properly around her, and frankly, he did not relish the distance such behaviour necessitated between them, both physically and emotionally. He decided he could give up the liberty of calling her by her Christian name as a compromise towards propriety. Confirming his resolve, Darcy nodded to himself. Before retiring for the evening, he summoned his valet to instruct him to prepare his trunks for departure the next day. He had thought of censuring the man for disregarding his privacy earlier with Richard, but knowing his cousin's talents at interrogation, the manservant may not have had much of a choice.

Elizabeth sat forward on her side of the carriage and eagerly looked out the window for the first recognisable signs of her beloved home county. Her excitement bubbled out to her companion who laughed frequently at her childlike glee.

"I am glad to see that you have come to your senses this morning, William. You are much more attractive when you smile and laugh than when you are so very serious."

Darcy lifted a single brow at her words. His amusement, though, could not be hid. "I am glad to hear it, Miss Bennet."

"Tsk-tsk." Elizabeth laughed. "You still insist on referring to me formally, I see. I might remind you, *sir,* that you are the one who first suggested that I call you by your given name."

"Even still, *you* might allow me this one concession to what is proper," he challenged.

Elizabeth smiled wickedly at him.

Darcy's low chuckle sent a thrill along her spine. She attempted to look serious, but she could not keep a smile from pulling at the edges of her lips.

"I should think that you would know by now that I have ways of punishing you."

Darcy crossed his arms, amused at her play of strength. "I am not afraid of you."

Seeing that he clearly did not believe her, she raised one hand and daintily waved a little goodbye to him as she allowed herself to acknowledge the softness of the red velvet carriage seat and the strength of the springs beneath and came to rest against the sturdy wood at the bottom—effectively disappearing from his view as she sunk into the structure of the carriage seat.

"Touché." Darcy laughed. "You fight valiantly, Miss Bennet, if a little devilishly."

The disembodied voice of Elizabeth came to his ears through the empty cushion before him. "Thank you, *Mr Darcy*."

The gentleman shook his head and looked out the window, amazed at her ability to pluck at him in ways no other lady had before. She could intrigue and delight him in one moment and vex him like no other in the next. Even now, he found her intellect admirable and her humour alluring even while he felt like grinding his teeth at her stubbornness.

After another minute, delaying just enough to make her worry, he leaned forward and tenderly called her name. "Elizabeth."

His smile grew, displaying the dimples, while he watched, enchanted as she emerged gracefully through the cushion with a slight pinkness to her cheeks. At first, she would not meet his eyes, and her modesty charmed him further.

Darcy shifted and changed seats so that he was positioned next to her. He looked down and, with a grin about his lips, leaned in to speak near her ear. "So what is your plan, Elizabeth? How are we to get you back together with your body?"

Elizabeth snickered. "What makes you think I have a plan, William?"

Darcy leaned back in the seat and, crossing his ankles on the seat opposite in a casual manner, laughed as he said, "Come now, my dear. The Elizabeth I know would have worked something out. Tell me; what role am I to have?"

Elizabeth then looked up at him and, with a smile, acknowledged that she indeed did have some ideas. Most of the rest of the carriage ride was spent in huddled conference, carefully considering and discussing their options. Elizabeth assumed her corporeal self was in her own room. This necessitated some strategising, for Darcy would have to get within ten paces of the bed.

"It might not be necessary after all, Elizabeth."

"Of course it is. You know that I am unable to venture far from you."

"But have you considered that perhaps coming home to Longbourn might release you from this bond we have?" This had only occurred to him while they discussed their scheme. He was not surprised to find he did not like the chance of that at all.

Elizabeth shrugged, unconcerned. "I doubt very much that Longbourn will have much effect on the bond at all."

Darcy frowned, intrigued at her confidence. "How can you be so sure?"

"Because Fate has destined us to be together."

Her words were so casually said and with such a frankness that they at once set Darcy's heart speeding and pounding out of his chest. "I would have to agree. Though would you care to share with me how you came to such a conclusion?"

Elizabeth could no longer feign nonchalance, and a blush began to spread from her neck to her hairline. She smoothed her dress with one hand and quietly spoke. "It is just a theory, mind you, but there are several instances that point to that conclusion."

Darcy could hardly breathe for listening to her words. "Go on."

"Well first, before the accident happened, I recall informing Jane that it was my New Year's wish to see you want something you could not have. I have seen something of that in your eyes when you attempt to touch me but cannot." She paused; her cheeks flamed further. Though she did not look up to see, his coloured as well. Shakily, she began again. "And when the accident occurred, whatever force that caused me to separate from my body placed this part of me —where else?—in *your* library, tethered by some magical force to you alone. Adding to this, you alone can see or hear me..."

"Fascinating conclusion," Darcy said simply. His feelings were warmed to the point that he could say little else. A man who felt less might have said more. For so long he had cared for her, admired her from afar, and despite foolishly trying to fight his feelings, she had come to him and forced him to acknowledge them. He did not deserve such good fortune.

As if she could read his mind, she said, "And my memory of the accident, thus my way of knowing how to get back to my true state, came only after I had acknowledged to myself that I loved you and was triggered distinctly by your declaration of love for me."

"You regained your memory just after I told you I loved you," Darcy repeated, spellbound.

Elizabeth nodded. "I believe I was in the middle before I knew it had begun, though I felt it coming on all the while you told Colonel Fitzwilliam of your feelings for me. I have thought of this since, and the only conclusion that makes sense to me is that Fate has intervened to bring us together."

Darcy was silent for a while, contemplating her words. He knew but would not say that, if she had not come to his library that evening, he might never have sought her out again. He probably would have continued to attempt to forget her. Whether or not he would have been successful would never be known. Perhaps they might have met again somewhere, and if that were to have happened, Darcy acknowledged that he would have been just as vulnerable to her as he had been upon discovering her in his library. He thought about her confession regarding her New Year's Eve wish, and he was grateful to have been given the chance to change her opinion of him. That wish was proof enough that she thought meanly of him before. He marvelled at her now, sitting beside him and talking of love and Fate. Darcy knew he owed a great deal to whatever force was responsible—God, Fate, magic—for bringing them together.

Thinking of her wish reminded him of his own New Year's wish. He had wished to see her again, and that also had been granted.

His reply came almost too quietly for her to catch. "And I made a wish to see you again."

After a full minute contemplating her astounding conclusion, he turned to her and, with marvel in his voice, said, "I believe you have the right of it, Elizabeth. How have I been so fortunate as to have secured your favour? I believe that, between the two of us, you have gotten the sham deal."

Elizabeth shook her head with good humour. "I do not quite know about that."

"How shall I make it up to you then, my dear?"

"Help me get by body back, and we can discuss it."

"Gladly!" Darcy said as he bent his head towards hers to discuss their plans until the carriage wheels rolled to a stop in front of Netherfield Park.

❧ 15 ❧

Jane gingerly knocked on her father's door as she opened it slowly. Peeking in, she found him at his chair by the fire. He smiled at her and lowered his book, taking off his glasses in the same practiced movement.

"Dear Jane, have you come to visit with your old father?"

"May I have a few minutes of your time, sir?"

Mr Bennet smiled kindly at his eldest daughter and, in a gesture of exaggerated welcome, encouraged her to come in. It never failed to amuse him that she always asked whether he had a moment to spare for her. He had never denied her, yet she always asked. It warmed his heart that Jane was such a gentle soul, never assuming and quietly content in her life. She was so different from his second daughter, and their differences were contributing elements to that love that, as a father of two such lovely ladies, he possessed in abundance. The comparison to his Lizzy brought a cloudiness to his eyes as he thought about her lying in her chamber. Though he felt confident she would recover, the protracted time was beginning to disquiet even him.

Jane walked gracefully into the room and took up the seat opposite him. He watched her fingers worry an errant thread on the shawl that was draped about her shoulders. After several minutes, it was apparent Jane wished to speak, but perhaps not knowing how to proceed, he ventured to put her at ease.

"Come now, dear girl. Tell your father what it is that troubles you so." He bent his neck a little to catch her down-turned head and encouraged her with a kind smile. "You may speak freely with me as you always have."

Jane returned her father's smile, her blue eyes pure and clear. "That is true, Papa; however, I do not believe we have as of yet had any discourses on the topic heavy on my heart today."

Mr Bennet sat back, surprised by her words yet concerned by her confession regarding the topic. He had his suspicions, and it was one he knew would be difficult for any father.

"Your heart is troubled, Poppet, is it not? Well, that is a serious matter, to be sure—one that requires fortifying."

Mr Bennet stood then and went to a chest near his desk, took out a key and, opening the wood panelled door, pulled out a lovely square tin. He turned around and gazed at his daughter; with a twinkle in his eyes, he put a finger to his lips to warn her to keep quiet.

"Should your mother gain knowledge of this little tin, there will be the end of it, no doubt." He placed the tin on his daughter's lap and laughed quietly at her puzzled expression. "Go on; open it, child, but save a few morsels for me. Matters of the heart, especially those of my daughters, affect this old man as well."

Jane smiled with humour at her father and bent to lift the lid of the tin. Inside she found an array of the most delicious-looking chocolates. Her smile broadened as she looked up in amusement at his merry eyes. "Indeed, Mama must not find out about these."

She selected one for herself and handed the tin to her father who also took one. For a minute, they savoured the sweet melting delights in silence. Jane was warmed by his kind gesture—his attempt at reducing her anxiety having some success, for she felt fortified enough to begin.

With a nervous laugh, she said, "I would normally speak of these things with Lizzy; however..." She met the eyes of her father, acknowledging their mirrored sadness before she continued. "Perhaps, though, you might advise me. You see—I know not what to think or feel about Mr Bingley's return."

Jane blushed pink, and her father rubbed his jaw.

"Ah, indeed, a matter best discussed with your dear sister, but alas I shall not let you down." Mr Bennet's attempt to appear unaffected by the topic was nearly successful, and that which his daughter detected only endeared him to her further.

"It is most puzzling, for I know not how, in what manner, I shall act around him. He has called now twice, and each time he has been most attentive, yet I fear at any minute that his attentions along with his presence in the neighbourhood might again end as abruptly as they did a few months ago."

Mr Bennet's jaw clenched, a surge of protective feelings wrapping their fingers around his heart. "Perhaps I ought to speak to the gentleman."

"No!" Jane spoke with energy, then collecting herself quickly, returned to her usual gentle tone. "That is, I thank you; however, I would not wish for you to do that, sir."

"And why is that, Poppet? I assure you that, after one brief interview with me, we shall know the gentleman's intentions on returning to the neighbourhood."

"Papa," Jane cajoled her father, noting the softening of his features as she addressed him. "When I sought your counsel, I wished for the ease of a friend, not the protection of a father."

It was difficult, but Mr Bennet acknowledged her words and attempted to restrain his impulses. He next listened to her speak of her warm affection—nay, love—for the gentleman. Her revelation was not a surprise though it did add to his burden of trying to keep his fatherly instincts at bay. Possibly sensing Mr Bennet's tenuous hold on his natural reactions, she only shared briefly the feelings she felt upon Bingley's previously leaving the neighbourhood.

"I fear that I have not ceased to love him at all during this separation. And while I am sure that the business that called him away before must have been important, I do not know whether I have it in me this time to see him leave again."

"Has he indicated to you that he has plans to quit the neighbourhood again?"

"On the contrary, he has made it very clear on several occasions that he means to stay for some duration of time."

Mr Bennet was silent for a minute, contemplating his daughter's words. He took up another chocolate, using it as an excuse to stay quiet as he sorted out in his mind that which he wished to impart to her. Although he understood her wish for him not to interfere with the gentleman, sensing that it would embarrass her, he also knew that the uncertainty was what was most distressing to her. Considering the delicate topic, normally applied to with ease to Lizzy, Mr Bennet wondered whether that daughter's plight might also be holding Jane back.

"Tell me this, dear one. Let us just say that Mr Bingley comes to call on you again on the morrow." Jane blushed at the thought, pleasure easily read on her features and also confirming to her father a fair bit more of the state of the matter. "And while he calls upon you, he happens to request your hand." Here he paused only briefly noting the silent gasp and brightened cheeks of his daughter. "What shall you say to the gentleman?"

Jane looked up through her lashes, a tender smile about her lips. "I should very much like to say, 'Yes.'"

He smiled too but, noting a hesitation in her words, questioned her. "However...?"

The lady noted his keen observation with a nod of her head. "However, I would not wish to be so happy when Lizzy is yet so... when her health is yet in such an uncertain state."

Mr Bennet nodded, that worried grief filling him again. He leaned back in his chair and lifted his eyes to the ceiling as he thought. "I wonder, however, whether Lizzy would feel the same way."

"I beg your pardon."

Mr Bennet then leaned forward and, securing his daughter's hand in his, looked thoughtfully at it. "We both know Lizzy would wish for you to be happy, and although I do not like to acknowledge it, there may be the chance that our dear Lizzy does not return to us."

His voice broke towards the end, and Jane's eyes filled with tears for her sister.

Mr Bennet cleared his throat after a moment and, determining to counsel Jane in such a way that Lizzy would approve—despite his own instinctual wish to lock all his daughters up in towers away from any gentlemen callers—thus continued, "I would advise you, Jane, to be resolved to act in that manner, which will, in your own opinion, constitute your happiness without reference to Lizzy or to any other person."

Before she could voice her protest, disregarding herself in her usual manner, he concluded resolutely, "And with one last note, I shall end my speech so that we might enjoy a few more of these chocolates before we are discovered. Your description of Mr Bingley's visits thus far has made me believe that you are in very great danger of making him as much in love with you as ever."

DARCY TURNED TO AWAIT ELIZABETH'S DESCENT FROM THE carriage before moving up the stairs to the Netherfield entrance. Glancing at his unseen companion, he noted her heightened colour and excited eyes, and his admiration grew still further in that instant. His private reverie was interrupted when he heard his friend's voice. Darcy looked up to see Bingley bound down the stairs to meet him.

"Welcome, Darcy. I am glad to see you have come."

"I believe it would have been impossible not to, Charles," Darcy said pleasantly as he again glanced towards Elizabeth at his side. She smiled brightly at him, and he watched enchanted as she bounced slightly on her toes in excitement.

Darcy returned his eyes to his friend, a smile still about his lips from watching Elizabeth. Bingley frowned at him and looked puzzled, but Darcy's spirits were too high to wonder.

"Shall we go in, or am I to expect to make up a camp outside. It is my cousin who is the soldier, Bingley, not I," Darcy said with a chuckle and a friendly pat on his friend's back. Darcy resumed his ascent up the stairs when Bingley numbly raised a hand to indicate he should continue. His friend's brows creased deeper.

The gentlemen—and lady—continued up the stairs until they were welcomed into the broad entrance hall. Elizabeth, like her travelling companion, was in high spirits as she considered how close she was to being whole again and, having had a pleasant journey, was now even refreshed enough to wish to move forward with their plan. Darcy, too, was jovial after enjoying his time with Elizabeth in the carriage. Her excitement and careful planning created in him a hope of their success that would soon make it possible for him to enjoy such pleasures as lifting her hand to his lips or touching the softness of her hair. The possibilities were numerous and endless in their ability to tempt or torment him.

Elizabeth looked about her and sighed happily. *"It is such a pleasure to be home—or nearly so."*

"Indeed, it is good to be here." There was only the slightest pause as Darcy remembered Bingley nearby—especially when his lady gestured towards the bewildered gentleman standing next to him. "Bingley. It is good to be here," he added lamely.

A quiet chuckle from the direction of the lady had a smile again pulling at Darcy's lips for his near error.

"Darcy...might I ask you to join me in the library?" Mr Bingley's voice was accented with wariness not typical to his usually carefree tone.

"I suppose we cannot take our leave for Longbourn immediately upon reaching his threshold, can we, William?" Elizabeth said with amusement. *"We ought to be gracious to our host."*

Darcy's lips twitched and, although he had something else in mind to voice, kept himself to only answer the gentleman in the conversation.

"Of course, Bingley, I am at your disposal."

Bingley nodded slowly and turned to lead them down the hall to his library. Upon entering, he poured Darcy a glass of wine and handed it to him. He watched with growing concern as Darcy raised it with a gesture of thanks before smiling broadly and taking a drink. He could not think why his friend was in such high spirits when the lady he loved was in a precarious state not three miles away.

"Darcy, my friend, did you perhaps receive my express?"

"I did just last evening. I thank you for being so prompt in writing it. It is, of course, the reason we are here so precipitously."

"We?" Bingley questioned.

"Oh, William, dear. You must endeavour to be more careful. They will send you to Bedlam before we can even put this whole mess to rights," Elizabeth teased.

Darcy cleared his throat and, with a casual scratch to the back of his neck, answered his friend, "That is, my servants and I."

Much to Darcy's relief, Bingley seemed satisfied with this clarification though his eyes remained concerned. Darcy, for the most part, remained oblivious to his friend's state of confusion.

After a minute, Bingley could take no more and blurted, "And are you not the least bit concerned, Darcy?"

Darcy started at his friend's vehement address. It occurred to him then that Bingley referred to Elizabeth's physical state. Having had the knowledge that her spiritual state was in no danger, and after planning with Elizabeth during their carriage ride from London, he was almost entirely successful at pushing the morose thought of Elizabeth's physical state from his mind. So certain he was that they would be able to bring Elizabeth to rights whole, he had lost all natural worry. He could see, though, that his friend was concerned, and knowing that Bingley could not know that Elizabeth in essence was well, or would be soon, he decided to temper his hopeful spirits.

Letting the smile drop from his face, Darcy said seriously, "Indeed, I am Bingley. You must excuse me for my indelicate behaviour. I am merely hopeful for a...a speedy resolution. It is this hope that has prompted my behaviour."

"How can you do it, sir?"

"What do you mean?"

"Even now, the lady you love is lying lifeless and has been in such a state for nigh unto a week—for six days to be exact! How can you hold to such high spirits?"

The mood in the room shifted then at the blunt words uttered by Bingley. Darcy looked over at Elizabeth, who also was feeling the weight of their situation again. Each wondered briefly whether they would know how the reunion was to be accomplished.

"Well, I would not have guessed it, but it seems Mr Bingley knows how to effectively sour the mood in a room," Elizabeth said in an attempt to laugh her way out of her suddenly gloomy thoughts.

Darcy agreed with Elizabeth and, turning towards his friend, said, "And would you have me pacing the room, fearful of the worst and agonizing over it? Though I am not noted for having the most happy of characters, allow me this one comfort of holding to a belief that all will be well and hopefully soon."

Bingley apologised then most feelingly. "I had not considered it that way. Truly, please accept my apologies. I am certain that Miss Elizabeth will be well soon."

"Thank you, Bingley."

Elizabeth sighed and walked about the room, looking at the collection of books. She tried most heartily to drive concerns from her mind and in the attempt uttered, *"Do you remember, William, when we spent near thirty minutes alone in this room together when I came to nurse Jane?"*

He remembered all too well; it was a lesson in patience and a trial of torture to be close to her for any length of time. He remembered her perfumed toilet water and its sly ability to tease his senses. He remembered the tapping of her foot and the way she bit her lip gently, creating a soft pressure that drove him nearly insane.

"I remember," he responded, then added quickly for Bingley's benefit, "When we were all here before the holidays."

Bingley accepted Darcy's wish to change topics and, taking up his seat, nodded wistfully. "It was perhaps one of the most pleasant times of my life. We have not met together since we were all dancing together here at Netherfield."

Darcy noted that Bingley's use of the collective meant he was now including the Miss Bennets as he had met with his friend numerous times during the interim in London.

"You see, William! He remembers it fondly and most accurately I would say." Elizabeth beamed with happiness for her sister. *"I wonder whether he has seen Jane."*

"Have you seen Miss Bennet then, Bingley?"

"Of course I have. How else would I have known about Miss Elizabeth's accident?"

Darcy shrugged. "These things often become neighbourhood gossip."

"I have been to Longbourn."

"Oh, please do ask after Jane," Elizabeth pleaded, suddenly filled with the intense desire to hear anything of her family and to know how Bingley was received.

Darcy nodded almost imperceptibly at Elizabeth and, turning to his friend, asked, "And how did you find Miss Bennet?"

Bingley sighed and slouched back into his chair. "She is just as handsome as I remembered and more angelic still."

Elizabeth laughed with merriment and tapped her slippered feet with excitement. Darcy's eyes grew tender at seeing her so happy.

"I have called upon Longbourn twice and each time was graciously received despite my poor manners upon quitting the neighbourhood."

"My mother must have been thrilled."

"Mrs Bennet, of course, was quite thrilled to see me, quickly ushering me to Jane's side."

Elizabeth coloured in embarrassment for both her mother's behaviour and for the mortification that Jane would have felt. It was only the realisation that she and Mr Bingley had said nearly the same thing that brought a smile back to her face.

"But that was only the first day. The entire house is quite subdued due to the accident and Miss Elizabeth's state. Mrs Bennet was a tad altered, though in essentials just as I remembered her. What will you think of my vanity when I tell you that I believe my return did brighten things a bit?"

"What are your plans then?"

Elizabeth leaned in, eager to hear his answer. The gentleman questioned was silent for some time though. She looked at Darcy with concerned eyes, and he, sharing her sentiment, gazed at his friend. Eventually, Bingley did speak.

"If you had asked what it was that I wanted to do, then I could easily give you an answer. I am not insensitive, though, to the pain that Miss Bennet has suffered over the past week as she agonized over her sister's health. It is all so precarious. If you had asked what I wanted," he repeated, "I would have told you that I want to saddle my horse this very minute, ride to Longbourn, and declare myself to her—give her the comfort of knowing my intentions and ask her to marry me." Bingley sighed again and, turning pained eyes to his friend, said, "But you asked what my plans are. I suppose, until Miss Elizabeth's health is less undetermined, my plans are to call upon Jane most frequently. I plan to convince her by whatever means are available to me that I am not as inconstant as my previous behaviour might have taught her."

Darcy sympathised with his friend. Although his own state of happiness with Elizabeth was much more determined, her ghostlike state made it at least still tenable. Where they had the benefit of some kind of understanding, they had not the ability to do anything about it. And where her sister and Bingley had the benefit of each other's physical presence, they had not the understanding of heart that Darcy had with Elizabeth. It was a troubling state of opposites.

"I think you have a good plan," Darcy responded kindly.

LATER, UPON RETIRING TO THEIR QUARTERS, ELIZABETH TURNED to Darcy and said, "I had not considered the state my family must be in. All this time, I have not considered them in the least. I have thought only of my own strange experiences."

She looked up at him with eyes so disappointed in herself that Darcy immediately stepped closer to her and shook his head. "You ought not to trouble yourself over this, Elizabeth."

"But does it not speak clearly to my character that I was not in the least bit concerned for how they might be suffering, worrying for me?"

"I do not think so. And you are forgetting, my dear, that until just last evening you believed that you were only dreaming."

Elizabeth considered this truth, and it did much to ease her feelings of self-reproach. The remaining feelings were transformed into a greater determination to be successful at her reunion. She was fairly confident that she would be able to manage it. That the wish of giving happiness to her family might add force to the other inducements that led her on, she did not attempt to deny.

"Come now, my dear. Let us speak on happier topics. Tomorrow we shall go to Longbourn, and you shall see your family." Darcy smiled upon seeing that his words returned that sparkle to her eye he loved so well. "And should we have the good fortune of manoeuvring all parties to our liking, we shall also be able to accomplish our plan. Perhaps even tomorrow you shall be restored to yourself."

Darcy successfully hid his apprehension at this. It was confusing in a most peculiar manner. He wished fervently to have Elizabeth be whole so that he might request the honour of her hand—literally—yet he also knew he would miss this time with her.

Elizabeth nodded and, with a more heartfelt smile, responded, "That is one point that we need to amend, William. Though we had planned for you to slip away when you called at my home, I begin to think you cannot simply stand up to take your leave in the middle of tea."

Darcy chuckled at the image that thrust itself into his mind of standing unceremoniously and leaving while Mrs Bennet served tea. "No, I suppose not."

Together they were silent as they considered options.

"You could excuse yourself to the necessary room."

Darcy coloured. "Indeed, I think not, Elizabeth."

"And why not? It is a plausible excuse."

"And one I am not accustomed to using. I can see you are as yet forming your argument, and I am telling you, Elizabeth, that in no uncertain terms will I excuse myself to use the privy."

Elizabeth chuckled at his self-conscious manner then and his blushing countenance. She took pity on him and disregarded that idea even though she thought it was the easiest and had much merit.

"Perhaps, I could suggest a walk," Darcy ventured, eager to move the topic forward.

"That would only make us farther from my body. We need to be closer to the house."

Darcy warmed to the idea still. "Not necessarily. We could perhaps stay in the gardens, and slip away when no one is looking. Is there not a back door that we might utilise to gain entrance?"

Elizabeth's eyes lit with excitement. "Indeed, I had not thought of it. There is a side door used only by servants and rarely still. It is opposite the kitchens, and since most of the comings and goings are through that part of the house, the servants seldom trespass there. It would be perfect."

"And may we access it through the gardens?" Darcy was hopeful as this idea seemed infinitely more comfortable to him than Elizabeth's previous one.

"Indeed! It is exactly off them around a little bend. It will be perfect." Elizabeth began to pace as she reviewed their plans to accommodate this part of the strategy. "We shall venture out on a walk with Jane and Bingley, who will surely agree to such a scheme as walking in the gardens. When they are not looking—they will be too in love with each other to notice—"

"Stay focused, Elizabeth," Darcy said, chuckling at the blissful look that stole across her features when she mentioned her sister and his friend.

"Right, sir. We shall then slip away to the side entrance. It accesses a back staircase to the bedchambers as well, which will help us to avoid notice from anyone inside."

"Then it is settled. A walk in the gardens."

Darcy relaxed into a chair and contented himself with happily observing his Elizabeth. Her countenance was brilliant and the bloom in her cheeks intoxicating. He could not believe he was there with her, and the sparkle in her eyes only added to those other sentiments that made him eager to be successful in their endeavours. He watched as she walked around the room, gesturing, lost in her thoughts with the excitement of their hopes for the next day.

"If I could, I would kiss you this very minute, Elizabeth."

He watched, charmed, as her energetic movements halted abruptly and she turned wide-eyed to him. The bloom so beautifully displayed before on her cheeks intensified and spread across her entire face. Darcy stood slowly, walking with measured steps towards her.

Elizabeth was rooted in place, her heart hammering in her chest and her mind sapped of all thought as she watched him approach her. Her eyes blinked rapidly, her pupils dilated. Unconsciously, she lifted a hand to touch the tips of her fingers to her lip. He made a sound then, and her eyes lifted to his just as he stopped before her.

The feelings overwhelming her made her laugh shakily. "Indeed, and what makes you think, sir, that I would allow you that liberty?"

Darcy tilted his head and settled scorching eyes on her, his gaze travelling lazily down to her lips. "It is the very thought that you might that haunts me even now, Elizabeth."

JANE HUMMED TO HERSELF AS SHE GENTLY AND TENDERLY washed her sister's hair. It was a task she had only allowed herself to perform, and she lovingly performed it with care. With only the aid of Mrs Hill in positioning Elizabeth near the side of the bed, Jane poured the scented water over her long, chocolate curls. She then towelled them until they were mostly dry before she plaited the hair prettily to lie along the side of Elizabeth's head down her shoulder. This service helped Jane to feel as if she were still connected intimately to her sister who had been asleep for so long.

"Thank you, Hill. I do not think we shall need anything further tonight."

Jane waited to speak to her sister until the housekeeper patted Lizzy's shoulder with affection and then her own before exiting the room. "There now, Lizzy, you look quite lovely. The gentlemen will be knocking down your door to see you," Jane said sweetly to her sister.

The silence then in the room settled like a blanket over Jane. Accustomed as she was now to hearing no response from her sister, she still did not expect to feel so alone.

"I spoke with Papa today about a certain gentleman. It is your own fault that you did not get to be my confidante as you will not wake up," Jane teased lightly, hoping to dispel the heaviness. "Did you know that he keeps a secret stash of chocolates?"

Jane laughed quietly; it was late enough in the evening that she did not wish to disturb the rest of the household.

"Indeed, with such advantages, I may always take my worries to him in the future."

Jane lifted her hand to smooth a small curl at Lizzy's hairline. She then adjusted and smoothed her sister's arms along the freshly laundered nightgown she wore. It had tiny purple flowers embroidered on it, and it was actually one of Jane's that Elizabeth had admired.

Jane turned when Lizzy's bedroom door opened and Lydia entered.

"Good evening, Lydia."

Lydia waved distractedly at her sister and walked to the other side of the bed to take up the other chair. "I did not know that you were in here, Jane. It is quite late, and I usually…"

"Do you come to talk to her, Lydia?"

The young girl avoided her eldest sister's eyes as she leaned in towards Elizabeth. With obvious embarrassment, she replied with a nod. "At night, when the others have gone to bed. There are ever so many things to do during the day."

Jane smiled at her sister, pleased that she showed such care for Elizabeth. She knew that Lydia's words were more an attempt to diminish the significance of her visits and lessen her own embarrassment at showing such feeling.

"I just finished washing her hair this evening. I might have sought my bed at any moment." Jane stood then to give Lydia some privacy, but she was stopped when she spoke.

"No, stay! That is, I would be pleased to have your company, Jane."

The awkwardness of the moment was felt by both parties since Lydia had never ventured to wish for Jane's company in the past. She usually only sought the attention of her mother, sister Kitty, or the officers.

"I saw Mr Wickham in town today," Lydia said coolly.

Jane settled herself in the chair again and, although not wishing to have another conversation about any of the handsome militiamen, was content to do so for Lydia.

"He asked after Lizzy," Lydia said as she reached up to smooth the same errant curl that Jane had smoothed moments before. Her tender action brought a smile to Jane's lips even when Lydia become conscious of it and awkwardly withdrew her hand.

"Mr Wickham is an amiable gentleman. He and Lizzy danced at the assembly and, if I do not mistake myself, enjoyed the experience."

Lydia nodded, frowning slightly though. "But have you noticed that, since then, he has not called here once to see after her health?"

Jane had not noticed that lapse on Mr Wickham's part due to weightier thoughts—especially in regards to another gentleman.

"I am sure that he was simply being considerate to the uncertain state here at Longbourn," Jane said kindly. Jane allowed herself to be slightly disappointed in Lydia for her concern with the lack of attention from Mr Wickham when Lizzy was so ill.

"I suppose you could be correct, only... I think there is more to it.

Our aunt Philips told me only today when I had mentioned speaking with Mr Wickham in Meryton that he is soon to be engaged to Miss King."

Jane's brows rose at such news. "I had not thought they were acquainted."

Lydia's frown deepened. "I introduced him to her at the ball."

"That was rather quickly done on his part," Jane observed. She looked at her sleeping sister and, knowing that Elizabeth had preferred Mr Wickham, was sad for her. "I heard that Miss King has just inherited a small fortune. If you look at it in that light, it is a prudent match for him," Jane offered in her usual way, absolving any wrongdoing for either party.

"I suppose you are right again," Lydia said unconvincingly though her expression told Jane she was still confused. Jane watched, surprised, as fire lit her youngest sister's eyes. "Only, how could he have forgotten Lizzy so quickly?"

❧ 16 ❧

Darcy and Bingley mounted their horses the next morning for the ride to Longbourn. There was a nervous energy about both gentlemen but for different reasons.

In an attempt to dispel his own uneasy anticipation at seeing Miss Bennet again, Bingley offhandedly asked, "How was your cousin the colonel when you left London?"

Darcy surprised his companion by laughing briefly before answering. "A little worse for wear, last I had the pleasure of his company."

Bingley raised his brow. "Was Colonel Fitzwilliam not feeling well then?"

Darcy looked sideways at his friend. "If I recall correctly, when I spoke with him yesterday morning, he was suffering under the effects of a night of rather poor judgment with regards to the quantity of spirits he consumed."

Bingley laughed, shaking his head at the image that came to his mind but not thinking much more on the topic. Darcy glanced behind him to where Elizabeth floated along. They shared a conspiratorial smile before Darcy resumed his attention on the road ahead. Recalling that morning, Darcy remembered Richard's rather pained attempt at confronting him about his strange behaviour. Darcy easily convinced the colonel—as he was well in his cups—that he had not observed things accurately. He further stunned his cousin by telling him that he was for Hertfordshire that very morning. This bit of intelligence seemed to calm and satisfy his cousin. Darcy had no trouble believing Richard would come to find the paltry excuses for his behaviour insufficient once the throbbing in his head eased, but by that time, Darcy would be well on his way and out of immediate reach.

As they continued to ride, Bingley noticed that his companion frequently turned to look behind them. Turning himself a few times, Bingley noted the empty road. Finally, unable to ignore such behaviour despite the amiable conversation, Bingley addressed his friend. "Darcy, do you imagine we are being followed?"

Darcy sat up straighter, his brows lowering in concern, and turned in his seat to scour the landscape behind them. The look of amusement that had graced Elizabeth's face previously now also turned serious as she looked about her while she floated along behind the gentlemen. After viewing their surroundings carefully, he turned to his friend. With a lowered voice and serious tone, he said, "I do not think so. Do you suspect something?"

"I had not until I saw you. You keep turning in your seat to look behind us."

Elizabeth's hearty laugh then reached Darcy's ears from her position a few feet behind. *"I think he refers to your incessant need to check on me, William."*

Darcy attempted to master the smile pulling at his lips. He had argued with her that they should take his carriage so she might ride along that way. She was most vexing in her stubborn resolve, arguing that he would be unable to make his escape should he need to leave alone. *Obstinate, headstrong girl!* He had not liked the idea of her travelling along behind him but could not very well suggest they walk when Bingley would surely prefer to ride. His concern for her had become a source of amusement to Elizabeth. Even when she was whole, walking such a distance was accomplished easily and with the greatest enjoyment on her part. Travelling behind Darcy's horse, at a greater speed and without the need for exertion was nothing in comparison. Still he could not like riding when she could not; the gentleman in him rankled at the idea.

"Darcy?"

Bingley's entreaty brought Darcy back from his thoughts and away from the charming smirk of Elizabeth. He turned again in his seat to face the road ahead. "I believe we are quite safe, Bingley. I was only admiring the verdant landscape."

Darcy sped up upon hearing Elizabeth's laugh again and to avoid Bingley's puzzled expression.

"*Yes, indeed, the frozen, frost-washed grey earth that marks Hertfordshire in January is most glorious to behold,*" Elizabeth teased.

WHEN THE GENTLEMEN WERE ANNOUNCED AT LONGBOURN, ALL evidence of amusement had been long erased from Elizabeth's features. She was overwhelmed by the sight of her beloved home and savoured every window, hedge, and stone; each was as familiar to her as a dear friend and just as welcome a sight.

Upon entrance, her senses remained fixed for the first glimpse of her family. Each servant who helped with the gentlemen's outerwear was named with squeals of glee as she acknowledged everything precious around her. They were led to the morning room and presented to the ladies within.

Elizabeth could not speak upon first setting eyes upon her family. Assembled before her were all her sisters, excepting Jane. Her heart hammered in her chest and spoke of the great love she had for each of them. Having not seen them nor knowing whether she ever would again, the moment was all encompassing. Softly, she whispered each of their names reverently, lovingly.

Darcy tried to appear attentive to his host but was transfixed by the look he saw in Elizabeth's eyes. He remembered then that, while he was first falling for Elizabeth last autumn, he had debated that he might be able to marry her if he could guarantee he would not have to encounter her family afterwards. Now he was filled with shame for such a thought and also a profound pain that he ever contemplated keeping Elizabeth from those who could provoke such a look of longing and love. These were her family, and he had stupidly

*—proudly—*assumed that they could not mean as much to her as his own small family meant to him. The very thought of never seeing Georgiana again pained him, and he put it out of his mind immediately.

His hostess was now welcoming him, and Darcy again focused his attention.

He bowed to Mrs Bennet. "Indeed, I am happy to be here, ma'am."

"She does not mean it, you know. She does not really welcome you to Longbourn," Elizabeth said offhandedly, almost affectionately, with regards to her mother.

Darcy startled slightly and turned to look upon Elizabeth while Mrs Bennet gushed forth with warm greetings and praise for Mr Bingley.

Elizabeth smiled at him then and shrugged. *"You displeased her when you refused to dance with me and called me merely 'tolerable.' She has not forgiven you for such trespasses."*

Darcy opened his mouth to protest, astonished to learn the whole of the neighbourhood knew of his folly. Before he could speak, Elizabeth shushed him with a slender finger to her lips, reminding him he could not talk to her without looking like a fool. *A great fool, I am.*

Darcy took up a spot near the window where he might view the room but not have to speak to anyone. His thoughts were in a jumble with regards to evidence before him of the incredibly poor manners he displayed a few months earlier. Ironically, he did not recognise his current behaviour as similar.

He watched Elizabeth rush from one sister to the next, looking upon each and declaring differences. She insisted one had grown taller, another's face looked older and still another was endeared by the way she wore her hair differently. A week could not really bring about such profound changes, but he loved seeing her so happy to be amongst her family again.

A few minutes after they arrived, the door opened again, and Miss Bennet slipped gracefully in. Darcy looked at her and then at Elizabeth. Elizabeth stood motionless, her eyes watering and her hand hovering about her mouth as if to hold in a cry. His heart grew more tender for her then, witnessing the great love she had for this sister. He could only imagine what depth of affection could produce such a look and was hopeful that, someday soon, he might claim to see that sisterly affection towards Georgiana. He stepped forward out of his location to greet Miss Bennet and bowed before her.

"Miss Bennet, a pleasure to make your acquaintance again."

"Mr Darcy, it is a pleasure indeed. Welcome to the neighbourhood, sir."

"Dearest Jane!" Elizabeth cried as she came to stand next to her sister, her usual spot when visitors called. *"I wish I could embrace you and never let you go."*

Darcy smiled affectionately at Elizabeth, his amiable expression noted by her elder sister and interpreted as a kind gesture of friendship.

"I was sorry to hear about your accident, Miss Bennet, and the injury of your sister."

Jane's eyes glistened, and she smiled warmly. "I thank you, Mr Darcy. Elizabeth is recovering, and although she has yet to awaken, we are all confident that she will soon."

"I have every belief that you are correct and will pray to that end," he said with compassion.

Standing beside Jane, Elizabeth turned to him and smiled. He returned Elizabeth's smile, making Jane speculate on his true feelings for her sister. It was something she had wondered during the autumn months, and indeed Charlotte Collins *née* Lucas had first suggested it.

"Thank you, Mr Darcy," Jane said, allowing herself then to be guided to a seat by Mr Bingley.

Darcy then took up the window behind them, looking out at the view beyond. He knew not how to understand his own unsettled emotions, being at Longbourn and seeing Elizabeth in her element. Whenever he had called before, they had not spoken, and she had been more reserved in her addresses to him. Looking back to that time, he realised how little they recognised each other's honest emotions. She assumed he enumerated her faults when he looked only for the pleasure it brought him.

"I should like to see my father, but I suppose there is little chance of that," Elizabeth said sadly as she finally came to stand by his side.

At his questioning glance, she explained. *"He does not often venture out of his study when guests come to visit. And I suppose it would be odd for you to request an interview with him at this stage."*

Darcy smiled at her teasing tone, noting again her habit of turning to humour to dispel an uncomfortable situation. He wished he could find some way to allow her to see her father but could think of nothing reasonable other than restoring her to herself as soon as possible.

He whispered then to her as he feigned interest in the view out the window. "We shall soon see you whole, and then you may not only see your father, but you may embrace him as well."

Elizabeth's eyes glistened again, and she thanked him, feeling grateful for his understanding. When she had recovered well enough to feel composed, she added, *"I think, sir, it is time to implement the beginning of our daring mission."*

Darcy raised his brows at her dramatic phrasing and, yet humoured by her enthusiasm, nodded. He too was anxious to see the other part of her again. "Indeed."

Darcy turned then and looked about the room. He had not been very sociable nor was it in his nature to be so. Apprehension stole into him at addressing the party at large. He looked at Elizabeth and noted that she was eager for their next step. Gaining strength by her confidence in him, he cleared his throat and awkwardly won the attention of those in the room as a result.

"I was noting the beautiful winter sun is out, and I thought perhaps Mr Bingley and I might accompany any of the Miss Bennets who so desired on a walk about the gardens. What say you, Bingley?"

As Elizabeth and Darcy had suspected, Bingley eagerly and immediately seconded the idea, looking hopefully to Jane for consent.

Mrs Bennet spoke aloud then. "I thank you, Mr Darcy, for the suggestion, but I am sure it is much too cold out."

"She is determined to dislike you," Elizabeth chuckled. *"Quick, pay her a compliment."*

Uncertain, Darcy turned to look at Elizabeth. It was clear he did not relish imparting any such flattery on Mrs Bennet.

"Quick sir! Or our whole scheme will be for naught. Look, already Jane is wavering."

"Mrs Bennet, I promise that should we find the environs too harsh for the delicate beauty of your daughters, we shall immediately return them to the safety and shelter of the house."

Both Elizabeth and Darcy held their breath as they watched Mrs Bennet puzzle through the unexpected attentions from Mr Darcy. Before she could say anything, however, Mr Bingley parroted again his approbation for the plan.

"Indeed, Mrs Bennet, I will personally see to it that Ja—Miss Bennet comes to no harm."

"Oh, Mr Bingley, sir. You are too kind. Come, girls; go and get your things. The gentlemen will take you for some air."

Elizabeth looked with excitement towards Darcy when her other sisters protested that they did not wish to go out, leaving them with the unexpected advantage of having only Bingley and Miss Bennet to lose *accidently*.

While Miss Bennet went up the stairs for her winter cloak and muff, Darcy and Bingley waited in the entry.

"Bingley, I have just felt the beginnings of one of my megrims, I fear. I do not wish to disappoint Miss Bennet or yourself by bowing out just now, but I think if I do not get the better of it while we take in the air outside, I may see myself home. Could you give my regrets should that become the case?"

"Certainly, you should take care, Darcy, but what shall we do without a chaperone?"

"Stay within sight of the house, and you will be perfectly proper. Besides, I daresay Mrs Bennet will not give you much trouble."

Bingley laughed in agreement.

"Very tricky, William. For one who abhors deceit of any kind, you are remarkably good at it," Elizabeth said cheekily.

It was little trouble then for Darcy and Elizabeth to slip away from the other couple whilst in the gardens. Even without the ruse, the scheming pair noted that the attentions of Bingley and Miss Bennet were focused entirely on each other.

"Come this way, William. The door is just around here."

Elizabeth confidently and with a skip in her step showed him around a hedge to a narrow door in the side of the house. When they reached the door, Darcy attempted to gain entrance but found that it was locked. He turned to Elizabeth for direction.

"It is locked, Elizabeth. We shall have to think of another way in."

"No, there is a trick to it. Lift slightly when you turn the knob and push with your shoulder."

Darcy looked at her sceptically but nonetheless did as he was told. When the door was manoeuvred open, he turned to her with a frown. "That is a security risk, Elizabeth. Your father ought to know that this door can be accessed without a key."

Elizabeth laughed at his distraction, considering the greater importance of their present task. "After we finish here, sir, perhaps you might wish to tell him that. I can just see it now." Elizabeth lowered her voice to impersonate Darcy. "Mr Bennet, while I was attempting to break into your house, I noted that your side door was not secure."

Darcy could only half smile at her teasing comment and, while acknowledging she had the right of it, still made a mental note to advise Mr Bennet at some future time. He could not like the idea that someone might be able to break into Elizabeth's home.

Gingerly, Darcy returned his attention to the door before them and opened it carefully. He peeked around it and sighed in relief to find the small space was empty of any person. Elizabeth indicated he should take the staircase to their left, and he quietly moved up the steps.

"This is so very exciting and more than a little shocking!"

Darcy ducked, shying away from her enthusiastic volume. "Shh!"

Laughing, Elizabeth said, "Do I really need to remind you, sir, that you are the only one who can be heard?"

Darcy paused then, realising how ridiculous his concern was, and could not hold back a quiet snort. "As ever, Elizabeth, you are right and beautiful."

"Indeed," Elizabeth confirmed merrily. They continued up the stairs a few steps in silence. "I have never broken into my own home before nor done anything so nefarious."

"Nor have I," Darcy whispered.

"We are quite the pair, are we not?"

Darcy sent her a quelling look that did little to hide the amusement he felt at her high spirits. His own heart was beating rather wildly in his chest, and he reached to loosen his cravat. He anticipated at any moment that he might encounter a servant, and the very thought of it sent a thrilling fear coursing through his veins. His ears were alert to any sound, and he ventured perhaps more slowly than Elizabeth wanted.

"Come; at this pace we will surely need to spend the night."

"Perhaps you might make yourself useful, madam, and go ahead of me to watch for anyone," Darcy whispered as he pulled a handkerchief out of his pocket and dabbed at the moisture on his brow. Elizabeth laughed loudly, and Darcy winced before again reminding himself that no other could hear her. He groaned inwardly at the easy part she had in this whole, underhanded affair. *She* would not be seen if they were caught.

Elizabeth reached the top of the stairs and turned down a small corridor, waving behind her for Darcy to follow. He felt much more at ease now that she was ahead of him. At one point, a noise down the hall caused Darcy to have to step into a doorway to hide himself. It was a passing maid at the end of the hall, and he could not like the way this close encounter caused his heart to lodge in his throat. Finally, after making their way up another set of narrow stairs, they reached a rough-hewn wooden door.

Elizabeth turned to Darcy then with a slight pinkness to her cheeks. Looking behind him, Darcy's anxiety made him question silently why she had stopped.

"Beyond this door, sir, is my chamber."

"Ah," Darcy said, finally understanding her blush and admiring her modesty. "I suppose it is only fair then."

Darcy opened the door to the room, pushing away a set of drapes meant to hide the service door. Once clear of the curtain, his eyes immediately focused entirely on the figure lying motionless in the small bed before him. He was barely aware of Elizabeth's squeal of triumph. He walked slowly into the room, his eyes devouring the very real, yet still ethereal, beauty of the sleeping figure. He took in her lustrous hair, swept to the side in an attractive braid and lying across her shoulder. It was the first time he had seen it thus, and it positively took his breath away. Her cheeks were pink, and the petal-soft lids of her eyes had a lavender shade that made him long to brush his fingers gently across them. He was spellbound by their contrast with the dark lashes resting peacefully against her smooth cheek. He had no words and could not utter a thing if he had them, for he was perfectly captivated by her magnificence. He walked as if in a trance towards the bed. All other elements of the room held no power over his attention, and he was perfectly fixated, his vision tunnelling to her.

When he reached her side, he stood immobile. Her beauty was astounding, and his heart was reminding him of that fact quite forcefully. Reluctantly, he raised his eyes from Elizabeth's sleeping form to her spirit standing opposite the bed from him. Quietly he compared the two visions. He noted that the Elizabeth who had been his companion over the past seven days had softened features. Her unconscious body was sharp in contrast. He could not have seen the difference without having both forms before him, yet both were mesmerizing in their allure to him.

He opened his mouth to speak to her. "You..." Words failed him, and he lowered himself into the chair nearest him. His eyes glistened at the evidence before him of these two Elizabeths. Unabashedly did he admire them both as he adjusted to the surreal experience. It was as fantastic a wonder as ever he imagined; yet, if he had not seen it with his own eyes, he might never have believed it. The experiences of the past se'nnight opened his mind to possibilities he would not, but for them, have believed possible.

Elizabeth was surprisingly less affected than she thought she might be seeing her body thus. She looked over her sleeping form and was pleased to see she looked healed though perhaps a little slimmer. She had wondered whether she might be shocked or unsettled; instead, all she felt was an extreme feeling of rightness as she beheld her room and stood near herself. She was enthralled with being at home again amongst her most treasured possessions.

Though embarrassed slightly by Darcy's flagrant admiration, she was still able to be grateful that he was occupied because having him in her bedchamber was by far one of the most profoundly stirring moments of this experience. As she looked about her, she realised how well she loved her odd possessions and special mementos. She noted that someone had placed a bowl of her lavender potpourri at the table near the bed, and she bent to breathe in its calming fragrance.

Whilst Elizabeth was occupied, Darcy, as if in a daze, uttered reverently, "You are so very beautiful, Elizabeth."

She was just about to stammer her thanks for his gentle words when she felt her hand tingle. She looked down at it and could see no reason for the sensation. She looked to Darcy to share with him this strange occurrence, only to see that he had taken up her physical hand and was holding it and looking at it as if it were the most sacred thing in the world.

Darcy held Elizabeth's small hand in one of his as he smoothed the top of it with his other. He had never held a lady's ungloved hand before, and the feeling was exquisite. The love that he felt for her then was so profound that he wished to tell her. He looked at Elizabeth and saw that she was turning her hand around to study it from different angles. It was the same hand he was holding!

A cool shock rushed through him as she uttered the very thoughts that he was having. "I can feel that. I can feel you holding my hand!"

Elizabeth's moist eyes locked with his. His chest felt constricted, and he was renewed in his determination to reunite these two forms of Elizabeth. For her part, Elizabeth was grappling with the urge to sob stupidly at the relief coursing through her at the knowledge, nay the proof, that she was still connected in some way to her body. Though the power of that intelligence was great, it was still less compelling to her than the actual feeling of experiencing the touch of Darcy's hand. It was something she had longed for and as yet had not had the pleasure.

"Elizabeth, you must attempt... I think you should try to reunite yourselves."

Elizabeth nodded her head, smiling at the tenderness in his voice, matched only by its twin in her heart. "Indeed, it is time."

"How is it to be done?" Darcy asked, stopping her from coming closer; a sudden panic seized his heart, the unknown causing him to fear.

Elizabeth shrugged. "I have never attempted it before."

She laughed then, and Darcy's frown turned into a smile. He

stood and, gently placing her hand at her side, stepped back. Elizabeth looked at her hand and felt the absence of sensation again.

"Very well, sir. I think if I just..." She walked through the bed and laid herself down, disappearing into her motionless body.

Darcy watched with rapt attention. All he could see was the sleeping form of Elizabeth. "Are you there, Elizabeth?"

He heard her voice, though her lips did not move. "I am here. However, I do not feel quite myself."

Darcy frowned, pulled his hands through his hair and rubbed his jaw. He was afraid to accept that this attempt had been unsuccessful, yet he knew in his heart that it was true. "Move your hand, Elizabeth."

An arm floated up from the bodily form below it. Elizabeth sat up and looked towards Darcy. She could see that she sat in the middle of her bed, her spiritual form seated, while her physical body still lay immobile. Elizabeth's troubled eyes met his, and together they anguished at their failure.

"Is there not something else you might try?"

Elizabeth shook her head sadly. "I know not what else to do. I thought it would be as simple as putting myself together like this."

Darcy sat again near the bed and took up her hand. He turned her hand to face up and he placed a gentle kiss in her palm causing Elizabeth to gasp at the sensation. He could not voice how very much his own hope had been deterred, for he could tell that her disappointment was great. He longed to solve her problem, take her up in his arms, and protect her from any hurt.

"We will find a way. You feel me; you feel my touch. We will find a way."

Elizabeth smiled wanly at him. "Can I ask something of you?"

"Of course, my dear. I have not the power to deny you anything should you ask it."

"Would you place my hand on your face? I have longed to feel it beneath my fingertips."

Darcy swallowed, nodded slowly, and bent his head to allow her hand to reach him. He cupped her hand to his jaw on his cheek. Though Elizabeth did not have the power to direct her fingers, he felt the exquisite touch of her hand, imagining she held it there of her own accord.

Elizabeth marvelled at the texture, heat, and feel of his skin. She had longed for some human contact, and this was quite the most glorious feeling. Neither spoke for some minutes as Darcy leaned his head into her hand. They let the moment be preserved in heartbeats and gladly would have stayed that way forever were it not for the sound of footsteps that brought them back to reality and high alert.

Elizabeth spoke first, her voice showing some of her concern. "Someone is coming. There is a set of stairs behind there, and I could always hear when someone was gaining this floor."

"Then I must go and quickly then." Darcy stood and, momentarily disoriented, looked about him as if he had completely forgotten how he had arrived at the place he was in.

"There is no time for that now. You must hide under the bed until they are gone."

His eyes snapped to hers as he shook his head decidedly. "I will not hide under the bed, Elizabeth."

Elizabeth laughed then and came off the bed. Darcy looked at her and then at her sleeping form next to her. He shook his head again when he saw her point to the floor underneath the ropes.

"No, I am not accustomed to hiding under beds. I will not do it."

Laughing, Elizabeth rushed around to the other side of the bed and waved her hands. "I fear you have little choice, sir."

"I am Fitzwilliam Darcy of Pemberley, for God's sake! I do not hide under beds! Come, let us rush out the way we came."

They both froze as they heard footsteps walk down the hall towards Elizabeth's door.

"There is no time for that. *Fitzwilliam Darcy of Pemberley*, get yourself under that bed!"

Darcy groaned heavenward and, shifting from foot to foot, his panic rising, quickly clenched his jaw and knelt down to climb under the bed. His pride was bruised, and he saw little humour in the indignant behaviour forced upon him. Elizabeth giggled as she settled herself next to him beneath the bed.

He turned his head so he could see her and whispered in a frustrated manner, "You have little need for disguise, Elizabeth. Nobody can see you. *You* need not hide."

Elizabeth smiled brightly at him and turned on her side, wiggling excitedly next to him. "I am aware of that, sir, but this is more fun, is it not?"

Darcy was silent then as he took in the view of her beside him. It was an improper position, and it certainly would be quite compromising had Elizabeth been in her natural form. Instead, he was left gazing at the softened features of her ghostly self and longing for her, in truth, to be lying beside him. *I would take you in my arms and...* The sound of the door opening startled him, pulling him away from those dangerous thoughts as he lay paralysed in fear beneath the bed. The dread of discovery began to slink up and around him like smoke, choking him and causing him to hold his breath.

He turned his head silently away from Elizabeth, who had held her finger to her lips needlessly. He could just see below the curtain of the bed frame a pair of delicate pink slippers. The chair scraped against the floorboards, and a rustle of skirts around the slippers told Darcy that their guest had seated herself.

"Oh, Elizabeth, I hardly know where to start."

Darcy looked at Elizabeth again, and she silently mouthed, "Jane." The fear in his heart decreased slightly if only to make room for the profound love he felt for Elizabeth then as they lay there listening to her sister speak.

"Mr Bingley called again today, and with him came his friend Mr Darcy." She was quiet for a moment longer before adding, "I would speak to you about that gentleman, Elizabeth. He asked about you, and it would take a fool not to see that he holds you in high regard."

Elizabeth smiled warmly at Darcy, whose eyes conveyed then what he could not say.

"I know you might say he felt only disdain, but you will have to wake for me to listen to that argument. But enough of that, Elizabeth; I am delaying." Jane paused, her heart full of emotion. "Mr Bingley...I do believe he may yet care for me. Am I a fool for hoping so? He all but said it today when we walked in the gardens. We were left quite alone for some time. Mr Darcy was to accompany us but was a very poor chaperone. We were not long outside before I looked and could not see him anywhere."

Elizabeth laughed aloud at this, and Darcy was quick to entreat her to silence, forgetting once again that she was mute to all others.

The sound of sniffling effectively silenced Elizabeth as her face twisted in concern for her sister. She left Darcy to hide by himself. Darcy could see her ghostly slippered feet opposite the bed from her sister.

"Oh, Jane."

"Lizzy, you must come back to me. I need you, dear sister. My heart cannot be truly happy with Mr Bingley's return if I cannot share it with a most beloved sister."

"I am working on it, Jane. I promise you, I will return."

Elizabeth watched Jane stand and exit the room, her shoulders slumping inward as she pressed a handkerchief to her face. Darcy remained where he was long after the door latched again.

"You may come out now, William," Elizabeth said dejectedly.

Darcy slowly pulled his great form from under the dusty bed, sweeping his hands over his clothing in the process. The dishevelled and dirty state of his clothes caused Elizabeth to dry her tears, and once again, she was quietly laughing.

Darcy could not be vexed at her humour, even at his expense, for he knew she dearly loved to laugh. "I am glad that you find such pleasure in ruining a good pair of trousers, Elizabeth, but I assure you, my valet will not."

His serious tone caused her to laugh harder, which was his intent. He shook his head as if he were annoyed and headed towards the hidden door they had come through. Darcy waited for Elizabeth to slip through the wood to the other side to check that the passageway was clear before he opened the door. He paused before passing through the doorway to take in one more glimpse of Elizabeth's sleeping form. Then together, quiet as shades, they slipped through the corridors and down the stairs, breathing only deeply when they finally exited the house unseen.

Only then did Darcy turn to Elizabeth. He looked deeply into her eyes, and promised, "Elizabeth, we will find a way."

Darcy turned to secure the door behind him, resting a hand against the cool wood; he stood with his back to the room for some time, thinking of what he might say to soothe Elizabeth. After stealthily retrieving Darcy's horse from Longbourn's stables, they walked together back to Bingley's estate. Elizabeth had barely said a word to him during their entire three-mile walk. He was able to beg solitude easily from their host, especially considering his earlier claim of a megrim. Indeed, when Darcy would request a tray in his room later in the evening, it would only add to Bingley's belief that Darcy did not feel well.

Though Elizabeth and Darcy had been left quite alone, they had spoken little. He observed in silence that she was deep in thought. Her brow puckered in consternation, and her bottom lip was often pulled in and bitten gently in distress. Though he found her just as enchanting in this state, he could not like the worry etched in her features and the cloudiness to those bright eyes he loved so well. He had offered words of encouragement, though little did he know whether they yielded any success. He knew that *her* lack of accomplishment that day was weighing heavily on her.

Tugging at the restrictions of his neckwear, Darcy eventually managed to loosen the folds. It hung limply around his neck as he walked to the nearest window and watched as the shadows at dusk crept further along the landscape. It was like observing the tide come in and devour the earth beneath it as it took its place for the evening. So many parts of this rhythmic cycle of night and day nagged at him in their inevitability and his lack of control over them. Night would come regardless of what he did to prolong the day. It felt like a fitting metaphor for his predicament with Elizabeth. He held no power over her state, yet he longed to be able to ease her burdens by reuniting her with herself.

Darcy turned when he heard Elizabeth's muffled sob. Immediately rushing towards her, he pulled a handkerchief instinctively from his breast pocket to offer her, her sad smile at his offering reminding them both of her acutely intangible nature.

"Elizabeth, we shall think of something. It is yet only the first day, the first attempt. Surely, you cannot stay this way forever."

Elizabeth met his eyes then and, lifting her hand to his cheek, allowed her mind to drift back to the memory of the feel of his face. "Forgive me. I am certain we shall find a solution; however, I was so very hopeful today, and now I fear you see the result of all that hope dissolving into utter disappointment."

Darcy nodded, knowing not what he ought to say. Her feelings mirrored his own.

After a lengthy moment of silence, Darcy, who kneeled at her side, reached for the book at the table next to her chair.

"Perhaps we need a diversion. What think you of books?" Darcy was gladdened by her knowing smile. "Shall I read to you?"

Elizabeth wiped her eyes, attempting to wipe away her disappointment too. She nodded to him and smiled lovingly as he turned and leaned himself against her chair. His strong, clear voice was like a warm summer breeze on her face. Closing her eyes, she rested her head and allowed that breeze to refresh her. She listened contentedly as he read poetry, all the while trying to allow the timbre of his voice to be her focus—and not her inability to run her hands through his hair as he read, as was her wish.

For a while, she half-listened, half-imagined evenings like this someday with him, comfortably ensconced near the fire, Darcy resting against her legs and reading. Without her notice, soft tears of longing rolled silently down her cheeks as she imagined reaching for one of his dark curls and twirling it in her fingers while he read. They had not once, despite their many confessions of the heart, spoken of marriage. It was as if neither wanted to think about the possibility that theirs would be a love destined for another time, incapable of earth's most long-standing act of devotion.

Darcy leaned back and arched his neck to look back at her. His smile fell when he saw her tears. Elizabeth offered him a silent answer in the feeble upturn of her lips, easing his worry, if only slightly.

Indicating the book, she said, "Do continue, please. You have a very soothing voice."

Though his brows were still lowered in concern, he nodded and, turning to his book, began to read aloud again. Late into the night he read, calming her spirit and soothing her pain. Occasionally, he would make some wry comment about one poem or another; he was encouraged further when he heard her laugh. He closed his eyes, allowing the sound to heal his heart and erase his fears.

"You are quite silly, Mr Darcy."

Darcy, who still had his back to her, turned and, countering her tease, said, "I beg your pardon, madam. However much I abhor correcting a lady, I fear I must inform you that gentlemen are never silly."

Elizabeth crossed her arms about her. "Is that so? I had not known it was entirely a female trait."

"Indeed it is. Imagine, Elizabeth, a bunch of 'silly' gentlemen at their clubs."

Hands coming to her mouth to cover her laugh, Elizabeth nodded. "It would be quite the scene."

Though he had introduced the topic, it reminded him briefly of his folly in taking her to such manly establishments, his actions once again causing him guilt.

Elizabeth noted his changed attitude and questioned him.

"I ought not to have taken you to those places. Your father could call me out if he knew, and he would be justified in doing so."

Elizabeth nodded in agreement, brushing a piece of her hair aside as she said, "I suppose it will be left to us to make entirely sure that he does not hear of it then."

"You would keep my secret?" Darcy chuckled, his heart beating at the very thought of a secret alliance with Elizabeth. Despite the intimacies of their situation, every new proof, every word and look that gave away her feelings towards him was welcome.

Elizabeth tapped her chin, broadening his smile at the charming way she looked, and pretended she would have to consider whether or not to protect Darcy in this manner. "I shall think very hard on it, you may be certain."

Darcy met Elizabeth's eyes, and together they held each other in the soft gaze of true companionship. After many moments of contented silence, Darcy sat upright and, with brows raised in eager anticipation, asked, "Would you care for a game of chess?"

"Ought not you to retire? It has become very late."

Darcy stood and, brushing off his trousers, walked towards the chess table resting along one wall of the room. Shaking his head, he answered her. "Indeed, not. I am not tired in the least."

Upon reaching her side again, he placed the table before her and pulled a companion chair to the other side. With a mischievous gleam in his eyes, he met her gaze. "Unless, of course, the lady protests for fear of losing."

Elizabeth's head fell back, and her laughter echoed in her companion's ears like a church bell. She pursed her lips and sent him a quelling look as she shook her finger at him. "You mean to frighten me, Mr Darcy, by coming in all this state to play me? But I will not be alarmed though you provoke so well with your challenge. There is a stubbornness about me that never can bear to be frightened at the will of others. My courage always rises with every attempt to intimidate me."

Darcy's lips twitched, though at first he said not a word. "Indeed, I shall not say that you are mistaken," he replied, "because you could not really believe me to entertain any design of alarming you. Shall we play then, Elizabeth?"

"I am not afraid of you."

Darcy laughed heartily and then turned smouldering eyes upon her. "Shall we put a small wager on the outcome?"

She pretended to be in serious thought. Frowning, she slowly scrutinised Darcy's person. When her eyes met his once again, she said, "Ladies do not place bets."

Darcy flicked a piece of invisible lint off his jacket sleeve as he said with a shrug of his shoulders, "True, my dear; however, I dare say that most ladies do not venture into gentlemen's fencing academies either."

"Unfair!" Elizabeth laughed. "You cannot claim guilt over exposing me to such scandalous places one minute and, in the next, hold it against me. It is very ungenerous of you—and give me leave to say, impolitic too—and is provoking me to retaliate, sir."

Darcy could not be distracted by her attempts, however. "You did not answer me, Elizabeth. Shall we wager?"

"What do you propose?" She answered, her heart beating now quite frightfully.

"Winner may ask for a favour to be granted at a later time."

His relaxed pose, as well as the indifferent tone of his voice, contradicted the heat in his eyes and caused her to look away, willing herself not to blush.

After a moment, she lifted her chin and attempted to match his gaze. The fluttering in her chest caused her words to pour forth rapidly. "I will have you know, my father taught me the game, and such moves may come out that will put your chess master to shame, sir."

"Indeed." He was undeterred. "A wager, Elizabeth?"

"Fine, I agree to the wager. Though I must say—"

"Ah, less talk, my dear. I think the lady postpones out of fear."

"Indeed not!" Elizabeth protested, laughing.

Since she could not touch the pieces herself, she indicated to Darcy which one she wanted to move and where to move it, thus beginning their game.

The game proceeded slowly after that, and despite their earlier fluency, they uttered hardly a word during the game. Darcy was pleased and impressed with Elizabeth's ability, and he was enjoying the game thoroughly. When it was her turn, she would consider, choose a piece, and tell him where to move it. Though her talent was obvious, his was far more practiced, and it allowed him to think on their situation further as he played the game.

While considering their earlier failure, he reviewed what they believed about their current state of otherworldly connection. His appraisal of the past week brought about a couple of observations. Elizabeth's spirit was transported to his keeping while her body slumbered. For whatever reason, they were fixed to each other for the duration as well. Neither was entirely correct as to why each was destined to such a state with the other. It was not until their struggle ceased that each was able to truly develop an understanding of the other's character.

This last observation caused Darcy to send a silent prayer of gratitude for the chance to work past his own stupid arrogance, conceit, and selfish disdain of the feelings of others, especially of Elizabeth. It allowed him to realise that *she* was the prize and *he* was her inferior. He became lost, then, as his internal observations became an external one of Elizabeth. He watched as she bent her head to examine the board, carefully looking at her options. Her lip tugged temptingly under her teeth, and her hand was unconsciously worrying a curl by her ear. She tucked her feet beneath her in relaxation. He could not regret the sweet picture of both elegance and innocence she presented.

He continued to watch, enchanted as she determined her move and, with a triumphant twinkle in her eye, told him her manoeuvre, and while he moved the piece on the board, she held a wicked smile. She then looked up at him expectantly, only to find his heated gaze.

"'Tis your move, sir," she said cheekily, grateful her voice did not betray the shakiness she felt on seeing him look at her with such devotion.

Darcy shook his head, as if to clear it and lowered his eyes once again to their game. After examining her play and selecting his own, he settled once again into considering their plight. He weighed the words she had said in the carriage about being destined together by Fate. Her memory of the accident, and thus their only way of knowing what truly brought Elizabeth to his side, came only after they had learned to really love each other. Significantly, she could only feel his touch in a connection to her physical state. Indeed, he realised, in every element of this marvellous, unbelievable path they were on, something was required of both of them. As he considered this element, an idea settled into his mind with such strength that he was, for quite some time, insensible to any other thought.

He leaned back in his chair, his hand coming to rest against his mouth, the game totally forgotten. His eyes again rested upon Elizabeth, and his heart beat faster as the idea became secure and gained strength. As he imagined what might happen should his idea prove to be the key to her reunion, his very being warmed with a love so tender that he could think of nothing but that he wanted to try it immediately.

He was not insensible, though, to what his part would be, and subsequently, his eyes could not meet her expectant ones after she told him what move to make for her. His cheeks coloured almost imperceptibly, and he struggled for clarity of thought. Breathing deeply to reconcile his emotions, Darcy looked again at the board. He knew it would be easier for him should he win the wager for their game and thus, duly motivated, considered his options. A path to victory soon became clear, and as he devised a course of action, a secret smile grew.

Within a couple of exchanges, Darcy's low voice spoke confidently. "Check."

Elizabeth quickly bent over the board and realised her precarious situation. With a triumphant shout, she was able to manoeuvre out of check with a little effort. Darcy smiled wickedly, making a move that forced the sacrifice of her queen to protect the king. Knowing that the end was in sight, Darcy was merciful and, when the time came, only whispered, "Checkmate."

Elizabeth sat forward, disbelievingly. "Indeed not!" she said, denying the sad fact of her loss until even she could see that nothing could be done. When that time came, she sat back in her chair and looked at her companion. A slow smile began to grow as she congratulated him on his win.

"And what is to be your prize, sir?" she said, knowing she could not avoid it now.

"We go to Longbourn again—indeed, this very evening."

Surprised at his answer, Elizabeth stood to look out at the pitch-black sky. She then looked at the clock over the mantel and, seeing it was only a few hours before dawn, frowned at Darcy.

"I believe you mean to say this morning. In a few hours, the sun will rise. Even then, it would be far too early to call at my home and hope to be admitted."

"I do not expect to be admitted, Elizabeth. Indeed, I propose that we go now and risk that forgiving door we passed through earlier today."

Elizabeth stood shocked, and looking once again from Darcy to the blackness outside, she challenged him. "Why do you wish to go to Longbourn now? Our lack of success is not to be questioned, William. It was no less than an utter failure."

Darcy stood then and walked to her. Wishing very much to cup her cheek with his hand, he instead clenched his hands at his side. Looking down at her, he said softly, "I have an idea, Elizabeth, that...I know not how but...I feel quite strongly that it may work."

"What is it?" she said with half eagerness, half fear.

"Do you not trust me?"

Elizabeth swallowed and considered his words. She trusted her very life with him, and she may very well give him just that. There were still so many unknowns to their plight that she could not rule out any outcome. Slowly, she raised her eyes to his and nodded. "I trust you implicitly, William."

His eyes gleamed in anticipation then, and he said, "Then let us be off."

DARCY PAUSED AT THE SIDE DOOR THROUGH WHICH THEY HAD previously gained access. He turned and tried to gauge Elizabeth's expression in the near blackness of the night. The only light available to him was that from the stars and the silver moon above.

"Would your family have hired a nurse to attend you at night, Elizabeth?"

Elizabeth thought about that for a moment before answering. "I do not believe we would have. More than likely one of my sisters or Hill would attend me."

Darcy frowned, his mind racing as he thought about how he

might get past this potential obstacle. He almost decided to go back to Netherfield and try again during a proper call to Longbourn. Before he could decide, though, he heard footsteps coming towards them.

Alarmed, he gawked at Elizabeth. She nodded, understanding his fear and ventured in the direction of the footsteps to determine their source and any danger they might signify.

"It is only Sue, our maid. She is one of our tenant's daughters and has come to begin her work for the day," Elizabeth said as she returned to him.

He stood motionless at the door as the sound of the maid's footsteps changed direction towards the other side of the house and the kitchens. He only drew in a relieved breath when Elizabeth confirmed the danger was gone.

"I am concerned, Elizabeth, that we may encounter someone in your room." Darcy finally voiced his fear.

"Let us go in, and I shall see. Perhaps we shall be lucky and it is only Hill that attends me. She will have to leave soon to instruct the other servants on their day's work."

Darcy wavered with indecision until his eyes settled on her face, lowering to her lips. He swallowed, and a hope began to grow in him that pushed the fear away as a light chases away the dark. He nodded and patted unconsciously at the small candle secreted in his pocket for when they got to Elizabeth's chambers.

Without a sound, they then repeated their actions from earlier in the day, entered the house, and were soon at the door leading to Elizabeth's chambers. Silently, she motioned that she would go ahead and see whether there was anyone to encounter. Darcy waited, his heart in his throat and his breathing laboured whilst she was absent longer than he thought necessary.

Eventually, she emerged through the wood door and said, "We are in luck. It is Hill, and she is just gathering her things, preparing to go down for the day. We have only a minute or so to wait."

Darcy's eyes bulged, and he motioned excitedly at the door. Elizabeth, understanding his worry, answered, "She will not come through this door. I told you it is so little used that we have nothing to fear. She will exit through the main door. She always has."

Darcy closed his eyes as relief once again washed over him. But as the possibility of implementing his idea settled into his mind again, his heart began to beat erratically for another reason entirely.

In another minute, Elizabeth confirmed that the housekeeper had left and they were free to enter without fear of discovery. She entered first as before, and when she noticed that Darcy did not immediately follow, she came back through the door.

"The way is clear," she said with earnest urging. "We ought to make haste; I fear we may not have long before she returns. Hill needs only to instruct the others in our service and will likely come again to watch over me. In fact, I am beginning to believe our earlier success was simply due to her attentions needed for Mr Bingley's arrival."

Elizabeth once again made to enter her chambers, but she was stopped when Darcy whispered her name. She halted and looked back at him expectantly. She was surprised and arrested at the look of tenderness that she found there.

"I would have you know, Elizabeth, that I love you."

Her face melted into a warm smile as she said easily, "And I you."

"Whatever the outcome...should this not prove successful..." Darcy's quiet accent faded away, not wishing to give voice to the chance of another failure.

"We will find a way."

Darcy nodded, his words lost in the thickness in his throat and the feelings manifesting themselves so powerfully within him.

Together they entered her chambers. Darcy took out the candle and quickly lit it. Immediately, the shadows in the room were chased to the corners, and once again, Darcy laid eyes on the delicate angel that was Elizabeth in life. They walked slowly towards the bed, and each took up a place on either side of it. Darcy looked down at Elizabeth and felt with greater conviction that he was the key this time to making Elizabeth whole again.

"You have not said what your idea is. What is it you want me to do?"

Darcy did not take his eyes from her sleeping form when he answered her. "Turn around, Elizabeth," he answered softly.

Elizabeth did not immediately follow his instructions and waited further to question him.

He slowly lifted his eyes to take in her ghostly beauty again as he answered her. "We were all wrong earlier. Before, it was just you trying to heal yourself. But it occurred to me that neither of us has really been whole without the other."

Here, he took up her earthly hand, and again Elizabeth gasped at the sensation that flew through her. She marvelled at it and, with moist eyes, looked at the gentleman who held her heart and now her hand. He looked down at the hand in his and patted it with such tenderness that her eyes pooled over.

Slowly he began to speak, all the while holding her hand, worshipping it as he lowered himself into the seat by her bed. "I have been a selfish being all my life, in practice, though not in principle. As a child, I was taught what was right, but I was not taught to correct my temper. I was given good principles, but left to follow them in pride and conceit. Unfortunately, an only son—for many years an only child—I was spoilt by my parents who, though good themselves (my father, particularly, all that was benevolent and amiable), allowed, encouraged, almost taught me to be selfish and overbearing —to care for none beyond my own family circle, to think meanly of all the rest of the world, to wish at least to think meanly of their sense and worth compared with my own. Such I was, from eight to eight and twenty, and such I might still have been but for you, dearest, loveliest Elizabeth!"

He lifted his eyes to her and she noted his too were glossy with tears. "You see, my dear, I believe you need me as much as I have needed you to be whole."

"What is it you plan to do?" Elizabeth whispered, surprised when the words escaped her mouth, as she was certain she was too overwhelmed with emotion to speak.

"Do you trust me?"

Though he had not answered her but instead posed another question to her, she knew what she would say.

"You have already asked me that once this evening. I trust you with my life and soul."

Darcy nodded, and together their eyes once again rested on Elizabeth's sleeping body. After a moment, Darcy looked up at Elizabeth again as she stood opposite him. "Turn around, my love."

This time Elizabeth did as he asked and turned her back to him. He took only a second to confirm she did not watch. He was not certain that it mattered whether she witnessed, but somehow he thought that, if he were not successful at bringing her to herself again, it would be easier not to witness the immediate disappointment on her beautiful features.

Slowly then, he leaned towards her body as it lay motionless before him. He drank in her comely features as they danced in the shadows of the flickering candlelight. Her lavender eyelids, closed in repose drew his eyes to her dark lashes, feather light against the alabaster softness of her cheeks.

His hand glided along her cheek then, and he paused when he heard Elizabeth gasp. "Stay where you are, my dear," he warned gently.

His heart was beating as he paused just above her angelic face. Closing his eyes, he drew a slow breath and lowered to press his lips to hers.

The warmth and softness of them entranced him, and he at once was devoured by the multitude of sensations coursing through him. As he pressed his lips to hers, slowly the feeling that grew in prominence against all the other exquisite sensations was that of extreme rightness. It was as if he was destined to this end.

Though the kiss was brief, it was no less powerful to the gentleman, who found himself quite breathless as he lifted his head. He looked down at the lady and was astonished, paralysed suddenly in shock, as he felt her stir beneath the hand still resting tenderly on her cheek.

"William!" Elizabeth's voice drew his attention to her ghostly self. She had turned herself during the kiss, and her hand was resting unbelievingly upon her lips. "I feel something. I...something is happening."

Wide-eyed, Darcy watched as her vision wavered before him. Never before had he had any difficulty seeing her, and now she seemed to flicker like the light from his candle. Though he felt a sudden excited triumph flow through him, he also knew panic. He disliked the idea of not knowing to where she was disappearing.

Again, the cheek resting in his hand stirred, and he was seized with a hope that drove him to bend over her lips again. This time the kiss he gave her held none of the reserve, worry, and doubt he had previously held—none of the nervousness and tingling anxiety that accompanies any gentleman upon his first kiss with the lady he loves. This time he poured forth all the love he felt in his heart and allowed it to manifest skin to skin as he connected his very soul to hers.

As he pulled away, the Elizabeth lying on the bed stirred. He looked up and beheld no one else in the room. He was half agony, half hope as he looked down again at the face he cradled in his hands.

Quietly he called her name.

Laughing tears of profound happiness and relief then rumbled up and out of his chest as he saw her eyes flutter and open to look at him. At that moment, he heard footsteps at the stairs on the other side of the wall and knew his time was now at an end.

He drank in the lustre of her dark brown eyes and smiled lovingly at her. He was speechless at first as they both gazed at each other.

"Welcome back, Elizabeth."

She reached a heavy arm up and took hold of his hand at her cheek. Pulling it off her cheek, with a slight pucker to her brow, she opened her mouth to question him.

He smiled at her, expectantly, though at that moment his attention was caught by the sound of footsteps nearing the door.

He turned back quickly to her and said, with warm humour in his voice, "I shall not hide under the bed again, Elizabeth." His soft laughter filled the space between them.

Then with a warm squeeze of her hand, he blew out the candle, encompassing the room in darkness once again, and departed silently through the secret door.

ELIZABETH CLOSED HER EYES AS DARKNESS FLOODED THE ROOM again. Her head pounded terribly, and she felt so very tired. She thought she heard someone open her door and settle into the seat near her bed, though she could not be sure of anything as the thoughts in her mind felt so very difficult to grasp. Almost immediately, she felt herself slip into a deep sleep once again. It was an hour or so later that she stirred again when she heard her chamber door open once more.

She resisted the urge to squeeze her eyes shut and tell the intruder to go away, that she was still so very tired. She heard Jane's voice as she quietly whispered to another voice she recognised as Hill's.

"How is Lizzy this morning, Hill?"

"Still much the same, I fear," came the reply.

Elizabeth struggled then, not understanding their meaning but feeling the most desperate need to alert them to her presence. Fighting with all the last strength she could pull from within, she opened her eyes once again and beheld her sister and Hill at the foot of her bed. She opened her mouth but could only manage a small sound.

Relief washed through her to see that they immediately turned towards her. She was not sure she had the energy to attempt to garner their attention again. She saw them rush to her side, heard their startled cries, and felt Jane's tears soak her cheek as her sister pressed against her in a warm embrace.

Again, Elizabeth felt she had to speak, to assure her sister that she was well. She closed her eyes and gained further strength from the warm devotion and love she felt from her sister's expressions of tenderness.

"Jane," she croaked, her voice feeling as if she had sand in her throat and had not spoken in ages.

"Oh, Elizabeth," Jane cried through her tears. "Thank God, you are returned to us."

Elizabeth saw through tired eyes that Hill had left in a hurry, saying she would alert the rest of the house. She felt so confused and unfocused. It took all her strength just to grasp at any one thought. Slowly, she turned to look towards the window. The sun was just rising, and its golden rays were puncturing the clouds. It was a beautiful sight, and as Elizabeth slowly gained more strength, she found her arms and carefully lifted them, though they felt weighted with stones, to return her sister's embrace.

Jane's happiness spilled into her, and she knew more than felt herself to be happy. When Jane sat back again, Elizabeth smiled at her sleepily. Sounds from the hallway then came to Elizabeth's ears, and she prepared herself for her family. As they each poured in, it was a reunion of sorts never before experienced in the Bennet family. Elizabeth was hard-pressed to give sentiment to it all. Part of her knew she felt happy to see her family, yet part of her felt still asleep. She hardly spoke as everyone around her rushed with their own words of relief and blessing. For many minutes, everyone celebrated, speaking at once, while Elizabeth just listened contentedly. She could not muster much strength to speak anyway.

Elizabeth felt someone take up her hand and looked to see her father holding it, a warm smile on his lips. "I am glad you are come back, Lizzy."

Elizabeth smiled though her head began again to ache terribly. She squeezed his hand by way of response. Eventually, she was able to convey to Jane, who had not ventured from her side throughout, that she wished to rest. Through some persuasion and much help from Mr Bennet, Jane was able to collect her family and guide them out.

When all was quiet again, Jane came to her bedside.

"How glad I am to see you awake again, Lizzy."

"You will have to tell me what has happened? How long was I asleep?"

Jane then gave her a brief outline of the past eight days and the worry they all felt for her. She told her how the doctor feared but encouraged them all to talk to her anyway. "There is much more to share, Lizzy, but I fear it will have to be for another time. I can see that you need your rest again."

"I am not too fatigued to see that gleam in your eye. Come, Jane, tell me what brings such happiness there."

"Can I not be happy to see you well?"

Elizabeth laughed, though her throat was dry, and it ended up in a coughing fit. Jane immediately procured a drink of water for her from the pitcher near the bed. When Elizabeth had cleared her throat she said, "Indeed, and I am glad to be well. I feel so much better than when I first awoke."

Jane was quiet for a moment, unsure whether to speak of Bingley yet or to allow Elizabeth to rest. Part of her wanted to share with her sister this news of importance from her life, but she knew also that Elizabeth longed for sleep again.

"What is it, Jane?"

Jane looked up at her with a slight smile on her face. "Mr Bingley has returned to Netherfield."

Elizabeth smiled broadly then. "Truly? That is something indeed. Some very significant things happened while I slumbered, it would seem."

"But I shall not speak another word of it until you have rested more. I would have you returned to full strength as soon as possible, Lizzy."

Elizabeth nodded, satisfied as a weariness began to creep up her limbs like a heavy blanket. A thought flitted through her mind then, and she asked sleepily, "And is he alone this time?"

Jane understood her and answered, "His friend Mr Darcy accompanies him now."

Elizabeth's eyes opened again, and she looked at her sister.

"Come now, Lizzy. We shall speak of all this later. Sleep. I shall not leave your side."

Elizabeth nodded and turned on her side so that she looked towards the dawn pouring through the window. Slowly she lifted her fingertips to brush against her lips, trying to dispel a tingling sensation she felt there.

Some ways off, on the other side of the window, though too far away to see, stood a gentleman gazing in her direction. The expression on his face could not be read, but if it were to be guessed, it might be considered happiness mixed with a hopeful excitement. He looked about him, expecting to see someone, and when he did not, he smiled, shook his head in wonderment, and slowly turned to walk across the field—alone—towards his friend's home.

❧ 18 ❧

Elizabeth pressed her hands to her face, grasping to hold on to the scene behind her eyelids. It was always brief, a flash of a room or a hallway, and then nothing. She viewed these places as if through her own eyes though they were places she could not recall having visited. The library was her favourite: robed in night, lit only by the warm glow of a fire. The furnishings were inviting, beckoning her to take refuge. Though the room itself was beautiful, it was the feeling it summoned that made her wish the image would stay. When her mind's eye was in this room, she felt whole, at home, and at peace. Since waking a few days ago, she had felt the love of her family, the fatigue of her long recovery, and an utter emptiness she could not explain—but oddly not whole, at home, or at peace in any way.

During the initial days after she came out of what she was told was a lengthy coma, she felt she slept more than she was awake. It had been a couple of days since that time though Elizabeth felt as if she could not sleep enough, as if she had not slept in a lifetime. Much of her time was spent asleep, but her wakeful hours were occasionally interrupted by those flashes of consciousness, distracting images of the room, the hallway and, most disquieting of all, of the retreating form of a gentleman and the pull she felt towards him. There was never enough time to recognise him, for as soon as she tried to focus on the fuzzy image in her mind, the entire scene would dissipate like a puff of smoke. The harder she tried to grasp these brief images, the quicker they seemed to evaporate into the recesses of her mind.

Elizabeth opened her eyes, disappointment and resignation settling into her bones at her inability to make sense of the images once again. She looked about and saw her sister Jane seated next to the bed where she reclined. Jane was looking at her strangely with concern in her eyes. Elizabeth sighed. She was becoming weary of seeing that same look in everyone's eyes when they saw her as if she were going to break at any moment. Elizabeth had not spoken of the room, hallway, or gentleman—nor was she likely to. After several days of looking into the concerned, fearful eyes of her family, she was not about to add to their burdens by admitting such a thing.

"Are you well, Lizzy?" Jane said with careful tones.

Breathing deeply, Elizabeth answered, "I am well. My head still hurts occasionally. I shall be glad to be rid of this room though."

"Every day you gain strength. It is a pleasure to see."

Elizabeth attempted a laugh. "Every day I get closer to the end of my enforced incarceration."

"Incarceration indeed!" Jane laughed. "You know Mr Jones said you must stay abed for at least another week because it will help you recover."

"Though I admit to feeling tired, I do not think it necessary that I be confined to my room. I should like to have some fresh air, to walk further than the length of this room—"

"Lizzy! You were not to get out of this bed! Do not tell me you have been attempting to walk?"

Elizabeth felt instantly guilty for her lapse and the distressed look in Jane's eyes. She pleaded then with her sister. "I must get my strength back, and that will only happen if I can take a little exercise."

Jane stood then and paced the room, her head shaking in disapproval. "You could have fallen and hurt yourself again. Did you not think of that?"

Though her tone was at first accusatory, it ended with a shaky fear pulsing through it. Elizabeth saw that her sister's eyes had welled up with tears.

"Jane," Elizabeth said softly, her hand extended towards her sister. Jane walked over to the bed again and sat, taking up Elizabeth's hand. "I am truly sorry to have caused you concern. However, I have been confined to this bed for four days now—"

"It has been much longer than that, Lizzy. You were unconscious for more than a se'nnight."

"Four days since I awoke, I mean. Four days that I recall. I must move about. I must!"

Elizabeth met her sister's eyes and watched as Jane looked deeply into hers. She was searching for something, and though Elizabeth could not tell whether it was to be found in her eyes or was something Jane was mulling over in her own mind, eventually she saw Jane come to a decision.

With a heavy sigh, she looked at her sister with a stern expression. "All right, but you must promise me that you will not try to walk unless I am here to help you. I cannot think... I cannot imagine what might happen should..."

Jane's eyes brimmed with tears again, and she pulled Elizabeth into a warm embrace. Elizabeth closed her eyes and returned the embrace. She felt terrible for troubling her sister, but she also knew her recovery would only be delayed by lying about all day.

When Jane pulled away, Elizabeth asked, "Would you help me now to walk?"

She nodded, and Elizabeth prepared by sliding her legs to the side of the bed and resting her feet on the cool floor. Jane helped her to stand, and together they made a slow, shaky journey across the room. Elizabeth's knees gave out but once, for which she felt gladdened. The first time she had tried to walk, she had needed to hold on to the side of the bed the entire way around it before falling exhausted face down on the other side. She peeked over at her sister, who shook her head slightly at the sudden trembling in Elizabeth's gait. Elizabeth determined then to take advantage of Jane's offer to help as often as she could each day, no matter how exhausting.

"Tell me, did your Mr Bingley call again today?" Elizabeth said, through a tight jaw. She was attempting to distract herself from the burning muscles in her legs.

Jane blushed and nodded beside her. "Both the gentlemen from Netherfield came again today."

Elizabeth said nothing; she drew in a deep breath and tried to push past the screaming in her legs.

"They were both very solicitous of news about you, Lizzy—Mr Darcy particularly."

Elizabeth could see the twitch of a smile on her sister's lips. Once before, Elizabeth and Jane had discussed the gentlemen's return to the neighbourhood. Jane shared with her the feelings she had regarding Mr Bingley's return in particular, as well as the way he acted. Elizabeth was happy for Jane, certain that Mr Bingley was as in love with her sister as ever. Jane also told Elizabeth that she thought Mr Darcy might have some tender feelings for her. Elizabeth tried diligently not to examine that notion. She was of two minds with regards to Jane's belief: one felt certain that the idea of Mr Darcy feeling anything but displeasure towards her was laughable and another, more absurd than the last, that his admiring her felt perfectly natural.

Elizabeth shook her head, dispelling the debate within, and replied flippantly, "I wonder whether he is curious to see how tolerable I am after being disfigured in an accident."

Jane rolled her eyes in a most unladylike fashion before smiling indulgently at her sister. "Disfigured, indeed! You hit your head, the bruise from which is all but gone."

"'Tis a more likely explanation than the one to which I know you hold fast."

"Unjust, Lizzy!"

Elizabeth stopped and looked at her sister, her legs trembling in relief for the break. "How so?"

"You give little credit to the good sense of your sister," Jane teased.

Appeased and amused, Elizabeth forced herself to continue towards the window; there she would allow herself a true break. "Your good sense is my dearest friend, Jane. However, I wonder to what realm it has gone with respect to that gentleman."

The sisters laughed at Elizabeth's words, and though the younger would have preferred to be done with the topic, the elder continued, her tone now serious. "You may disregard his often having looked at you when he was last in the neighbourhood. You may disregard that you were the only lady outside of his own party he asked to dance at the Netherfield ball. But you cannot disregard the look I saw in his eyes—and have seen every time he has come to call and ask after you."

Elizabeth was silent. Though she wanted to protest, she could not form the words. She felt certain she was missing something, some valuable piece of information, and though she could not think why or what it could be, missing it was. So many things since waking were difficult, strange, and new. Her body felt as if she did not know how to use it, as if she had lost power over it for a long time and was having to relearn everything. Her mind created images of places and persons she had never known, and her heart beat rapidly when they flashed through her consciousness. Now, with regards to Mr Darcy, she felt a rope about her, tethered tightly to some secret, reluctant to accept Jane's observations yet unable to absolutely refute them as she would have before the accident.

Thankfully, they reached the windowsill, and Elizabeth was not forced to make any response. She carefully settled herself on it and rubbed her tired legs. Jane watched her with a frown on her face, concern and pity again in her eyes.

"I am well, Jane, truly. They are tired, but did you not see that I was able to manage well enough? I shall be walking these lanes"—Elizabeth gestured out the window to the garden below—"in absolutely no time at all."

Jane lowered herself to sit beside her sister. "It is very wrong of me to indulge you in this. If Mr Jones or Papa finds out..."

"I should not worry about Papa. If he proves to be upset, I shall tease and smile him out of his ill humour."

Elizabeth patted her sister's leg beside her own and changed the topic. "Tell me about Mr Bingley's visit." Elizabeth's smile brightened when she saw her sister blush.

"He was very amiable again."

"Come now, Jane," Elizabeth whined. "You might as well tell me nothing at all for how little 'amiable' really says. Just how *amiable* was he? Was he *amiable* enough to ask for your hand?"

Jane pushed her shoulder into her sister and laughed. "Not quite that *amiable*, I am afraid. Though he did say he was very much enjoying his visits and hoped that I was too."

"And you replied that his visits were the very thing to bring the most pleasure to you all day."

Jane laughed but coloured at the very idea of such a bold statement. "I did no such thing, I merely answered kindly that I looked forward to his visits." Even that admission had felt bold.

"There are very few of us who have heart enough to be really in love without encouragement," Elizabeth began. "He may never do more than like you if you do not help him on."

Jane laughed uneasily. "You sound very much like our friend Charlotte."

Elizabeth startled a little at that, realising her words were nearly those Charlotte had said many months ago. "Perhaps I have given too little credit to the truth of her beliefs, though I should not like to be married to Mr Collins, no matter how true. I am merely saying that this accident...it very nearly killed us both and has taught me that life is entirely too short. If you like Mr Bingley, as I know you do, then make it absolutely clear."

Jane turned and held her sister's gaze. Her eyes watered at the mention of the accident. She knew her sister to be telling the truth and felt a courage grow within her at even the thought of sharing such tender emotions with Mr Bingley. At the very worst, he might be offended and leave the neighbourhood—again. She had endured that once before, even with the idea that he did not care for her at all. Should that happen, she would at least have the benefit of experience to ease her way.

"I will confess, the very idea makes me tremble, but I shall do as you say. I shall, as you put it, 'help him on.'"

Elizabeth smiled and laughed quietly. "Then I feel certain you shall be an engaged woman by the end of his call tomorrow."

"How can you be certain he will call tomorrow?" Jane said in an attempt to dispel the fluttering in her breast.

"Has he not called every day since his return?"

Jane looked down, a pink glow spreading across her cheeks answering for her. Elizabeth nodded and turned to gaze out the window. Her own future could not be so certain. Though it was yet early in her recovery, she felt disconcerted about her state of health, about the strange visions of unknown places that flitted occasionally across her mind like a leaf in the wind. She thought perhaps marriage may never be an option for her.

A thought skittered through Elizabeth's mind: the library again, its treasures muted rectangles on the shelves in the low light. A sound to her right and she turns... Elizabeth blinked, the scene gone once again. Immediately the sense of warmth was replaced with longing and a sensation that she was lost—or maybe had lost something. She could not decide.

Her eyes turned from the gardens outside her window to look about her room. She recalled when she first woke.

"Jane, there is no possible way..." Elizabeth blushed at the very idea, yet it seemed so real. "Mr Darcy could not have been allowed to visit me here..."

Though she had put voice to the thought, still it mortified her to consider Mr Darcy or any gentleman in her chamber with her. Her hands came easily to her face to cool the sensation there, her heart beginning to beat unsteadily.

"I do not take your meaning." Jane said in astonishment mixed with disbelief. "Do you mean here in your chambers?"

Elizabeth coloured a deeper red though said not a word.

Jane, scandalised by the very idea, also blushed though she laughed shakily. "Indeed, I should think not! How could you suggest such a thing?"

"I... It was perhaps a dream then."

Jane raised a brow at this, still unbelieving, her own mind unable to consider such a breach of propriety. A memory then came to the rescue and Jane, relieved, breathed deeply. "I spoke to you about Mr Darcy a number of times while you were yet unconscious. On the very day he called, I came up here and talked to your sleeping form about him. You must have heard me, as Mr Jones had thought possible, and somehow dreamt that he was here."

Elizabeth lifted her eyes to take in her sister's face. A slow smile grew on her lips. "Oh, that is a relief. That was just the day before I awoke, yes?"

"Yes, the very day before," Jane confirmed, now quite recovered.

Elizabeth nodded her head. "I dreamt I had awakened to see him seated by the bed. He said something though I could not immediately understand."

"What did he say?"

Elizabeth began to laugh. "He said he would not hide under the bed again."

She doubled over then in laughter, her sides beginning to hurt. Jane laughed as well, shaking her head at the absurdity of her sister's dream.

"Well there is your proof, Lizzy, if there ever was a need for it. Mr Darcy, I am positive, would *never* hide under a bed. It must surely have been a dream."

Elizabeth nodded. "The only thing I remember after that was waking to seeing you and Hill at the foot of my bed."

"Then it was the last dream you had before waking."

"Indeed. But answer me this most troubling question: Why do I dream of Mr Darcy?"

Jane raised a brow at this, and together they fell into laughter again.

Darcy's legs fell into a familiar pattern across the length of the library at Netherfield. He paced five steps, turned, and paced five back, his hands clasped behind his back and then separated and clasped again. He remained in this agitated repetition for the better part of twenty minutes before his friend spoke, interrupting his pattern and bringing him to a halt.

"I think you have little to worry about now, Darcy. You heard Miss Bennet yourself this morning declare that Miss Elizabeth was recovering well."

Darcy looked about him as he had done many times since leaving Longbourn in the early morning mist several days before. He was alone—except for Bingley, of course. Yet it mattered little how many people were in the room. Darcy found that he constantly felt truly alone since being separated from Elizabeth. He had grown accustomed to her voice, her gentle laugh, the graceful movement of her figure, and the connection between them. He would turn to share a joke with her, expecting to see the humour he knew would be in her eyes, only to remember where she really was. He knew he ought to feel relief for her reunion and eager anticipation for *their* reunion, yet still a part of him felt that, in bringing her back to herself, a part of him had been stolen. Indeed, he knew his heart had been left at Longbourn that morning. That was why he was so very anxious to see her again—to share a secret smile, take her hand in his again, and maybe even ask for that hand in marriage. He blinked twice, realising his silence had been noted by his friend.

"And you would tell me, should it be Miss Bennet recovering and you could not see her, that you would be so very calm. For God's sake, Bingley, I have not seen her in days!"

Bingley turned then, his brow lowered. "You mean weeks, nay months really."

Darcy coughed and rubbed his chin. "Of course, a slip of the tongue, I assure you."

Bingley laughed in his carefree manner, stood up to pat his friend on the back, and walked towards the sideboard to pour some tea from the tray that had arrived a short time ago. "Indeed, I see your point."

The night before, Darcy had almost convinced himself to return to Longbourn, to the side door he had scolded Elizabeth about but now saw as heaven-sent. But he could not do it. He was a gentleman. When they were earlier in their very unearthly bond, neither had any choice but to break with propriety, but Elizabeth would not thank him now to embarrass her or to compromise her in such a way. Now was the time for the rules of society to be enforced again, and he cursed them. What a fool he had been to care a jot for propriety before she woke. Now he was bound by that same propriety, and he hated every bit of it.

The little intelligence he gathered from Miss Bennet when Bingley and he called upon Longbourn was too little. Though he felt that Elizabeth's sister was being kind and sharing more than was merely polite, he still wished for more. His heart begged for the confirmation that she had missed him, had thought of him during their separation. He longed to look into those eyes and gather for himself whether she was truly well and recovering. He could not think how he managed not seeing her for so many weeks when he left

Netherfield in November. Now the separation felt like a prison, a torture even.

A week, he was told. She would be confined to her chamber for a week. It was absolute agony.

Still, he would call upon Longbourn daily and live on what little sustenance he could until he could drink in her beauty again. He could not know then that his fasting would be relieved sooner than he thought.

The next day, they entered Longbourn to call and immediately heard a commotion in the morning room where they were to be presented. Only scattered words and phrases reached Darcy's ears, but he could surmise some sort of disagreement. The closer he came to the room, the more he felt uncomfortable for their impending intrusion on what appeared to be a private family matter. He looked at Bingley, who returned his look with a frown.

Stopping, Darcy held his friend back. "Perhaps this is not a good time."

Darcy could see that his friend wavered, his face turning towards the closed door ahead of him and back to his friend several times. He understood the longing in Bingley's eyes and knew that Bingley only hesitated out of a wish to see Miss Bennet.

Then Darcy's ears picked up a voice, clear and pure, through the door. It was a voice more beautiful to him than any other, and his heart beat nearly out of his chest as it recognised her.

"I assure you I am quite well enough and will not spend another day locked away in my chamber!"

Darcy involuntarily took a step forward, and he was caught this time by Bingley's hand on his arm. He looked back at him, half mad with want to see her and unhappy with his friend for preventing it.

"Steady, Darcy, listen."

Darcy turned again towards the room and heard a chorus of other family members protesting Elizabeth's declaration and insisting she return.

His eyes pleaded with his friend, but Bingley uncharacteristically held firm and insisted they depart and come again later. Darcy watched the door dejectedly, knowing that just beyond was the treasure he longed to see again. Even as Bingley quietly informed the servant who had escorted them to the room that they would call again and that there was no need to present them, Darcy almost begged his friend to take back the words. Though he ached to see her, he knew his friend to have the right of it, and reluctantly, he straightened and prepared himself to turn and go.

"I walked down here on my own, Jane, Mama, Kitty, Mary, and Lydia." Elizabeth's voice sounded exasperated, and it brought a smile to Darcy's face, her distinct pronunciation of their names pointedly giving proof of her impatience with them. He envisioned her as eager to see him as he was to see her, and his rapid heartbeat grew stronger. He turned again towards the door, just as he heard her speak again. "The gentlemen have been seen at the gate and will no doubt be here presently, and I should like to be here for their call."

He raised his eyebrows in triumph for his friend and even laughed a little with relief when he saw Bingley sigh and relent, his own wish to see Miss Bennet no doubt helping Darcy's case. Together they turned to the servant and agreed to be presented.

❧ 19 ❧

I mmediately, his eyes were arrested by Elizabeth's as she stood with her family to welcome them. A slight smile breached his lips as he bowed in return. She wore a yellow gown, and he blinked in surprise at it. It was not new to him; he had seen her wear it once before. In fact, he recalled it was one she had worn at Netherfield when she stayed to nurse Miss Bennet. What startled him was the mere fact that it was not the dress he had become accustomed to seeing her wear during her sojourn with him in London. This reminder of how immediately tangible and perfectly earthly their situation was now delighted Darcy. She was a spectre no more though she held him still within her spell.

He walked with Mr Bingley to her, his lips muted by the living, breathing, physical Elizabeth before him. Her eyes were a deeper brown, her skin, though, still delightfully creamy, not eerily pale any more. *Her lips...* Darcy snapped his eyes back up to meet hers. His small smile grew until he was positively beaming at her.

"Miss Elizabeth, what a great pleasure to see you well again."

Darcy was jolted by Bingley's words, unable to understand how his friend could have managed to speak first. He turned again to Elizabeth, noting a slight question in her eyes as she examined them both.

"Indeed, Miss Elizabeth. It is a pleasure," Darcy repeated lamely, a little frustrated with himself for being unable to think of anything more significant to say. He was glad, however, to find that his ingrained sense of decorum did not fail him by permitting him to call her by her given name.

Elizabeth curtseyed and said, "Thank you Mr Bingley, Mr Darcy."

It was less than he would have liked to hear, but he understood that, while they stood amongst others, they could not speak in the manner to which they had grown accustomed. Though he did not want to admit it, he was a little disappointed that she had addressed her comments almost entirely to his friend, glancing only briefly at him when she said his name. Perhaps she had been merely directing her response in this manner since Bingley had spoken first.

There was an awkward pause then, and the gentlemen took the opportunity to claim seats. Darcy was disappointed to find the seat next to Elizabeth occupied by one of her sisters, and he was thus left to stand some way off near the fireplace. He did not wish to take up another seat and to be stuck there for the duration of the visit. Should Miss Catherine choose to stand at any point, he might have a chance then to claim the seat next to Elizabeth.

From his place by the fire, he was bothered that he had no share of the conversation with Bingley, Miss Bennet, and Elizabeth. He could only content himself with her frequent smiles, her pleased observations of her sister and his friend, and the sound of her delightful laugh as it whispered to him across the room. He was glad she could observe the fruits of their labours in London when he confessed to Bingley of his interference. Now she could see all would be made well in that quarter. What joy that would bring, and he was happy to witness its transformation on her features.

Occasionally, she cast shy glances at him, and each time he tried to convey the depth of his feelings for her through his gaze. He had the pleasure of seeing that his look would almost overwhelm her, for she would turn away quickly, a slight pucker to her sweet little brows. He imagined kissing that small spot and smoothing it out. Their enforced separation and their new state of being had brought about a return of her reserve, and he found it charming.

Thankfully, not many minutes after their arrival, a tray was brought in and placed at a table near him. He waited and watched as the ladies stood and prepared the tea; Miss Mary brought him a cup as Elizabeth sat contentedly on the sofa. He was gladdened she was willing to rest, for if the concerns voiced by her family prior to his entrance had any merit, she ought to save her strength until she was fully recovered.

To his greater pleasure, after preparing tea and plates of cake, Miss Catherine chose then to take up a seat with her youngest sister. He watched for a few minutes as they hovered in close conversation, wanting to make sure that her change of seat was not temporary. When he saw her settle in to work on the ribbons of a bonnet, he smiled to himself and carried his plate and teacup to take up the seat next to Elizabeth.

He was encouraged when she turned from her sister and Mr Bingley to accommodate him into the circle.

"Indeed, Eli—Miss Elizabeth, you look remarkably well; I hope that you will soon be in perfect health."

"Thank you, sir," she said politely. Without looking at him, she kept her eyes modestly at the plate on her lap. "And what have you been doing since we last met, Mr Darcy?"

"I have been rather bored actually," he answered artlessly, watching for the glimmer he expected to enter into her eyes. She looked up, but he only saw a slight puzzlement.

"I have missed the pleasure of companionable conversation," he hinted further for clarification. He could not very well say he missed her, not in front of so many people. She must understand that.

"Is not your sister capable of companionable conversation, sir? I should think that, given Miss Bingley's estimable praise, Miss Darcy would be found to be so."

Darcy was a beat behind in his response. He was not prepared for the reference to his sister. Elizabeth knew Georgiana, and she had proclaimed her charming. Still it was the tone of her voice that disquieted Darcy. It was everything civil, to be sure, but he had not anticipated her coolness.

"Georgiana is a most capable conversationalist," he said slowly whilst his mind worked around Elizabeth's behaviour. "Though we... I left her in London to come to Hertfordshire."

Elizabeth nodded and, picking at a piece of her cake, said as if in dismissal, "Well, I hope, sir, that you find your stay in our county a pleasurable one."

Astounded, he watched as she turned slightly to take in Bingley's conversation with Miss Bennet. Darcy sat there in silent contemplation as a small fissure of alarm picked at his heart. He beheld Elizabeth as he considered the painful, fearful thought that she might not remember their time together. It was an outcome that had never occurred to him!

He was oddly reminded of a time as a little boy that he watched a foreman carry hot tar up onto the roof of the stable. He was patching a leak there, and Darcy found the process fascinating. As he watched, however, the foreman lost his balance briefly and toppled over the bucket. The steaming, black tar slowly poured a path down the slope of the roof. Its sluggish, all-encompassing path captivated him as a child, and he had stayed rooted in the spot as he watched it eat away at the length of the roof towards the edge. When it reached the end of the roofline, it built up a small mass at the edge, clinging to it as it gained volume. It had cooled slightly on its way down the roof and had lost some of the momentum. Slowly, the mass of cooling tar rolled over the edge, hanging like an evil arm off the side, gravity forcing it to extend and stretch. He watched it fall and drape irregular and ugly scorching stripes across a barberry shrub. He remembered that, eventually, the gardener had to remove the plant as the shrub never fully recovered from the attack.

The destructive thought of Elizabeth not knowing of their time together was like tar on his heart; he could not fathom the idea of it any more than he could prevent the pain. It would render their time together a dream—his dream, of which she remembered no part. How was he to tell her about it? How was he to help her remember if, indeed, she could be made to remember? His face grew stern, contemplating this fear, and he felt the caustic coating of the tar over his heart. He would be unable to speak to her of their time in London. Which portion could he even mention: the horribly compromising part of their presence together in their bedchambers, the gentlemen's clubs, the fencing? She would not remember any of their extraordinary experience tethered together. The room felt all at once suffocating, and Darcy brought his cup to his lips to swallow the tepid liquid, hoping to dislodge the lump in his throat.

Our kiss. He almost groaned in pain, thinking she remained ignorant of their intimacy. *He* had thought of little else since placing his lips upon hers. Indeed, the more he thought on it, the clearer it became that now she acted the part of a woman untouched by love. He was growing more certain by the minute; she remembered nothing of their time.

Out of the corner of his eye, he detected her gaze. Looking up to meet her eyes, he saw a fire there. He recognised at once from the early days with her in London that it was anger and frustration. If she truly did not remember, then he could see his behaviour then was unforgivably rude as he sat next to her, silent and scowling. He attempted to lift the gravity off his face and hide the despair swallowing him.

"You have not touched your tea, Miss Elizabeth. May I refresh it for you?" Darcy asked, relieved his tone was gentle and tender still.

She shook her head. "No, I thank you. I have not a taste for tea at present, sir. Refreshing it will not change that, I fear."

If only I could have some kind of clue, some kind of hope that she was the least bit altered by our time together, he thought, *I might be able to prevent myself from drowning in this misery.*

He had to know for sure then, the uncertainty weighing most on him. He leaned into her, ignoring as best he could the way she immediately tried to pull away. He lowered his voice so that nobody else could hear and asked, "Miss Elizabeth, do you remember when last we were in company together?"

He watched her eyes meet his, and he saw all at once that she was thinking of something and it gave him hope. The faraway look in her eyes could not mean that he was totally lost to her. All at once though, he saw a change enter her eyes, and she said, "We have not met, sir, since the twenty-sixth of November when we were all dancing together at Netherfield."

Darcy sat upright then, his head nodding numbly. The pain rising in his breast was bound to drown him, and he knew he had to get away lest his bereavement become too much to hide. He did not know what he said then or how he excused himself, but soon he was standing and taking his leave of the rest of their party. He did recall assuring Bingley that he need not leave as well, stating urgent business he remembered that required his immediate attention or some other such nonsense. He looked at Elizabeth one last time and tried to memorise every detail of the very life that was in her.

He bowed to her last, and with a final, heartfelt farewell, he said, "Forgive me for having taken up so much of your time, and accept my best wishes for your health and happiness."

He then turned and walked stiffly out the door, not looking back and unable to bear the searing of the hot tar as it coated his heart.

ELIZABETH SAT MOTIONLESS, STILL STUNNED BY MR DARCY'S close proximity only moments before. She could detect his lingering cologne and felt almost as if she recognised it from somewhere. Perhaps her uncle Gardiner wore the same. She could make no sense of it. And then he had asked so carefully, yet almost urgently, about their last meeting—as if it held every importance in the world to him, though she could not think why. His reference to when they last saw each other had brought to mind her dream of him by her bedside, and she had been momentarily transfixed with the image of him so close to her.

When she had realised the length of her silence, she had cleared away the puzzling dream and answered him honestly. She could not understand why he seemed so entirely altered after that. He had mumbled some polite words on seeing her again and then stood to take his leave. She watched mesmerised by his formal manner, not unlike his accustomed behaviour to be sure, but somehow incongruent at the same time. While she puzzled over this, she was again startled to hear him address her as he bowed goodbye. His adieu was everything amiable, yet the tone of his voice sent shivers down her back. The finality felt there disquieted her though she could not think why.

But it was when he turned to leave that she was most shaken. She watched his silhouette, and it conjured the other gentleman, the one in the image that now flashed in her mind. Their gait and the sway of their shoulders matched perfectly. It all combined to create so great a turmoil in her mind that she soon was pressing small fingers into her temples.

Jane immediately sensed her distress and leaned towards her with concern. "Lizzy, are you well? May I help you back to your chamber?"

She suddenly longed severely for just that, the security of her room, though she could not say so. She remembered her earlier battle with her family to stay in the room to receive the gentlemen. She had wanted to observe Bingley for herself. She could not very well retreat to her room now that she had gained this freedom.

Shaking her head, she said, "I shall be fine, Jane. I only wish for some other refreshment."

Jane took her cup from her immediately.

"Shall I pour you some more tea?" Bingley asked kindly, trying to be of use.

Elizabeth smiled at him, grateful for his return and the joy it brought her sister. She shook her head though, and as a thought flitted through her mind, she knew what she wanted. "Jane, I think I should like a cup of coffee."

Jane blinked but did not move. Bingley stood then to find a servant and make the request.

His lady stopped him when she said, "You do not drink coffee, Lizzy. You detest the stuff."

"Still, I should like to have some all the same."

Elizabeth could not like the way Jane's eyes filled with a nervous worry. "Truly, Jane, I am well. I suffer only from a slight headache. I know it is strange, but coffee sounds appealing to me now."

"My father used to drink coffee when he got a megrim," Bingley offered, happy to contribute.

Jane looked at him and again at her sister and finally nodded. She stood to ring the bell to request a cup of coffee for Elizabeth.

When the tray came, Elizabeth began heaping spoonfuls of sugar into the brew. She did so almost instinctively, as if she knew exactly how she would like her coffee. She stirred it quickly and brought it to her lips. The dark liquid immediately was drunk with pleasure. The taste was heavenly to her, and she pulled the cup away to look at it in astonishment. Jane had been right when she had declared that Elizabeth did not like coffee. But it would seem now that, for some inexplicable reason, Elizabeth Bennet had developed a taste for the brew.

If only the gentleman who had just left had stayed! He might have had the sign, the hope he sought. But by that time, he was already issuing orders for his trunks to be packed and readied for his departure. A note lay on his friend's desk with an inadequate excuse for his hasty removal.

❧ 20 ❧

Within days, the news of the gentleman's departure made its way to the inhabitants of Longbourn and the surrounding areas though only his friend had puzzled much over it. *He* had thought Darcy's purpose in the area was of a more lasting type. Bingley's own long-term hopes for one lady of the area were sufficient to distract him from the abruptness of his friend's departure and instead to focus entirely on bringing about his own happiness.

Thus it was that, with a swiftness known to his character and without any further delay, Bingley set about to determine the heart of Miss Bennet and, once sufficiently encouraged, to secure it for himself. The happy news of her shy but eager acceptance was soon spread about the house with all the exuberance that such news often encounters. Such as it was, the excitement associated with her change in situation prevented the newly betrothed from having any private audience with her favourite sister. Not until later that night could Jane give a proper accounting of how the deed came about.

The two sisters retired to the eldest's room; attired in their sleeping gowns and warmed by their shawls and slippers, they prepared for a lengthy discussion of all the finer parts of the event.

"So, Mr Bingley was amiable enough this time, Jane," Elizabeth said by way of introduction and in reference to their discussion earlier in the week.

Jane's cheeks grew rosy, but she took up both of her sister's hands in hers and squeezed. "He is the very best of men, and I cannot think that I should be so happy."

Her sister smiled and expressed her own satisfaction in terms only a sister most beloved could. Pulling her feet up and under her, she leaned in with eager anticipation. "Tell me everything that happened. Do not leave out a single breath."

With contentment radiating in every way, Jane set out to describe the few minutes that changed the direction of her life and secured all the hopes of her future happiness. Mr Bingley had taken no gamble with the probability that they might find a quiet moment while on a stroll in the gardens and had quietly asked for a private audience from the start. This request was granted with all due haste by Mrs Bennet, who amused everyone as she ushered them out of the room, leaving her eldest daughter with a kiss on her blushing cheeks and a heart thrumming quite out of control.

Elizabeth listened with warm tenderness as her sister detailed the all too important moment.

"It was all I could do to shakily nod my head. My eyes were already betraying the emotion I was feeling."

Elizabeth smiled, retaining Jane's hand in hers, and encouraged her to go on. Her sister's happiness was, next to nothing else in this world, the most important thing to her. Having known the suffering Jane had endured during her separation from Mr Bingley, this was a most satisfactory end to a lengthy ordeal.

"Once confident of my assent, he shared with me something that quite surprised me."

"And...?" Elizabeth urged with a smile. "Come, Jane, do not delay, I am all anticipation."

Still her sister paused before continuing. "I am concerned with your reaction. I fear you may be angered."

"Angered?" cried she in surprise. "I fail to see how any part of such a charming proposal could anger me."

Jane eyed her sister with concern. "It has something to do with his friend Mr Darcy."

Elizabeth was silent, unsure of what to say. It was no secret that, before her accident, Elizabeth did not hold that gentleman in any favour, but since waking up, she felt slightly differently. It was not as if she admired the man—that did not seem a likely thing—but it was almost as if she could no longer find within her the dislike she had once held so staunchly.

She did not share this ambivalence she felt with Jane because it was all a part of the growing list of different sensations since waking. Deny it though she would, she felt a listlessness about her that could not be explained by fatigue or continuing recovery. She had preferences that were decidedly not the same as before her accident, her peculiar taste for coffee being foremost among them. This ennui, combined with the other changes she bore, as well as the troubling flashes of places and persons she did not know, were enough for Elizabeth to keep her own counsel. She feared the return of the wariness so previously prevalent in the eyes of her family and only recently beginning to fade. It was as if, in the couple of days since she first ventured down to the drawing rooms to await the call from the gentlemen from Netherfield, her family had begun to trust in her recovery, and Longbourn had taken a collective sigh of relief. Elizabeth was not about to stir any more worry on her account over a few trifling changes, troubling though some may be.

Elizabeth also knew of her sister's suspicions regarding Mr Darcy, and hesitantly, she thus began, "I know that you have your beliefs about Mr Darcy, and I beg you not to repeat them. The man does not favour me."

Though not what she was about to reveal to her sister, Jane felt she needed to defend her opinions.

"Lizzy, you are entirely too quick to dismiss your own charms in general. I do believe that Mr Darcy esteems you. He was much too solicitous of your health to be—"

"Yes, Jane, because gentlemen who are enamoured often flee the neighbourhood wherein the object of their desire resides," Elizabeth interrupted with a sigh and a disbelieving smile.

"Mr Bingley once did just that, and I believe at the time you were insistent that he was in love with me," Jane said pointedly.

Elizabeth bit her lip, holding in a laugh. "Indeed, and fortunately for the both of us, though more so for you, I was correct in that opinion."

Jane gave her sister a look that said she ought to see the similarities.

"Jane, their manner is entirely different. When Mr Bingley took his leave last autumn, he did so after quite clearly showing his preference for you in front of all of Hertfordshire. When he returned, he took up exactly where he left off. And today we have seen the evidence of his admiration for you as he has asked for your hand."

"I think it is only that you do not like Mr Darcy, that you are so determined to dismiss my thoughts on the matter."

Elizabeth sighed and, giving her sister's hand a squeeze, said kindly, "I apologise if you feel that I have dismissed your opinions on the matter as naught. I simply cannot see anything in Mr Darcy's manner last autumn or during his *brief* visit most recently that would suggest he favours me."

The two sisters looked intently at each other. It was the only point of contention they had ever really had, and each looked at it with so different a view that it was impossible they should come to terms with the other's stance.

Jane suspected the gentleman's preference though she would admit that his manner of wooing lacked a certain finesse, and though she could not prove it with any finality, she very much hoped that it was the case. She had always thought better of Mr Darcy than had her sister and had felt that, should her sister look beyond his initial poor impression, then Elizabeth might find in him an equal partner in intelligence, passion, and wit. Besides, it made perfect sense to Jane that two persons so well favoured by herself and her betrothed might come to care for each other.

For Elizabeth's part, she held no animosity towards the gentleman, puzzling though that was given her previous sentiments. And while she could not account for *that* change in her feelings, she could see quite plainly his own. While in company with him, he was often grave, serious, and silent. True, he did often look upon her, but Elizabeth felt as if that might be interpreted as abstraction of mind on the gentleman's part. She knew of her sister's hopes for a possible match, and she was endeared to her for her sentimentality given Jane's current state of happiness. It was quite natural that, once assured of their own joy, people often wished to ensure that of those close to them.

"Come, let us not quarrel about this tonight, Jane. You were just speaking of your happy moment. You have not finished what Mr Bingley said to you that you found surprising." Elizabeth could see that her sister still hesitated and thus said, "If you are concerned for my reaction, you need not say."

Though her curiosity was piqued, Elizabeth was sincere in her statement.

"I do wish to share with you what Mr Bingley said. Only I fear that you will be too much upset by the beginning that you may not see the virtue in the end."

"I promise to withhold judgment then until the end. Will that satisfy?"

Jane was a moment in answering and, with a nod, thus began. "Mr Bingley explained to me his absence last autumn and his delay in returning as soon as he had planned."

Elizabeth's brows rose at this, and she pursed her lips, interested to know his explanation. She could see, though, that Jane was nervous, and that made Elizabeth suspicious.

"Once in town he was persuaded to stay by his friend and sisters. They believed it was in his best interest to quit the neighbourhood entirely."

"Is that so?" Elizabeth said with some heat, but upon seeing her sister's stern look, she was reminded of her promise.

Jane then related the extent to which Mr Bingley had missed her in the meantime, but having been convinced by his friend and family that she did not return his affections, he instead agreed to remain in town.

Elizabeth was surprised to find, upon examining her feelings during this revelation, that she could not be angered at the gentleman's interference. Though she believed she ought, instead she felt an uncharacteristic hesitation to condemn Mr Darcy. Did she not counsel her sister days ago to be more open to Mr Bingley and leave him in no doubt of her feelings? If Mr Darcy was concerned that Jane did not care for his friend, would it not be natural that he might wish to save Mr Bingley the pain of discovery upon a later date? Elizabeth was slightly startled by this reasoning and by the objectivity on her part.

Jane took advantage of her sister's silence and continued. "I wished to share not the reason Charles left"—Jane blushed at her first use of his Christian name with her sister—"but the astonishing intelligence of what brought him back to the neighbourhood. I had thought that perhaps news of our accident had reached him through my letter to his sister, but when he returned, he seemed genuinely surprised and upset to learn of it as if he had not known beforehand. He shared with me today that his friend persuaded him to return."

Elizabeth looked up at her sister with interest.

"Mr Darcy came to him and confessed that he thought he might have been in error and was concerned that, indeed, I might care for Mr Bingley. He came in hopes that Charles might decide to find the truth of the matter himself by returning."

Abruptly Elizabeth's eyes became unfocused and her mind distracted by a fleeting image. It was so swift to pass through her consciousness that it was gone before she could grasp it. She shook her head to clear the haze and returned to the present conversation.

"What could have been Mr Darcy's motive in doing so if, as you said before, he had doubts sufficient to make him give the initial advice for quitting the neighbourhood?"

"Charles said he was not at liberty to say exactly but that his friend wished only to right a possible wrong and to hope for his happiness. Do you not think this singular proof of Mr Darcy's goodness?"

Elizabeth eyed her sister with amusement but was silent for a minute. "It is quite a singular thing to discuss during a *proposal*, to be sure."

Nodding, she looked down at where their hands were clasped together. "I cannot deny the truth of that; however, I shall be glad forever that he shared this with me. For it went a long way to proving his constancy, which I believe was his motive in all."

"I think you may be correct."

Seeing her sister's cheeks begin to flush, Elizabeth suspected there might be more of the proposal to relate, and though the hour was late, their evening was not yet over.

"And...after this most serious revelation..." Elizabeth prompted.

"He made a promise never to leave me again."

"But I suspect there is yet more. Indeed, I can see from your cheeks there is. Come now, sister; tell me all!"

Elizabeth watched as Jane shot her a wicked smile, and though she still could not quite meet Elizabeth's eyes for any length of time, she said, "Let us just say that, were it not for Mama's immediately bursting into the room not long after his explanation—"

"She could not be persuaded not to listen at the door though I tried!"

Jane shrugged and pulled at a loose thread from her shawl. With a tremor to her voice, she continued, "Were it not for her interruption, I believe that Mr Bingley may have attempted to...be even more amiable."

Elizabeth chortled in hilarity and hugged her sister. "I have no doubt. Mr Bingley is a very amiable gentleman."

"Lizzy!" Jane laughed. Though just thinking of receiving a kiss from Mr Bingley was enough to bring Jane's cheeks to full bloom and send them both into sisterly speculations as to how it might be accomplished and what it might be like to be kissed by a gentleman. Elizabeth unconsciously tasted her lips during the course of the discussion, feeling a tingling sensation.

As the days of January faded into the early weeks of February, Elizabeth found that, although she slowly regained her physical strength, the strange blanket over her emotions remained. It was not that she did not feel things; it was that, with some things, she felt differently, and at other times, she felt as if she were totally disconnected from her heart.

She was walking around the garden in contemplation of these changes when she heard footsteps on the frosty ground coming from behind her. Turning, she welcomed the visitor with surprise.

"Mr Wickham! It has been an age since we saw you last, sir!" Elizabeth said, laughing.

The gentleman bowed to her and said, "Miss Elizabeth, I am truly gladdened by the scene before me! For here you are, standing in perfect health once again."

Elizabeth felt an unease begin the moment she heard his voice. Unable to account for it, she pushed it aside. "As you see, sir."

"I hope you will forgive the tardiness of my visit," he said with a flirtatious smile that spoke of his assurance of her absolution. "My duties as an officer have not readily made it possible for me to call upon you until now. I had heard that you were very ill, but it seems you have made a quick recovery."

"It was not quick, I assure you," Elizabeth said amiably. The unease she felt earlier increased; nothing in his actions or manner of speaking were improper, yet she felt much apprehension.

"May I escort you inside? My friends have come with me to call and are already within."

Elizabeth nodded; yet, when she reached to take his arm, she immediately felt a panic bloom within her breast that she ought not to trust this man. It alarmed her enough for her to pause with her arm extended not quite to him. Her eyes flew to his, and she saw nothing there that was unfamiliar. He still had an open countenance, and he was clearly waiting expectantly for her to take his arm. The disquiet she felt in this discovery of yet another change within her made her pull her arm back and return her hand to its mate within the warmth of her muff.

"I had not realised how very cold it is, sir. I think I should like to allow my hands the benefit of my muff if you do not mind."

His easy smile was incongruent with her feelings, and she winced.

"Not at all. Shall we?" He gestured towards the walk that led back to the house, and soon they were enveloped in the warmth of Longbourn.

After divesting their outerwear, they made their way to the sitting room with a slightly awkward silence that the gentleman easily accepted was due to the length of time since they had been in company together. Wickham smiled to himself at her obvious feelings for him. He could tell that she was more timid towards him, perhaps even punishing him for his negligence. He liked her for her intellect and looked forward to bringing the bloom to her cheeks again as he charmed his way back into her good graces.

Elizabeth only needed to be among her family again, and she instinctively knew that, once void of Wickham's sole company, she would feel better. She was relieved that the constriction about her chest released, and she felt more at ease once they entered the room.

She looked for a place to sit among the many officers, and just as her companion was about to guide her to a secluded set of chairs on the side of the room, Elizabeth noted with relief that Lydia made her way to them in haste. Elizabeth could not be more thankful for her youngest sister's enthusiasm for officers and was pleased to see Lydia wedge her way between them.

"Mr Wickham, it is such a surprise to see you here," she began. "You have not paid a visit to Longbourn since before the new year."

Elizabeth noted a slight edge to her sister's voice but put it off as her imagination. She looked at the gentleman and could see that he, too, had perceived something in her sister's tone, and at once Elizabeth wondered whether Lydia really was displeased with Mr Wickham.

Wickham, indeed, had noticed the sharpness in Lydia's voice and smiled to himself at the evidence that yet another Bennet lady had missed him. Lydia was a wild one, and he enjoyed her sauciness as much as he was stimulated by Elizabeth's ready wit. And both had figures that pleased him. He was not concerned over any apparent change in their behaviour towards him. It mattered not as he was quite capable of winning over both of them, and he would take pleasure doing so.

"Miss Lydia." Wickham bowed handsomely and raised her hand to his face. Though he did not place a kiss on it, he looked seriously at her. "Please forgive me. As I was telling your sister earlier, an officer's time is often not his own when in the service of our king."

Elizabeth was surprised, then, to see her sister pull her hand out of his grasp with a decided shake of her head. Lydia took up Elizabeth's arm, pulling her firmly to her side. "Indeed, it would *appear*, however, that Miss *King* is the only sovereign whose favour you seek, Mr Wickham."

Wickham started at this and still had the politesse to colour.

Though he did not like that either Bennet lady might have reason to withdraw from his attentions due to his engagement to Miss King, he did, however, find pleasure in the idea that now formed in his mind. A catlike grin formed as he presumed that the ever-entertaining, ever-cheeky Lydia was jealous of his transfer of affections to Miss King. Indeed, as he looked at Elizabeth's pinched brow, he could see that she might be feeling the slight as well.

"Ladies," he purred, "do not be angry with me." Here he gave them each his best look of contrition before continuing with his seduction. "The ladies of Longbourn have held and will always hold a special place for me. But you must concede that handsome young men must have something to live on as well as the plain."

Elizabeth was struck with the mercenary sound of his words despite his teasing efforts. Her unease in his presence remained, however, even with her sister holding dearly to her arm. Elizabeth observed Lydia, who looked quite put out. Upon consideration, Elizabeth could not comprehend why such would be the case unless Lydia was perhaps jealous of Miss King's good fortune. She knew her sister's nature would be to behave petulantly with Wickham in an attempt to regain his attention. But still more likely, Elizabeth thought, Lydia might just as easily turn her own attentions towards another.

While Elizabeth puzzled over her sister, Lydia was far from confused. She had seen her sister come in with Wickham, and it had brought to the fore all the growing resentments she had for the man. His worst sin in Lydia's eyes, however, was his blatant disregard for the feelings of others when he cared not an ounce to come and call in the aftermath of the accident. Even now, it was nearly a month since Elizabeth had awakened, and he was only just calling!

Lydia stepped closer to Wickham then, and by virtue of her hold on Elizabeth's arm, her sister was brought forward too. The gentleman leaned in, encouraged by the fi re in Lydia's eyes but misinterpreting it.

Lydia lowered her voice, so that she might not be heard, and passionately began to speak. "Mr Wickham, let us be clear and not make excuses. You cared not to visit us when our family would have welcomed a kind ear. You cared not to show any constancy in your regard for any member of this household. I will not embarrass you, however much you have offended me, by asking you to take your leave immediately, but I will say this: you are not welcome, sir, in this home any more." Elizabeth felt her sister's grip tighten even as her own jaw fell in astonishment. She listened, positively amazed, as her sister poured forth a grave warning. "And should you choose to disregard this and attempt to associate with us outside of these walls, I will notify my father immediately."

Wickham's brows rose in bewilderment as if he had never before been spurned by a lady. Elizabeth was quite stunned yet delighted by Lydia's pronouncement. Though she had not thought to condemn the gentleman—given that she was not particularly troubled by his absence—she could see that her sister was offended and rightly so when his sins were put forth in such a manner. Elizabeth was filled with a familial sense of pride for the uncharacteristic show of maturity and loyalty on Lydia's part, and she gave her arm a squeeze since words were beyond her.

Mr Wickham at that time had the good grace to blush and quietly bowed as he backed away, feigning a new interest in the view outside the window for the remainder of the visit.

After watching him retreat, and upon gaining her wits again, Elizabeth turned to her sister. "Brava, Lydia. Whatever caused you to champion me against the gentleman in such a way?" Lydia looked down at her shoes, and Elizabeth realised she had never before seen her sister demur. Elizabeth tilted her head until she could see into Lydia's eyes once more and said, "Come, dear sister, I am proud of you."

"I did not like...that is, I...I could not like it when you were so ill."

Elizabeth, who was filled then with a feeling of tenderness for her often impulsive, always passionate sister, reached to place a hand on Lydia's cheek.

"But as you see, I am well now."

"I may not always show it," Lydia said as she straightened and affected composure. "But I do care for my sisters, and I did not like the thought of...of losing you. Furthermore, that gentleman"—she gestured with a flick of her fan—"acted as if nothing had happened."

WITH A DEFINITIVE STROKE OF HIS QUILL, DARCY MADE A CLEAR black line across the ledger, delineating the end of the section before he signed and dated it. He paused before placing his pen once again in its holder and handing the book to his steward.

"What is next, my good man?" he said with more briskness than he intended.

His steward did not react but merely answered in an even tone. "That is all, Mr Darcy. We have finished the last of them and in good time too."

"That is all? But surely we cannot be finished," Darcy said, looking about, aware that a slight panic was worming its way into his consciousness. He needed to stay busy, or he would never be able to move on.

"We have in three weeks finished the audits that usually take us two months, sir. I have no doubt that, with the hours you have devoted, you are now in need of some well-deserved leisure."

Leisure was the last thing Darcy wished for—or needed. He looked at his steward and was aware that he was acting with uncharacteristic exertion regarding his estate matters. Still he needed further distraction. Hoping it did not come out like a plea, he said, "Surely, there is something else that needs to be done. This is a great estate, Jacobs. What is next on the list?"

The older man laughed and began to pack his books into his satchel. "For you, nothing. Even I do not have much left to do, thanks to your studied employment these last weeks."

"What is on your list still? Perhaps there is something..." Darcy's voice died away at the man's strange expression.

"I assure you, Mr Darcy, it is nothing that I cannot handle. You need not concern yourself, and I must earn the wages you pay me, sir," said Jacobs good-humouredly with his long-time employer. They had always had a comfortable working relationship stemming from a mutual respect of the other's talents.

When he could see that Mr Darcy looked momentarily disappointed at his statement, he paused. He had wondered at the increased energy with which his employer had attacked their work over the past few weeks since his unscheduled arrival at Pemberley.

Knowing that it was not his place to ask, Jacobs held his tongue and studied his master's face.

"Tomorrow, I shall oversee some preparation on the land east of the river in the lower fields."

Darcy looked up eagerly. "What time shall I meet you, sir?"

"I had thought to ride out at eight."

Darcy stood, and with evident relief, he shook hands with his steward and walked him to the door. "I shall see you tomorrow then."

Mr Jacobs paused at the threshold of the master's study. He looked up at the young man and again thought to say something. Mr Darcy had worked relentlessly for weeks and looked as if he had not slept the entire time. A break was perhaps warranted though Jacobs knew it was not his place to suggest it. "Perhaps, sir, Miss Darcy might wish to come to Pemberley as well? I could arrange for her transport."

Darcy smiled kindly at his steward and patted him on the back as he ushered him through the door. "I think we are far too busy to consider that option for now. I would hate to have her come all this way and find that I have no time to spend with her. Besides, she is quite happily ensconced at Darcy House with Colonel Fitzwilliam."

Knowing that to say anything more would be out of line, Jacobs nodded, bowed to his master, and left him to walk to the steward's office at the back of the house

Darcy watched until the man was out of sight before turning around and closing himself off in his study. It was still midday, and until that moment, he had eagerly distracted himself with estate business from sunrise to sunset since coming from Hertfordshire.

Wincing at the thought of his most recent travels, Darcy paced to the window to look out at the winter scene. He could not and he would not think of Elizabeth.

He had thought at first to go to London upon quitting Netherfield and had written to that end when he had left a note for Bingley. But he knew as soon as the first change of horses that he could not bear to go there. He informed his coachmen, and they changed direction to travel directly to Pemberley. It was a fortunate change of plans, for he had only to inform his butler in London of his location in case of an emergency, and he was left alone. Bingley thought him in London, his cousin and sister would think he was in Hertfordshire. A part of him knew he ought to better inform them. Of course, he would eventually.

Though Pemberley was certainly a longer carriage ride—one that was made more difficult by the empty seat opposite, mocking him—it was exactly the place he most needed to be.

He had to escape to a place he could find solitude despite his loneliness. He needed to be away from the worried eyes of his sister, outside the prying observations of his cousin, and most certainly, absent from the home where *she* had haunted him, quite literally.

❧ 21 ❧

E lizabeth bent distractedly to pick up a long, grey branch lying across the path as she walked in solitude about her home's gardens. All around her, the grip of winter was showing signs of loosing its hold on the landscape to the warmer days and verdant hues of a budding spring. Her eyes were unseeing as her fingers twisted and turned the thin branch back and forth, a remnant of a dying season. There were scattered branches, brush, and general debris left about from many months of snowy hibernation.

Within the coming weeks, as spring took up its stewardship over the land, the gardeners would again come to clean, prune, and coach these pathways into their normally wild, yet beautiful splendour.

Her mind was focused elsewhere, however, as she twisted the branch in her hands, occasionally letting her arm drop to sweep it across the barren ground. Try as she might, she could not shake the grey grip of winter on her heart. She took joy in her family, in Jane's felicity, and in having her strength completely restored to her, yet she could not feel truly well. Occasionally, she still experienced a dull ache in her head, but it was the hibernation of her heart that was responsible for the majority of her concern.

Though she had grown used to some of the changes in herself, she could not yet account for any of them. It made sense to her that, with the seriousness of her injury, she might find some things changed. Yet she also felt as if she were missing something, as if she were not really experiencing a change in herself but mourning a part of her that was gone.

A sudden well of frustration pressed against her ribs from within, and with a quiet cry of agitation, she lifted the switch in her hand and swiped it through the air in front of her. The aggression lifted her spirits slightly, and she felt the tiniest bit of relief from her oppression. Eager for more, Elizabeth began shifting back and forth with her feet as she raised her arm level with her shoulder and swiftly slashed the stick through the air, a satisfying swishing sound accompanying it.

"Ah-ha!" cried she as her movements grew more deliberate and forceful. Her heart began to beat fiercely, and for a moment, she felt quite a bit more alive than she had in recent weeks.

For several minutes, she thrust, shifted her feet, and swiped again, unaware that she had an observer not many feet behind her. Her arms ached with the exertion of her impromptu exercise, yet she could not command them to cease, so great was the relief she felt from it.

Born of her frustration, the strike of the branch across the valiant opponent of the bush she now fought was cathartic and satisfying. She felt connected to that troublesome organ within her as it beat loudly in her ears. She felt exhilarated by the movements of her body, surprised by her agility and the practiced movements she had never before attempted. Elizabeth poured into each strike and swipe of her garden-forged sword every last bit of her listlessness over the past couple of weeks, her confusion over the feelings in her breast, the unreachable images that flashed in her mind, and the feeling of loss she experienced.

When her arm could take the onslaught no more, she allowed it to fall to her side as she breathed heavily. She reached one hand up to wipe her brow and found, much to her astonishment, that her face was wet with tears. This discovery stole her recent bout of strength. Her shoulders drooped inward as her head dipped, allowing her tears to fall unhindered to the disturbed ground.

Her observer sighed and walked slowly towards her. He had been watching first through the window of his study as his daughter walked the grounds as if in a daze. He was troubled by this change in his beloved Lizzy. She used to be so vibrant with life, and now she seemed masked in a haze that kept her smiles from reaching her eyes. When she began to fence an imaginary foe, his concern turned into amazement to find her skilled. He had come to ask her about this new accomplishment of hers, wondering how she came to learn it. It did not occur to him that he ought to frown at any lady knowing the finer points of a gentlemen's sport. It was not until he saw his daughter's distress at the end of her match with the hedge that he grew concerned again.

Slowly Elizabeth became aware of strong arms surrounding her, and she allowed the comforting scent of her father's cologne to wrap her like a blanket as she cried into his shoulder.

Surprised and worried further by her tears, he patted her head, gently brushing away the tangled ringlets at her ear. "Come, my dear; put down your foil."

He gently removed the branch from her tight grasp and tossed it aside. As Mr Bennet looked down at her, his anxiety grew again. She felt so fragile in his arms, yet he had seen the fierceness with which she had attacked the demons in her heart.

"Come, my child; let us go in. Though March is upon us, there is yet a chill in the air that these old bones cannot abide."

Elizabeth nodded numbly, and as they turned to walk the path back to the house, she made use of the handkerchief he held out to her to wipe away her tears. She could not describe her feelings then though she was grateful for the strength of her father's arm as they made their way inside. She was not surprised to see him wordlessly guide her directly into his study.

Mr Bennet deposited his daughter gently into a chair near the hearth and went to close his study door for privacy. He stoked the fire, placed a blanket about her now trembling shoulders, and then went purposefully to the chest near his desk. He unlocked its treasures and knelt on the hard floor before his daughter, the tin of chocolates placed reverently on her lap.

Elizabeth, upon seeing his offering, could not help but give a watery laugh and reach to place a cold hand on his cheek.

Mr Bennet pulled her hand from his face and began to rub some warmth into it as he looked into his daughter's shiny eyes. "Lizzy, my dear, shall you tell me what troubles your heart so terribly?"

Elizabeth smiled tenderly at her father, warmed by the love she saw so clearly in his expression. Suddenly, she wished fervently that she might tell him of her troubles—that she might share the burden she carried.

"I hardly know, Papa."

"Come, you are chilled. I shall order some tea, and we shall have a cosy chat by the fire like we used to, and you shall tell your Papa about this great black beast you carry on your back."

Elizabeth breathed deeply and nodded, prepared to tell him her concerns and encouraged by his tender words. Mr Bennet stood to pull the cord and, when the maid came in response, began to request a tray.

Elizabeth's brows puckered slightly when she heard her father order a pot of coffee with the tea and knew then that he had observed this and likely others of the changes in her. When the tray came, without a word he poured her a cup of coffee and, with a bemused face, passed the sugar bowl to her.

"I find it entirely unbelievable that you should prefer coffee now."

Elizabeth shrugged. "I cannot account for it myself, only I find that, although I do not dislike tea, coffee has a certain comforting appeal now."

"Interesting," was all he said as she prepared his cup of tea to his liking.

When they were both seated near the fire, the warmth of their cups in their hands, he spoke again. His eyes were on her as she gazed into the fire. "Lizzy, the coffee is not the only change I have witnessed in you since your accident."

Elizabeth turned and gave him an apologetic smile. "I know. You mentioned earlier our talks by the fire, and I realised I had not come to visit with you like this since before the accident."

"I am glad you are here now," Mr Bennet said with some emotion.

Elizabeth nodded, acknowledging the more significant meaning behind his words. It pained her to know how much her family worried for her, and it was the primary reason she tried to hide her disquiet so determinedly.

"Papa..." Elizabeth began, pausing slightly and pulling her gaze back to the fire. "I do not quite feel myself. Ooh, that is not quite it either," Elizabeth stammered in frustration. "It is almost as if I am missing something or more like I feel I have misplaced something of great value."

Mr Bennet observed his daughter silently, a frown at his brow. "I have worried that you have not been happy, Lizzy."

"I am not *unhappy* exactly," Elizabeth tried to put words to her puzzling feelings. "There are so many things for which I have to be happy—Jane's felicity in particular. Yet I still feel... It feels as if..."

"You still feel asleep."

Startled, Elizabeth looked up at her father. That was almost exactly how she felt, yet she had not found words to describe it until then. "Yes! It is like I am still sleeping, dreaming of all this yet not really experiencing life."

"I wish I could mend it for you, Lizzy, this strangeness you feel. I fear it will not be as easy as when you would come to me as a child with scrapes about your hands from falling out of a tree."

Elizabeth laughed half-heartedly as he had hoped she would. She fumbled with the tin on her lap and took out a chocolate, toying with its paper wrapper for a minute and turning it about in her hands.

Her quiet tone was barely heard by her companion. "Do you think I shall ever be well again?"

The tremble in her voice nearly broke her father's heart. It was not fair that he should be so incapable of fixing her troubles. It was a father's right and responsibility to do so. Even now, Mr Bennet felt the frustrating helplessness that all gentlemen feel when faced with the tears of a lady. His inability to right the wrongs and slay her dragons pressed upon him. Though he often relegated himself to his book room instead of being in company with his family, it was not from lack of feeling for them. It was due to a surfeit of this impotency he felt when confronted with their trifles, troubles, and tears. His Lizzy was special in that way to him for she very rarely cried, thus very rarely rendering his heart broken.

"I think so, my dear." As he reassured her, he wished to reassure himself.

His gaze roamed the room as he tried to puzzle through possible solutions in his mind. When his view reached his desk, he happened upon a letter there. It was from his ridiculous cousin Mr Collins. The cleric had written many weeks ago to express his obnoxious pontifications regarding the news of the carriage accident. The letter itself held nothing of concern for the welfare of his cousins but only the many suggestions kindly given by Mr Collins's benefactor, Lady Catherine de Bourgh, as to how he might better instruct his coachmen to drive in the snow so as to avoid a reoccurrence of the tragedy. Mr Bennet remembered he had quit reading when Mr Collins had offered, quite magnanimously, to officiate over Elizabeth's funeral should that "unhappy, though quite likely, event take place," all the while stating that it was through the benevolence of the great lady from Rosings Park that he should be allowed to extend them this great mercy.

Though angered again at the odious pomposity of his cousin, seeing the letter did bring an idea to Mr Bennet's mind. With a flicker of hope, he turned to his daughter. Elizabeth was drinking her coffee slowly as she snuggled into the seat.

"I believe what you need is a change of scenery."

Elizabeth looked at her father with a crease between her brows. "I do not take your meaning."

Mr Bennet, now warmed to this idea, felt invigorated by the possible solution he felt he had found. "It is yet dreary here, Lizzy. It will still be many weeks before the colours of spring are full upon us here in Hertfordshire. It would be better to distract yourself."

Elizabeth began warily, "And what are you suggesting, Papa."

"Mrs Collins née Lucas extended an invitation to you, did she not?"

"Yes, but that was many weeks ago at her wedding and before she quit the neighbourhood with Mr Collins."

"I do not believe she has withdrawn her invitation."

"No, she has not," Elizabeth said slowly. The idea of visiting Hunsford was not exactly appealing to her. Though renewing her friendship with Charlotte held some allure, renewing her acquaintance with Charlotte's husband, not so much. Still she pondered her father's suggestion. A change of scenery might actually help distract her from the troubles weighing on her.

"I believe Sir William and Maria leave in only a se'nnight. Should you like to go to Kent?"

Elizabeth smiled at her father. She could see he held a hope for this, and it was that spark in his eyes that made the decision for her. While she had almost shared with him a more detailed account of her concerns—namely, the troubling flashes of rooms, places, and people she could not explain—she was glad now that she had not. It was difficult to keep that to herself; yet, seeing the worry leave her father's eyes was enough to convince Lizzy to keep her counsel again when it came to *that* change.

"I think you may be correct. A change of scenery may be what I need after all to pull myself out of this heaviness."

Mr Bennet clapped his hands and stood with an eagerness born of a man relieved to have something of use to do. He went to his desk and wrote immediately to Sir William to inform him of Elizabeth's accompanying them. Once finished, he quickly placed a writing desk on his daughter's lap, a pen and paper at the ready.

Elizabeth laughed and looked up at him, amused at his enthusiasm.

"Write to Mrs Collins, Lizzy. Accept her invitation, and I shall post it today."

A feeling of rightness seeped into her heart then, and whether it was her father's conviction that stirred her own or something else, Elizabeth felt then that at Hunsford she might find what she had lost. Laughing, she bent her head to quickly pen a letter to her friend.

"Mr Bingley! Well met, sir!" Colonel Fitzwilliam said brightly as he encountered the man exiting White's.

Bingley looked up at the sound of his name and smiled cheerfully at the colonel. "Hallo, Colonel Fitzwilliam. It is a pleasure to see you again."

Colonel Fitzwilliam laughed and, patting the other gentleman's back, steered him back up the steps of the club. "Have you a minute to share a drink with me, sir? I should like to have news of my cousin. But first, my good man, how is it that you are in London?"

Bingley frowned slightly before laughing with his companion. "I have but a minute, Colonel. I am in London on very important business."

The manner in which he said this made the colonel pause as he divested his outerwear to the waiting attendant. He looked at Mr Bingley, his lips twitching in amusement as he saw the gentleman's glowing smile. "Am I to wish you joy, Bingley?"

Mr Bingley beamed and stood taller, pushing his chest out proudly. "I must ask that you do, Colonel, for I am bound for leg shackles and cannot be happier."

Colonel Fitzwilliam laughed heartily at this, expecting nothing less from the energetic gentleman before him. When they found an empty table, the colonel extended his hand in genuine congratulations.

"I am well pleased to hear it, sir. When shall be the happy day?"

"We plan to marry in May, sir, and you must come to Hertfordshire for the wedding. I insist!"

A deep chuckle resonated in the colonel's chest as he settled himself into a seat and ordered a drink, all whilst nodding his assent to Bingley. "I would not miss it; you may be sure of that. So I assume this important business in London has to do with your fortuitous new change in situation?"

Bingley smiled widely. "That is does, sir. I came to review the final copies of the settlement papers and then hope to be back in Hertfordshire immediately."

"Good, good. Now, sir, I demand you give me news of my cousin. He has been a dissolute writer since going to Hertfordshire though I suspect his *reasons* have been quite pressing." Colonel Fitzwilliam laughed somewhat wickedly at his own wit and awaited Bingley's report on Darcy's success with Miss Elizabeth.

Bingley frowned, making Colonel Fitzwilliam frown.

"Darcy is not in London?"

"My cousin is not in Hertfordshire?"

"Indeed, not. He left some months ago on urgent business to London. I have not heard from him since." Bingley's grimace deepened. "Though, I confess I have been a poor friend, my own mind quite occupied."

Colonel Fitzwilliam sat up at this news. "But he has not come to London and still has all his post forwarded away."

"Well, it is most certainly not forwarded to Hertfordshire. I had hoped to see Darcy while in London. One of my tasks was to ask him to stand up with me. You do not fear some misfortune to have come upon Darcy, do you?"

Colonel Fitzwilliam shook his head though he worried. When his cousin had informed him he was going to Hertfordshire to win the heart of the lady who had claimed his, Richard had assumed that was exactly what he was doing. Remembering his strange behaviour in the weeks before leaving London, the colonel was again filled with dread.

"I had thought, considering Miss Elizabeth's recovery, that Darcy would be elated. We all were certainly well relieved. But he stayed hardly long enough to see her before leaving on business. What business could he have, sir?" Bingley speculated with concern.

"I have not a clue, but I assure you I plan to find out just as soon as I find out where in the blazes he is."

Colonel Fitzwilliam stood then to leave, determining to question his cousin's staff as to Darcy's whereabouts, assuming correctly that they would know where they were instructed to send his cousin's post. "Mr Carroll ought to know—" Colonel Fitzwilliam stopped as a thought flashed through his mind. "Bingley, you referred to Miss Elizabeth's *recovery*. Has some misfortune befallen the lady?"

"She was in a carriage accident on the New Year with her sister— my betrothed—and was in a coma for quite some time. She had only awakened a few days before Darcy quit the neighbourhood."

Colonel Fitzwilliam pondered this as they exited the club and hailed a hackney. "And my cousin—did something happen to him while he sojourned with you?"

Bingley shook his head, frowning. "I cannot think of anything, sir. He stayed but a se'nnight."

For the majority of the ride to Darcy House, the gentlemen were in silent accordance of their fears and concerns regarding Darcy. Upon reaching his house, the gentlemen scaled the steps quickly and immediately asked to speak with the butler. Their concerns were alleviated slightly to learn that, though Darcy had not had any kind of accident himself, he had quite abruptly secreted himself away at Pemberley for the better part of the last two months.

"Colonel Fitzwilliam, sir. If I may say something?"

The colonel looked up from his impassioned pacing to see that Mrs Carroll had entered the room to join her husband, the butler, in his interview regarding their master.

Colonel Fitzwilliam slowed to a stop and nodded to the housekeeper. "Have you something to add, Mrs Carroll?"

He watched, somewhat more alarmed, as the usually composed, and frankly a little imposing, housekeeper wiped a tear from her eye with her apron. "I have been in contact with Mrs Reynolds, sir, at Pemberley. We fear that the master is troubled by something. He works himself most exhaustingly during the day and then paces his chambers much of the night."

"I see. Thank you, Mrs Carroll."

Colonel Fitzwilliam began to have some suspicions regarding his cousin's behaviour and was not best pleased by his stubborn determination to fight his inclination for Miss Elizabeth Bennet. When the servants left the room and the gentlemen were once again alone, Colonel Fitzwilliam turned fiery eyes to Bingley.

"I could easily and quite happily box his ears!"

"I do not believe I understand your frustration, Colonel. I agree that whatever is troubling my friend must be grave indeed for him to be so uncharacteristically reclusive but—"

The colonel laughed, effectively halting Bingley's speech. "Uncharacteristically reclusive? Do we speak of the same man? Darcy's very character is defined by his reclusiveness! He prefers to keep his own counsel, especially when he ought to do the opposite—the bacon-brained buffoon."

Bingley sat silent for a minute. "I suppose I would have to confess that I am usually the one seeking counsel."

Colonel Fitzwilliam waved away Bingley's guilt-ridden words. "He does not wish to burden others and is arrogant enough to believe it is his responsibility to fix everything himself."

"What do you suppose is troubling him?" Bingley said as he

helped himself to a generous measure of Darcy's port. Though the colonel had brushed off his concerns, Bingley was acutely aware that he had never quite been as useful a friend to Darcy as his friend had been to him. He sought now to remedy that in some way.

"I haven't a clue, to be sure, but I would wager my quarterly earnings it has something to do with this lady."

"Miss Elizabeth?"

"Indeed, it is my experience that a lady is almost always to blame when a man acts foolishly. Delightfully charming, little wicked darlings. God love them."

"It is a wonder you are still a bachelor, my friend."

Colonel Fitzwilliam smirked at Bingley's wry tone. He went to pour himself a measure of port too and took up a relaxed pose in a chair by the hearth.

Bingley noted his companion's change in anxiety. "Are you not concerned for your cousin any more?"

Richard shrugged and brought the glass up level with his eye as he watched the colours from the fire dance through the liquid. "Not in the least, my dear sir. There is nothing as easy as working my cousin. It takes only provocation."

"I confess I am not following your logic in the least. Kindly explain what you mean regarding Miss Elizabeth and Darcy. What is it you suspect of him?" Bingley was baffled as he took up the chair across from the military man.

Colonel Fitzwilliam looked over to his companion with a smile. "The way I see it, my cousin has again determined in his mind that there is some impediment with regards to this lady."

Bingley's brows rose though he said nothing.

"Darcy is fantastically able to imagine problems of his own invention and skilled at stubbornly standing behind them."

"And you plan to provoke him past his stumbling blocks?"

"Indeed and get his addle-pated arse back to Hertfordshire to win the lady's hand so that we all might enjoy a damn drink and stop worrying about him."

Bingley half smiled, detecting the familial bond the gentleman before him felt for his cousin. Despite his easy manners just now, Bingley could detect a small amount of concern lurking behind the colonel's eyes. Glad to have some useful part to play, Bingley said, "In that, you may find some difficulty, Colonel."

"And how is that?"

"Because I escorted the lady here in my carriage with her sister short of a se'nnight ago. Jane is shopping for her trousseau, and Miss Elizabeth was to travel on to Kent for a few weeks."

"What the devil is she doing in Kent?" the colonel asked with some frustration. He was beginning to feel like a director having to deal with the emotional fits of his actors.

Bingley's brows lowered in reflection as he lifted his glass in preparation to take a drink after he finished speaking. "She travelled on from London with her neighbour to visit his daughter, her friend. She has been out of sorts since her accident, and her father felt she needed a change of scenery, so he sent her to Hunsford."

"Hunsford?" Colonel Fitzwilliam sat up, a smile growing at his lips. "This friend of hers, she resides in that village?"

"She is lately married to the vicar there. Mr Collins lives at the parsonage in Hunsford. In fact, I believe his patronage is through your aunt Lady Catherine de Bourgh. The parson said as much when I was introduced to him in November."

"Indeed? Interesting. So Miss Elizabeth is in Hunsford, a mere mile from Rosings Park."

"Yes, and I am sorry to say I do not know the duration of her stay. I could ask my betrothed about her sister's travel plans if you wish, sir."

Colonel Fitzwilliam waved the offer away with a smile, strategies already formulating in his military-trained mind. "I believe, Mr Bingley, that it is quite time for Darcy and me to make our annual visit to Lady Catherine. Indeed, I believe I shall depart tomorrow and collect my chuckle-headed cousin from Pemberley."

❧ 22 ❧

"M iss Darcy, Colonel Fitzwilliam, you are most welcome to
Pemberley," Mrs Reynolds said tenderly as she embraced the
former and patted the cheek of the latter. Barely reacting to their
unexpected appearance, she turned quickly to issue a few clear
orders to the servants regarding chambers for the new arrivals before
she turned once again to them. "I do not believe the master is
expecting you and will, no doubt, be very pleased at your surprise."

Colonel Fitzwilliam laughed at this. "I am certain you are correct
at least with **some of** your prediction, Mrs Reynolds. He is certain to
be much surprised, though 'pleased' remains to be seen. Where
might I find the dear man?"

The housekeeper eyed Colonel Fitzwilliam with a knowing glint
after recognising the slightly forthright tone in the gentleman's voice
and actually found herself sighing with relief. Her master's constant
exertion was troubling. Colonel Fitzwilliam at least seemed on a
mission to look into its cause, but if he were piqued at Darcy for
another reason, she knew the colonel could be trusted to take notice
of her master's distraction and demand some kind of explanation.

"He is currently in the library, sir. Shall I notify him of your
arrival?"

Georgiana spoke up then. "Not just yet, Mrs Reynolds. Let us freshen up a bit from our journey, and we shall surprise him afterwards."

Colonel Fitzwilliam looked at his young cousin with surprise and a little chagrin as he had planned to charge into battle directly upon reaching Pemberley. He was also a little unhappy with her use of the collective when it came to speaking to her brother. He anticipated a heated skirmish and did not wish to offend her sensibilities by being witness to it.

The housekeeper smiled and nodded, lifting her hand to indicate they were free to ascend the steps to their usual quarters.

Upon reaching the landing, Colonel Fitzwilliam made to go right towards his usual chambers while at Pemberley when he felt Georgiana forestall him, pulling him in the opposite direction towards hers. When questioned, she shot him a stern look but did not answer until they were securely enclosed in her sitting room.

Rounding on her cousin, Georgiana crossed her arms about her and spoke fiercely. "I certainly hope the thought has not occurred to you to confront my brother without me."

Colonel Fitzwilliam started at this and, with an amused smile at her show of temper, replied, "Indeed, I had, Sprite. There is no need for you to concern yourself with this. I shall have your brother sorted out in no time. Lord knows I have plenty of practice at it."

Richard laughed to himself though the humour died on his lips when he looked across at his cousin, expecting her to share in his wit, and instead found a face devoid of humour and quite stridently fixed in a scowl. He sobered immediately, frankly a little intimidated by this new side of his young cousin. He had always experienced her tender and timid character with pleasure, almost as one might automatically love a sweet, little puppy. Before him stood an angry terrier in a periwinkle muslin travelling gown.

"Georgie, you said you were pleasure-bound when you requested to accompany me. I regret to inform you that I am not here on a pleasurable holiday. Your brother's behaviour of late has been more than disconcerting, and I intend to root out the source of it," he said carefully though indulgently.

"I am surprised that you bought that bouncer, Richard."

"Georgie! A lady does not say such words," admonished the good colonel, shocked by her language. He was certainly out of his element when it came to training females. His expertise and comfort lay in unruly youth enlisting in the army. Young men were infinitely less foreboding than young ladies. Although he was her guardian, Georgiana had always had governesses or companions for that sort of feminine stickiness. He looked at her and saw that his rebuke fell on deaf ears.

"Not without me, you will not, Richard. I am not a child any more, and he is *my* brother. My claim on him is greater than yours."

Colonel Fitzwilliam's brows rose at her unyielding tone. He rubbed his jaw, uncharacteristically discomposed by her and realising, with a touch of sadness, that she was correct at least partially; she was no child any more. He walked to and fro another minute, contemplating her request—nay, demand. Although he was inclined to indulge her, especially after this show, he did not want her to know the extent of her power over him at that moment. After making her wait another minute, he stopped and fixed her with his own fierce glare, usually found disconcerting to any of his soldiers. Georgiana did not so much as blink an eye as she waited, delicate arms crossed about her chest, a dainty slippered foot tapping the carpet.

"Very well, Georgiana."

He watched, baffled, as she smiled broadly, bounced up and down in excitement, and ran up to bestow a sweet kiss upon his cheek. This transformation back to the sweet puppy left him speechless.

"Oh, thank you, Richard! I am certain that together we shall help my brother be well."

"On one condition, Sprite!" Colonel Fitzwilliam said, clearing his throat and the confusion from his mind. "We will do this my way. I know you love your brother, but in this, you must trust me to lead the way."

She nodded eagerly and dismissed him with gentle, though determined, nudges towards the door. "Splendid, now go. I shall require a half hour to refresh myself and will meet you directly thereafter."

Before Colonel Fitzwilliam could say another word, he found himself deposited outside her sitting room and the door at his back closed with a decided click. He stood there stunned for a minute, trying to decipher what had just happened and how he had been so browbeaten by his young cousin—and frankly a little proud of her. An amused smile began to tug at the edges of his lips as his bafflement transformed into good humour. He shook his head in wonder as he took himself to his own chambers to freshen and prepare for his—their—interview with Darcy.

Colonel Fitzwilliam eyed Georgiana with slight circumspection when she approached him, looking demur and docile in a refreshed gown of sage green. Never again would he underestimate her. It seemed that his young cousin had a bit of her brother's stubborn determination, and it was as frightening as it was delightful.

Together they approached the library door and entered only to gape at the scene that met them. Stacks of books were piled high on many of the tables around the room, and the usually brilliantly maintained and warmly furnished room was in complete disarray. The most astonishing part of the scene before them was that of William standing on a ladder in his shirtsleeves and waistcoat, covered in dust, his hair sticking up in complete disorder. A few servants were scattered about below him, and his steward sat tiredly at a large table with many papers strewn about him.

At the sound of their entrance, all activity stopped, and the occupants of the room looked at the newcomers. Immediately, the steward stood, and the servants assumed their usual subservient positions, hands at their side, prepared to exit. Darcy stared, frozen on his perch. Then, blinking a few times before coming to life with an uneasy laugh, he came down from the ladder to welcome them.

"Georgiana, Richard, what a pleasant surprise. I had not known you were coming."

Richard could see through the pinched smile and appearance of delight that Darcy bestowed as he came towards them. Clearly, his cousin was surprised but did not necessarily find it "pleasant."

"Brother," Georgiana began hesitantly, walking carefully into the room and looking about at the mess. "What have you done to our library?"

Darcy brushed awkwardly at the grey sleeves of his shirt, dirtied from their usual pristine white to that hue, straightened his waistcoat, and laughed a little uneasily. "As you see, my dear, we are cataloguing the books. There was no order to the room, and Jacobs and I are putting it all to rights."

"Forgive me if I speak out of turn here as I am but a simple soldier, but this does not seem like the normal job for a steward, let alone the master of the house," Colonel Fitzwilliam said with a disbelieving look about him.

Darcy coughed, clearing his throat with discomfort. He was not happy for the interruption and certainly not happy to see his cousin at his door asking all manner of questions. He was bound to ask questions that Darcy did not want to answer. "Indeed, you are correct. But we have had an unusually efficient few weeks, have we not, Jacobs? I cannot comprehend the neglect of a family library in such days as these."

"Sir, I shall leave you now to visit with your relations. Welcome home, Miss Georgiana. Welcome to Pemberley, Colonel Fitzwilliam." Jacobs motioned to the servants to leave with him, feeling all the strangeness of the situation and relieved for the break it provided.

"No, no, Jacobs. I am sure that is not necessary. My sister and cousin will likely wish to refresh themselves after their journey. We can resume while they do so," Darcy said with an expectant look sweeping from his steward to the new arrivals.

"We have already refreshed ourselves, William," Georgiana said with a frown as she took in the cluttered tabletop near her.

Darcy feigned pleasure at this news and said, "Ah, wonderful. Well then, perhaps you will excuse me a moment. I should like to clean up myself. As you see, I am a disaster."

"That you are, Darcy," Richard said with more significance than Darcy thought necessary for a simple agreement. With a worried swallow, Darcy nodded to his relations and made to walk out the door. If he could just have a few moments to compose himself in his chambers, he felt certain that he could come up with some ruse to avoid Richard's inquisition.

"On the contrary, William, I think you ought to stay."

Darcy's head whipped around, stunned at the uncompromising tone of his sister.

"You may wish to pay heed to her, Darcy. To my misfortune, I have already experienced your sister's new proficiency in temper, and it rivals even yours."

Darcy frowned at his cousin and looked again at his sweet, young sister. The look on her face caused Darcy to involuntarily step back, nodding numbly as he instead led the way to the secret door to his study. "Very well then, let us escape this jumble and retire to my study."

Georgiana batted her eyes sweetly at her brother and took his arm so he might escort her. As they walked, she threw a look behind her at Colonel Fitzwilliam, a mischievous smile on her lips. It was all the colonel could do not to burst into laughter. He was beginning to admire this new side of Georgiana as long as it was directed away from him.

Darcy left his sister on a comfortable sofa as he poured first two glasses of sherry and then, upon consideration, poured a third. Still not sure what it was that had spurred Georgiana, he distributed the glasses and decided he would play along until the two of them were successfully satisfied with their interrogation—and interrogation, Darcy had no doubt, it would be.

Colonel Fitzwilliam looked towards his young cousin to remind her that she should allow him to lead the discussion before he turned to look Darcy squarely in the eye.

Darcy had just lifted his glass to his mouth when his cousin spoke.

"Miss Elizabeth Bennet."

Sputtering, Darcy spilled his drink down his already dishevelled shirt and coughed to clear his throat. He winced at the sound of her name, a pain lancing through his chest as profound as it had upon first discovering she had no memory of their time together or their love for each other.

When he achieved some semblance of control over himself, Darcy lifted tortured eyes to his cousin, the misery apparent. He did not speak, the heart in his throat preventing it.

Though Richard was moved by the tormented man he saw in his

cousin's eyes, he knew that, if he did not press at the wound Darcy was suffering, it would never have a chance heal. It was swelling deep within, and his cousin would suffer greater pain should he not release the pressure.

"Darcy, tell us about this lady."

The gentleman turned and went to place his glass upon the side-board. His fingers rested on the polished wood lightly as his head fell forward. "There is nothing much to tell."

"I very much doubt that. Come on man, why do you resist this?"

Anger burned rapidly up through Darcy's chest, at both Fate and his cousin's intrusion. "Blast it, Richard! There is nothing to tell!" Hearing a gasp and seeing the startled face of his sister, Darcy remembered her presence, and he was immediately deflated. "For-give me, Georgie," he offered in defeat.

Georgiana stood then and crossed to her brother. Tears welled in her eyes as she saw the grief reflected in his. Wordlessly she wrapped her arms about him and pressed her face to his chest. Darcy slowly lifted his arms to return her embrace, patting her back softly.

Pulling away slightly so she might see his face, she pleaded with him gently. "Will you not let us help you? We love you and do not wish to see you so burdened."

Darcy said not a word at first; his gaze lifted slowly from her tender entreaty to his cousin. There he saw the same compassion reflected, and the fortress he had been attempting to construct around his shattered heart tumbled down with one silent look of compassion from his family.

Feelings and emotions he had attempted to keep in check for several months poured out of that stronghold. He disentangled himself from his sister and collapsed into the nearest chair. With his head in his hands, he said nothing for several minutes while his cousin and sister looked at each other for help.

A faraway voice emanated from between Darcy's hands. "I very much doubt you will believe me even if I were to tell you."

Georgiana kneeled at her brother's feet and pulled at one of his hands so she could see his face. "Will you not trust us to try?"

Darcy moved the hand she held to her cheek and brushed it tenderly. He only realised then that she had used words very similar to ones he had said to her when in the anguished aftermath of Ramsgate.

Acquiescing, Darcy helped his sister to rise and brought her again to her seat before returning to his. As he formulated words and decided how to tell such a fantastical tale, he again allowed his head to fall into his hands, overwhelmed.

He looked up at his sister first. "Do I assume you have been told who Elizabeth is?"

Georgiana shook her head and looked at her cousin.

"She is a lady your brother met in Hertfordshire last autumn while visiting Bingley. He became enamoured and admired her a great deal."

Joyfully, Georgiana turned to her brother for confirmation. Darcy nodded blankly.

"Your brother's object of admiration comes from neither esteemed connections nor any wealth. For that reason, he did not pursue her. Instead, he left Hertfordshire with the express hope of forgetting her and finding someone more suitable. How do I do so far, Darcy?" Richard asked kindly.

Darcy finally found his voice and continued from there. "She was so very beautiful." He paused to draw in a strangled breathe. "So very lively...and I was completely under her spell. For some time while in London, I found it impossible to forget her. The distraction drove me to madness, or so I thought." Darcy laughed without humour, causing his companions to frown. "The rest of the story will seem rather impossible to believe, I fear. I wonder a little now whether I have only imagined it myself."

He then began to relate, with tender, yet painful recollection, his first discovering Elizabeth's spirit in his library. He told of the happiness and fear that mixed within him at seeing her before him and his conviction that he had lost his mind. His narration of the ensuing days of struggle and denial, and then acceptance and reconciliation with Elizabeth over their strange connection was shared with the utmost reverence on Darcy's side. He spoke as if seeing it all in his mind. Speaking of the thrill of falling in love and the discovery of his feelings being returned was a bitter tonic for Darcy to swallow. His throat often constricted, almost preventing his giving voice to such sacred moments.

"All the while, she thought she was dreaming, and you thought you were going mad," Georgiana summarised, clearly wanting to believe such a heartfelt story. The tone of her voice told Darcy that she did not condemn him even if she had yet to be convinced.

He nodded and told of how they argued over it, laughing once at the memory of their quarrels. Their time together was related with warmth. He talked of her love for lemon tarts as if it were the most charming thing in the world to him. His profound love for Elizabeth made this confession near impossible at times, his occasional pauses bringing tears to his sister's eyes.

At one point, Darcy stopped talking to collect his thoughts for the next part of the improbable story. His family remained silent, occasionally exchanging glances between them. He then began to tell how Elizabeth regained her memory, seemingly because of his declaration of love for her. As if in a dream, he related how they discovered why she was there on the same night that Colonel Fitzwilliam had confronted him over his strange behaviour.

"She was there then? I was ape drunk that evening, but I do remember something of this part."

Darcy half smiled in remembrance. "That you were."

Richard took up a seat near Georgiana as Darcy began to relate his and Elizabeth's elated discovery of her accident. Though worried for her, Darcy and Elizabeth were glad to have some kind of explanation and eager to reunite her with her body so that they could realise their fondest wishes. Laughing, he shared their first attempts at reuniting Elizabeth and his concealing himself under the bed, the indignity of it having dissolved into a fond memory by now. Unbeknownst to him, the other occupants of the room looked at each other with utter astonishment at this part of the story as if it were the most unbelievable part!

He recounted only briefly their last day together, keeping certain parts to himself—a private treasure just for him. When it came time to speak of the reunion, he excused himself to the window as a well of emotion overtook him and made it quite impossible for him to speak.

Recollecting privately that tender moment, their last minutes together, and the kiss they shared was profoundly bittersweet in its agony for Darcy. He had not allowed himself the tortured pleasure before now. They had declared their love again mere moments before as they stood outside her door. The kiss they shared was still etched on the memory of his lips. Yet, he could not have known that his actions would set in place the binds that restricted his heart now in powerful agony and besieged him daily for the past two months.

"That evening, an idea came to me as to how we might be successful in reuniting Elizabeth with her body. We secreted ourselves to Longbourn in the dark early hours before dawn. When we got there...well, I—we—engaged in the measures I had thought might bring about the solution."

"What was it? What did you do?" Georgiana said in eager antici-pation, having become transfixed in this marvellous tale of love and devotion.

Darcy looked at his cousin, a silent communication between them confirming to him that Richard knew what it was that Darcy had done. He moved his eyes to take in her youthful merriment and wonder that expressed itself so beautifully on his sister's face then. Knowing her to be quite grown, if her earlier show of determination were any indication, Darcy still felt a brotherly instinct that made him uneasy telling her of the kiss.

"Suffice it to say, Georgie, it worked."

Georgiana made to protest, knowing that her brother was censoring his story for her benefit, but the firm grasp of her cousin's hand on hers forestalled her. She looked at Richard with frustration only to see him shake his head slightly at her, the look in his eye telling Georgiana that he would not relent in this case.

With obvious reluctance, she turned back to her brother and encouraged him to continue, suspecting her brother's actions. "So Elizabeth was restored to herself! Oh how wonderful! What happened next?"

Darcy swallowed, grateful that his confessions had worn at his emotions enough to render him quite numb. With a detached voice, he told of tea at Longbourn and his discovery of Elizabeth's having not remembered a thing.

After several profoundly quiet minutes, Darcy drew in a deep breath; feeling a little less burdened, he turned to his companions. "And that is the end of the story. I came directly to Pemberley and have kept myself quite busy, attempting to will my own recalcitrant heart to follow Elizabeth's example and forget our time together." Nobody spoke for several minutes more. Darcy stared with unseeing eyes out the window, his heart far away in another part of the kingdom.

"I believe you, Brother," Georgiana said softly. He acknowledged her words with a smile and looked at Colonel Fitzwilliam.

"Well I think it does you little good for us to believe you, or more to the point, it does the *situation* little good. What are you going to do now?"

"I do not have the pleasure of understanding you. There is nothing left to do."

"I would have to disagree with that, Cousin. How is your current method working for you? You are exhausting yourself—and your servants—and to what end? Has her memory faded in the least?"

"No," Darcy said pointedly.

"Then I think there is naught but one thing you can do, my erstwhile Romeo."

Darcy was not amused by Richard's teasing and, having no patience for it, glared at him.

"The way I see it," Colonel Fitzwilliam began, unmoved by the warning in his cousin's expression. "You have wooed her in the spirit and now you must woo her in the flesh."

"Richard!" Darcy scolded, sending shocked, wary eyes towards his young sister.

Colonel Fitzwilliam began to laugh then, shaking his head. "I certainly did not mean that in the way in which you took it, but if that is what is on your mind—"

"That is quite enough, Richard!" Darcy growled, his ears growing pink as he avoided looking at his cousin or sister then.

Georgiana began to laugh, catching the attention of both gentlemen. "My dear sirs, I have read more scandalous things in my novels! Let us not become distracted from our course over a few wicked words. William, I believe you take our cousin's meaning. You must go to Elizabeth and make her fall in love with you again. You must make her remember."

Georgiana's words settled on the air with a heavy significance that stirred Darcy's heart. He felt it beat once, twice, as if coming to life again. Hope was a fickle lover, and he was not sure he wanted to place his trust in it. Yet the idea of seeing her again, of regaining her love was a temptation that his frail heart positively yearned for.

Darcy looked at his companions, profoundly relieved and grateful that they seemed to believe his confession. *That* at least was a small miracle; he would need a much larger one to do what his cousin suggested.

"I am afraid I do not know how it is to be done." When he had gained her heart before, she had had no choice but to spend time in his company due to their bond. That was certainly to his advantage then, but now he had no such mystical ally.

The sentimental advice he received then came from a surprising quarter: not his romantic, tender-hearted sister but his war-hardened cousin.

"Elizabeth told you that she believed Fate had destined you two to be connected. Whatever force brought you together in the first place will aid you in the second. The way I see it, you might be part of the greatest love story ever known. I cannot think that two souls so joined in life or death can be easily separated. Her mind may not remember, but her heart will."

Darcy bit his lip, hesitant as hope began to encompass more of the hole in his chest. After a time, he looked at both his companions and cautiously nodded.

"I shall go to Elizabeth and try to make her fall in love with me again."

Georgiana squealed and jumped to her feet to rush to his side, and he found himself encompassed once again by her delicate arms. He looked at his cousin and allowed him to see the fear that still lurked in his heart as he returned his sister's hold.

Darcy attempted some levity. "I suppose I ought to tell Jacobs the library will have to wait."

"I most seriously doubt that man cares one jot about your library." Richard walked towards them and pointed out the window. Under a tree some distance off, his steward leaned against its trunk, quite asleep.

Darcy looked a little embarrassed as he said with a small laugh, "I have been working him quite relentlessly."

Georgiana laughed as she wiped the tears from her face with a square of linen from her pocket. She swatted her brother with the fabric. "Well then, what are you waiting for? Make haste and bring me back a sister."

"I shall direct my valet to begin preparations to leave for Hertfordshire early tomorrow, Georgie. I shall do my best, I assure you."

They began making their way out of the study when Richard cleared his throat. "A fat lot of good that will do. Miss Elizabeth is in Kent."

"Kent?" Darcy stopped, surprised at the news. "How do you—"

"She is currently visiting her friend, the good vicar's wife—the vicar of Hunsford parish."

"Indeed!" Darcy said, a genuine smile about his lips. He was feeling lighter than he had in months. "Is Easter not almost upon us, Richard? Lady Catherine will be expecting us soon."

Richard sighed dramatically and patted his cousin's back. "A necessary sacrifice, I fear, for the cause."

Georgiana rolled her eyes and left the two with a parting hug and a skip in her step as she went off to her room.

"Darcy..." Richard called his cousin, his tone serious, after they watched Georgiana disappear up the stairs. Darcy looked at him, his brows lowered.

Richard eyed Darcy squarely. "You know that I do believe you."

"I do, and I thank you."

"Good, good." Richard cleared the unanticipated emotion from his voice. With the return of his usual carefree tone, he added, "Into battle we go, comrade."

Laughing, the smile reaching his eyes for the first time since the night before Elizabeth's reunion, Darcy patted his cousin's back and declared with vigour, "Onward!"

❦ 23 ❦

"Well that went rather badly," Colonel Fitzwilliam said after calling on the parsonage shortly upon their arrival in Kent.

Darcy followed after him, dazed as he thought about the magnificence of Elizabeth and the pleasure that stole through him when he was first able to rest his eyes upon her again. He paid little attention to his cousin's words while he savoured a warmth that was speeding the tempo of his heart and healing its hurt just by having seen her.

"To Mrs Collins you paid your compliments with your usual reserve, and whatever might be your feelings towards her *friend* met her with every appearance of composure," Colonel Fitzwilliam mocked with frustration.

He was disappointed in his cousin and in the visit as a whole. Darcy had sat nearly mute during the visit, content to look upon Elizabeth with that damned enigmatic smile upon his face while Colonel Fitzwilliam was left to carry the conversation with Miss Bennet. It was a chore he did not feel too put upon to perform; nonetheless, it was his cousin who was supposed to be wooing the lady. The only outcome of the visit that satisfied Colonel Fitzwilliam was that now, having met the lady, he could feel completely at ease with his cousin's affection. She was everything that was charming, all unaffected airs and graceful yet witty conversation. *And beautiful—gads, she was beautiful,* he thought with no little envy for his cousin.

Unbeknownst to the gentlemen walking around the side of the parsonage as they made their way to the path that led back to Rosings, a window above them was opened for fresh air, and the lady currently being discussed sat upon its sill. Looking down, she pondered the two gentlemen. She had been surprised to have them call so soon upon their arrival in the area. Charlotte suggested it was due to her that they paid such a compliment, but Elizabeth could not but protest such an absurd idea. Strange as it was, though Mr Darcy did not speak much to her, she felt an awareness of him that she had never felt before. Not true—she had felt something of it when she last saw him at Longbourn, but that was such a short visit and quite some time ago; she had put it off then as nothing. Briefly, Elizabeth wondered whether there might be some truth to Jane's suspicions.

The gentlemen stopped just below her, and Elizabeth sucked in a short breath when she heard her name—her Christian name.

"Elizabeth," Darcy said, speaking it like a caress.

"Are you attending me to me all, Darcy? Your manner of wooing just now could not convince a—"

"She is every whit as beautiful as I remembered," Darcy interrupted, still not paying his cousin any attention.

"You are every whit as beautiful as I remembered." Elizabeth stumbled backwards off the sill, almost losing her balance completely —and not just physically. The remembered words flashed through her mind, triggered by his actual words outside. Neither occurrence could she believe was possible to have been uttered by such a man. Yet, somehow, unfathomable as it was, she could remember his saying once directly to her the sentiment he had just shared with his cousin. The fleeting memory was jarring, and all at once, Elizabeth felt unsettled and discomposed. Her hands flew to her head and her eyes squeezed shut as she tried to hold on to the memory, but to no avail. It was as unreal as a dream and just as slippery.

In her confused state she stayed, trying to shake the distraction of such implausible words from such an implausible source. That they gave her pleasure, she could not deny, for she felt the excited fluttering in her chest. She had not yet recovered from the surprise of what had happened—it was impossible to think of anything else—and by the time she recovered enough to remember the gentlemen outside, they were gone.

She sat shakily upon the sill again and attempted to gather her thoughts. Warmth settled upon her like a blanket as she replayed the gentleman's praise in her mind. Shocking as it was, Elizabeth clung to that warmth as it was the only thing that seemed to bring life to her heart since she woke. It was quite some time before she allowed her mind to dwell on anything else.

DOWN THE PATH, DARCY WAS PULLED FROM HIS PLEASANT ruminations by the firm grasp of his cousin's hand upon his arm.

"Darcy! For goodness sake man, wake up!"

Darcy frowned at his cousin and said tersely, "What are you upset about?"

Colonel Fitzwilliam looked almost close to apoplexy. "Pardon me, but were we in the same parlour just now? You hardly spoke to the lady, and I begin to wonder how it was that you managed to make her fall in love with you in the first place if this is the extent of your romantic abilities."

Darcy smiled then, infuriating his cousin further. What began as a small chuckle turned into a full-fledged laugh as he patted his companion's back and began walking with great strides towards Rosings again. "I assure you, I am fully capable of wooing the lady." At Pemberley, once he committed to go to Elizabeth, Darcy had thought seriously about how he might make her love him, effectively erasing his previous insecurities.

"You will, of course, forgive me if I have my doubts," Richard said as he caught up.

"Today I was simply overwhelmed by the pleasure of seeing her again."

"Then how are you to win her heart, sir?"

Darcy stopped and looked at his cousin with bright eyes. "Come now, you do not expect me to give away all my secrets!"

By way of response, Darcy received only a grunt and a shake of the head. Together they continued down the path. Darcy asked his cousin what he thought of Elizabeth, and the rest of the journey was spent in pleasurable conversation as the two enumerated her manifold attractions.

MORE THAN ONCE DID ELIZABETH, IN HER RAMBLE WITHIN THE Park, unexpectedly meet Mr Darcy. She felt all the perverseness of the mischance that should bring him where no one else was brought. Conscious that the compliment of overhearing herself *complimented* was affecting her rather more than it ought and in the hopes of its happening again, she took care to inform him that it was a favourite haunt of hers. When it happened again thereafter, she hid a secret smile and felt a little guilty for her better knowledge.

Though she did not mind his company, she knew her perspective on it had been altered positively by knowing, as she did, that his opinion of her tolerability had changed. This little proof of vanity on her part could not make her completely comfortable with her machinations either, but her motives for seeking Darcy's company ran deeper than just vanity.

Although she would admit it to nobody, her gratification in his company was also a private one. With him, she often felt calmed, with less of that listlessness she had known in Hertfordshire, and though she did not understand why, she felt almost as if theirs was an acquaintance of longer standing than it was. She felt safe. With him, she began to feel a sense of peace that had been missing, and with him, her world was reborn. Coming to Kent had been her father's idea, and in the first few weeks there, she felt an increase of her spirits, but it was not until she began spending a meaningful amount of time with Darcy that she felt any real improvement.

For the gentleman's part, he was simply pleased beyond measure to be in her company whenever the blessing could be brought about. The edicts of propriety were against him this time, for any chance with her was limited to a daily walk or call upon the parsonage. Occasionally, his aunt would invite the party from Hunsford to tea or dinner, and he would see her then. On those occasions, he would have to be more circumspect in his discussions with her so as not to draw the attention of his aunt. Colonel Fitzwilliam served as a distraction during those evenings and often went with him to the parsonage to play the same role with Mrs Collins.

His avowed plan was to see whether he might get her to fall in love with him, and his strategy was to remind her bit by bit of their time together by talking of the subjects they had shared before. He hoped to spark some kind of recognition in her, and at times he knew that words he spoke affected her rather strongly, for her eyes would become unfocused and her hand would drift gently to touch the side of her head where she had been hurt.

Though he could not exactly know whether he was successful—and at times found the process torturously slow in bearing fruit—he was gratified that, as the weeks passed, she came often to look forward to his visits. It warmed his heart beyond measure to see her eyes light with happiness upon his approach in the grove or to see that her smile was directed at him when he called.

On one occasion, Darcy visited the parsonage, and when the door opened, to his very great surprise, Miss Elizabeth—and Miss Elizabeth only—occupied the room. He was astonished to find her alone and apologised for his intrusion by letting her know that he had understood all the ladies to be within. Secretly, he was gratified for this little blessing. They then sat down, and when her enquiries after Rosings were made, they seemed in danger of sinking into total silence. Darcy found himself, due to the surprise of being alone with her, again transfixed with her beauty and at first did not notice the growing awkwardness of their silence.

"Shall I call for tea, sir?" Elizabeth's quiet voice awoke Darcy from his trance.

"I should not like to trouble you," he said automatically.

Elizabeth stood and went to pull the bell, summoning the tea, all the while assuring him in her gentle voice that she was just about to have some refreshment herself and he might stay to share it with her.

When the tray came, Darcy's eyes lit upon seeing that the maid had brought coffee as well as tea. He thought at first that Elizabeth was remembering his preferences. When she asked which beverage he would favour, he was momentarily disheartened. His dismay lasted only until she had poured him a cup and then poured herself the same refreshment.

"I did not think you liked the taste of coffee," he said immediately.

This seemed to startle her, and he realised that it would be odd for him to know this about her. Though perhaps a bit confused, she answered him with only the slightest shake to her voice. "I...I have developed a taste for it, I suppose."

"Since when?" Darcy spoke quickly, his heart beginning to beat rapidly.

Elizabeth met his gaze and, though she felt a little embarrassed to be sharing any of the strange changes about her since waking, answered him honestly. "Since I woke from my injuries, sir."

Darcy smiled brilliantly at her, and at first, he could see she was stunned by it. Shyly, she returned a small smile of her own, wondering at the strange flicker of something she saw in his eyes.

Elizabeth looked away first and resumed preparing her coffee the way she liked. Her head bowed, she could not see the smile her companion wore as he watched her stir several lumps of sugar into the brew. If she had encountered his eye, she might have seen how well the expression of heartfelt delight, diffused over his face, became him.

"And how are you, Eli—Miss Elizabeth, since your accident?" Darcy asked, his love for her gentling his voice.

Elizabeth placed her cup in its saucer and smoothed the edges of the napkin next to it. Though in truth, she knew little about Darcy, she had come to trust him, and his company did bring her comfort. "I have been well, thank you. I..."

She looked up and saw kindness in his eyes, not the worry she had expected to see or was used to from her family. She continued then, devoid of her usual embarrassment. "I have felt a little strange, to be truthful." She laughed half-heartedly. "You were correct; I did not always favour coffee. Some things feel different now."

Darcy nodded, contented at her candidness and pleased that she felt comfortable sharing this with him. "Such significant events do often change us."

He could see that his words had made her happy, and he thought she seemed a little more at ease the rest of the visit.

ON A PARTICULARLY WARM SPRING MORNING, DARCY FOUND Elizabeth walking the groves again, just as he had hoped. She spied him and waited with a smile as he joined her.

She eyed the parcel in his arms with an amused smile, wondering what he had planned for that day. Their unspoken arrangement to walk the groves each day was exciting and much anticipated for Elizabeth but partially because she came to expect some sort of surprise from the gentleman. On one day, he had brought her a handkerchief full of lemon tarts from Rosings. A few other times, he had brought books with him. The strangest by far had been when he had brought a fencing foil with him, wondering whether she might be interested to see it. His claim that it had just been purchased seemed peculiar, for even her inexperienced eye could see that it was much too small for his stature and meant to fit a smaller student, a young boy just learning the art perhaps.

Though interested in the piece, she was careful to keep her interest to the degree appropriate for a lady and kept her tone neutral. It confused her then to see in his eyes some expectancy that she did not know how to fulfil.

"What do you have there, Mr Darcy? Another of your treasures to share with me?"

Darcy bowed, and when he looked again at her, she felt a shock fly through her. His gaze was steadfast and immovable, and it made her insides twist unexpectedly with pleasure.

"Indeed, I have brought along with me today a chess set. I thought we might play a game or two."

"What? Here in the park?" Elizabeth looked about with a laugh.

Darcy looked down at the blanket in his arms, wrapped around the travel chess set. Colour infused his cheeks as he felt slightly embarrassed by his forwardness; nevertheless, he answered, "I know of a small clearing not far from here. Would you permit me to take you there?"

Elizabeth smiled and indicated he should lead the way. Her heart hammered at the thought of being alone with Darcy, alone in the way of a secluded glen.

Darcy offered his free arm to her, and she took it, colour infusing her cheeks. He escorted her down a smaller path she had not previously noticed, and true to his word, a moment later the trees opened to a little clearing, just beginning to bloom with spring wildflowers.

"Oh what a beautiful little secret Eden," Elizabeth declared as she let go of his arm. She turned about in the soft grass of the clearing, bending to brush her hands across a few of the flowers peeking up above the green carpet of earth.

"I am pleased you like it. I used to hide here as a boy with Colonel Fitzwilliam and his brother. We played pirates and other such games."

"And were there never any maidens to rescue?" Elizabeth asked with a laugh.

"Not until now."

Unable to say anything at first, she watched him spread the blanket and sat when he set up the chessboard.

"How do you know that I even know how to play? It is not exactly one of the accomplishments usually taught to young ladies."

She watched him seem to stammer, undecided as to what to say. She took pity on him then and tapped a gloved hand on his bent knee.

"It so happens, sir, that my seminary consisted of my father as teacher, and I have, indeed, learned to play the game. Shall we?"

Elizabeth looked at him and saw his gaze was fixed upon the light pressure of her fingers on his knee. Quickly she pulled back her hand, embarrassed to have been so forward and appalled that she should not have given it a thought before noticing his distraction.

He looked at her then, and though she wished she could hide her own eyes beneath her hands, she met his gaze. There was a powerful secret he kept in his eyes. She saw it, and she was drawn closer, as if she could read it—understand it—if only she could see it better. Unconsciously, she allowed herself to lean towards him, mesmerised by that secret within. The gentleman lifted his hand as if to touch her cheek, to guide her closer.

A warbler's call snapped the tenuous thread pulling them together, and they both sat back, warmth imbuing their cheeks and emotion choking any words. Elizabeth pulled at the ties of her bonnet, suddenly finding it excessively tight. She looked down at her lap, and she was grateful that the head covering was at least useful in hiding her blush. She did not know what had just happened and dared not think what might have had not the bird sounded its call.

Her companion cleared his throat and, with a little more gravel to his voice than was perhaps usual for him, spoke softly. "Shall we play, Miss Elizabeth?"

She nodded and, when he indicated she should go first, made her move. Their game began at first with heavy silence as both players attended less to their strategies than to the emotions whirling within them. But soon the morning and game progressed, and they regained their normal ease.

As Darcy packed away the pieces of the chess set, his fingers paused with the last one. Elizabeth watched him play with it nervously, finding him at that moment, much to her surprise, utterly adorable.

"Miss Elizabeth?" Darcy finally spoke, looking up at where she stood. He was crouched on his knee to gather the blanket and game.

Elizabeth swallowed, seeing him kneeling before her and knowing in her heart that she was quite in danger of falling in love with him. She forced herself to meet his gaze and raised her brow by way of response since her throat was too thick to speak.

Darcy stood, bringing himself before her. He looked at her with open tenderness. "Will you walk with me tomorrow?"

Elizabeth bent her head, unable to encounter his eye. Her heart raced, the knowledge that this was the first time he had so openly asked for her company the cause of its increasing tempo. They had met often, almost daily, but always under the guise of accident.

"I would like that," she whispered, finally meeting his eyes.

Darcy smiled and expressed his gratitude with a nod. He led her out of the grove and back to the parsonage. Slowly, as their visits grew in frequency, their familiarity with each other grew like the spring about them to be like unto when they were together in London. Darcy was nearing the point where he felt he ought to say something to her of his feelings, if indeed they were not already altogether obvious.

AGAIN, AS SHE WAS WALKING IN THE GROVE IN SECRET HOPES OF

seeing Darcy, Elizabeth contemplated their time together over the past couple of weeks. She was at times confused by her feelings with regards to that gentleman. She knew her heart was in some danger of falling in love with Mr Darcy (if indeed it was not already), yet she also felt a sort of disloyalty to the mystery gentleman who flashed through her mind. During the day when she was with Darcy, she felt elated for such attentions, conscious of the compliment from a gentleman of his standing. Indeed, she had her doubts that a man of his sphere would even consider someone from hers. Elizabeth found that he was everything charming and, although not as conversant as his cousin or Mr Bingley, had a pleasantness about his lips when he spoke, and the low rumble of his voice often mesmerised her. She noticed he was altered from the way he used to be in Hertfordshire though Elizabeth came to understand the difference amounted mostly to reserve. Indeed, Mr Darcy definitely improved upon further acquaintance.

During the day, Elizabeth's thoughts were saved for Mr Darcy, but the nights were for a different gentleman. Dreams of the retreating form of the unknown gentleman-spectre as she followed him through a beautiful house disturbed her sleep. The frequency of the dreams matched that of her time with Darcy during the day. Every night she wished that shadowy gentleman might turn around so she could see his face. If her waking hours were increasingly devoted to Mr Darcy, her nightly hours were certainly for the other.

Whatever or whoever *he* was, she knew he also held some property of her heart, for she felt the same feelings of peace and contentment during her dreams as she did while walking side by side with Mr Darcy. Indeed, as the weeks in Kent passed and her acquaintance with Darcy became more intimate, she felt this tug at her heart that she could only credit to worry that she was somehow being unfair to one gentleman over the other.

Elizabeth heard footsteps behind her, drawing her from her thoughts. She smiled to herself as she recognised the cadence of Mr Darcy's strides against the gravel walk. She stopped to allow him to reach her side and curtseyed when he did.

"Good morning, Miss Elizabeth," he said over a bow as he pulled her gloved hand to his lips.

Elizabeth flushed, smiled prettily, and attempted to be composed despite the riot within. As their familiarity with each other grew, so did the warmth in Mr Darcy's eyes and expressions. Elizabeth looked at his hands, noted he wore no gloves for some reason and wondered what it might feel like to have him touch her without the barrier of fabric, his or hers. Cheeks bright, Elizabeth shook her head slightly to dispel the thought and replied, "Good morning, sir."

"You looked as if you were deep in thought when I came upon you just now. I am afraid I interrupt your solitary ramble."

"You certainly do," she replied with a smile. "But it does not follow that the interruption must be unwelcome."

Together they resumed walking, and Darcy, ever conscious of Elizabeth beside him, looked at her to see her gaze was again faraway. "Might I enquire what it is that you contemplate so seriously this morning?"

"Spring, sir," Elizabeth said to him with a sparkle in her eye.

Darcy smiled in return though he raised a brow in question.

"I was just thinking how marvellous it is that the ground, the bushes, and the trees come to life in the spring."

"It is quite beautiful," he said, not fully understanding the marvel in it that she did but enjoying the beauty the subject rendered her expression.

"After many months of winter, the spring comes and, with it, all the plants—slumbering for so many months—remember their true purpose and come to life."

Darcy swallowed the emotion that this speech wrought upon him. She could not know the images and hopes her words conjured up for him. *How I wish you would awake and remember your true purpose, Elizabeth...*

"You do not bring with you any treasures today, Mr Darcy?" Elizabeth teased, effectively pulling his attention back to her.

A smile came to his lips, and he looked at her with open affection. "I did not. Sadly, you are left merely with me today."

"I shall bear up as best I can, sir."

Darcy laughed, and she soaked up the sound, ever eager to hear it again. Wishing to hear it more, or more than she ought, she considered the tumult of emotions the sound produced in her.

Together they walked companionably for some distance, engaged in pleasant conversation, when the toe of Elizabeth's half boot caught on a stone, and in her distraction, she tripped.

Instantly Darcy reached out to steady her, his bare hands coming in contact with the silky skin of her arms—skin to skin for the first time since he had kissed her at Longbourn. Darcy sucked in a breath as they froze, knowing he ought to release her but less certain whether it was in his power to do so.

The moment his hands touched her skin, Elizabeth felt a whooshing sensation, and her vision darkened as images and thoughts flew through her mind, echoing one by one like drops from the sky settling into her heart. That organ, long asleep, skipped a beat, two, and then she felt it restart with a glorious tattoo of reawakening as she remembered every emotion, word, and look of her dream in London with Darcy. Her arrival in his London library, her magical ability to experience books, his words of love and devotion—all came rushing back, filling up the empty spaces within her. Instantly she remembered and felt the moments anew; she experienced the contentment of acknowledged love and at once was overwhelmed with a shaky power from within as it fused her heart again to her spirit.

Mesmerised by the marvellous truth settling in her soul, she breathed, "William."

Darcy's heart hammered in his throat, and he dared not believe his ears. He knew she would not have called him by his Christian name, not unless... *Oh God, please let it be!* Slowly he pulled Elizabeth backward to rest against his chest, his arms stealing around her as he buried his head in the crook of her neck. His face was against the softness there, breathing in her delicate scent and furiously praying he had not heard wrong.

"William!" she said again, this time with all the tenderness he had known of her before. He felt her small fingers reach up and press his head to hers.

Darcy trembled with the emotions pulsing through him, a part of him fearing that this was all a dream. Overwhelmed by the beautiful possibility it was not yet still conscious of being discovered thus, Darcy wordlessly withdrew his arms, took her hand, and began leading her into the forest, his destination clear even if the riot of emotions were not.

Upon reaching the little clearing, he turned to her and pulled her to kneel with him. Hand in hand, they knelt, facing each other, leaning back on their heels, and gazing into the other's eyes for the first time with that new awareness.

"Elizabeth," Darcy said reverently. "Can this be happening? Do you really..." Emotion choked off his words.

Elizabeth burst into a watery laugh then as she leaned forward to touch a hand to his cheek. "It feels just as I remembered," she murmured, exploring his cheek with her fingers. Her eyes searched his, and a sob bubbled up then as she comprehended the love there that she recalled now with such vivid conviction.

Her head collapsed against his shoulder, and his arms immediately wrapped around her, desperate to hold her close and never let her go. While Elizabeth's body wracked with relieved sobs, Darcy pressed his head to hers, lifted it almost as quickly to remove her bonnet, and then rested himself again against the softness of her curls. His relief demonstrated itself in the fierceness of his hold. He would not let her go for anything.

Nothing could describe the utter disbelief and rapture he felt. Part of him had despaired he might never make her fall in love with him again, or that she might never remember the time it first happened. His touch had stirred something when he reached out instinctively to catch her from her fall, and he could never be more grateful that he had forgotten his gloves in his rush to see her that morning. Hugging her closer to him, he sent a silent prayer of gratitude for this miracle wrought upon them.

Elizabeth felt complete for the first time in many months. She was no longer lost or sensed a loss. She was exactly where she was meant to be. Her mind raced through each of the days with Darcy in London over and over again as if to commit them to her memory—to secure them in her heart, never to be lost again. That organ beat rapidly as she listened to his. She recalled listening to it that evening in the library when she had embraced him after he recounted his history with Wickham. She had so longed at that time to truly feel his embrace and indeed give him comfort. The realisation that she was now experiencing what she had so wanted then only increased the tempo of her already frantic heart and warmed her cheeks.

When at length they separated, Elizabeth smiled with glistening eyes as she wiped a tender hand across his tear-stained cheek.

"I am so very glad it was you," she said as she assimilated now the gentleman from the brief memories she had been having as being Darcy, one and the same. When she saw his puzzled expression, she explained how she had had flashes of different scenes, *memories* she now knew. She told him how she had known she felt very fondly for the mysterious gentleman in her mind. "I knew not how to account for him, but I am glad now to know it was you."

"Elizabeth..." he said again, hardly able to give voice to the happiness building within him. *A part of her knew! A part of her remembered!* He allowed his eyes to travel all over her, as if to assure himself that this Elizabeth was indeed reality. "You are well? Pardon me, but I must know for sure. Do you remember London?"

Elizabeth tilted her head and shifted so that she sat against him. "I remember every minute, every heartbeat..."

Attempting to commit her words to memory, Darcy tilted her head up so he could see her eyes. With a sigh, he released the last of the worry, heartbreak, and sadness that had gripped him during the last months. "I have missed you so very dearly, my love."

It was a minute before Elizabeth said anything. "I am sorry that I did not remember, that I caused you pain, William."

Darcy smiled at her use of his name; he would never get used to it. "So am I."

"How you must have suffered when I awoke," she said with feeling as she sat up again and enthusiastically wrapped her arms about his neck to comfort him.

He laughed, holding her close and savouring the exquisite feeling before pulling back to look at her. "I am sorry that I did not stay to help you remember. I was foolish enough to think I had lost you."

"How came you to Rosings then?"

"You alone have brought me to Rosings. For you alone, I think and plan, though it was Georgiana and Colonel Fitzwilliam who convinced me to try. Will you forgive me?"

"If you will forgive me," Elizabeth said with a smile.

"I would forgive you anything, dearest, loveliest Elizabeth, if you will consent to marry me. If at last you will be my wife, my companion, and never again leave my side."

Elizabeth's hands brushed gently across his cheeks and came to rest on his shoulders. "My spirit, you have bewitched and in my flesh likewise. I love... I love you."

A rumble emanated from Darcy's throat as he looked down at Elizabeth and could resist no longer. He leaned into her and placed his lips upon hers again after so many months of anguish. She returned the kiss with equal passion. Theirs was a love that transcended life, conquered the spiritual world, and could not be lost, evermore.

EPILOGUE

E lizabeth looked at her reflection in the mirror and smiled a secret smile. Today was the day she was going to leave the name of Bennet and take up the name of Darcy. She knew herself to be happy, and the pleasure she felt radiated throughout her being.

"You almost glow, my dear!"

Elizabeth turned to bestow a smile upon her Aunt Gardiner, in town with her uncle for the wedding. She watched her aunt take in the dress with a smile.

"It looks very lovely on you, Lizzy. I am so very glad that I thought to have it made."

Elizabeth nodded and returned her gaze to her reflection in the mirror. Her aunt had come across a swath of the most beautiful ivory silk and had commissioned a dress before the carriage accident. The dressmaker, familiar with Elizabeth's measurements from previous work, had created a gown of such pristine beauty that Elizabeth was in awe when she first saw it.

Though the dress itself was quite stunning, Elizabeth was mesmerised in truth because it was the very dress she wore while in London with Darcy in her dream-state. She knew while in London that she had never owned such a dress, and when her aunt first presented her this gift upon hearing of her engagement, Elizabeth immediately recognised it—declaring the dress was destined to be her wedding dress. No suggestions by anyone to add a ribbon here, or a patch of lace there would be listened to. Elizabeth knew exactly how it ought to look, and she would brook no alterations. Fate had decided its look already, and Lizzy would not tempt Fate.

"It is time, Lizzy. Jane is ready and has already gone down to the carriage."

Elizabeth, suddenly overcome with emotion, flung her arms around her aun. "Thank you so very much for the dress. It is perfect, more than you know."

Aunt Gardiner's eyes glistened, and she pulled away with a watery laugh. "I knew from the first moment you liked it. I am honoured you have chosen it as your wedding dress. Mr Darcy, I am certain, will find you heavenly."

Elizabeth started at first and then laughed to herself. "That, I believe, dear Aunt, is assured. I happen to know he will love it." Her aunt looked at her oddly but nevertheless escorted Elizabeth down the stairs.

Once at the church, Elizabeth drew her father aside before it was time for him to escort her and Jane down the aisle for their double wedding.

"You are well, Papa?"

Mr Bennet nodded, patted his sweet daughter on the cheek, and said, "I can hardly believe such a story. Or any man worthy of you, Lizzy, but I am overruled. Who am I to argue with Fate?"

Elizabeth quickly embraced her father. She had needed to convince him when she and Darcy returned from Kent engaged. Mr Bennet worried that her state upon leaving was influencing her decision to marry Mr Darcy. He did not want her to make decisions of such magnitude or lasting effect before she was completely recovered. Together, Darcy and she had shared the miraculous and unbelievable story. Stunned, he had sat silently through it all, watching the exchanges of looks between the two as they each revealed parts of the implausible tale. Elizabeth remembered, with fond amusement, her father's first uttered words after hearing the incredible account.

"Young man, there will be no more visits to my daughter's chambers," Mr Bennet said strictly—and, it must be said, still with a hint of humour—successfully assuring the younger ones he believed them and also attempting to shake the shock from such a story.

"Then you ought to see to fixing that door, sir," Mr Darcy replied definitively and without embarrassment, effectively bringing a wry smile to her father's still staggered expression.

In the end, Mr Bennet could do naught but believe it and grant his blessing, for his eyes beheld a love so magnificent that to do otherwise would have been quite impossible—though he did see to the side door immediately.

"Thank you, Papa. I shall be quite happy with him."

Together with watery eyes, they turned to join Jane. Elizabeth had struggled whether or not to tell Jane about her phantasmal history with Darcy and, in the end, shared the whole of it. She had so longed for her sister during the most confusing of the times in London as she fell in love with the last man in the world she ever would have thought to marry; to keep Jane in the dark would have been irreverent to the story.

Jane gave Elizabeth a triumphant smile, very like the one she wore after learning her suspicions regarding Mr Darcy's admiration for Elizabeth were correct. It was unlike her dear sister to gloat, but Elizabeth found it endearing in that case.

"Yes, yes, yes, Jane. You were right all along, and I shall never live it down, I see. But in such cases as these, a good memory is unpardonable."

Jane laughed at the playful glint in Elizabeth's eye and kissed her cheek. They both knew the immense value of Elizabeth's recent return to "a good memory."

"Come, my darling girls; let us meet these gentlemen of yours."

WHEN DARCY SAW HIS BRIDE COMING DOWN THE AISLE TO HIM and recognised the dress, his love for her grew boundless, and his eyes told her exactly how heavenly she looked. Here was his angelic vision now in the flesh.

Darcy and Elizabeth spoke their vows with conviction and feeling, neither wishing to place doubt in the powers above of their willingness to devote themselves to the other. Each was mindful and possessed the warmest gratitude towards the powers that be who, by bringing her to his library in London, had been the means of uniting them

When the ceremony ended, Darcy brought Elizabeth's hand to his lips and said with feeling, "At last, Mrs Darcy."

Elizabeth smiled at her new husband, grateful for their strange, *spirited* courtship. Their solitary moment was soon disrupted, however, by the glad tidings of their guests.

Among the first to congratulate the newlyweds were the groom's sister and cousin. Instrumental in their reconciliation, the two were tenderly embraced and congratulations accepted with welcome hearts. Colonel Fitzwilliam, upon learning of the good news of Elizabeth's returned memory, had been quick to aid his cousin in defusing their aunt's displeasure at the news of Darcy and Elizabeth's engagement, though it was not their efforts that made the final difference. That honour went to Darcy's cousin Anne, who levelled her mother's combative vitriol by reminding Lady Catherine of the knowledge they both had that she, because of her condition, had been told many years before by their physician that she was barren. This news, of course, was received with sympathetic exchanges from her gentlemen cousins, and knowing that Darcy could not leave Pemberley without an heir, Lady Catherine had unhappily relented. She never displayed any remorse for wishing to deceive Darcy in the matter before and never uttered any form of acceptance for Elizabeth after.

"Mrs Darcy, what a pleasure it is to see everything come to rights. If only I had met you first," Colonel Fitzwilliam said with a gallant bow.

Elizabeth smirked. "Thank you, Colonel. Might I give you a bit of advice?"

Surprised, Colonel Fitzwilliam nodded and waited for her to speak. Darcy eyed his wife with interest, and Georgiana listened attentively too.

"You ought to watch your language when in the presence of a lady, Colonel, if you ever hope to catch a wife."

Darcy erupted in loud laughter, followed a beat behind by his cousin as they both remembered the time in Darcy's study when

Colonel Fitzwilliam, not knowing of Elizabeth's manifestation, had allowed quite a few ungentlemanly oaths to pass his lips.

"And perhaps you ought to be a bit more temperate too, Cousin," Darcy added with a slap on the shoulder.

Georgiana looked at her companions for clarification. "I do not understand."

"I do not feel that I can be held accountable for my actions that evening. Darcy's port is of the highest quality," the colonel quipped in good-humoured defence.

Georgiana, remembering something of this from Darcy's account at Pemberley, tapped her cousin's arm with her fan and bestowed upon him a scowl that sobered him immediately. "Richard! Do not tell me you spoke rudely in front of my new sister?"

"I did not know she was in the room, Georgie!" Colonel Fitzwilliam defended.

With smiles, the newlyweds left them to argue alone as they greeted their other guests.

DARCY LAUGHED UNCONTROLLABLY AS HE WALKED BACKWARDS across the threshold, pulling Elizabeth along by her hand. She looked at him with a mock frown, causing him to laugh harder.

"I do not find it humourous in the least, Mr Darcy. And I should think you would not wish to upset your wife so soon upon your nuptials."

Darcy attempted to rein in his laughter. "I am sorry, Elizabeth, but I find it infinitely funny and perversely fitting that the tables have turned so delightfully. For once, it is not I who provokes strange looks."

Elizabeth harrumphed and crossed her arms about her. "It was a slip from decorum on my part, and I find little humour in it."

Darcy drew her to him and wrapped his arms about her waist then. With one hand, he lifted a curl at her brow and twisted it in his fingers before lovingly tucking it behind her ear. Though he was no longer laughing, good humour coloured his gentle tone. "The look on their faces was priceless."

Elizabeth's lips twitched, and she relented. "Mr and Mrs Carroll certainly were quite startled, were they not?"

Darcy chuckled again, nodding. "I am certain they will think little on it except to believe their new mistress is exceedingly friendly."

Elizabeth laughed then, unable to pretend displeasure any more. After their journey from Hertfordshire to London following the wedding breakfast, it had been an impulse, an instinct rather, that caused her to embrace the housekeeper and kiss the cheek of the butler upon first entering Darcy House minutes before. She had been so pleased to see them again and gladdened to be back in a place that held such cherished memories. Elizabeth simply forgot that *her* state when she had met *them* was a little less corporeal.

The rumble of laughter in Darcy's chest was felt against her own, and Elizabeth suddenly became aware of their current location. It had been natural to be led by Darcy through the house, so natural that she had thought little of their destination until now. With a sudden and extreme blush, Elizabeth noted that he had brought her to his bedchamber.

Darcy, seeing the bloom on her cheeks and suspecting its cause, tightened his hold on her. His voice turned gravelly and low. "Welcome back, my dear Elizabeth."

She was all too aware now that they were alone and in his chambers, and for the first time, both of those instances were combined with the fact that neither of them was ethereal in nature. Elizabeth struggled to raise her eyes to meet his and turned to look beside them. Her eyes caught on something, and she began to smile widely. Thankful for the distraction, she said impertinently, "You have not moved your bed back, sir."

"No, I have not."

Somehow, his voice seemed yet lower, her momentary equilibrium lost again. She looked at him then and saw his eyes burn with love and desire, once again bringing heat to her cheeks. Emboldened by his look, she stood on her toes and bestowed a brief kiss, one to which he instantly reacted, pulling her back for another not quite so brief one.

Though her heart was beating quite fiercely, Elizabeth threw a mischievous glance his way before trying to disengage herself from his arms.

"I recall your saying to your valet that you preferred to sleep alone."

Darcy's lips twitched in remembered humour, but his arms tightened about her waist, keeping her from leaving him. "You misheard me, Elizabeth. If you recall, I said that a man deserves to sleep alone if he wishes."

Laughing, Elizabeth managed to squirm away and, backing away towards her door, gave a quick curtsey. "Then I shall leave you to it, sir. Good night."

She turned then and, before she could depart, felt his strong arms steal around her. Darcy's voice was husky in her ear as he whispered, "I do not wish to sleep alone tonight, Elizabeth. Or ever again."

"So I presume you would wish for me to stay?"

Darcy kissed her neck, sending shivers down her spine. Each word he punctuated with another gentle kiss. "As ever, Mrs Darcy, you are right *and* beautiful."

THE END

ACKNOWLEDGMENTS

I never imagined I would write a novel, let alone a few. However I know all these words would still be locked inside if not for the encouragement of a great many people.

My editor, Christina Boyd, deserves my thanks for fixing all my grammar issues. Her ability to tweak the sentence or coax a scene made my writing seem so much better after and her faith in this story made it come alive. Thanks are also due to Ellen Pickels for her unparalleled expertise all things grammar and regency.

Quills & Quartos Publishing for their fan-girling me through my insecurities in the process of rereleasing this book and for unflinchingly lending their knowledge and support throughout the process.

Gratitude must also be given to my kids who never complained once about having to watch a movie (wahoo!) or suffering pizza for dinner (yippee!) or even being asked to endure it multiple times (Moms the best!) while I wrote this book. My son once asked me if in my books Mr Darcy and Elizabeth Bennet always (insert little boy exasperation) end up together. Yes, darling they always do.

Lastly, a most devoted thanks to my girl Miss Austen. I make no claim to match her abilities or her talents. I simply love her stories enough to want to try.

ABOUT THE AUTHOR

KaraLynne began writing horrible poetry as an angst-filled youth. It was a means to express the exhilaration and devastation she felt every time her adolescent heart was newly in love with "the one" and then broken every other week. As her frontal lobe developed, she grew more discerning of both men and writing. She has been married to her own dreamboat of a best friend, Andrew, for 17 years. Together they have the migraine-inducing responsibility of raising five children to not be dirt bags (fingers crossed), pick of up their socks (still a work in progress), not fight with each other (impossible task) and become generally good people (there's hope). She loves escaping into a book, her feather babies (the regal hens of Cluckingham Palace), and laughter.

She has written four books and participated in many anthologies including: *Falling For Mr. Darcy; Bluebells in the Mourning; Haunting Mr. Darcy: A Spirited Courtship; Yours Forevermore, Darcy; The Darcy Monologues; Rational Creatures; & Sun-Kissed: Effusions of Summer.*

For more information about new releases, sales and promotions on books by KaraLynne and other great authors, please visit www. QuillsandQuartos.com

ALSO BY KARALYNNE MACKRORY

Falling for Mr Darcy

The simple truth is proven that sometimes a gentleman never knows his heart until a lady comes along to introduce it to him. When Mr. Darcy encounters Elizabeth Bennet injured after a fall, his concern for her welfare cracks the shell of his carefully guarded heart, and a charming man emerges. Elizabeth sees an appealing side of him she never believed possible from the stoic, proud master of Pemberley. They find the simple gentlemanly act of assisting her home will test both Mr. Darcy's resolve to keep his heart safe and Elizabeth's conviction that this is the last man on earth she might have ever been prevailed upon to marry. Soon, falling for Mr. Darcy becomes a real possibility.

Bluebells in the Mourning

Jane Austen's beloved Pride and Prejudice is readapted in this regency tale of love in the face of tragedy. Mr. Darcy is thwarted in his attempt to propose to Elizabeth Bennet at Hunsford when he encounters her minutes after she receives the sad news from Longbourn of her sister's death. His gallantry and compassion as he escorts her back to Hertfordshire begins to unravel the many threads of her discontent with him. While her family heals from their loss, Darcy must search London for answers – answers that might bring justice, but might also just mark the end of his own hopes with Elizabeth. Is it true that nothing can be lost that love cannot find?

Yours Forevermore, Darcy

Mr. Fitzwilliam Darcy has a secret. The letter he presented to Miss Elizabeth Bennet after his ghastly proposal is not the only epistle he has written her. In this tale of longing, misadventure and love, Jane Austen's dearly loved Pride & Prejudice, is readapted as our hero has learned a powerful way of coping with his attraction to Miss Bennet. He writes her letters. The misguided suitor has declared himself, and Elizabeth Bennet has refused him, most painfully. Without ever intending for these letters to become known to any soul, Mr. Darcy relies on his secret for coping once again. However, these letters, should they land in the wrong hands, could amount to untold scandal, embarrassment and possibly heartbreak. But what would happen should they fall into the right hands?

Made in the USA
Coppell, TX
15 August 2022

81480638R00184